CW01151914

KNIGHT ETERNAL : BATTLEBORN

Published by River Styx Project
Devon, United Kingdom.

RIVER STYX PROJECT

www.riverstyxproject.co.uk

First Published: September 2023

Hardback Print Edition - ISBN: 978-1-7395340-0-4
Paperback Print Edition - ISBN: 978-1-7395340-1-1
E-book Edition - ISBN: 978-1-7395340-2-8

Copyright © 2023 River Styx Project, Knight Eternal and related logos,
names and character likenesses thereof are trademarks or registered trademarks of
River Styx Project. All rights reserved.
This is a work of fiction.
All of the characters, organisations and events portrayed in this novel are either products
of the author's imagination or are used fictitiously. Any resemblance to actual persons,
living or dead (except for satirical purposes), is entirely coincidental.

Interior illustrations & artwork by Matt Buckett, Copyright © Matt Buckett 2023
Ian P Marshall asserts the moral right to be identified as the author of this work.

No part of this publication may be reproduced, stored in a retrieval system, or transmitted,
in any form or by any means without the prior written permission of the publisher, nor be
otherwise circulated in any form of binding or cover other than that in which it is published
and without a similar condition being imposed on the subsequent purchaser.

Printed and bound by Dart Print Ltd, Tavistock, Devon, United Kingdom.

Cover Art by Matt Buckett
Book design, interior layout and type setting by River Styx Project

riverstyxproject   River Styx Project

**RIVER STYX
PROJECT**

LIMITED EDITION

No. *90*

Ian P Marshall

Matt Buckett

Inspiration

I was asked recently where the idea for the Knight Eternal came from. Well, as a youngster, I was an avid reader and my stable reading in the early days was the pulp fiction of the thirties or even earlier, notably Edgar Rice Burroughs, H Ryder Haggard and my all time favourite, Robert E Howard. I was captivated by the characters within these stories, John Carter of Mars, Tarzan the ape man, She who must be obeyed, Allan Quatermain, Solomon Kane, Kull of Atlantis, and, of course, Conan the Barbarian. Every story was filled with adventure, monsters to overcome, ancient ruins and treasures to be found, death defying escapes and thrills aplenty. Each story was a page turner, with the hero somehow coming through in the end against incredible odds, and despite they were written nearly a hundred years ago, the stories still feel vibrant and read well to this day. You will find that a lot of these influences have filtered through into my writing and especially this tale of the Knight Eternal.

So, my answer would be that John was born from all of these great hero's of yesteryear, a little piece of all of them perhaps, thrown together to form a new pulp hero. This book is dedicated to all these great authors and others to boot. My hope, is that in a small way, I can carry the torch for them into the 21st Century, showing everyone that the age of the pulp hero is alive and well in the form of the Knight Eternal.

Dedication

To my family, for their support, who have put up with my constant typing, deep into the night, on many occasions. Of course, to Matt for his wonderful artwork and his faith in my writing skills enough to put his time and effort into the project.

And to you, the reader, thank you for purchasing this book. I hope you enjoy this tale as much as I have enjoyed writing it.

Ian P Marshall
August 2023

I'd also like to dedicate this body of work to my family, who always support my projects and encourage my creative output, even when I ask them to pose for character shots when I need reference material!

Most importantly I'd like to thank Ian for suggesting our partnership and bringing me into the world of the Knight Eternal, I can't wait to see where the adventure goes.

Matt Buckett
August 2023

KNIGHT ETERNAL
BATTLEBORN

BOOK 1

Written
By
Ian P Marshall

Illustrated
By
Matt Buckett

Other Titles By The Authors

Ian P Marshall

The Creeping Dread
Mr Lucky
The Last Of The Fairy

The Together Forever Series:
The Dragon In The Stone
A Call To Arms
Orphans In Time
(Also available as a Trilogy: **The Books Of Time**)

Matt Buckett

The Weapon - A Graphic Novel
Ink Sketches Vol I.

KNIGHT ETERNAL
BOOK 1
BATTLEBORN

CHAPTER 1 ~ IN THE COMPANY OF GIANTS   11

CHAPTER 2 ~ A PURPOSE   33

CHAPTER 3 ~ ORIGINS   57

CHAPTER 4 ~ DEVINE INTERVENTION   84

CHAPTER 5 ~ THE HARKNESS INSTITUTE   100

CHAPTER 6 ~ EGYPT   122

CHAPTER 7 ~ ASSAULT ON THE INSTITUTE   141

CHAPTER 8 ~ ST JOHN   160

CHAPTER 9 ~ VILLAGE OF THE DAMNED   179

CHAPTER 10 ~ ROYALTY   196

CHAPTER 11 ~ DEVASTATION   210

CHAPTER 12 ~ THE CALLING   232

CHAPTER 13 ~ THE LAST WISH   263

CONCEPT ART   293

KNIGHT ETERNAL

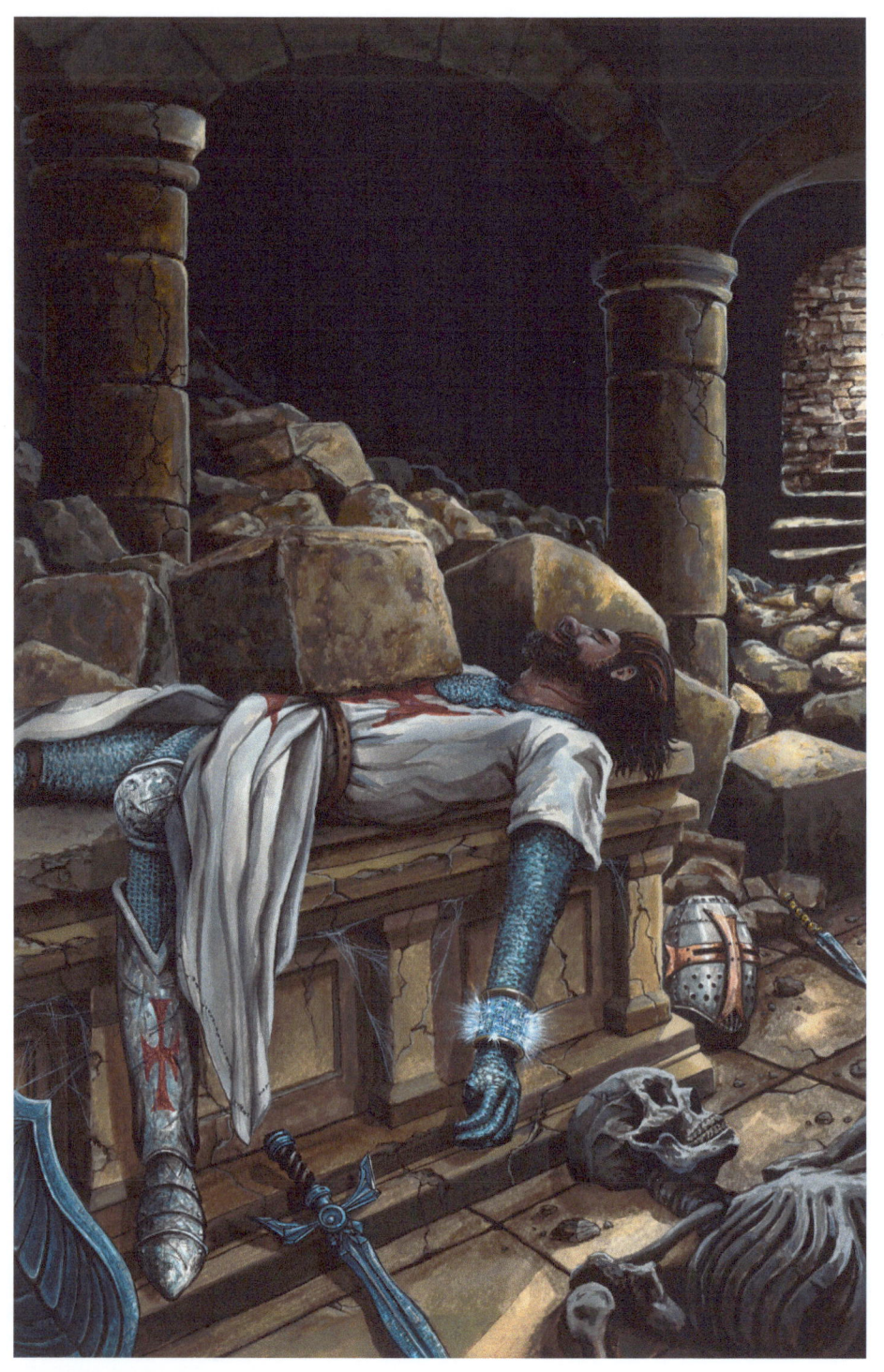

Plate: 1

1

IN THE COMPANY OF GIANTS

"You want me to tell you about my first mission for the crown. OK, I think the year was 1579, or something like that, you've probably got it on your files somewhere, knowing you guys. Anyway, it was a strange affair that involved a witch, a giant and a talking goat. The talking goat reminds me of you, Arthurs," I say with a deep chuckle, knowing I'd get a rise from the meathead. The man stirs in his seat and looks as if he is going to come at me, but a steady hand on his arm from the woman next to him, stops him. In the end, he just looks at me with those deep-set eyes, and bushy eyebrows, as if he wants to burn me at the stake. 'Good luck with that one, flyboy,' I think. Arthurs is a strange one. You'd think that after eight hundred years I'd be able to read people better but my intuition is as it was, when I was found in that tomb in Acre with a block of masonry on my chest, big enough to fit in the great pyramid of Giza, no better or worse than before. I went on gut instinct, always have, always will. And something in my gut tells me, that Arthurs isn't just a highly trained operative, there is something the agency are not telling me about him. Sure, I've read his file, but who made up the file, the agency, so even his name might be a lie. It does say he is male, so I guess that fact is true, although you never know, I think, smiling. He has the sense of humour of a mad goat, he'll rather charge at you than trade insults.

"What are you smirking at?" his gruff voice came to me through my daydream. 'Do they train them to speak like that in the forces or is it in-built? Or maybe you have to talk like that to get in, in the first place' I think with a wry smile.

"Nothing, tough guy, just my own private joke." He probably thinks 'tough guy' is a compliment.

"So, you got a sense of humour, then?" he replies gruffly. "When did you pick that up? Was it the 1700s or the 1800s, or perhaps it was just yesterday?"

"Actually, it was when I met you?" I say quietly, "I realised then, that..."

"Enough!" the woman next to him said loudly.

"Actually, it's my wise cracking sense of humour that has kept me sane over the centuries... and young at heart, of course, no pun intended."

"OK, OK," the woman says, raising her hands for peace. Her name is Susan Harkness, director and leader of this small band of brothers... and sisters. She is in her mid-thirties with the longest black hair I have ever seen, even though at the moment it is tied in a bun that looks like she has a burnt loaf of bread on her head, and I am definitely not going to tell her that to her face, she scares me. Those piercing green eyes are like Medusa's. You look into those, and you may as well turn yourself to stone. Come to think of it, her hair can easily hide a few snakes!

"What are you looking at?" she says, raising her eyes to the sky.

"Nothing, nothing," I say far too quickly, speaking first was often an admition of guilt, as I well knew.

"OK, so can we get back with the program, tell us about your first mission, please. And no more interruptions, OK, Godiven."

I smile and nod in compliance, for now, anyway. I have no intention of hanging around long, that is for sure. I feel like telling her that my name is not actually Godiven but think better of it, this time. I don't know my real surname, only that my Christian name is John. Sure, I've been called Godiven for nearly seven centuries, but it hasn't really stuck in my mind for some reason. Perhaps I need to give it more time. I mean, the reason I'm called Godiven in the first place, is because when they found me buried in that tomb beneath Acre, I was dead or in limbo, or something else, I don't know what. But my body was preserved as if I'd been there for only a couple of hours, rather than a hundred years. I wasn't moving, probably something to do with the fact that a large chunk of the roof's masonry was sat on my chest pinning me to the altar, where the Saracen magician had been performing an arcane rite to resurrect an ancient demon that would slaughter the infidels who were attacking their sacred land, namely us! Anyway, that's a story for another time. When they found me, they thought I was some demon, I still had my crusader armour on, my chain-mail hauberk, my white surcoat with the red cross, my iron helmet and mail mittens, all still in perfect condition. Even my leather belt was whole and intact. A sword and shield are lying next to the altar. I remember looking wide eyed at a metallic armlet attached around my left forearm, which I could not recollect ever seeing. It was only when they managed to lift the stone off my chest, with the help of six men, so I've been told, that my heart started to beat again. I remember waking to see light above me, and incredulous horrifying looks from all the people present as I started to rise. I tried to say, "God in Heaven," but my mouth was dry and full of dust from lying there for over a century, my throat was sore beyond belief. What came out sounded like 'Godiven'! And that's been my name ever since! And will be until I find my real name! John Godiven, ex-crusader and immortal warrior. I peer around at the group, an odd mix, if ever I saw one. A woman who is probably a witch, an army man, a boy that must only be about fourteen at the most and a woman that looks like she couldn't open a packet of crisps without help. However, I do know from past experiences, of which I have more than anyone, that appearances can be deceiving.

I gather my thoughts and start my story.

"Little did I know that this was just a prelude to even more stranger things to follow. It was wintertime, nearly Christmas if I recall correctly, and I was sent to Yorkshire. The department, as you would call it now, had received reports that the bones of a buried giant were affecting the soil, causing nothing to grow, and making the earth lifeless. We were informed that the ground stank of a morgue, or burial vault, and worse still, the stench and lifelessness was spreading at an alarming rate. A great mass of nothingness, heading directly towards the castle of Lord Ashworth, who was a friend of Elizabeth I. Hence, why I was sent. Accompanying me on this journey was Elizabeth Harkness, your founder member, benefactor and inspiration for everything that has followed. She was one crazy lady, but I loved her dearly. The day she passed was a sad day.

We arrived in the small village of Lower Westcombe, on a bitter December morning. I remember it being freezing cold. Snow was swirling around, trying to settle, as we were directed up the hill towards a lone cottage that sat just off the road below a cairn of stones, upon a headland. The road was a slippery mess of frozen mud and patches of ice, making the going really tough. The wind was strong and biting, throwing us this way and that, as if playing with us. Tendrils of cold seeped between our clothes, stabbing us with sword-like efficiency. Through the swirling snow shower, which felt like it would soon turn heavy, I glimpsed the tiny cottage for the first time. Everything was in darkness as if it was derelict, but we knew otherwise.

Strapped onto my back and hidden under my thick black cloak was the shield I had found lying beside me. On my left wrist, the thick metallic armlet that had attached itself to me when I had awakened in Acre. I felt the reassuring coldness of the metal on my wrist and the faint tingle that we were getting close to some supernatural force.

My sword, the one made from the same strange material as the shield, was in its hilt under my cloak, concealed from prying eyes. Below my woollen cloak, I wore a tight-fitting jacket that was buttoned down the front. On my head, I wore a thick, black-rimmed hat with matching black leather gloves. I was obviously into black leather in those days." I say, and wink at the group. None reply, so I carry on. "Beneath this, I wore a thin white linen shirt that rose high on my neck, covering the great scar that the scimitar had made, when it had nearly decapitated me four hundred years earlier. I also wore a dagger on the right-hand side of my belt, just in case," I add with a smile.

I see Arthurs shake his head and raise his eyes all in one motion. Amazing, he can multi-task.

"Elizabeth was wrapped up tighter than a hibernating squirrel. She was already sixty-six when I met her, but she was so young at heart and fit of body and mind, you would think her half that age. Her beautiful dark brown eyes were the only things visible, beneath a scarf that was tightly wrapped about her face. Specks of ice and snow clung to it, and more clung to her woollen hat. She was only five foot tall, compared to my six foot four, but her size hid her strength, she sure was one strong lady. I didn't realise she was a witch then, but I was soon to find out. For some unknown reason, my armlet never sensed her gift, a mystery I never unravelled. We must have looked some sight, if anyone had been watching, slipping and sliding our way up that hill towards the cottage to meet its occupant, a certain Effe Cuthbert. Now, if that wasn't a witch's name, or a witch's cottage, I would have eaten my hat. I suspected it and the armlet, which tingled on my arm, seemed to think so too. As we neared, my armlet started to thrum and vibrate.

Having worn it for nearly four hundred years now I had got pretty used to its strange vibrations, so that I could understand its different warning patterns and what they implied. On many occasions it had saved me from a nasty surprise. How it attached itself to my wrist is a mystery that I am yet to find out. Remember folks, this was my first mission for the crown, not my first mission ,OK, remember that, because I'd already been around for three hundred years and I have seen and done some incredible things, and also a lot of things I'm not proud of. I've searched high and low to try and find out who I am or where I come from, but there is nothing. All I know is my Christian name is John. The weird thing is I remember most of my last day before everything went bat shit crazy, as clear as if it was yesterday, but apart from that it's one big fat blank." I see Susan Harkness flinch just a fraction at my words, I see Arthur's shuffle ever so slightly in his chair and I know they know something. Over the centuries, despite my intuition remaining the same, some of my other senses have reached a different level. I have become far more aware that body language does not lie, ever. If you know what to look for, you can read a person like a book, except witches, they are the exception. My eyesight is also off the chart, my vision is like a pair of strong binoculars. Add that to a sense of hearing that can hear a pin drop, and I am pretty difficult to creep up on, unless you are invisible and silent. Which unfortunately some ghosts are, especially the ones who have lost their material forms and are just floating about trying to find a way to the afterlife. I hate immaterial ghosts most of all, they really suck!

"Anyway, we reached the cottage and Elizabeth went to knock on the door, when it slowly opened. With witches' houses that happens every single time. I tell you they may as well leave the door open, before anyone gets near it. I looked at the door and realised I was going to have to stoop pretty low to get in. I remember pondering whether my sword would get through, without me having to take it out and man handle it through. I thought the old lady might throw a fit if she saw me stepping over the threshold with a sword in my hand. As per any witch's house, no one was at the door to greet us, and the customary "come in, come in, my dears," croaked faintly from a room at the back of the cottage. A dim glow could be seen down a dark hallway, and I hoped the old lady had a fire going, I couldn't feel my toes now. I crouched low, my body touching both sides of the passageway, while my head was bent so I didn't bang it on the ceiling. I heard a chortle behind me and without turning around, which I couldn't anyway, said 'it's not funny!' "

"It is to me, you look like an oversized bear who got stuck getting in his cave before hibernating," Elizabeth said to me.

I look at the group, reading their minds, and say, "And don't even mention Winnie-the-Pooh, he's not going to be invented for centuries to come, so that wasn't the comparison!" I see Susan lips curl up a fraction in a half smile and the girl chuckle embarrassingly. I decided to continue without any more wisecracks.

"I leant forward, opened the door, and saw the oldest woman I have ever seen in my life standing beside a big open hearth, warming her hands beside a blazing fire. I mean old, really old. She was so old, she had wrinkles on her wrinkles, and that's old. A trio of copper pots stood in a wire frame beside the fire. As I entered the room and saw this, my senses immediately told me something was not right here. Even my armlet was going crazy, and for once I couldn't read what it was trying to tell me. The old hag, for that was about the best description I could give her, turned and smiled at me, her dark rotting gums showing one solitary black tooth. She was a looker all right. Her hair was grey and straight, falling to her shoulders in tufts. She wore a black cloak, which had definitely seen better days. Like a lot of the earlier witches, she had an enormous nose. It almost seemed that as they got older, the nose continued to grow while everything else shrank! Yes, she had a big, hooked nose, with warts all over it, that seemed to cover most of her face. Her tiny little eyes were deep-set, and dark brown. Witches only have two different eye colours, dark brown or green. It all depends on your birth sign, from what I've been told. Elizabeth's were dark brown by the way, but I'm sure I've already told you that. If you didn't know, and because you are already here, I'm suspecting you do know, but witches were quite common in the Middle Ages; as many as one or two in each town or village. It was only the fear of the unknown, and the fervour of the church, which started to drive them out, and into the hands of the zealots. Most witches were good folk, healers, knowledgeable of the land and the magic it can provide. For the ordinary folk, fear of the unknown and mistrust of what they couldn't understand, soon escalated to hatred, banishment and worse. Religious fanatics, hellbent on control of the common folk, stoked this fervour to fever pitch. Witches became hunted, captured, tortured and killed without any investigation or thought. Most were elderly women who stood no chance and were quickly silenced. Family members and close friends were also thrown into the mix, with whole families being wiped out just because grandmother healed someone's rash with a salve mixed with herbs from the forest. Villages became places of fear and mistrust, with everyone looking over their shoulder. It all started, and finished, in the name of the Lord and was carried out by his Witchfinders. Sure, they were witches, and some were very powerful, but most were good people just trying to use their powers to help others. Now, only a few remain, spread far and wide and still afraid to use their knowledge. All because the church decreed that witchcraft was evil and should be done away with. They don't even know the true meaning of the word. Religion is a dirty word in my book, just look at all the wars we have fought in the name of one religion or another, it sickens me.

Humans have been fighting wars since the dawn of time, instigated by one word to cover up the real reasons, which are mainly control and power. I look at what I was in my past life, and I am disgusted at myself. That was no Holy War, none of the Crusades were, it was all about power and controlling the masses. Saladin and his army weren't the real enemy, the real enemy were hiding in their papal halls, or roaming their mighty cathedrals or white stone mosques.

The Saracen's were just fighting to get their land back, after all it was not ours to take in the first place. People will do anything to protect their homes, their land, and rightfully so. Atrocities have been committed on both sides, sometimes in the heat of bloodlust, but mostly by fanatics who have gone beyond the reason of what they are fighting for to a different level of war, or maybe persecution is a better word. These fanatics are dangerous, they can create wars as well as fight in them. I roamed Europe through the Middle Ages, and man, did I see some crazy fanatics. Take those Templars for starters, they were nuts, they fought under that holy banner to protect their way of life, which actually boiled down to living in big frigging castles, drinking and womanising themselves into early graves. Protecting and hiding holy relics, was just a front for their wanton debauchery. Didn't work out too well for them, did it?"

Again, I see Harkness nervously shuffle in her seat at my words. What does she know? Looks like I'm going to have to stick around here a while to find out.

"Religion, that's the word that has cost more lives on this planet, than any other," I said pausing for dramatic effect. "Look at the crusades for instance, thousands killed on both sides, innocents slaughtered all in the name of religion. I still feel ashamed for the part I played in this, however small a cog I was. I renounced my position as a crusader a long time ago, once I realised religion had nothing to do with our holy wars."

"So, I take it you are not a God-fearing bible basher then?" Arthurs asks.

"I've bashed a few false gods over the years, but no, I have no faith left in me," I reply feeling somewhat hollow inside at the words, knowing even then that I didn't mean it, I just didn't want them to know that, yet. I'd seen enough to make me believe something is out there beyond the veil. Something, I want to believe in. Something, I need to believe in. I know there is power in the sacred word and hallowed ground, but not just in our religion.

"But some supernatural force has kept you alive since the 12th century. Not only alive but enhanced and better in many ways." Harkness blurts out. I could see that she was annoyed with herself as soon as the words had been uttered.

"Peachy," I reply in jest, smarting at the truth. "Perhaps I'm the next evolutionary step in humanity," I add sarcastically to cover up my discomfort. Arthurs snorts at this. He and I are going to have issues if I stay here too long.

"Shall we continue with your story?" Harkness says with a nod to me.

"Yes, yes, of course. Anyway, when I..."

"Do you always say, 'Anyway', in front of everything you start saying?" The young kid says. I turn and glare at him, and I think my big bushy red eyebrows, and staring blue eyes got to him. He shrinks back into his seat with a frightened look, as if I am going to eat him. Good God, he is an annoying little punk. And what is he doing here anyway? This isn't kids' stuff!

"Anyway," I say slowly, looking at the kid, "when I walked towards the fire to warm myself up, I realised she was not only a witch but she was a dead witch."

"You're dead," I said to her, which is not the best greeting in the world. I was fixated on her single tooth. It looked like it was going to drop out at any time. She lifted her crooked frame and stared up at me, waving her right hand dismissively.

"Of course, dear," she said, and her single tooth wobbled some more. I snapped out of it when she clicked a finger in front of my face. "So, you are the one they call the Eternal Warrior, eh? Not much of a looker, is he?" she said turning to Elizabeth. "It's so good to see you, dear, I've been waiting a long time to get you here? Why don't you sit down and make yourself comfortable, and I'll make you a nice little witches brew?" What, I thought?

"Hang on a minute, Lady, I..., we came here to sort this giant problem out, not sit in front of a ghost fire that gives off no heat, talking to a dead woman, while my toes start to go blue! I hadn't controlled my anger issues by then." I say with a raised eyebrow, and wink towards the kid.

"My oh my, so impatient for one so important," she cackled back, turning towards the stove. "Why don't you wander up to the cairn and sort it out, dear. You'll know what to do when you get there."

"Will I now," I thought. "OK, I'll just go back out into the cold, then," I said as I headed towards a door at the end of the room, that I expected would lead out onto the moor.

I heard her talk then, but she had her back to me and was dipping a ladle into one of the pots and was bringing something out that was steaming. I knew it

had to be fake ghost steam. She was good, this witch, the whole illusion thing was impressive. Trust me, I've seen some bad ones in my time!
"What did you say?" I asked as I reached for the handle and swung the door open. The light from outside started to penetrate into the small room, its rays moving across the dusty floor. Snowflakes followed in, drifting and settling on me, even as the old hag turned to me and repeated her words.
"I said, mind the..."
And that's when something hit me right in my midriff, sending me flying back through the air, through the ghost of the witch, which gave me another icy chill through my bones, through the ghost pyramid of pots, to crash into the imaginary fire in the hearth.
"goat," she said, finishing her sentence.
I came up fast, covered in soot and ready for anything except what I saw.
The silhouette of a goat stood framed in the doorway. I reached down to my chest, which was hurting. I felt like a few ribs may have been broken, and I knew I would be bruised for weeks. I took a deep breath and felt something rattle within me. Great, I thought, taken out by a goat! The goat, which was white in colour, had its head lowered so that it could show off the big bastard horns that had just sent me flying. It didn't advance, but just stood there on the threshold, as if waiting to be invited in. Wait, I thought, "That's not a vampire goat, is it? Tell me that's not a vampire goat?" I asked the witch.
And then it spoke.
"I am not a vampire goat," it said with a young feminine voice, "in fact, I'm not even a goat, am I, witch?" It said with bitterness and anger towards the dead witch, who cringed and looked towards Elizabeth.
"This day was getting weirder and weirder, and I hadn't even tackled the giant problem yet!" I say to the group. "Like I said, this was one crazy first mission!"
"Anyway," I say slowly and deliberately," the goat turns to me and said,
"Sorry, I thought you were her." It said this in a spiteful malicious tone and twitched its head towards the witch in a human like fashion.
"Do I look like her?" I said, pointing to myself with both hands out in front of me.

"I said, sorry, I've been waiting twenty years for her to open that door, that's a long time."

"Tell me about it!" I said, raising my eyes. It's then that I saw that the goat was tied by a rope to a piece of iron set into a low dry-stone wall, which denoted the end of the cottage's garden from the moor. "OK," I said, "what's the story? I'm not going anywhere until I find out what is going on here. Ghost Lady, Effe, witch, whatever you want to be called, what is going on here? Come on, spill the beans." I said, rubbing my chest, where it was hurting. What I did know was that the regenerative powers that had kept me alive, were already at work, healing me.

"She forgot to turn me back before she died!" The goat said from the doorway. "Now I'm stuck like this forever." The last word was said with a sob, but because it was coming from a goat's mouth, it sounded more like a snort.

"Why do you think I summoned you two?" Effe said to them, ignoring the goat. "We are not called witches for nothing you know... even dead ones! You are here to help with the giant problem, yes, dear. Elizabeth is here to put right a wrong I did, so that I can rest at last."

I looked at Elizabeth, who by now had removed her scarf and hat, and was looking at the witch with a bemused look. "Me?" she said quietly.

"Yes, of course dear, you? You are a Harkness after all," she said as if that made everything crystal clear.

Things were starting to fall into place in my mind. I had already seen incidents like this in Europe. You see, when someone dies, not everyone goes straight to heaven or hell, or whatever you want to call it. Some get stuck in a limbo type area and become ghosts, restless spirits that wander the land of the living, waiting, looking for someone to ease their pain; to relinquish them from whatever is holding them in this plain of existence. I don't know if it comes from within the person or from some higher force, but something needs to be done here in our world to free them. Only then can they be released on to the next part of their journey, whichever direction! Effe fitted into this category, like a bucket into a well. And I knew exactly why, in this case?

"So, you cast a spell that turned this girl into a goat and then died leaving her like this for twenty years, yes?" I asked. "That's bad timing, unlucky on you," I said to the goat. "Anyway, what's your name? I can't just call you goat!"

"Charlotte Ashworth," the goat said proudly. Well, as proud as a goat could, anyway, I thought.

"Ashworth? As in related to Lord Ashworth, who's castle is just over the other side of the hill?"

"He started it," Effe said, turning to look at the goat for the first time. "If it wasn't for your father stealing our land, this wouldn't have happened. It was only meant to be a warning. I didn't know I was going to die! I'm sorry dear, I never meant to leave you like this, it was only meant to be for a day or so. I couldn't face what I had done to you, it haunts me every day."

A ghost being haunted, I thought, that's a first.

"So, you locked your ghostly form in your cottage and pretended nothing happened?" Charlotte Ashworth said, and then added "So, why now, why bring them here now?"

Effe turned to Elizabeth, who returned her gaze with one of shock and a little sadness.

"She doesn't know, Effe?" Elizabeth asked rhetorically.

"Doesn't know what?" I asked. It was right then, that there was a knocking at the front door with what felt like a sharp object. The knocking was a series of quick raps, in a staccato manner.

"I know you are in there," a loud aristocratic voice bellowed. Effe looked at Elizabeth, who looked at me with a tight-lipped glare.

"You didn't read the files, did you?"

"What files?" I asked, stalling for time to come up with an excuse and failing miserably.

"The ones in the carriage, I asked you to read on this case!" she said, her eyes wide in condemnation, her head shaking in judgment of my failure.

"Ah, well yes, I thought I had, I must have missed a page! Enlighten me?" I said with my most charming of smiles, which fell on her deadpan face like snow on a hot tin roof.

"Pick it up yourself, soldier boy," she said to me as she went to let the caller in.

"Elizabeth always called me 'soldier boy', when I was in the dog house," I say to the group with a wry smile.

Elizabeth came back into the room accompanied by a man, who was dressed in the attire of someone of wealth. The man was grossly overweight, about five foot six, with round cherry red cheeks and short squinty eyes that seemed to hold a feeling of anger. A small button nose and large red lips gave me the feeling that this was a man who had never done a proper day's work in his life. He wore white gloves, and in his right hand he held a black painted cane with a brass end, that he must have used to rap on the door. He wore a ridiculous purple coloured suit and white shirt. It looked like he was the lead in a Ribena advert.

"Daddy!" the goat said, pulling on the rope to enter and reach her father.

"Charlotte, my dear, what has she done to you?"

"It's nothing that can't be undone, now that Elizabeth is here!" Effe butted in, spittle falling from her mouth. And she called me, 'not much of a looker!' I thought, raising my eyes to the sky which actually was the ceiling, and was only a few inches above me. My back was really starting to ache.

He took a step into the room, and I immediately realised that he was also not of this Earth. My eyes turned to Elizabeth who gave me the 'told you to read the files' look.

"Lord Ashworth," she said calmly. "Why don't we all just sit down and talk this through. I know John here might need your help shortly, which in turn might help you out of your predicament too."

"Daddy!" the goat said again pleading for his attention, but it came out more like a stuck in the mouth neigh.

"Just hold on, my love, I'll have this rectified in a few moments, I assure you," he said looking me up and down with a haughty glare of disapproval.

"I've been holding on for twenty years," she bleated out.

Effe turned to me and spoke quietly, her voice less of a cackle, and more one of understanding. "Please," she said, "take the girl with you and deal with what you came here to do." She emphasised the 'you', to say that this was my part of the mission, not Elizabeth's.

"OK, OK," I said, raising my hand, "at least I'll be able to straighten up outside, even if it is freezing cold."

By now the snow was falling in big sweeping waves, making visibility low and the going tougher. Already it was settling against the cottage, and if it continued, it would soon cover the land in a frozen sea of white horses.

"Right," I said, "I'm on it," as I marched out the door. Actually, it felt more like I popped out the door and straightened up, feeling the cold winds and icy threads of snow hitting my exposed parts. I looked down at the goat, reached down and yanked the rope free. Before I leant down to untether the rope from the goat's neck, I said.

"You are not going to kick me again, are you, 'cos that still hurts a good 'un."

"Of course not, I know who you are now," Charlotte replied, "I couldn't see properly in the darkness of the cottage, and goat's eyesight is different, but I can see you now for what you are?" she seemed to pause then as if she had said too much.

"And?" I asked impatiently, feeling the snow starting to settle on my clothes.

"It is nothing. Thank you for freeing me," she added, changing the subject. "Come, I will lead you up to the cairn."

We trudged through the snow, me and the goat, huddled together, making a fine pair. The weather had now turned into a blizzard. Great blankets of wind and snow struck us full on, as if you were on the deck of a ship in the high seas. You automatically tried reaching for something to balance yourself, and at one stage I grabbed one of Charlotte's horns by mistake.

"Hey," she bleated back over the cacophony of the storm.

"Sorry," I shouted back, while putting one arm across my face to protect me from the oncoming snow, which was attacking us like a sandstorm. We had gradually been climbing for what felt like forever, but was probably only twenty minutes, when I felt the ground under the snow turn more solid, as if we were walking on a road. I peered up through the blizzard, seeing nothing apart from a white moving blanket of snow. Charlotte was struggling too, her legs were covered by a foot or two of snow. I looked down at my feet and could see that my footprints were leaving a red tint. I looked at Charlotte's prints, and

IN THE COMPANY OF GIANTS

Plate: 2

they too were red. It was an eerie sight. It looked like we were bleeding as we climbed, but I realised that it was the giant's blood mixed with the earth and the compact snow under our feet, which was making this effect.

It was then, just as the thought of turning back entered my mind, that we broke through what I can only describe as a barrier and entered an area where the snow could not enter. I looked around taking in a deep breath, my eyes wide in disbelief. The storm was continuing around us unabated in its full force, but in here, where we were, nothing was getting through. We were not underground, but some unearthly force was holding the storm at bay. A complete clear semi-circle covered the top of the hill and the cairn. It was an amazing sight, even the sound of the storm had been muffled out. I could still see it outside, but nothing was getting through this field of whatever it was? It was like being inside a glass house during a storm, with the volume turned off.

Anyway, Charlotte shook herself down, and I brushed myself off, then looked towards the cairn. This was one crazy day, but it was going to get even crazier in a moment.

"I'll wait here," she said, tilting her head to one side.

"Why, thank you," I replied sarcastically.

The cairn was made up of a series of huge granite rocks set on top of each other and placed in a particular fashion that made it look a bit like a long flat house. I strode up to the cairn of rocks thinking how on Earth these rocks had been placed like this, when I spotted a dark opening to one side between two large boulders. The ground was hard and compact underfoot, and I could see thin tendrils of what looked like a red weed stretching in all directions. I straightened up and saw that it was everywhere. The grass was dying, the soil turning into some sort of mulch once it was in contact with the giant's blood. 'What is it with giant's blood,' I thought.

With a newfound strength that I was nearing the end of my quest, I leant forward and entered the darkness, cursing myself for not having anything to light my way. A narrow, tall shaft led downwards to a dark opening, which reminded me of one similar to when I encountered a nest of vampire like demons, a few centuries earlier. As I neared the opening, I thought my eyes were becoming accustomed to the darkness, but I realised that a phosphorescent lichen, attached to the ceiling, was giving off a dim light. I stopped, when I heard a deep moaning somewhere in the distance. It was the sound of hopelessness and eternal suffering, all rolled into one. My armlet was telling me nothing. With a deep sense of foreboding, I reached the end of the corridor to look out upon a large chamber, which must have covered almost the whole size of the cairn above me. The room was lit with more lichen covering the walls and ceiling, giving the scene an almost eerie green glowing effect. The ceiling was painted in a deep ochre with white stones set into it, depicting a representation of the cosmos. A series of black monoliths, about five foot high, surrounded a raised piece of ground and pinned on top of this mound was a figure at least ten foot in length. I was surprised to see that the thing was alive, I had expected to encounter another ghost, or fight a huge skeleton, but the sight before me was far worse. This was humans doing what they are so good at, inflicting pain and suffering.

The figure looked human and was spread eagled and pinned to the floor by heavy chains, tied around its legs and arms. The figure had wavy red hair and was bearded. His clothes hung about his thin sticklike frame as if they were ten times too big for him. When I neared him, his head shot towards me and I stared into his white, unseeing eyes, knowing he had heard me and not seen me. "Who is that?" he asked weakly in a low voice. "Is that you again Ashworth, come to taunt me!"

I immediately felt pity for this poor creature that had been tied here. I felt revulsion and anger when I neared and saw that his wrists had been cut, his feet also, not by much, but just enough for his blood to seep down into the soil. This man was barely alive, I could sense that he had been this way for a long, long time, kept alive by some sort of magic. I looked at the chains around his wrists and ankles, and realised that if he was strong enough, he could easily have slipped his wrists and feet through and been free; but he was too weak to even do that.

"I am not Ashworth," I said, feeling my voice tremble. "I have been sent up here to stop whatever is happening, your blood is poisoning the land. What happened here?" I asked.

It was at that point, I sensed movement behind me, and I turned to see the goat standing at the entrance to the cavern.

"It's cold outside," Charlotte said.

The giant didn't respond at once. I could see his once great chest lifting and falling with each breath. I heard his breath rasping for air. His face looked pallid and near death, but for how long he had been this way, I wasn't sure.

"Every year we would come here," the giant started, turning his head towards the ceiling, "to honour our dead and lay a single stone as homage to our ever-dwindling race. We had a good relationship with the locals, trading and swapping wares, helping them with heavy lifting tasks. Ashworth, the Lord of the Manor, wanted this piece of land for his own aims but was opposed by everyone. He swore that if he couldn't have it, no one could. He captured me one day, drugged my drink, I think, and with his friends initiated an arcane right, holding a service right here in this cavern, our most sacred of places. Trapping me here and stopping any other giant from entering our holy of holy's. Many times, I have heard them calling down to me from the tunnel entrance until eventually, to ease their pain, I lay silent. Eventually they did not return. My eyesight went shortly after that. You see, we giants need sunlight to keep our eyesight whole, without the sun, we would all go blind. Ashworth knew this and often came here to taunt me. He always hated the giants, because of the help we gave to the local people who opposed him. He is an evil, greedy man with very little respect for anyone."

"My father did this," Charlotte said quietly in dismay. "I feel ashamed."

"Is there someone else there?" he said, crying out in shock.

"Only a friend," I replied.

"Something has happened," the giant continued. "The curse has been lifted; I feel my life slipping away. At last, I will be free to join my ancestors in the great halls of Valhalla. Has something happened to Ashworth, I have not seen him for some time, that's why I thought it was him coming to taunt me again?" his voice was weakening even as we stood there.

I turned to look at Charlotte, my head bowed. "Lord Ashworth is dead."

"What?" she bleated out. "I've just seen him! We have just seen him. Daddy, no," she said shaking her head.

"Is that a goat, I hear in here with us?" the giant asked. "I love goat meat. Oh, to have one more decent meal before I go. That, and the chance to feel the sun on my face one more time before I die would be all I ask?" he said and starts to cough.

Getting Charlotte's attention, I put my finger to my lips to insist on quietness and turned to the giant.

"I think I can help you with one of those," I said.

"I hope it's the second one," Charlotte whispered, "or I'm out of here as quick as my four legs will take me."

Despite all that had happened, I smiled at her plucky response, the girl had guts, I liked that. I motioned for her to go out, then returned and freed the giant. His eyes were shut now, and his breathing was slow and shallow. I picked him up and was amazed how light he was, he was just skin and bones. I carried him up through the shaft and came out into the brightness of the day. My eyes watered and cleared, and I realised that outside the dome, the snow had stopped, and the sun was doing its best to break through the dispersing storm clouds. I felt the giant sigh and move in my arms. I reached a part of the cairn where I could sit him upright, with his back to the stone, facing the sun. I sat beside him, making sure that he was comfortable and would not fall. Charlotte moved towards us and sat down. "Thank you," he whispered and smiled. "By the Gods, I feel the sun on my face and the wind in my hair." It was then that I realised that the dome was collapsing. Cold air seeped in, and a breeze ruffled the giants red hair. His body trembled. "Thank you," he said again and I saw his eyes open. I watched as he seemed to squint at the sunlight. His body went rigid, one hand reached towards the sun. "I see a light," he whispered in awe, then his hand dropped to his side and his head slumped to rest on my shoulder.

We sat like that for some time until I felt the earth tremble and a shadow fall across my form. I sensed movement all around me. I must have fallen asleep because when I opened my eyes, there were at least twenty giants, all standing around us in a semi-circle, looking at me. No, not me, they were looking at the dead giant leaning against me, whose name I didn't even know. I had never thought to ask. Charlotte was tucked in next to me, shaking in fear. I feared the worst and was about to raise and draw my sword, when all the giants knelt down on one knee, and bowed their heads for a few moments. Without a word, two of the giants approached and picked up their fallen comrade and carried him past me, behind the cairn and over the hill, the rest following, apart from one, who rose and approached us. Charlotte began to shake even more, and the grip on my sword tightened. He came within a few feet and stopped, his shadow covering both our bodies. He stood at least ten feet tall, had a human appearance, but was basically just bigger in every aspect. He wore trousers, a loose-fitting shirt and a faded multi-coloured waistcoat that was fraying at the edges.

"Thank you," the giant said in a quiet and deep voice that sounded full of sorrow, loss and tiredness, all rolled into one. He had one of those warm welcoming faces that made you feel safe, and that everything was right in the world. His demeanour was of one who did nothing in a hurry, everything would be done in his time, slow and deliberate. If God had a human face, then this was how I would like it to look. I was awestruck and didn't reply at first.

"I didn't even know his name," I said, "Who was he?"

"His name was Bran. He was my son."

"Oh, I'm sorry for your loss," I replied.

The giant peered down at us, a frown forming on his face as he looked me up and down.

"You have done us a great service, my people thank you. You have freed my son and released the dark energy that kept us away from our sacred shrine. If there is anything you need of us in your future, do not hesitate to ask. My name is Bron. Return here and sing the calling song and we will come."

I nodded my acknowledgment, tongue tied for once. He looked at me again, his eyes seemingly looking past my human shell to what lay deep within. Then he smiled, nodded his head to me, turned and left on the same path that his fellow giants had taken.

We sat there in silence, awestruck.

"Now that's something you don't see every day!"

"Nor is a talking goat," a young woman said in delight, from beside me.

"You're back," and then I looked down at her feet, "well, nearly." The girl was in her late teens and was dressed in the clothes I assumed she had been wearing when she had been turned into a goat. Everything had returned to normal apart from her feet. She looked down and saw two hooves where her feet should be.

"Oh!" she said putting her hands to her mouth.

"I'm sorry about your father," I said.

"It's OK, I didn't really know him, to be honest. He wasn't a very nice man, was he?"

"No, he wasn't, and I'm going to tell him that as soon as we get back to the cottage."

I stopped then, taking a deep breath to say I'd finished my story.

"And?" the boy says, wanting to hear more.

"We returned to the cottage, through the snow, to find Elizabeth stoking a real fire in the hearth. She was alone, the witch had moved on to wherever she was meant to go, and I hope Ashworth moved on to wherever he didn't want to go. I don't know what went on when we were with the giant, and Elizabeth never mentioned it, which was fine by me. We took Charlotte in, and Elizabeth raised her as one of her own. Charlotte now had the Ashworth estate, and she used that money to fund Elizabeth's operation at the institute, the very same one you are attached to now. I don't know what happened to Charlotte, whether she wed and had children. I always wondered if her kids would be born with hooves," I say with a wink towards Arthurs. Not a single muscle moves on his face. He stares at me, unflinching, his dark eyes showing no emotion. This guy was hard to read, I think.

"I often think of the giants, where they came from? How do they keep their anonymity? Where they live?"

"Did you ever go back?" Susan asks.

"Yes, a couple of hundred years later, I was near the place and decided to visit the cairn. I was very surprised to see that the cairn was bigger again, more huge rocks had been placed upon the original ones. The entrance had been covered up by boulders that only a giant could lift! It was good to know they were still around. You know, it seems there are still some secrets and mysteries in this world. It would be pretty boring otherwise, now, wouldn't it?"

"You said you came across a nest of vampires, real vampires?" the boy asks.

"You want me to tell you another story, about the vampires? That's two for the price of one. Well, OK, but then I want some answers?" I say, turning to look at Susan, and seeing her nod in agreement.

2

A PURPOSE

"I think the year was 1350, I'm not sure. Anyway, at that time, I travelled across Europe like the Angel of Death, meeting out my own justice to all those that I felt deserved to die. I hunted down murderers, rapists, overthrew despots and murderous dictators only to, more than often, see them replaced by someone more villainous than before. After a while, I realised that it was pointless, the justice I was serving out, in my name, was turning me into the very people I was chasing. I was angry and hurt, until one day when I rode into a small village near the edge of the Carpathian Mountains and met Christina. She would be my first true love. She saw my scars, external and internal, and took me in, never asking questions. She calmed my restless spirit and angry heart, turning me into a kind, caring and loving husband. It was the happiest time of my life... until the Black Death swept into the village, on a horse drawn cart full of infected rats. It took hold of the whole village, and destroyed it in three short months, taking my wife and unborn child. She and the priest, Yarimesh were the last to go. It was he who with his dying words asked of me to make a promise, which would set me on the road to joining you here, centuries later. He said that the church had sent him on a mission to exorcise some demons from Castle Torenbec, a day's ride from the village. He was babbling and in fear of his soul, because if he did not carry out this order, he would have failed God and would rot in hell for all eternity. He had just been too scared to follow through with this order. Whether he was scared of catching the plague, or of facing the demons he had

KNIGHT ETERNAL

Plate: 3

been ordered to exorcise, I will never know. On his deathbed I nodded a promise to him, only to return and find my wife cold and unmoving. I buried them in the church grounds in one of the few remaining plots left. I remember standing in front of the freshly dug graves to this day, the smell of the soil, the mud on my hands and the tears running down my cheeks, as I said a final prayer.

You know, you never get used to losing someone, it never gets any better. I have loved and lost, and loved and lost again, and each time a piece of my heart hardens to the emotional strain of seeing your loved ones die in front of your eyes; while I keep going, never ageing, never changing, until there is just nothing left... but hurt. Eight hundred years is a long time up here," I said, tapping my head with my forefinger.

"I left the rest of the villagers where they were, there were too many to bury. The place stank, bloated and decomposing bodies lay in great heaps, piled on top of each other. Blood ran in rivulets, up and down the muddy streets. Flies hovered and settled in their swarms, with rats and mangy dogs chewing on the carcasses. I left town with tears in my eyes, and a mission to complete. My heart was heavy, my loss complete. I think those demons I met were in the wrong place at the wrong time, they didn't stand a chance."

"Hang on a minute," The boy interrupts. "You really mean to say that they exist, and you fought them. Real demons?"

"Weren't you listening? Yes, of course they do... they still do." I reply. "But they are not like the demons or vampires you see in films, not the ones that look like humans and have fangs like Count Dracula. Sure, they had fangs all right, but these things that I came across were very different from that, monstrous in comparison. Let me tell you the story and all will become as clear as mud, or should I say blood.

"I left the village with a heavy heart, with anger welling up inside me like a volcano waiting to burst. Who was I most angry with? At the time it was God, for abandoning us in our time of need. All the suffering, all the agony and death that I was witnessing, and nothing or no one to stop it. Why did he not raise a finger to help to stop the suffering? And then there was me, unaffected by the plague, by ageing or death, seemingly immortal and impervious to any disease.

Reports had reached me that the plague was now infecting the whole known world. Some thought that this was the end of the world, an act of God to destroy the human race, brought on by our own evil ways. I could vouch for that; I'd seen enough of that to agree with those terms. Evil festers in the hearts of all men. For some it never surfaces, held in check by the good deeds of those around them, while for others, it is set free with gay abandon to wreak havoc. There is goodness and wickedness in all of us, of that, I am sure. Anyway, I digress, I will return to my vampire encounter.

I followed the dirt track out of town, away from the stench of death and decay. Although it was high summer, it had been raining the night before and the road was heavy going. My boots and britches were covered up to my knees in mud, when I rounded a corner and came to a crossroads. One road headed east towards Poland and Russia, while the other led west into the heart of Carpathia and the Castle. I was the only one on the road, the sun was out and there was not a cloud in the sky, it was a beautiful day. Birds were singing in the trees, and everything looked like the world was at peace. I took a deep breath and turned westwards to honour my promise to a dying priest.

I travelled all day at a fast pace, my rage forging a way across a barren but stunning landscape, stopping only at a stream to drink some water and chew on some dried beef. I felt as if I was the last man alive. The countryside consisted of rolling hills and farmland, with large swathes of trees and forests stretching into the distance. A range of mountains stood proudly on the horizon, their peaks covered with snow. I skirted a village that gave off the smell of death, seeing no movement and fearing the worst, I moved on. A few farms stood silent with large red crosses painted on the barn doors. A pack of dogs yelped at me but kept their distance. The letter from the Vatican and a Bible, were tucked in my britches. I had a rough map of where I was going, and I used this to check my direction. I knew that I wouldn't reach the castle till nightfall but paced on regardless. The muddy road, which was no more than a cart track led onwards, winding its way through the countryside, until, as night began to fall, I rounded a corner and saw a wagon and its contents. I tensed, as nothing moved. My armlet began to tingle sensing the presence of something supernatural. The smell hit me first, the smell of death, but this was a little different. I drew my sword and reached behind my back for my shield. I crouched low and looked into the shrubs on either side of the road, looking for any sign of movement. Night was falling fast; the shadows were stretching, and a full moon was starting to make its way into the clear night sky. I listened but heard nothing apart from an owl hooting in the trees off to my left. It was as if the world was holding its breath, waiting for me to start the clock. I crept forward, reached the back of the wagon and peered around the side to see a crumpled figure. Beyond that, another figure lay on the earth, unmoving. The stench of death was worse here, but there was an underlying smell I could not fathom. I turned and looked down the other side of the wagon and could see nothing amiss. I crept down this side as silently as I could until I reached the head of the cart and stared in horror at the sight before me. Two oxen had been pulling the cart, but now they were just skeletons, stripped to the bones where they stood. The only clue that this had happened recently was a dark wet stain that glistened in the moonlight, blood. In shock I raced around to the two figures and was horrified to see that these two humans had also been stripped to the bone. Clothes lay scattered and shredded all about their skeletons, as if they had been torn off in a frenzy, to get at the meat within. I shuddered, feeling a fear like nothing I had felt before, creep into my psyche. What had happened was a complete mystery, the like of which I had never seen before. What manner of creature, or creatures, could do this? Could this be the unholy demons that the dying priest had told me about? I left that scene as fast as I could, fearful of what I might find on the road ahead. But my resolve was unwavering in my mission to rid the world of such evil monstrosities that could skin a man to the bone.

I was more than pleased to reach a bend in the road and leave the sight of those unearthly deaths behind me. I replaced my shield behind my back, as if that action would shut out the horrors I had just encountered. As soon as I rounded the bend, I saw a copse in the distance, and beyond that I could see the silhouette of a castle, I was nearing my destination. I realised I had been holding my breath, and I let it out slowly and quietly. My armlet began to tingle again, sending tendrils of alarm up my arm, and I peered towards the castle looking for signs of anything unusual. The air hung heavy, as if a storm was about to arrive. Not a sound could be heard, it was so quiet; no bird, no insect, it was as if I was looking at the beginning of life on a new planet, waiting for it to burst forth. The copse was made up of huge trees, as if planted by some rich landowner to create a garden that would be the envy of all around. The road led through the copse to a crossroads that skirted the castle, then continued into a forest. In the distance a wisp of smoke hung in the air, and I wondered if it was the fire of a home or funeral pyres. Outcrops of rock jutted up out of the trees, increasing more as the ground rose to the summit. A path, now overgrown and littered here and there with boulders, led up to the castle. The armlet continued to thrum and pulsate on my wrist, signalling that something supernatural was near me. Beside the crossroads, I picked out the unmistakable look of a hanging tree. Most villages and larger settlements had one. It was the easiest and cheapest way to punish wrong doers. Justice and retribution were swift and merciless in the Middle Ages. Many a person would be wrongly convicted and hung for a deed they did not commit. I've seen many a hanging, and no one died well. It always brought out a crowd and I remember seeing kids running and playing around the hanging tree. I even saw one kid climb a hanging tree and use the noose to swing, much to the cheers of the crowd and annoyance of the hangman, who was normally the local sheriff or one of his deputies. Hangings brought the worst out in people. The macabre sense of watching someone die at the end of a rope, has a strange effect on you.

Normally, it was a large tree with a big enough branch to hold the weight of a few men, or women. Women were often hanged, especially witches! Corpses would be left to rot there, as a warning that this was a God-fearing place and to watch your guard. Crows and magpies would sit upon the rotting dangling carrion, fighting over every tasty morsel.

The moon was up and full, casting an eerie glow upon the castle. It sat above the castle like a huge pearl, illuminating the landscape in a monochromatic picture. Shadows stretched across the ground from the trees where the moon hit, and the ground looked as if it were covered in a silvery sheen.

Gripping my sword tighter, I strode forwards, towards the castle, on aching limbs that were in need of rest; that they would not get that night. As I neared the hanging tree, I saw the unmistakable line of ropes hanging from it. The branches stretched and covered the road, enshrouding it in darkness that even the moon could not penetrate. As soon as I entered beneath its branches, my armlet began to throb even more, the temperature dropped, and I saw my breath forming in front of me. I paused, tensing for action but sensed no movement. My eyes pierced the gloom and came across something out of the ordinary. High up, and hanging from a long branch, I saw what looked like six silent dark forms, swaying ever so slightly, as if on an imaginary breeze. What they were I had no idea, all I could make out were the six dark shapes, human in form, but hanging upside down, swaying ever so slightly.

My foot crunched on something as I tried to get a better view, and I peered down to see that I had stood on a bone fragment, crunching it under my boot. A yard in front was a pile that looked like more bones. With trepidation, I sheathed my sword and found some dry wood so I could make a torch. I lit the torch and as I did so, I took a step back in horror. In front of me lay the carcasses of two horses, one larger than the other, both stripped to the bone. I was a lover of horses and was disgusted at this sight, as much as the human skeletons I had seen earlier. The earth beneath the bones was stained, and I knew why. Beyond that I saw two more figures. I moved towards them and saw that it was the skeletons of two youths, probably boys, picked to the bone and left where they died, their clothes shredded and scattered all around them. I fell to my knees, 'what manifestation of horror was going on here?' Instinctively, I reached out to touch the skull of the nearest youth. My arm straightened instantly, my head flung back, and my eyes rolled, as I felt the last terrifying moments of this poor child."

I paused then, seeing that the group were open mouthed, enrapt in my story.

"You see, one of my new found skills, or curses, is that when I touch someone that has died, I get to relive the person's final death throes. It's such a lovely gift! I live out their last moments as if it is me dying, it's pretty intense and not one for the faint hearted," I said sarcastically. "I don't use it much but when I do, it can come in handy, despite the nightmares that follow." I pause momentarily, letting them take this in, then continue the story.

"I remember seeing the terrified look on one boy's face as something came at them from the night sky in a swirling mass of wings, claws, teeth and red eyes. I watched helplessly as his friend was lifted into the sky, his clothes stripped off him in tattered shreds. I hear his screams cut off quickly as he was torn to pieces. I felt myself being lifted at the same time by taloned black hands. I felt the beating of wings and rushing of air. I felt my clothes being ripped from me, my flesh following, bodies and wings all around me. Mouths filled with sharp pointed teeth, and with bloodshot eyes, attacked me. The pain was intense as I was pulled to pieces in seconds. And then a darkness filled me, before I woke back in the real world. I'd seen what foul demons had done this deed, and in his dying moments I'd seen what they looked like. The reaction of the vision made me jolt upright and stumble backwards, only to get my heel stuck in the other youth's ribcage, causing me to fall on my backside, beneath the ropes of the hanging tree. I heard a stirring above me in the trees. My mind was still haunted with the horrifying images of the dying youth, eaten alive by flying demons. I felt a wetness seeping through my britches, that I knew was blood and gore from the demons feasting. I look up through the foliage into six sets of bloodshot red eyes, barely twenty feet above me. Something wet and sticky lands on my face, and I realise that the demons have not left.

Why they were still there, I'm not sure. Whether they were just gorged on their meal or just hanging out, no pun intended, I don't know, but they had not left the killing ground. Why they didn't attack me straight away, again I don't know, perhaps their hunger had been satiated, but when I clattered back onto my backside, I certainly got their attention. I saw movement above me, an unfurling of wings, and a rustling in the leaves.

They came at me as one, as I got to my feet and backed away into the open, to give me room to defend myself. I drew my sword and braced myself to face these demons from hell. My mind was one of anger and vengeance, anger for the horrors I had seen these creatures perform, and vengeance for the lives lost and never to be lived, because of these flesh-eating horrors.

They swept down and under the lowest branch, a seething mass of moving darkness. These creatures in some weird way looked human, most six foot or taller. They wore no clothes and had black shiny skin that gleamed as they appeared into the moonlight. Their heads looked angular, were hairless and had tiny bat like ears covered in the same black skin. Bloodshot red eyes peered at me with a ravenous hunger, the likes of which I had never seen before. They glided under the branch, their huge wings unfurled, then flapped once, twice and shot forward at an incredible speed, with long clawed talons reaching for my throat. But no innocent peasant was facing those creatures, no lamb to the slaughter, but a lion with claws that had a bite. I harnessed my anger, gathered my thoughts, my training and experience taking over. I pulled my sword up to waist height and swung it in one fluid motion. Two of the demons came at me from the front and my sword sliced through the first and continued on through the next one without a pause. A single agonising screech echoed from their opened mouths, which showed rows of pointed teeth with two large fangs. They fell to the floor with a thump and turned to dust before my startled eyes. I turned as another rose above me, clawing at me as it passed overhead. I felt it's long talons brush through my hair. I swivelled, thrusting my sword upwards into the demonic creature's hide. The sword was wrenched from my hand as it tried to pull away, its powerful wings flapping quickly to escape. But it was to no avail, the creature fell to the ground with a high-pitched screech. As it hit the floor, it instantly turned to dust, leaving my sword stuck in the earth, rocking back and forth.

Three more of those incarnations of evil remained, swirling in the sky above me, looking for an opening. I wonder if they felt a hint of fear at my prowess in killing three of their kind. I hoped so. I reached for my shield, took a few steps, retrieved my sword and turned to face them, even as a form bundled me over and pinned me to the ground. The speed in which they moved was astounding. I grabbed one taloned hand as it reached for me. My shield was pinned between myself and the demon, my sword hand held by its other hand. I was gripping the taloned hand like a vice, trying to keep it from slitting my throat. Out of the corner of my eye, I watched as the other two settled to the ground, furling their wings behind their backs in one smooth motion and walking towards us, moving in for the kill. The demon I was grappling with had its face above me, its fetid breath and blood smeared fangs inches from my face. I saw it's bat like ears and the tops of its wings above its shoulders. I rolled to the left and then the right, looking to gain some leverage, but gaining no purchase. The demon was incredibly heavy and had the advantage. These demons were overwhelmingly strong. In over fifty years I had not met a man that could best me in hand-to-hand combat, but these demons were like no man I had ever met. Not a sound came from the fetid mouth, at least I could be grateful for that. I sighed, relaxed my grip on the taloned hand, giving the impression that I had given up the fight. The creature thinking this, relaxed ever so slightly, a bad mistake that was going to prove costly for it. I wrestled my left arm free and bludgeoned it with my armlet, hoping to knock it off me. But to my amazement, and utter relief, the demon gave a dying screech and turned to dust, covering me in a thin film, that I brushed away in disgust.

I rolled and rose, gripping and swinging my sword wildly at the remaining two demons. My sword cut deep into one, and that one didn't even have time to cry before it too, turned to dust. Only one remained and this creature backed off, its red eyes never leaving mine. I glimpsed my torch still spluttering on the floor a few yards away.

"Come on, you filthy demon," I screamed at it, my blood rage up.

The thing hissed at me, crouched and tensed to spring. As it did, I dropped and rolled, swinging my sword but hitting fresh air as the demonic creature lifted itself skyward. My hand fell on the handle of my lit torch and instinctively I lifted it and threw it at the creature. It was twenty feet above my head when the smouldering torch struck its wing, ripping through the thin, vein like skin and setting it alight. The creature dived, twisting in the air as it plummeted towards the Earth. Before it struck, it righted itself and glided off towards the castle, its wing still smouldering and damaged. The creature was screeching wildly in agony as it rose and was momentarily silhouetted against the moon, its winged form looking like a evil version of Icarus. I watched as it flapped its wings frantically to keep above ground, every sinew in its body desperate to keep it aloft. With a great effort, it rose towards the castle, then dived and disappeared into the ruins.

I slumped to the floor, exhausted and bruised. One demon remained. I remember thinking that tomorrow I would hunt this foul creature down and end this outrage once and for all. Five down one to go, it's not been a bad night's work. Little did I know what was to follow. I found shelter in some brush underneath the overhang of a rock, and with the stone to my back I settled down to eat and drink. Dawn was fast approaching when I finally managed to sleep, my dreams filled with demons, vampires and heinous dark omens. I think it was me that coined the phrase 'sleeping with one eye open', because since that night I've always been a light sleeper, hearing everything around me as if I was fully awake and alert.

The sun was already high in the sky when I started climbing the rocky path up to the castle. Not a cloud could be seen. It was as if God had decided to shine a light on the darkness that was eating away at the edge of my thoughts. It was tough going, with some of the track completely covered in rubble, thick brambles and heavy vegetation. Sometimes I'd have to climb over a few rocks, or skirt through the undergrowth, to rejoin the track. The day was getting hotter by the hour, and not just because of the climb; summer was just beginning with the promise of warmer days to come. I was sweating and breathing heavily when I reached the top of the path and looked upon the ruins of a once grand castle. I had no idea why this place had been left to turn to ruins, its destruction was almost complete. Another hundred years and it would be gone forever. One tower stood defiant against the decimation, and one corner of the castle also still remained; it was these two that I had spotted the previous day. Huge blocks of stone were scattered everywhere as if it had exploded, throwing stones far and wide. A line of crows sat on top of a half-ruined gate, cawing at me as soon as I crested the rise. I ignored them and entered what was left of the gate, into what had once been an open courtyard. In the castle wall that was still standing, was a dark opening, almost totally concealed by the shadows and it was here that I sensed I'd investigate. I strode across the cobbled courtyard, the noise of my footsteps echoing off the high walls. As I neared the opening, a foul stench reached my senses, one of death and decay. I was used to this now, but this smell was slightly different, just like at the wagon, and where the boys had been butchered. This was the demons lair, and this was where the last creature was going to meet its end, one way or the other. I could see a straight shaft heading gradually downwards into the earth, but beyond that nothing. I decided to enter and find out more. But I wasn't just any foolhardy naive warrior, I was a seasoned campaigner by now. I knew down there it was in its own domain, I was the intruder. Darkness was its sanctuary. I scanned the area looking for any sign, and when the warmth of the sun climbed over the top of the wall, I was given one.

I waited a few minutes longer, then drew my sword, lit another torch, took a deep breath and strode into the darkness.

The shaft led down for about thirty paces to what would have been a lower level of the castle, possibly the dungeons. I kept looking behind me at the thin beam of sunlight and knew that I didn't have much time. I came to a halt as the ground levelled. The stench was almost unbearable, even my eyes were watering as I held the torch up above me and scanned the area. My knees went weak at the sight, and a creeping dread filled my mind. I had reached the dungeons. Huge iron gates lay strewn across the floor. Columns of stone, like the arches of a cathedral, swept into the distance to a far wall. These were the foundations that had once kept up this great castle. But none of this really registered in my mind at the time, as hanging from every piece of stone were hundreds of the bat-like demons. On the floor were heaps and heaps of bones, all intermingled into pyramids. I swallowed hard, knowing that I had made a mistake that might very well cost me my life, or maybe something even worse. A faint stirring echoed around the chamber, I sensed movement all around me. Before I had time to retreat a line of the bat-like demons unfurled their wings, and blocked my path, while even more surrounded me. I took a stance and raised my sword, preparing to sell my soul dearly. I looked over my shoulder and thought that if I could survive the next few minutes, my plan might just work. I swished my torch around forcing the creatures back, to give me room to swing my sword. They certainly didn't like the light. I saw the creatures tense and ready themselves to pounce when suddenly, they paused. I sensed movement from the back of the cavern as something came towards me through the throng. They parted like a wave on either side, making way for what I suspected would be their leader. The thing came out of the shadows and walked right up to me, showing no fear whatsoever. This creature was different. He was at least nine foot tall, and completely dwarfed me. His black skin was dappled with white spots, even his face looked drawn and old. His body though was like one of the statues that adorned the amphitheatre in Rome. With thighs as big as my trunk and arms as thick as my legs, this creature was the definite alpha male in this parlour! He looked at me with the curiosity of a lion who has found a new prey but is not sure what to make of it.

"What have we here?" it said, sniffing the air in front of me, it's red glowing eyes never leaving mine. I didn't respond, the question seemed rhetorical, so I didn't want to upset the guy! And then things got interesting. "You smell of the plague but it doesn't affect you, you are like us... brother," it said with a lengthy pause before the last word.

"I'm no brother of yours," I spat out.

"A human, yet not a human. A demon, yet not a demon." The thing hissed its words out, looking me up and down. "A demon in a human form perhaps?"

"There's only one demon here... and it's not me? Actually, I think there's more than one," I said, stalling for time, looking at the hundreds of red eyes all around me. Behind me, I glimpsed my salvation. A thin line of sunlight was gradually making its way down the shaft towards me. I'd stopped in this point for one purpose and wasn't going to budge. Not yet anyway!

"So, you think yourself human, do you?" the demon said with a snort of disgust.

"Looks that way to me, every time I look in the mirror." The demon recoiled ever so slightly at the words, taking a small step back.

It was then that all hell broke loose. One of the bat-like creatures, the one closest to the opening suddenly screeched in agony and burst into flames, setting alight the creature next to it. The rest scattered out of the way of the advancing sunlight, giving me a direct line to safety. The demon king, or whatever it was, lunged for me but it was too late. I had stepped back, and into the safety of the light. I had banked my life on the hope that they wouldn't be happy in sunlight

KNIGHT ETERNAL

Plate: 4

and had made a good choice this time.

The creatures hung back just out of the light, hissing at me, until they were quietened with a silent command from the demon king, who appeared again next to me.

"Fancy a dance?" I said with a smile.

"You'll be the one dancing tonight, human, on the end of a rope where I will eat you alive!" it hissed in annoyance.

"Thanks for the compliment, but I don't think so. I'll be long gone before you can come for me." I had no intention of leaving but I wasn't going to tell him that.

"You can't travel far enough for me not to find you. Give up this feeble body, join me and become my second-in-command. I promise you much, you'd be a fool not to accept." Now he was trying to stall me.

"Thanks for the offer, but I'm not keen on stripping the flesh of a living human and eating it. So, call me what you like, I'll stick to this body, thank you."

He screamed at my insults, reached out at the nearest demon picked it up and threw it at me. As soon as the sunlight touched the thing it turned to dust with a screech that stopped abruptly.

"Feel free to keep doing that." I said, with a smile, brushing dust off my clothes.

The demon king screamed again, a screech that echoed around the chamber, causing bits of rubble and dust to fall from the walls and ceiling. I had to cover my ears with my hands and as I did so my armlet, which had been under my sleeve, caught a glint of the sunlight and lit up the darkness in the chamber above the throng of creatures. In an instant, it was gone, but the seeds of a plan had formed, all I had to do was survive the night!

Already the sunlight was starting to move. In moments, the sun's rays would be gone completely. I backtracked up the shaft towards salvation, fresh air and away from the smell of that evil nest.

The demon king's screams followed me up the shaft as I ran to get ahead of the diminishing sunlight.

"I'll find you, human," he was pretty pissed off by now. "I'll find you, and eat you alive." It screamed up the tunnel at me.

I came out into the courtyard and was never happier to see the sun than on that afternoon. I knelt and thanked the Lord for his salvation, then rose with a purpose, and a plan. It's funny how when you face impending death and survive, we all thank the same Lord we had been cursing earlier.

Time was against me; I had the remainder of the afternoon and evening to find a way to survive the night. I returned down the track to the vale, and to where I had slept the night before. I hacked away the undergrowth around the area, exposing a semi-circle of open ground. I dug holes in the earth and placed stakes that I had cut and shaped to a point, forming an impenetrable barrier. I then covered the stakes with the undergrowth I had hacked out. The overhang of the rock gave me some protection from above. I left a small area clear, my killing ground, where they could only come at me one at a time. I made as many torches as I could, placing them between the stakes and around the killing ground. I also made spears and stuck them all around the semi-circle of open ground. A calmness had come over me, one of the warrior before a great battle that doesn't know what the future holds, but realises he has prepared as best he can, and that some divine entity will now roll the dice to decide the future.

Every muscle and bone ached as the evening drew to a close, and the main event hadn't even started. As the sun started to fall over the horizon in an ominous red glow, I set light to the hanging tree in many places. I raced back to the safety of my area in time to see a dark wave erupt out of the castle. I turned to the flying demons and roared a battle cry. The tree was now fully ablaze, bathing the whole vale in a flickering picture show. I started lighting my torches, turning just in time to see the first demon impale itself on a stake, its screech suddenly cut short as it turned to dust. More quickly followed, sweeping low on wings of hate. In their eagerness for human flesh, especially the one that had already killed so many of their kin, they came at me in a moving mass of red eyes, beating wings and glistening fangs.

How I survived that night unscathed, I will never know. They attacked in a relentless wave, striking the hidden stakes and turning to dust, only for the next to do the same, never seeming to learn, the blood rage so strong, it seemed to blind their senses. How many died, I can not guess. Whether it was the fire

from the hanging tree and the torches that made them foolhardy, or perhaps they were driven on by the demon king, I know not. But they threw themselves towards me, dying in their hundreds upon the stakes. When one did get through, I met it with brutal efficiency. As the sky turned towards a new day, so their efforts became even more frenzied. At one point, I impaled four on one spear as they charged through, all of them turning to dust with screeches that could have woken the dead. The air was thick with dust that crackled and spat as it made contact with the torches. A strong smell of burnt flesh hung in the air. The hanging tree was now a smouldering wreck, blackened and never to hold a hanging rope again. My torches were nearly dead, their light dwindling into nothingness as the dawn approached, and I saw much to my relief the remaining demons swarm back to their nest. It had happened just as I hoped. Then something glided towards me and spoke.
"Why?" was all it asked.
"I made a promise to a dying priest," I replied, "he was a good man, one of the few."
"A priest?" Dawn was minutes away. If I could distract him, capture him or stall him in any way, I could stop him here, I thought.
"The opposite of you," I said with spite, and I meant it. I lifted my sword, my arm aching with the effort. I advanced out of my cauldron of safety, towards the demon king, ready to engage, wanting to finish this now.
He stepped forward and I thought he was about to attack, when he unfurled his wings and swept above me, heading back towards the castle. If he wasn't some horrifying demon from the pits of hell, it would have been a magnificent sight. His wingspan was massive, taking up the whole sky as he passed over me.
"Priests, ha!" he said as he flew off, "I've met my fair share of priests and most of them are very like me, the only difference is, they just wear a collar and carry a book."
He paused in mid-flight, hovering above the ground and turned back to face me again. "I ask again, why?"
"Because what you do is an outrage to God, and must be stopped." I shouted at him.

"Is that what you are? A weapon of God, ha!" he snorted, "A wolf in sheep's clothing, a demon within a human who fights for a God who has forsaken this planet for centuries. You fight alone and unseen and will die alone. What if I said that we are just trying to survive, to live and procreate, like any species? What if I say that you have invaded my home and all I am doing is protecting my brood? Would you not do the same?"

"You are abominations and must be destroyed." I managed to retaliate but I was rattled, his words had got to me.

"That is what you humans say to all things you do not understand." he said and peeled away, leaving me dazed and confused. Blood was seeping from many cuts and scratches on my body, my legs were shaking with the effort just to stay upright. My adrenaline had dropped, and I was starting to feel faint.

I watched him go, his wings flapping gracefully up and down like some ancient dinosaur from a forgotten era. As dawn broke, I watched as he dived down and disappeared. I let out a sigh and crumpled to the ground in exhaustion. How many had I killed; It was impossible to tell.

Again, the day was bright and sunny, the clouds a distant memory, when I reached the castle keep and looked towards the hole that led downwards into their nest. The crows were still there sat on the broken gate, cawing away at me as if I were trespassing, or perhaps, beckoning me forward towards the gates to hell.

I checked the time by the rising sun, sat down in the sunlight to wait and almost immediately nodded off; the night's adventures, and the morning climb, catching up with me. My dreams and visions were dark and horrifying, lost in a labyrinth of catacombs chased by red eyed demons. I don't know how these visions came to me. Perhaps it was the close proximity to the demonic lair. Perhaps it was the thousands of dead humans butchered here, whose blood had seeped into the ground and tainted the soul of this castle. *At one stage, I remember seeing space, a great vast expanse of stars with Earth in the foreground. But not the Earth that we know of today, one of a bygone era. The land masses were completely different and the poles were free of ice. Within that vision, I glimpsed an armada of ships heading towards the planet. Time seemed to shoot forward to a ship landing on an outcrop of rock, before a vast sea of trees. A forest that stretched for as far as the eye could see, in every direction. As the sun rose, so an opening appeared upon the ship, with steps descending to the stony ground. A swarm of black demons erupted out of the craft, which looked like the same creatures I now fought. Even as my mind tried to ask whether these were the pilots of these ships, then humanoid forms started to appear down the steps, one holding a glowing white staff. Other life forms, reptilian in nature scurried around the humans. It became apparent, that these reptilians and the black skinned demons were slaves. I can't remember how I knew this, but I did. Again, time seemed to stretch forward to a scene of carnage, a great battle had taken place, an uprising where the humanoids managed to defeat the combined forces of demons and reptilians, banishing them from the face of the Earth for all time, changing their DNA so that just the merest touch of sunlight was deadly...*

I awoke with a start, and looked to the sun, my eyes wide. I feared that I would miss my chance and have to survive another night. I hurriedly rose and raced to the opening, with only minutes remaining. I took out my shield and exposed my armlet. I kept my sword sheathed and ready to use, but today I had a better weapon and the tools to use it.

My heart was still heavy, and my mind confused with the vision. These were beings from a different world, who had tried to overthrow their masters and failed, only to be banished into the shadows for all eternity. Was it my right to end their lives? And then I saw and heard in my mind the dying boy's screams as he was ripped to shreds, and my resolve hardened. With each step, so my determination grew. They were not of this Earth and were demons. No more humans shall die by their hands, not while I still lived.

I reached the bottom and skidded into the same spot as the previous day. A beam of sun was already warming my legs as I roared another battle cry. I heard the unfurling of many wings, and the glint of red eyes in the darkness. There was still so many of them left. Before they could even move, I knelt and held out my shield to catch the sun, angling the ray into the shadows. Like a laser beam, the sunlight ripped through the throng of demons, destroying them even as they started to come at me. A cacophony of screeches, which left my ears ringing for the rest of the day, echoed through this chamber of death. As the sunlight hit the creatures, so they screamed in agony and burst into flame, often setting alight the ones closest to them. As I angled the shield, I spread the rays around the room catching anything that moved. And as the sunlight increased, so I rose and stood with my armlet also catching the light. Like two eyes, piercing the darkness, one large and one small, the beams of sunlight wreaked a heavy vengeance on the nest of demons, until the room was silent, and a layer of dust hung in the air. I stood there, bathed in the sunlight, a destroyer of demons, basking in the warm glow of the hunt. Had I killed them all? I hadn't seen the demon king die, but he could have been engulfed without me knowing. But somehow, I felt that he wasn't there he was somewhere else, somewhere deeper."

"In their fright to escape my 'sun gun,'" I say and look at Arthurs. "Good name, eh?" I ask, goading him, but getting no response. And then I realise he was too engrossed in the story to care, so I continue.

"In their fright to escape my 'sun gun,'" I say again, "the creatures had tried to escape, and in their panic flown into some of the columns. As the last one screeched and turned to dust, so I heard a faint rumbling. Masonry started to fall from the ceiling, dust and brick crashing to the stone floor in ever increasing amounts. I felt the Earth shake under my feet and saw one of the columns waver then settle momentarily, before starting to collapse. I turned and ran back up the tunnel as fast as I could. I reached the top as a dust cloud erupted behind me. More rubble began to fall, and I saw huge parts of the courtyard collapse inwards and disappear into the depths. To my right, the huge tower and corner section of the castle, started to fall. I ran a gauntlet of stone and rubble, before heading down the path towards the burnt hanging tree. A great roaring, followed by a large column of dust, that billowed into the sky like an erupting volcano was replaced by an eerie silence. Only the murder of crows broke the quiet, circling above the rubble, angered that they had lost their perch.

I stood at the crossroads, bloodied, dirty and covered in the ashes of the creatures. My whole body ached, each movement an effort. My eyes caught the thin whiff of smoke on the horizon along the road that led parallel to the hill, so rather than retrace my steps, I stumbled on, entering a line of trees. I soon came across a fast-flowing river with a stone bridge crossing it, leading to the column of smoke I had seen earlier. I left the road, headed to the water and found an area that was secluded by brush. I stripped and washed myself in the river. The water was cool and clear, and I remember drinking, feeling the energy of the water giving me a boost, as if it were some magical elixir of life. As I washed the blood away, I looked at my cuts and wounds from the previous night and saw that they were already healing, the open cuts and slashes of the demons' claws closing over, leaving thin white lines of scars that would eventually disappear completely. Only my neck wound, the long white scar that had nearly decapitated me before I had been changed, and would certainly have killed me, remained upon my body. I reached up with my right hand and traced its rough edge, feeling the line of the cut. How had I survived such a wound? What had happened in my final moments before I was transformed? I remember the day as if it were yesterday, but the final moments are a blur, a mystery that needs to be unravelled.

My thoughts returned to the bat-like demons, and I pondered on the fact that they had come from the stars. This alone was something that did not compute in my mind at the time. Only with today's knowledge can I comprehend this a little better. Had I the right to meet out this justice to a race of beings that were just trying to survive? Whatever form of brutal life they lived? Did I have the right to destroy them?

I came out of the water refreshed and clean but still unclean within, my thoughts troublesome and at war with each other. I found a safe spot, lay down and slept. When I woke, it was morning. I had slept long and felt refreshed, but ravenous. Perhaps the village I had glimpsed would have food for a warrior who had destroyed the horrors that had surely terrorised them.

I crossed the river, following the path up another few yards before I turned a corner in the forest, and looked down on an amazing sight. A village lay before me, and one unlike anything I had seen in many a year. Houses were scattered far and wide, all with signs of life. Children ran about playing. Chickens scurried and screeched to get out of the way, and dogs ran in and about the kids, barking and wagging their tails in joy. People were everywhere, going about their everyday lives as normal, as if the plague didn't even exist. There was no sign whatsoever of the Black Death, no doors painted with a red cross, no funeral pyres, it was as if the plague had somehow skipped this oasis of calm. My heart leapt with seeing such normality, and I remember making a quick thanks to God for showing me that hope still remained.

With a spring in my step, I started down towards the village, my thoughts on food and perhaps even some wine, when two forms slid out from either side of the tree line. They held the longest spears I had ever seen and wore masks that covered most of their faces.

"Stop right there," the one on the left said to me.

"Don't come any closer," the one on the right added.

"That's not a nice greeting to a traveller simply looking for a good meal, and a flagon of wine," I replied angrily, my hand going to my sword hilt.

"Rest up in yonder valley for the night and then come again in the morning, and we will let you pass," the one on the left said, nodding his head to the way I had just come from.

"What?" my mind was already starting to put things together, but I didn't want to believe what it was telling me.

Behind the two guards, I saw a crowd gathering, heading our way. Not one looked sick, they all looked healthy.

"By whose authority?" I asked.

"By mine, stranger," a voice said as the crowd parted to let someone through. It was so like the meeting in the castle dungeons, that it sent a chill down my spine at the thought of it.

A man appeared, coming out of the crowd to stand alongside the two guards. He was at least six foot tall. His wavy silver hair and trimmed beard showed he was old, but he had an imposing presence. The people looked at him and quickly scuttled out of his way, giving him a clear line to me. I could almost smell the power he had over these people, the fear he empowered.

"And you are?"

"I'm the village Elder, stranger, and that gives me the authority. Because of what we have heard, all that come to this village must at first be purified by the divine spirit in yonder valley. In the morning you will be most welcome."

"Divine spirit!" I said in contempt and laughed.

"You dare laugh at our customs."

"Customs," I laughed again incredulously. "And what custom is that?"

At this point, a woman broke through the crowd and raced towards me but was caught and held back by one of the guards.

"Please, stranger, have you seen my boys, two twins, Demetri and Yusef?" she was crying and trying to break free. "Please, they were taking the sacrifice to the..."

"Silence, woman," the Elder boomed.

And then all the pieces finally fell into place, my thoughts and doubts, my hopes shattered, my anger again boiling over.

"Custom, you call it! You are in league with the devil," I shouted to the crowd, and then added quietly, "or you were?" and spat on the road in front of them in disgust. "You make innocent traders, travellers on the road, stay the night in the hanging tree valley so that your 'friends' can satisfy their needs if they are infected by the plague, or let them pass if they are not. That's it, isn't it? Was it you who signed this pact? Do they somehow protect you from the plague, and in return you offer up travellers, or if none come for a while, you offer up cattle or horses instead?" I said, pointing at the Elder. "And how do you know if they only take the tainted ones? Tell me? How do you know that they don't just eat anything that takes their fancy, like two young children," I spat out the last words with a heavy-heart.

The woman fell to her knees, sobbing uncontrollably and although I felt pity for her loss, I did not show it. For was she not a part of the whole, however big her loss had been.

"You disgust me," I said and turned and walked back down the track. I did not bother to tell them that the demons were destroyed. By the time they'd find out, it would be too late for them. At that point, I realised that not all demons have fangs and wings, some walk on two feet, in broad daylight and pretend to be human."

I pause, my story complete. I looked down at my hands and see them shaking ever so slightly. Reminiscing on this tale has released some emotions that have laid hidden for many years.

"And now, it's about time you gave me some answers?" I ask.

"It seems you had a sense of humour for some time there, hos," Arthurs nods in appreciation of my efforts. "You are one hell of a fighting machine, I'll give you that," he says with awe. I am beginning to warm to the guy, and then he blows it, "That's if any of it is true. We haven't got one scrap of evidence to prove otherwise, now have we, just your centuries old arse on it!"

In reply, I just laughed at his stupid stubbornness, and shake my head, which makes him even more angry.

"Have I run your pet bunny over or something? What have I done to make you hate me so much, Arthurs? You do want me on your team, right?"

3

ORIGINS

The car drove up the short private road with a neatly cut verge on either side of a woodland. Beyond the verge, a line of firs swayed and creaked in annoyance to the strong winds that were buffeting them. Almost complete darkness holds sway within the overhang of trees, interspersed by the odd ray of sunlight that has managed to break through the canopy and make a faint light between the massive trunks.
I sense my heart beating fast as we approach a huge set of black wrought iron gates. Above the gates, a plaque with a raven holding a branch emblem reads, 'The Harkness Institute'. On either side of the gates, a high wall stretches away before disappearing behind the trees. I know it surrounds the whole estate, or it did in my day.
Much to my surprise, the gates open automatically as the car approaches.
"Stop," I say, before the car drives through. Arthurs stops the car just before the gates, then turns to look at me quizzically.
Susan turns her head towards me, her eyes scanning my features.
"Anything wrong?" she questions.
"No, I would just like to walk in through the gates if you don't mind?"
"OK, no problem," Susan replies.
She gets out the car as well, but I don't complain, she is a part of this as well.
"We will see you at the house," I hear her call to Arthurs, waving him on.
I stand there, between the gates, my back to Susan and the car.

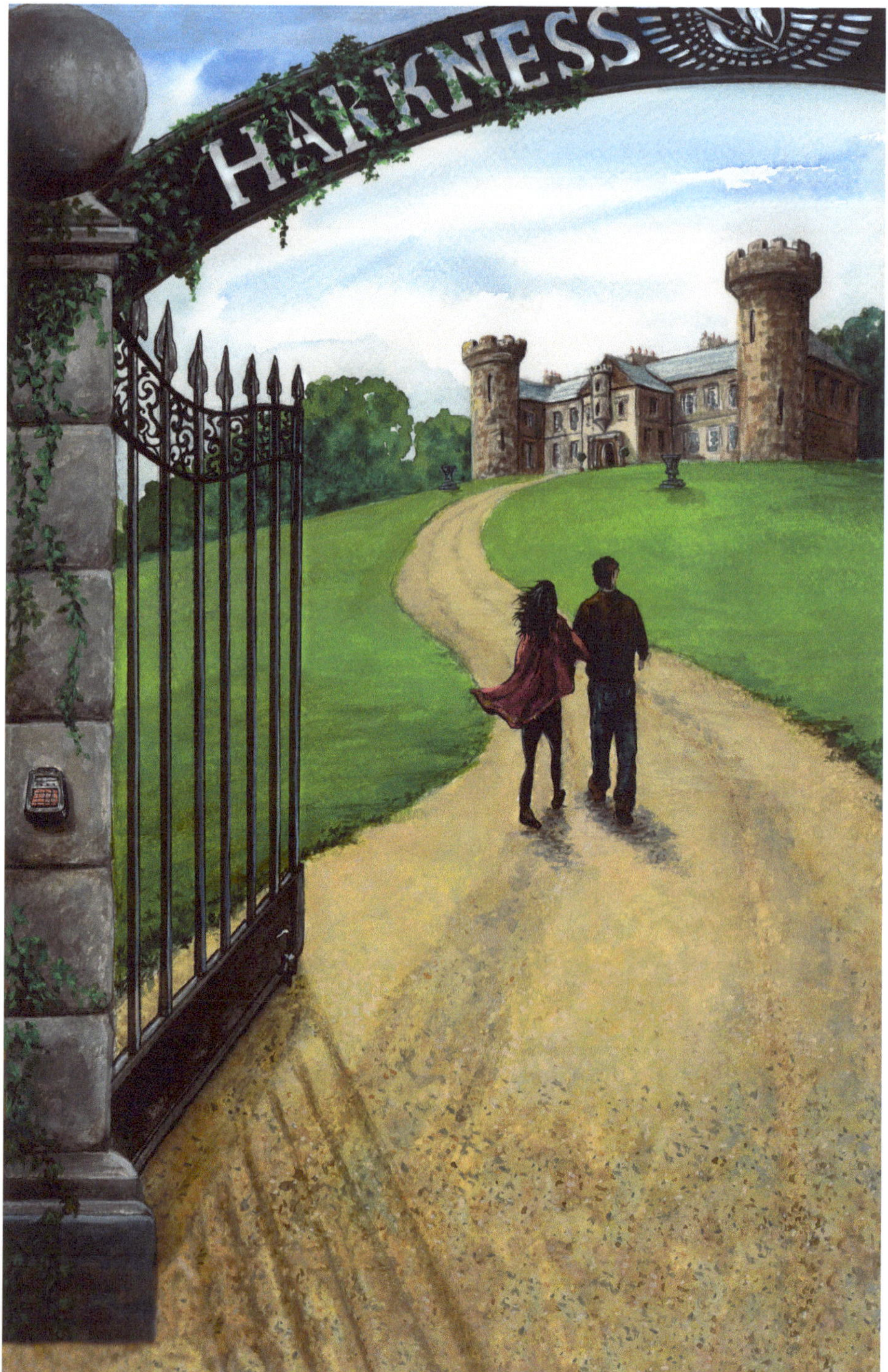

Plate: 5

"It seems that you've upgraded since my last visit, you have electricity now!"
I sense Susan smile, making a tiny snort of laughter. Again, she did not reply, she was good at that, most witches were; they had the knack of not replying and making you the one who continues the conversation. Which is exactly what I do.

"You know the last time I walked through these gates I was carrying Elizabeth. I thought I could save her, I thought my powers would protect her, but they didn't, and I couldn't. I thought if I could get her back to Dr Phobius, he could save her. Somehow, deep down, I think I knew, I just didn't want to let her go! Not like that, not like that," I repeated the last words as if it had just happened. I look down at my arms which have formed a cradle, as if I am carrying something. Just then I think I see the bloodied and torn features of Elizabeth, her face deathly pale, her lifeblood soaked into my clothes. Her eyes were closed as if at rest, and at the time I thought she was just sleeping.

"I swore that I'd never return after that, but that was over four centuries ago! I suppose it's time to put that ghost to rest," I raise my head, my gaze looking towards the house within the grounds of the estate. The smell of freshly cut grass drifts past on the wind, and I can hear the faint noise of a lawn mower in the distance. A huge stately home, the once ancestral home of the Croft's who's last known relative Lord Archibald Croft, was lost in some expedition somewhere in South America in the early 1900s. Built like a fort, it was all square shaped with turreted corners. The building was battleship grey, and built with brick from a local quarry, only five miles away. I was nervous to be returning after so long, I had always avoided the place, even though I had been close on several occasions. The house has too many skeletons for me to look at with anything but a hint of dread. I thought of all the people I have known and lost, the team we had formed, all destroyed on that one awful mission back in 1599. And as if to drive out my demons, I turn to Susan, surprised to see her eyes filled with tears. She could sense my anguish, my fears, my thoughts. She is going to make a fine witch one day, if she isn't already.

"That's why we thought we'd meet up in the pub," she replies.
"The Royal Oak! That was quite ironic," I say, with a snort. "That's the name of

our carriage. I'm sure I never heard of a pub called the Royal Oak until we started travelling around the Kingdom." I squint, looking towards the house and the shadows covering the parking area, expecting to see the old carriage and horses, waiting to take us out on another adventure.

What do you see?" Susan asks.

"I see the past like it was yesterday, I see all their faces as we set out on that day, never knowing it would be our last together. We were a happy bunch. I had settled at last after so long. I'd found a home and friends and the love of a good woman again. We weren't a couple, of course, but we were family and I loved Elizabeth as much as any man could love a woman. I can see Brother Matthew, a giant of a man. Frederick the German, another powerhouse who wielded a large, two handed, murderous looking axe. Then there was Staunton, the best archer I had ever seen, hardly ever missed, amazing he was. All battle-hardened warriors with good souls plucked from society by Elizabeth and given a purpose. I knew it couldn't last, of course. Eventually, they would age and die, and I would go on. I had prepared for that and was ready for it. But it didn't happen like that. It ended so suddenly and bloody, losing everyone in one awful night in the forest of Cannock. We didn't stand a chance.

We called ourselves 'Battleborn', as we were born and trained to fight from an early age. Elizabeth hated the name, saying that it gave off the wrong impression of what we were trying to achieve. We were there to protect people from the supernatural forces that were at large across these ancient isles. We weren't there to destroy them, that was a last resort, she would remind us. And that's what killed her in the end, wiped out our whole team, all except me! She had this inherent faith that all creatures could be swayed away from the dark, educated to live in peace. When we lost everyone, I walked away and swore never to return… and here I am, on the threshold!" I paused, then plucked up the courage to say what had been on my mind since we had met.

"Why am I here, Susan? What's the real reason?"

"It's complicated," she says, looking at the house.

"Then uncomplicate it!" I reply.

"Something big is taking place around the world, something catastrophic. We were asked to bring you in. We need you, John."

"You need me, you mean the Government need me?"

"No, not the Government, the Crown. The Government don't know much about you, I don't think. In your day, with Elizabeth, you worked for the Crown. To this day we work for the Crown, we always have. Even the monarchy has their secret organisations, and we are one of them. It was the Royal envoy that spoke to me, insisted we bring you in. We've kept tabs on you for a long time."

"Really, how surprising?" I reply with a hint of sarcasm. "The Crown!" I half say to myself, "Amazing."

I was still standing under the arch of the gates, almost as if I was afraid to take that next step because if I did, then I felt that there would be no turning back. I owed no one, I'd done my bit, I didn't need to be beholden to anyone. Walk away, John, I told myself, you don't have to do this.

"We think we know who you are, where you came from?" Susan says quietly from beside me.

"Oh, OK," I reply, not knowing what to say.

"You need to see it, to believe it. There was a disturbance at Canterbury Cathedral that uncovered something. It relates to you", she didn't elaborate any further. Just like Elizabeth, I think with a smile.

"Well, if that isn't a big enough carrot to dangle in front of my snout, I don't know what is," I reply.

"It's really exciting," she says raising her eyebrows.

"Now you are just teasing me. This is as bad as bribery," I add, my heart somehow lightened, my dark thoughts broken. She was good, this girl, she knows which buttons to press, just like Elizabeth.

I took a nervous step forward then took another more assured one, before turning to Susan.

"Come on then, time to get back to work by the sound of it," holding my arm out for her in the old-fashioned way for a man to escort a lady.

She smiles and places her hand through the crook of my elbow to hold my arm. I immediately felt the 'witch tingle', as I call it. It feels good for once.

"Ooh, you old romantic," she says with a smile.

"Less of the old, if you don't mind," I reply.

"Well, you are probably the oldest man on the planet, alive!" she adds with a smirk.

After that, we walk on in silence, reaching a bemused looking Arthurs. He was waiting for us with a scowl on his face, when he spots our arms entwined. I return his gaze with my own smug smile of satisfaction. Living for centuries still hasn't made me any more tolerant of people I don't like. I feel Susan withdraw her hand just a little too quickly and realise that these two are perhaps more than just co-workers.

"There's something else," Susan says, as we approach the huge double wooden doors of the house.

"There's more?" I say exaggeratedly.

"I'm not sure if you are aware, but Elizabeth kept a diary of everything. Of all your adventures."

"A diary, wow, slipped that one by us, didn't you Elizabeth! No, I didn't know." I reply. Now Arthurs was giving me the smug look.

"All your missions, all the different creatures she documented, naming them, putting as much down as possible, like a blueprint for anyone that followed. A lot of it relates to you, and how you became what you are. She was trying to figure that out and had made progress. There is a lot of stuff in there that might be of help in finding out who you are? It seems she was going to tell you once she returned from that final mission. It seems she was following a lead on that mission that related to you! Can you remember her saying anything to you about it?"

My mind had gone numb at the thought. 'A diary. Elizabeth, why didn't you say something? I never knew she was documenting everything. Elizabeth, you always were ahead of your time,' I think. "It was a long time ago," I reply, still in shock.

"I wonder if you would take a look at it and see if it triggers anything?"

"Of course," this was a day of surprises, that's for sure! And at my age, surprises are hard to come by!

Her room has hardly changed at all, right down to the desk, the wooden floor and the stacks of bookshelves. All sorts of books from alchemy and witchcraft to herbal remedies, and more. It was like I was stepping back in time, and I almost expected her to walk in and join me, but I knew that those days were long gone. Wooden shutters had been drawn back casting the room part in shadow and part in light. Dust particles hung in the air as if time was standing still. My boots made a loud noise on the wooden planks as I approached her desk with a fleeting moment of apprehension. I reach out and touch the wood, feeling the smooth polished grain of the seasoned oak, a distant smile of happy times drifting across my thoughts, seemingly calming me with its touch. On her desk lay an old leather-bound book, which I had never seen before. The seat behind her desk was still the same one I'd seen Elizabeth sit in so many times in the old days. I sit in it and pull it towards the table, scraping the legs on the floor as I do so. Reaching for the book, I can feel my hands trembling. I look up into Susan's eyes, then at the others in the room, the thin girl that didn't say anything, the boy, Arthurs and finally back to Susan.

"You've all read this, I assume."

"Yes," Susan replies, coming to join me. "There's certain pieces that I think might be of importance. If I may?" she says, reaching for the book.

"Be my guest," I reply. As she reaches across, her scent came to me. She even smells like Elizabeth!

Flicking through the book, she stops on a chapter and starts reading. Within seconds, I could hear Elizabeth's voice filtering down through the ages as Susan began to talk.

"May 1581. I still cannot fathom how John seems to be a force for good not evil, as he was reborn to be. Something does not make sense. I have researched all the arcane rituals on summoning demons into human hosts, and no one comes out like John. He has the powers of a demon but is not demonic, there is no badness in him, it's as if some other force has created

this superhuman force for good, for light. He does not see it in himself, of course, but we do, he shines through like a solitary star in the heavens."

Susan flips some pages forward and starts reading again, before I even have time to ask a question.

"January 1590. At last, a breakthrough. Robert has found an inscription on a church altar pertaining to a certain Holy Cleric called John. I know John was a common name, but I now know he was a part of Richard's inner circle and a close confidant. Perhaps John was this Cleric? I will go to this church at Chester and see for myself.

March 1590. Robert accompanied me to the church and together we entered the inner sanctum and found what I had come to see. The inscription tells the story of a Cleric from the royal household who arrived at the diocese in the year 1197 and began to perform miracles. Taking on the mantle of bishop, he banished the resident clergyman, saying that he was corrupt and unclean. His flock were many, and the miracles he performed were mentioned far and wide within the county. Before long, he was swamped with all kinds of visitors from all over the land. It says that at the height of his popularity, a group of Kings men seized him, and returned him back to face the King. Every carving, every story about him states that this man had come from the court of the King. And on his person, he always carried an old wooden staff that some people said was the source of his holy power to heal."

"Does this ring any bells?" Susan asks, turning to look at me.
"No, not a thing," I answer.
"Susan, we are wasting our time here," Arthurs interrupts.
"Enough, Frank," she replies sharply, "Can't you see John is trying to help here. Give him a chance!"
'I know who wears the trousers in that relationship, if indeed they are a couple,'

I think, and chuckle to myself.

Susan opens the book again and my stomach turns when she reads the date.

"**May 1599. One final clue needs to be confirmed before I show John my findings. This time, I will take the team with me, including John. Perhaps, in Cannock, he will finally find out who he is. He deserves to know, and I still can't believe who I think he is, it is amazing and fitting to now realise. Robert will meet us at Fairhaven to escort us on the final part of our journey, and I look forward to his conversation on the way…**"

And that's it, her final entry."

I was staring down at my hands which were locked tight together, the knuckles white, a cold sweat seeping from my pores. I look up, seeing the group before me, not the modern group, but the original 'Battleborn'.

"We started out at first light," I begin. "Four of us in the 'The Royal Oak', drawn by four black mares. We were heading towards Chester. The roads were not like nowadays, they were dirt tracks, some with stones in places, and sometimes the old Roman roads. Anyway, the going was tough, bumpy and very uncomfortable. Many a wheel was broken, and we would have to stop before we turned the carriage over. We came to the outskirts of Cannock Chase Forest. It was nighttime, bitterly cold and a near full moon cast an eerie glow over the land. A thin mist seeped out of the ground, covering the bracken. Our breaths formed before us in the carriage.

Everything happened so suddenly. It doesn't matter how well trained you are or how good you are, because if you are taken by surprise, all that goes out the window. And in this case, it was the carriage window. Everyone was in good spirits, rubbing their hands together and cursing the cold, but happy to be out on a mission. Only Elizabeth seemed quiet and distant, her demeanour was one of contemplation.

The first sign of anything going wrong was the sound of a spoke buckling, and a slight lurch in the carriage. I then felt the tingling of my armlet denoting something supernatural was on hand. As we slowed, we heard the unmistakable sound of terrified horses. One was screaming. I heard Crookshank, our regular driver and a former soldier, cry out to the horses while trying to slow them. The carriage lurched again and shot forward. I pulled the curtain back to look out, just as something heavy landed on the opposite side of the carriage. I heard Crookshank scream in agony, then the sound of the horses screaming and tearing free. Suddenly, I felt everything leaning towards my side of the carriage as we toppled off the side of the road. Elizabeth thumped into me, her breath leaving her. She looked into my eyes for the last time that I can remember. As the carriage started to tilt like a sinking ship, I gathered up Elizabeth and cradled her from the impact. Matthew, Frederick and Staunton were all holding on for dear life as with an almighty thump, the carriage hit the earth and broke apart throwing us everywhere. I felt myself rolling, feeling every bump and bang, but doing my utmost to protect Elizabeth. We rolled to a halt, and then I saw a piece of the carriage falling towards me. I rolled Elizabeth away from me and to the side, as the piece of carriage landed on my legs, pinning me to the cold earth. I screamed at the pain and tried to break free. In my peripheral vision, I saw and sensed movement all around us, but couldn't focus on what I was seeing as my head was still spinning. Out of the corner of my eye, I saw the 'Battleborn' rise groggily to their feet, even as something careens into Matthew, and he is no longer of the living. He crumbled to the floor, his neck gushing blood across the rest of the 'Battleborn', dropped his staff and tried to stem the flow, but I know it is too late for that. Staunton, still with bow in hand, draws and fires in one fluid motion. I hear the roar of some creature as his arrow strikes home. He pulls and fires again, then again, each arrow finding its mark, each mark bringing a roar of agony. Fredericks lifts his axe above his head and roars, even as something strikes into him with so much speed that his axe drops to the floor with both hands still holding it, his arms shorn off at the elbows. He screams in agony, looking wide-eyed at the two stumps that are fountaining blood. A dark blur of motion before him produces a final choke of life and he is down in a heap, quiet and unmoving. Staunton, without a thought, races towards us even as something bowls him over. Somehow, he rolls and rises as one, and stabs an arrow repeatedly into his unknown assailant. The creature screams, rolls and disappears into the darkness. At the same time, I hold Elizabeth's gaze as she rises to her feet, while I was desperately trying to free my pinned legs. My head was throbbing, and I could feel blood dripping from a cut above my eyes. I got one leg free and used that to lever the other one free, as I saw Elizabeth stand and turn to face a muted form coming at her out of the darkness.

"Elizabeth," I screamed, urging her to move, but she stood there and raised both hands in a sign of peace, palms facing her assailant. I saw the creature slow down and halt in front of her, and I gasped. I've seen werewolves before, but this one was huge. It stood about ten foot tall and walked upright on two crooked hind legs. Its whole body was covered in a silver fur that shone with an unearthly brightness. Its arms were human looking, apart from the large, clawed hands that were dripping blood. Its head was that of a wolf, a long snout with rows of sharp teeth. Its eyes had a yellow tint and looked almost reptilian, transfixing Elizabeth with a inhuman fascination.

Two more appeared beside the first creature, equally as big and ferocious looking as the first, arrows protruding from their bodies.

Out of the corner of my eye, I saw another gorging on the remains of one of the mares. It was tearing great strips of flesh off with its hands, to get to the softer treats beneath. My stomach turned at the thought of what these creatures could do to us!

I saw Staunton had raised his bow and notched an arrow. He stood poised and ready to move into action at a moment's notice, his eyes never leaving the werewolves. No fear showed across his face, only focusing on the job in hand.

"Aim for the heart," I said quietly.

"What do you think I've been doing?" he replied in his Yorkshire accent. "I have read your notes, you know!"

I didn't reply. Tension hung in the air, like a thin sheet of ice, ready to shatter at the slightest touch of movement.

Elizabeth stood her ground. She was so brave, it was unbelievable. She always thought she could talk anything down, and many times she had been proved right. But not this time. The werewolf reached her and lowered its head to sniff her, moving from one side of her head to the other, its fowl breath forming steam to rise and cover the long line of sharp teeth within its gigantic jaws. The werewolf's snout was literally covered in blood and gore but Elizabeth seemed not to notice, her stare remained unfaltering, her demeanour one of calm. I heard Elizabeth say something to it and it paused, rising to its full height, towering over the small woman. It turned back to its two brethren as if to speak, then in one incredibly fast movement, it lifted one clawed hand up and knocked Elizabeth off her feet and towards me. I had freed myself by now and was rising, just in time to catch her stricken form in my arms. I saw deep cuts across her front and face, where the claw had raked her. Already her clothes were changing colour and growing wet with blood. A line of gashes continued up her neck and across one side of her face. Her eyes were shut, she appeared to be unconscious. I heard the unmistakable twang of arrows being fired in a quick staccato fashion. I saw one creature fall and then another. 'Good lad, Staunton,' I thought. One creature came at me, lowering itself onto all fours and charging. I transferred the still form of Elizabeth into my right arm, stood my ground and swiped at the advancing werewolf with my armlet hand, bludgeoning the thing as it pounced. The creature howled in pain, flying through the air to land in a heap at the trunk of a tree. It lay there whining as I drew my sword, advanced on the still forms of the two, shot by Staunton, and proceeded to cut their heads off with a couple of swipes. Even as I did, I waited for the transformation back to human form, but nothing happened, no change, the first time ever that this had not happened. This was a mystery I had no time to look into. I turned and shuffled towards the one I had struck, when I saw a form appear behind Staunton. I glanced towards the corpse of the horse and saw no movement.

"Staunton," I screamed, turning to race towards him, but I was too late. He sensed it as well. These creatures were so fast and so silent, even he had not felt its presence until it was just too late. A swipe of its great hand and Staunton's head sailed through the air to roll and land at my feet, his eyes still showing a look of surprise. His headless body sank to the ground, his trusty bow snapping as he fell. The creature bounded onto the stricken carriage and roared at me. I still held Elizabeth tight, a thought of how I could save her already forming in

ORIGINS

Plate: 6

my mind. That's if I could survive the next few moments!

I see the creature tense ready to pounce, when the carriage beneath it collapses, pulling the creature down, so that it was momentarily trapped. Staunton's body had fallen forward, and his broken bow lay in front of me. In one motion, I sheathed my sword, dropped to one knee, slid along the turf and gripped the bow. I knew it was made of yew, he'd told me that many times, this was his favourite bow which never left his side, even when he slept. I also knew from experience that yew was the most potent wood to kill a werewolf with. The creature howled trying to break its way free of the carriage. It took its eyes off me, searching for what was trapping it. Bad idea!

I brought the bow up and thrust it towards the werewolf.

"This is for Staunton," I said to the thing, wanting to get its attention. It raised its snout to me and opened its jaw to roar, just as I rammed the broken bow down its throat, as far as it would go. The creature's eyes went wide in fear and pain, and it started to thrash around with only its body visible. I took a step back, unsheathed my sword.

"And this is from me," I yelled, and swung the sword in an arc that took the werewolf's head clean off.

I turned to face the remaining werewolf only to see it disappearing into the trees, hobbling on one leg, as the darkness swallowed up its silent retreat.

I still held Elizabeth tight. I was exhausted, my head was aching, but the blood from the cut above my eye had stopped dripping, the wound already starting to heal. I reckoned that with the power that kept me alive, that it kept everything inanimate, and hopefully animate, in perfect condition as well, this might suffice. When I had been found in Jerusalem, everything I wore, everything that I had been touching was in perfect condition. Could this work with another soul, if I was touching them? I thought that if I could get Elizabeth back to Dr Phobius, without losing any more blood, he might just be able to save her. So, as long as she was attached to me, held by me, she would not die. All I had to do was get her home. Already, I could sense, the flow of blood had stopped. I could see the cuts on her neck and face were no longer bleeding. It was working. I looked around at the carnage. The 'Battleborn' were gone, slaughtered in the time it took to down a flagon of ale. Once Elizabeth was safe, I would return for them and give them the burials they deserved. Then I would hunt these creatures down and wipe them off the face of the Earth. The carriage was destroyed, Crookshank and the mares dead. Three werewolves lay dead, a fourth was injured and still at large. I don't know how many miles we had travelled, but we had been travelling since daybreak. There were no other travellers on the road at this time of the night. I had more chance meeting smugglers or bandits, than anyone who could help me. It wasn't like today where you could get your mobile out, or flag down a passing car. I was alone in the dark, with a dying woman in my arms. I hadn't even known our final destination. Should I carry on and find help on the road, or turn and head back to the institute? Could I make it that distance on foot? I knew I'd done it before, many times. But carrying Elizabeth as well?

My armlet tingled again, my eyes staring towards the deep shadows made by the line of trees. I saw a dark form moving amongst the trees heading my way, vulpine eyes glowing. The last werewolf was returning to finish me off. I turned, cradling the still form of Elizabeth, and ran.

I kept running, only stopping occasionally to listen for my pursuer. The armlet kept tingling, forewarning me that the beast was still on my trail. If I could just put Elizabeth down for a short while, I could end this. But I didn't want to risk the consequences, I didn't want to risk Elizabeth's life. As day broke, I left the forest, reaching the open moor. There was very little cover, so I just kept moving, following the track and the marks made by the carriage. A thin mist hung over the moor and as I crested a rise and looked back, so I saw a man leave the safety of the trees heading along the road in my direction. I watched him approach with great interest. The figure was tall and moved with a gangling stride, which ate up the miles. 'A fellow traveller on the same road or something not so nice,' I thought.

I pause to look at the silent group around the table.

"Do all your adventures end in bloodshed and death, there seems to be a common denominator in all of this?" the boy says. I'm looking at the girl, she still hasn't spoken but she's looking at me with pity in her eyes. I sense a sadness about her as if she carries the weight of the world on her shoulders.

"Can you speak?" I ask her, interrupting the conversation and my story. Everyone turns to look at the girl.

"Sometimes," she says quietly, her lips hardly moving.

"Well, I'm glad we've cleared that up then." I say, "then perhaps you can introduce me to the rest of this conclave who are listening to me bare my soul," I say to Susan.

"My apologies, this is Ayesha," she says opening her palm towards the young lady. "Arthurs, you know, you read his file on the way here, and the person sitting next to you is Billy." They are all employees of The Harkness Institute, and all have the highest possible clearance."

"Well, that makes me feel better!" I reply sarcastically, "Nice to meet you all. So, what have you got that makes you special? This is a team right, that's what I'm assuming. You do realise, I don't do teams. If you haven't already noticed, people tend to die who hang around me too long, and I've got enough blood on my hands to last many lifetimes. I work alone, so if you want my help, I'll do it on my own."

"I don't think he likes company," Arthurs says with a chuckle.

"Shut up, Frank," Susan says sharply. Arthurs clamps his mouth shut as if he's been struck. 'Good girl, Susan, he deserves that,' I think. 'What is his problem?'

"And the answer is, no, by the way, not all my adventures end in bloodshed and death. Most of them seem to, though," I say with a wink to Billy to lighten the mood. "Now, let me finish, please, I don't want to repeat this again," I say with finality.

"I was tiring, my arms were aching, and I was parched from lack of water and food. Even the powers that had kept me alive for so long, were not limitless. The sun was out, and a cold wind swept across the moor, ruffling the few hardy shrubs that clung to the land. Fern and gorse clung to the ground on either side of the track, fighting for control of the moor. Skylarks whistled merrily above my head, singing in their joyful way, seemingly oblivious of the human tragedy that was unfolding below them. The road wound around a small headland, through a series of rocky outcrops. I peered back towards the traveller and saw that he was gaining on me. As I rounded a corner and lost sight of him, I pulled off the road, moving undercover of the rocks, my eyes on the road. I unsheathed my sword and held it at the ready. I had been constantly swapping Elizabeth from one arm to the other to keep them from going numb, so while I waited for the man to approach, I did this again. My right arm which had been cradling Elizabeth, ached as I stretched it out, trying to work life back into the joints. I peered again at Elizabeth and tried listening for her heartbeat but couldn't hear anything. Was she already gone, or in the suspended state I was hoping for? Would everything kick back in again once I laid her on Dr Phobius' table, and let her go? All these questions went through my mind as I waited for the traveller. With my elevated senses, I heard the approach of the man from some distance away. He wasn't trying to hide his approach, he seemed to be moving at a quick pace, as of one in a rush to get somewhere. A messenger perhaps? Messengers were frequently around in that era and were well paid for their time. It was often a hazardous job, fraught with much danger. Many never reached their destinations. I listened to the man approach, draw level with us and carry on. I leant back out of view. Was it my imagination that he paused? Did I hear him sniff the air, or was my over tired mind playing tricks on me? In a second, he was past my hiding place and gone. I listened to his onward journey as it grew fainter and fainter, and then I let out a deep sigh of relief. I leant against the rock, taking in my surroundings. It was a small grassy area, completely enclosed by rock but open to the sky. One entrance in, one out. I slid to the floor, my back to the rock, holding Elizabeth close. Making sure she was secure, I put my head back looking towards the blue sky. My gaze picked out a buzzard gliding on a thermal. My mouth was dry, and I was desperate for a drink. My stomach grumbled with lack of food, and I felt faint. My eyes felt heavy, and I knew I needed to rest. I always slept with one eye open, knowing I could rest up and renew my energies before making my way back to the Harkness institute. I looked at Elizabeth first. Like me, as soon as I had picked her up the bleeding had stopped, the wounds holding fast as if in suspended animation. They weren't healing over like mine, but they were not getting any worse. She still seemed alive, despite the lack of breathing. Her eyes were shut, her face serene and at peace. I sighed and shut my eyes. Her body was still warm.

The hour that I slept, I dreamt of Elizabeth facing off with the creatures, it was almost as if I was reliving it through her eyes. *I saw the creature approaching me, stalking forward on two legs that were not made for walking upright. I felt it's fetid wreaking breath as it lowered its head towards me, its long blood-stained whiskers brushing across my cheek, first on one side of my face, then the other. I sensed it sniff me, breathing in my scent.*

I speak to it in Elizabeth's voice, which was calm and steady, with no hint of fear. "Please stop this, we are not a threat to you. We come to make you an offer that can help both our races," I said, with her voice.

The creature turned its back on me, and I see the hair on its back, matted with dark wet stains. And then in a blur, it turned again, and I see a clawed arm flash towards me.

I awoke with a start, my eyes watering as I peered up into the noon day sun. I had slept too long and would now not make it back before dark. I looked at Elizabeth again and saw no change. Getting to my feet, I headed out of the stones and rejoined the road. I felt refreshed despite the lack of food and water and marched at a quick pace. At the first river I came to, I drank deep feeling the energy the water gave me, as if it was more than just water, but some restorative magic potion. I stood up feeling renewed and looked towards the dropping sun. I will get you home Elizabeth, I promise.

I passed a few travellers on the road always keeping my distance, as did they. Everyone was wary of travellers in those days. Unless you travelled in large groups, or were well guarded, you took your life into your own hands when you travelled far. Single travellers, like messengers, were always a good target for thieves and brigands. No one was safe.

We had left the moor far behind and had entered into the semi-darkness of a woodland. I'd skirted a few villages and towns, steering well clear of any prying eyes. I knew we had no chance of reaching the institute before nightfall, but I kept moving forward, determined to get there as soon as I could. The trees had now become a dense wood with the last rays of daylight being stifled by the thick foliage overhead. My eyes soon became accustomed to the darkness, and

I strode forward, listening for any sign of trouble.

Before long I spotted the faint glimmer of a fire. I left the path as quietly as I could and entered a thicket of trees, from where I could see a light flickering in a grassy glade. I peered into the glade to see the fire, and sat on a metal frame was a pot, with something bubbling away within. A figure sat facing me. It was the man who I had seen earlier. He sat with a hood covering his features, his head bowed, as if he was in deep contemplation, his features hidden.

"Come join me," the voice said with a heavy French accent. "You have nothing to fear here, monsieur," he added.

I was amazed that he had heard me approaching. I was renowned for my stealth, but I was carrying Elizabeth, so I thought that perhaps I had not been as silent as I normally was. The man had not moved, he was not afraid of me. I could be anyone, yet he showed no fear. By now a near full moon had risen and was basking the night in its eerie glow. The clearing was open to the sky and I could see, and sense that no one else was nearby.

"Come, monsieur, join me for some broth, and we can enjoy each other's company, it has been a long time since I spoke to another human," he said, "and I welcome your company."

I left the trees and approach the fire, standing the other side of it, giving me the time needed if I had to react. The man lifted his head and drew back his hood. Long black hair and a thin angular face with a long nose, and thick moustache, greeted my stare. His deep penetrating eyes reflected darkly in the firelight, like a candle held in front of a tarnished mirror.

"Sit, please and we can share some broth. Do you like squirrel?" I could smell the broth; my mouth was watering at the thought of it.

The man was wearing a long, hooded cloak that covered him from head to toe. On his feet were slip on boots of some sort, ankle length and of a design I had never seen before. Even sitting, I could see he was a big man, taller than myself, I guessed. He looked at Elizabeth in my arms, and only showed the slightest hint of interest. His eyes met mine, and held for a moment, before looking back into the flickering flames.

I sat down, my eyes never leaving him, my senses looking for any untoward movement. His body language was of someone who was at ease with a stranger in his presence. His whole demeanour gave me the impression that he was arrogant or foolhardy, or both.

"I'm Godiven," I said introducing myself, sitting down opposite him.

"Le Loup," he said and nodded his head.

He passed me a cup of broth and I gobbled it down, burning my throat in my eagerness to consume the stew. It tasted amazing, reviving my senses, and giving me a renewed lease of life. He watched me eat in silence, his thoughts his own. I planned on thanking him and moving on, when he lifted his head and sniffed the air, his eyes darting into the trees, his body tensed for action. He rose quickly, as did I, and we stood there looking at each other across the dying embers of the fire. He smirked at me, one side of his face turning into a smile. And then his body relaxed again, as if whatever had troubled him had passed.

"I think we need to build that fire up if we are to keep it going through the night. We need to keep the predators at bay don't you think, Godiven? If you excuse me, I will go search for some more wood."

And with that, he glided into the trees like a creature of the night. My senses picked up his movements for a few moments, and then he disappeared as if he had fallen off the face of the Earth. My armlet tingled and my senses came alive when I heard a voice from behind me at the far end of the glade.

"Well, what 'ave we 'ere?" a voice said.

Three figures appeared out of the trees, all holding swords. The closest figure was the one that had spoken. He was barely five foot tall, wore a ragged set of clothes and was thin and mean looking. A sneer covered his unshaven and dirty face. "Looks like we got ourselves an 'ansome little prize 'ere?"

They kept coming towards me. In the dying embers of the fire, I saw that the next figure was only a young boy, about fifteen years old. He was trembling in fear, his sword hand shaking, making the dirty steel flicker in the firelight. I suspected that this was the first time he'd ever been out on this type of adventure. It was to be his last.

My armlet was pulsating now as I saw a dark shadow glide through the woods behind the advancing robbers, yellow eyes glowing in the darkness.

The third man who was bringing up the rear was an older man of similar stature to the first, but fatter. His grey wispy hair hung in patches on his head. He looked old but moved with an arrogant swagger. Here was the leader of the group, putting his gang out first to case the joint, as they would say in later years. He was the first to die. The figure swept out of the trees in a blur of motion, catching the man completely unaware. A swipe of a claw followed by a choking sound and the man was down on his knees, clutching at what was left of his throat. Seconds later he sank onto his front, quivering in the final throes of death.

The boy turned and saw the werewolf disappear into the trees. I saw his knees sag and he let out a pitiful whimper that brought the first bandit to an abrupt halt. The lad was pointing towards the stricken figure on the grass, who was still quivering in his final death throes, his eyes already glazing over. The lead bandit looked wide eyed from his dying accomplice to the boy, his head swivelling in fear towards a movement behind him, when the werewolf pounced. It landed on top of him and started ripping him to pieces. He didn't even have time to raise his sword before he was disembowelled. His screams broke the brain freeze of the boy, who stared open mouthed at me. I'd never seen someone shake so much in my life. I saw the front of his breeches dampen with the fear of the moment and I felt for the lad, despite what he and his fellow bandits had planned for me.

"Run," I shouted to him, and I meant it.

Wide eyed and with tears rolling down his cheeks, the boy dropped his sword and fled. The creature's head turned at my words, pausing in its actions. Its hide was covered in blood and gore. The werewolf seemed to be enjoying the moment. It lifted its head and howled to the moon, its head silhouetted against the light, its rows of sharp teeth dripping blood.

It sprang off the second victim and shot into the trees before I could even say anything. The first robber's body sank to the floor with a squelch, like a fallen tree landing in mud. I lowered my head, my senses picking up the boy crashing through the undergrowth, his heart beating fast. He'd lost all sense of direction and was now headed back towards us. I closed my eyes when I sensed the werewolf's approach, and all I could think at the time was 'please make it quick.' When it appeared, I heard the faint cry of help to a God that was not listening, and then a gurgled scream, then it went deathly quiet. It wasn't long before the werewolf appeared at the edge of the glade. I had already drawn my sword and held it point down to the earth. It walked towards me and as it did, it started to transform before my very eyes. Its hind legs straightened. From its slouched posture, it seemed to lean backwards as its spine contorted into a straight position. The talons that had just dealt out so much death, retracted and formed hands, even the snout retracted turning it back into the face of the man called Le Loup. Within seconds, the naked form, covered in blood had become fully human. His neck made a cracking noise as he approached the fire, then Le Loup sat down opposite me as if nothing had ever happened. His naked body was covered in a fine layer of hair from head to foot, giving him the look that he was almost dressed. His hands were covered in blood, his nails still retained bits of flesh, which to my horror, he put into his mouth and picked at with his teeth, as if he were picking the last meat off a chicken bone. The last thing that changed was his yellow eyes which dulled and returned to black. The tingling of my armlet ceased as his dark eyes stared across the dying fire at me.

"Did you have to kill the boy?" I said in disgust.

"Grief, my friend, affects us all in different ways!"

"What do you mean by that?"

"When you lose someone close, your family, or your friends, you never know how you might react. You have just seen how I deal with my grief. Vengeance and revenge are the normal traits of all of us, would you not say, Godiven? Please sit, I mean you no harm. I sensed from our first encounter that you are different, you even smell different! I am intrigued."

"Intrigued? You've slaughtered my friends. Killed those three bandits. One of them was just a boy, you could have let him go. They didn't stand a chance. You are a monster. When I get Elizabeth back to safety, I'll come looking for you, don't you worry."

"No doubt you will, but you will not find me, and there will be bigger things for you to worry about than me," he said with a calm assurance. "You also have taken something from me, the only family I had, gone."

"You attacked us without provocation!" I retorted.

"Really, monsieur, we were only trying to stop you getting what we want, what we need?" Le Loup said. "Her contact said she had information, but she was just trying to find out where the artefact is. To keep it for herself to use."

"I don't know what you are talking about!" I said vehemently.

"You really don't know, do you, monsieur? Well, when you get back to wherever you are going, ask her, she'll explain."

"I'm going to. Why don't you explain?"

Le Loup paused, looking into the dying embers, as if contemplating what he should do. "Very well," he said, looking back at me.

"We are being exterminated, Godiven, wiped out by an unseen enemy. We came here in search of something that might help, a weapon. All we have found is a riddle, an inscription on a pagan stone that shows that the artefact exists, nothing more."

"Exterminated! How? How can that be?"

"Do you know much of our history, monsieur? Non? Well, let me tell you a little of our race. The great forests of Europe hold many secrets, hidden from the prying eyes of man. The forests of Germany and France are where our brethren live, where we originate from. Many clans live at peace with humans, hunting wild game to sustain their blood lust. Some turn rogue and become a menace to our harmony. These are the ones that create your legends and myths," he stopped then, looking at me again. "You have fought us before, eh, monsieur? I can tell. I can see it in your eyes, your actions yesterday. What are you?"

"Just a man," I replied stoically.

"Ha, you jest, monsieur. You are much more than just a man."

I didn't reply.

"You know, you look very like the figure in the stone carving, monsieur? Perhaps, you can live forever, eh, Godiven?" he said with a snort.

Again, I didn't reply.

"Your silence gives you away, monsieur. Do you know of the staff we seek?"

"No," I replied with as much composure as I could muster. "Who's exterminating you? How can creatures as powerful as you be killed off?"

"Have you ever heard of the 'worms of the Earth'? 'The little people', Non? Nor had we until a few months back. The great forests of Europe are vast. Yes, you humans are cutting them down for timber, for houses and ship building, but they still stretch for hundreds of miles, an uncharted wilderness. Our clans live in the depths of the wilds. Sometimes, you wouldn't see anyone for days on end. We often travelled at night between the settlements. We lived in small groups and had to spread wide, otherwise the wildlife could not sustain us.

We came across one settlement swallowed up by the Earth, with no sign of our families. At first, we thought it was a freak of nature. These things happen, eh, monsieur, but it wasn't. A week later, we came across another one with no survivors, as if they had disappeared into thin air. I was sent ahead to the next settlements, to warn other groups, but I was too late. Everyone was gone, not a soul remained. How can you fight something you cannot see? I came to one of the last settlements and found an opening within the side of a cave, which seemed like it had been carved by hand. We sent our best warriors down to investigate. None returned."

I sat in silence trying to make sense of what he was telling me.

Susan interrupts my thoughts.

"Have you ever heard of the Hollow Earth theory?"

"I'd once met up with a French explorer who was keen to map some uncharted caves in Germany. We spent some time together and I even accompanied him and his team to the caves' entrance. It was a huge hole in the ground, so deep that the tiny valley below seemed to have its own ecosystem. I wished them, 'Godspeed' as they were winched down to the valley floor and disappeared into the shadows, never to be seen again." I say, reminiscing on the young adventurer, Francois Tolenbach, who always greeted you with a roguish smile. "So, yes, I've heard much about the Hollow Earth theory and thought nothing more of it." I see Arthurs stir nervously in his chair, his hands rubbing together, slightly faster than normal, to denote that he was sub-consciously uncomfortable. I see Susan look to the floor for the briefest of moments, and then realign the papers in her hand for the umpteenth time. They are hiding something. I let it go for now and continue, wanting to get this out of my system, and move on. I saw the group look at me expectantly, so I oblige by carrying on.

"Le Loup told me of his customs and strict laws, and I listened intently until I started to nod off. My eyes felt heavy and Le Loup's words became an almost hypnotic lilt, his story telling skills far surpassing my own. Eventually, he said for me to rest, and he would take watch. It took me a lot of effort to relax, but I thought that if he wanted to attack me, he would have done so by now.

Again, I dreamed of Elizabeth's encounter with Le Loup and its outcome. "We come to make you an offer that can help both our races." she had said. What did she mean by that? They were her last words. Of someone trying to join forces with werewolves, to unite against what? What possible foe could make Elizabeth want to join forces with werewolves? How bad could they be? When I woke, Le Loup had put on his shoes and hooded jacket and was sitting in the same spot opposite me, with the burning fire between us. He nodded as I awoke and slipped into the trees with an 'adieu' on his lips.

With the day breaking I rose stiffly, Elizabeth still silent and unmoving in my arms. It took me until mid-morning to reach the gates of the institute. I sensed Le Loup stalking me all the way back. No, not stalking me, guarding me and protecting me until I reached safety. This certainly was a real turn of events. Only once did my armlet tingle, when I heard a distant scream suddenly cut off. It was then that I realised, he was clearing the path of any obstructions that might get in my way. Whether the cry was human or animal, I never knew.

Dr Phobius was at the gates waiting for me, his assistant as well. A stranger had appeared and warned him of my approach."

"And Elizabeth?" Arthur's asks.

"She was dead. By the time I'd picked her up, she had already gone. My powers had stopped the flow, paused the aftereffects, nothing more. The dreams I was getting were her last moments. Le Loup, the creature that I'd sat down with, had killed her."

"I'm sorry John," Susan says sincerely. Even Arthurs didn't have a sarcastic reply to this, he knew when to stop. He lowered his eyes to his hands.

"You know, you never know when it's going to be the last time you see or speak to someone. Life is so fleeting." I say contemplating Elizabeth and the 'Battleborn's' demise.

"Not for you?" Arthurs said quietly under his breath.

I ignored him. "One minute you are with someone, the next, in the blink of an eye, they are gone. And there's always so much you want to say, but it's too late, that moment is lost forever. It's a hard pill to swallow, as they say. Someone once told me that life is like a fast-flowing river, it's forever changing, and no time can be retraced, it flows forward, ever onwards towards its final resting place, never to be repeated."

A nervous silence greeted my final words, as if everyone was contemplating their own fragile existence.

"I stayed until we buried Elizabeth the next day. I couldn't believe how many witches turned up to the funeral, it was incredible, I never realised how many witches there were, and how quick they had got here to pay their respects. After that, I left... and haven't returned since." I pause, staring out the window to see swallows darting to and fro under the eaves.

"Would you like us to leave you to read the rest of the diary in peace?" Susan asks.

"No, that's fine," I say, gripping the book in my hand and lifting it up to look at the cover. Only the Harkness emblem of the Raven sitting on a branch embossed into the faded red leather, greeted my stare. The book felt light, the paper within it dry and brittle to the touch. What secrets lay within, I ponder.

"I think, I'll leave it here, I've done enough reminiscing for now," I say, placing the book back on the desk and rising.

"John, there's something else, there was a disturbance at the Cathedral in London, an earthquake actually. It was only a minor one, but it was enough to uncover something that we have been looking for, for a long time. And again, it relates to you."

"Lucky old me," I said sarcastically, "it seems like it's my lucky day!"

4

DIVINE INTERVENTION

The Cathedral appears through the gloom and rain, like the menacing ramparts of a huge castle.
"You're saying that we are going to find my coffin in there, next to my father's, but you are not going to tell me who it is? That's like offering me ice cream without a cone," I reply with the worst analogy ever.
It was raining hard, the drops coming down thick and fast, the noise really loud as the rain hit the pavement. Already, puddles were forming, and fast flowing rivulets were running down the sides of the road, to be gobbled up by the eager mouths of storm drains. Good old British weather! Even the streetlights couldn't penetrate the torrential downpour. The pavements were still busy though, as people rush around trying to find a place to get out of the rain. Rush hour in London definitely wasn't over in an hour. But 'rush hours', didn't really roll off the tongue very well! Susan produces an umbrella and pops it over her head. 'Did she magic that up? Or had she just seen the weather forecast and, come prepared?' I guess it was the latter.
Susan nods, her eyes raised, as if I was being led to a surprise birthday party. She was so like Elizabeth; it almost scares me.
"But I'm here, I'm not dead, so how come the coffin?" I was shouting now to be heard over the downpour. Again, no reply. She knew how to keep a guy on the edge! 'Well, lead on, young lady, it will take a lot to take me by surprise,' I thought and shrug at her lack of reply.

We reach some tall wrought iron gates that were locked. A security guard, who was wearing a yellow anorak and leggings, and a pair of galoshes, stood on the other side, hunched over and sheltering himself as much as he could. Susan raises some sort of pass.

"Harkness Institute," holding up her wallet, "we have an appointment with Roberta Sands."

The man squints at the wallet, holds up a torch that dazzles us all momentarily, before lowering it and letting us in with some faint mumblings. A young smartly dressed woman in her mid-thirties, greets us, then disappears out into the rain after a quick conversation with Susan.

"I hate going in churches," I grumble, as we enter into one of the stone arched doorways along the side of the great building.

"You see, he isn't religious," Arthurs says, removing his hood and jacket, and placing it over his arm. As he did so, I notice the tiny impression of a concealed gun. 'Why bring a gun to church? Unless he always carries it,' the thought made my senses stir. The others took their coats off and left them hanging on the back of some plastic chairs littered about the vestibule. We pass through another door entering into the nave of the Cathedral.

"I said, 'I hate going in churches', not that 'I hate churches', numbnuts. It's because of them," I say pointing up to the roof of the church. They all follow my stare, their eyes straining to see things only I could see. After a few seconds and a few creaking necks, the group turned to look at me, frowns forming on their faces. Even Susan couldn't see them yet, but I knew she would one day soon. Above our heads, floated dozens and dozens of ghosts, restless spirits, looking for a way to end their eternal search for the afterlife. They floated around in the rafters like fish in an aquarium, endlessly going round and round. I hadn't taken my coat off, I very rarely did when I was working, it was like my 'Linus blanket'. As soon as I saw the ghosts, I kept my head down and eyes on the floor in front of me, but it was too late. I heard their cries, a deep moaning whine that reverberated around in my head like a stuck record. Multiply that by the number of ghosts there, and it became like the screams of a 19th century madhouse. I was almost glad the rest of the group couldn't hear the wailing; I was used to it over

KNIGHT ETERNAL

Plate: 7

the centuries, but it still grated on my nerves.

"I can hear them," a young voice says from beside me, Billy. I'd forgotten about him, or perhaps I'd tried to forget about him. He'd been standing so close to me that I'd not even noticed him.

"How?" I ask him, looking down at the small boy, seeing him properly for the first time. "You're not a boy, are you?" I ask. His body language had been wrong from the start. His whole demeanour, the way he moves, the way he interacts, his facial expressions, they never looked childlike. 'Whatever he looks like on the outside, he wasn't the same on the inside. Pretty much like most of us, I suppose,' I think candidly.

"It's a long story," Billy says.

"And not one for now," Susan butts in. "What do you see, John?" she asks turning to me.

"Just ghosts, that's all," I reply, nonchalantly.

"Ghosts, up there?" Arthurs says with an incredulous look, but I see his hand slide towards his gun in an instinctive reaction. 'That's not going to do a damn bit of good,' I was going to tell him, but cut him some slack.

"I see them too," Billy says to Arthurs.

"Come on, we are wasting time," Susan says ushering us along, but it really was too late, the ghosts had spotted me. They came swooping down, straight at me, as one long procession of wraithlike shadows. In the swirling semi-translucent state that they were, I glimpsed pained and anguished faces of all different ages. A young girl with a child in her arms led the cavalcade, and I could see anxiety mixed with hope on her dirty face.

"Back off," I say to them. "I haven't got time to help you today, I'll come back another time and see what I can do, but not today." They came on, oblivious to my offer. This had happened so many times before, ghosts very rarely listen to the living, unless they want to. It normally took something a bit more severe to challenge their wraithlike minds. So, I did what I do best and put a stop to this, for my sake and for the sake of everyone there. I raised my left arm and slid my sleeve back, revealing the armlet.

"Enough," I shout, my voice echoing around the silent Cathedral, causing some pigeons in the rafters to take-off and fly around amongst the ghosts, before settling down again. The ghosts stopped stone dead, their wailing becoming unified in their horror at seeing my armlet. The whole line of ghosts simply disappeared, only to reappear moments later back in the rafters, swirling round and round in their tight circles again, as if nothing has happened.

I turn to face the group who were again staring at me with open mouths.

"Now you know why I hate going into churches," I say, "happens every time! As you can guess, ghosts tend to congregate near to where they have been buried or wronged, so most churches are packed to the rafters with ghosts hoping to find a way out of their limbo. I spent many years in Europe helping ghosts find a way home to whatever end they deserve. So, when I say, 'I don't like going into churches', that is the reason why, OK! And nothing to do with the fact that most churches are built on the sites of other religious deities dating back to the dawn of time, of course. And they normally produce even more lost spirits!" I add for theatrical effect.

Susan smiles at me and shakes her head, her eyes glistening with a hint of mischief, one cheek raised in a half smile.

"Come on, soldier boy," she says, and a shiver went down my spine. 'So, like Elizabeth,' I think again.

We left the nave and entered a narrow corridor, then climb down a spiral staircase that had a rope pinned into the side of the wall as a handrail. We seem to circle down for quite some time before levelling off into a larger tunnel, which was an arched catacomb, with dark openings on either side. There were iron railings set into the stone and above my head a small inscription was chiselled into the rock.

'Crypt of Kings'

"I've never heard of a 'Crypt of Kings'?" I say quizzically, "and I've been around a long time." I add.

"Some things are kept from the public and have been for a long time, things even you, who have been searching for your family history would not find if you had thousands of years." Susan says.

"Well, that makes me feel better," I say, "it only means I've been wasting years and years trying to find out who I was, and I was never going to get anywhere, great!" I exclaim, a little sarcastically.

"At least, you didn't sign up to the ancestry website and pay monthly?" Arthurs says with another smug smile.

'Is that another part of army training now,' I thought?

"At least, I've got a past, it looks like you were created out of a test tube as some sort of army experiment gone wrong," I retaliate. He was really getting to me, this guy. His reaction also throws me off, I see him pause, look at Susan, then return his glare to me. Before he replies, Susan places her hand on his arm again, to calm him. Were they lovers? Their body language almost seemed to prompt me to think yes, but they concealed it well if they were. She gives me the quick eyebrows raised, 'you should know better' look then turns and walks off, expecting us to follow. I was beginning to like Susan, she wasn't scared of me, and could definitely put me in my place. Like Elizabeth, she had balls. At first, I had been a little scared of those brown eyes, I always was a bit scared of witches on first encounter, to be honest, you never quite knew what to expect. Although I knew they were mainly good folk and harmless, they had the unsettling knack of knowing how to manipulate people; often getting them to do things they didn't want to do. A thought then crossed my mind. Is this what was happening now, I wondered?

We entered a crypt, a small room with a low ceiling, which had a line of alcoves set into either side of the rock. Inside each alcove was a stone sarcophagus. A dais in the middle of the crypt had an even grander sarcophagus with the carved figure of a Knight on the lid. But not any Knight, the inscription in ancient Latin which I read effortlessly, as I could read, write and speak pretty much every known language on the planet was:

'Here lies Richard, Lionheart and King'
1157-1199

"Hang on a minute," I say, "Richard the Lionheart is buried in France, I know that for a fact, I've been to his crypt and seen his sarcophagus. I thought he might be the link to helping me find out who I am?"

"And he will, my dear," Susan says, smiling and walking to stand beside me. Arthurs moves to the head of the statue, while Ayesha, who had not said a word since we left the institute, moves to stand beside Arthurs. Billy stands next to me as Susan begins speaking.

"Two days ago, there was an earth tremor that was actually monitored as 6.2 on the Richter scale, at the institute."

'She has a seismograph at the institute!' I think.

"The tremor was felt across most of the country, and it even made the local and national news, as some buildings were damaged. It's the highest we've had in Britain since records began, and there is a reason for that which I will explain later. For now, we have this to occupy us with," she says, pointing towards the coffin. "This is the true resting place of Richard the Lionheart, his bones lie inside."

I noticed the lid was slightly off-centre. In fact, the whole sarcophagus looked like it had been moved. From the unsettled dust and markings on the floor, I could state as a fact that it had definitely been moved recently.

"Richard's coffin slid off its dais, nearly falling and shattering on the ground, but its secure now," she says. "What we found underneath is the reason we are here, particularly you John. It's one of the reasons we called for you to come in," she says with a tight-lipped expression on her face. She was still hiding something beyond whatever was happening here tonight.

"We found another coffin underneath," she continues, "I think you'd better come and have a look." She takes my hand and I feel that same tingle you always get when you touch a witch for the first time. That's one of the things that gives them away. If in doubt offer them a handshake, and hey presto, you've found a witch. Susan leads me around the side of the King's sarcophagus to view a coffin lying on the floor in the shadows. "This was hidden directly beneath Richard's," she says as I knelt down to look at the inscription.

Here lies the remains
of
John, beloved son of Richard and Eleanor.
Go with God
1165-1191

"As I said earlier, we think this could be you," Susan adds quietly.

I took a step back, my mind reeling. For so many years over the centuries I had sought my lineage and now, at last, something new, something concrete. For the first time in ages, I was speechless, confused and excited, all at the same time. My heart was pounding away like a bass drum, and I felt adrenaline flowing through me like I'd drunk too much caffeine.

"But how can it be me? I'm here!" I say, thinking aloud.

"Your remains were never found. In that instance, they would often place a coffin in the crypt, filled with artefacts belonging to that person. Especially ones who were dear to them."

Her words seemed to come to me from far away. My mind seemed to be in a vacuum, I couldn't concentrate, it was like I was here but in a different time loop.

"We haven't opened it, we thought you might like to have that honour," Susan says, stepping away from the coffin. It was a plain slate grey coffin with the inscription on top. The lid looked heavy. Arthurs, much to my surprise, looks at me and says, "I'll help you, big guy."

Together we bend down at either end of the coffin, taking a firm grip with both hands. With a silent nod we lift the stone lid and placed it on the floor beside the coffin. My eyes peered into the coffin, and I was relieved to see that there was no skeleton inside. Instead, two items lay inside. An ancient looking staff, about three foot long, with inscriptions carved all the way around its length, sat where the body should have lain. Where the head should have been lay an ancient parchment with a red wax seal, still intact. With shaking hands and a nod from Susan, I reach for the parchment, feeling how light it felt, how brittle the thick paper was. The seal, which had the King's Lionheart emblem upon it, disintegrated in my hands as I very carefully unwrapped the paper to see a handwritten note. The words were written in Latin, in a beautiful and flowing calligraphy. I translated them and read them out in a way that everyone in the group could understand.

> "Forgive me for not protecting you in your hour of need, my son. I know in court I could never call you my son, but you were always my proudest moment. I longed to tell you and hold you close, but it would have been your downfall. It was my wish that you were to become my successor. Eleanor was my one true love, and you were the result of that union. We had to protect you, so even though you could never know, I made you my closest Knight. I kept you close to protect you, to see you. Only when you announced your hatred of all the fighting and became a man of God, did I lose you. We fought a holy war, and you had become a man of God, but even then, you wanted nothing to do with it. It was I who called you back and sent you on that mission into Acre, that night we stormed the city. Your faith was so complete, you took no sword with you, only your staff that had been with you since an early age. What powers that thing had I do not know. Once while you slept, I tried to burn it, only to find that fire could not harm that strange white wood. I don't know what happened, but your quest succeeded even though we lost you, and most that went with you. You stopped them, you saved us all. All I found was the staff, so I lay it here as a reminder of you, and our love for you. I hope you are now at peace. You were trained a Knight and became my best warrior but became a priest instead. You truly were the best of all of us, John.
> Rest well, my son, my Knight Eternal.
> Richard."

Beside Richard's name was the royal stamp of the King, the Lionheart.

"Oh my," I hear myself say, as my eyes water. I feel myself go all weak, my legs turning to jelly. I grip the side of the coffin for support as my vision blurs, my thoughts a complex mass of pictures from a bygone era, frittering across my mind like some 1900s black and white picture show. I reach out for the staff, my hands wrapping around the shaft like I was gripping an old favourite sword handle. But as soon as I did, my eyes roll, and everything goes black.

When I came too, I was sitting on my backside, looking out over a desolate landscape of destruction. Before me had once been a great city, but now it was a tomb of rubble and half destroyed buildings. Everything was in darkness, apart from some fires burning out of control. Through the flickering flames, I glimpsed the remains of human bodies, some clothed, others like they were on a butcher's counter. A wide flowing river passed through this city with two destroyed bridges, their broken ends like small piers jutting out to join each other but never reaching. I saw countless bodies floating on the river. I sensed movement out there in the darkness, and I hear something that sounds like an animal's cry, followed by more distant cries, almost like they were replying. The sounds were so unusual and eerie, sounds I had never heard before. A cold clammy hand of fear grips me and forces me to rise to my feet.

'What is this?' I think, 'some vision of the future, where am I?'

"It's alright, John, there is nothing to be afraid of here," a deep voice says from behind me. I turn to see a man walking towards me. But not any man, it was Richard the Lionheart, King of England, and more importantly the father I never knew I had! For a moment, I am speechless. I look at the figure approaching me. He was six foot tall, strongly built and wore a long dark cowl that swept behind him. A Crown of Gold sat on his red unruly locks, and his deep-set grey eyes and warm smile greet me as if I had spoken to him only yesterday, rather than centuries earlier.

"I see you have found your way home, my son," he says, reaching down with one hand to help me up. His grip is strong and assured, especially for a ghost. Most ghosts struggle to even make a solid form, so I am guessing I am having some sort of vision, or worse, have I, at last...?

"Am I dead?" I ask, because it would be about time!" I add.

The King laughs. "Always one with a sense of humour," he replies wistfully.

"No, you are not dead, you are very much in the land of the living and we need you to remain that way. I am here to tell you that a new age is dawning. One in which the Earth's future lies in the balance and on the turn of a friendly card." he sweeps his hand wide to encompass the burning city.

Plate: 8

"*What is this? A vision of the future.*"
"*The shape of things to come, yes, a possible future that can be prevented. Creatures from a bygone age are going to make their play for the Earth, and all who live upon it. You are the divining rod, the game changer in this struggle. You, and that staff,*" he says. pointing towards the staff that was still in my hand. I look at it incredulously. I could not remember anything of its history, or where it came from. Any knowledge of my previous life, prior to my resurrection had been wiped clean. "But I don't know anything about it, my life before, nothing!" I say. "Only that final day up to the mission's end and then, that's it, nothing!"
We were standing face to face now, and I can see the lines on his face close up as he frowns, as if this was news to him.
"*Then you must find your history to save the future,*" he says after a pause.
"What, how?" I was taken aback, and not sure what he was meaning.
"*Son, I have so much I want to tell you, but already, our time is running out,*" He was starting to fade now, his form becoming transparent. I could see the fires of the city flickering through his image, the red of the flames almost matching the colour of his hair.
"*You must use your powers, cast out your inner demons, only then will you find your true calling, only then can you turn the tide...*"
He was gone, his final words echoing on the breeze. I looked down at the staff, feeling a slight vibration.
And in the blink of an eye, I was back in the real world again, as if the staff had woken me from my sleep.
"He's coming around," I hear someone say.
"Hey, John, you gave us quite a fright there!" I hear Elizabeth say. No, not Elizabeth, Susan. My head was in her lap, her hands on either side of my head. Arthurs stood over me like some victorious gladiator, his silhouette menacing. Within the darkness of his gestures, I see his eyes glow orange momentarily. My armlet tingles in reply. I shoot upright, looking at him, eyes wide. He shuffles back, a frown on his face.
"What's wrong, crusader boy, seen a ghost?" he asks sarcastically.
Had I seen what I thought I'd seen? Or was it some trick of the light. The bulbs

had a dim red tint, perhaps it was that. My senses and armlet told me otherwise. But a chill went through my body as I remembered those glowing eyes from before. I rise to my feet, lifting myself up, the staff in my hand.

"John, the staff," Billy says from beside me. He was like my shadow!

The staff was made of a white petrified wood, almost bone like. A ring of metal, similar looking to my sword and shield, wrapped around the shaft at its centre as if holding it together, or joining two parts of the wood together, I pondered. Strange inscriptions adorned the metal band with pictures of planets and stars forming some sort of text I had never seen before. I looked at it again at the wood, bringing it closer to me to read the inscription etched into the wood. It was written in Sumerian, an archaic language, but one that I could read. Certain letters seemed to light up as I turned the staff in my hand, reading something out to me that I could not completely understand. Had this happened to me before, in my previous life? Billy was wording it out aloud as I twisted the staff, his voice low and assured, but I could not comprehend what he was saying. Who is this kid, I think?

"I think we will take that," a deep voice says from the doorway.

We all turn as one.

At the entrance to the crypt, were three figures. Two of them held guns, pointing towards us. A fourth person, stood outside, the lady who Susan had met at the church entrance, Roberta Sands. Obviously, another double-crossing rogue who had sold her soul. The man that was speaking seemed to be the leader whose large muscular frame blocked the doorway and the only exit.

"I don't know who you are, but we can't let you have it, it's too important to let it go," Susan says resolutely.

"I'm going to count to ten, and then my men will start shooting," the man replies without emotion. He means it. I see the two men raise their guns and tense, ready to brace themselves against the recoil of their weapons. Trained assassins, what the hell was going on?

Tension hangs in the air, ready to ignite into a bloody frenzy. I looked towards Arthurs, whose body is tensed for action. One hand hangs close to his concealed weapon, while the other tightens into a knot. I hear him snort, his face grimacing in absolute hatred for what was happening. My armlet tingles again. I feel myself tense for the fight. 'Could I protect them. Is Arthurs what I think he is? If so, we might stand a chance?'

"One," the big guy says.

I sense Ayesha shuffle closer to me. Thinking that she wants protection, I automatically move in front of her, but she calmly reaches out and ever so gently touches my hand. A tingle shoots up my arm and again, in the matter of a few seconds, a scene unfolds across my mind in the time it took the man to reach 'five'. I see myself reach for my gun as Arthurs starts to turn and leap at the gunmen. I gasp as I see silver bullets rip him to pieces. He drops in mid-air, half changed, his snout dripping blood, his orange eyes glazed over before he'd even stopped moving. I feel bullets striking me, the force of them, throwing me back into the crypt, where a dust covered coffin collapses atop of me. Susan is struck, her hands held out in surrender, offering no protection. Ayesha and Billy dive for cover behind the dais and as I lie beneath the coffin, I hear the man say, "Kill them all." I hear footsteps approaching, and more gunfire. Out of the corner of my eye, *I see my staff lying beside me. One of the gunmen reaches down and looks at me, and in my half-dazed state, I see reptilian eyes staring back. The creature smiles and picks the staff up, his gun still trained on me. The next instant he stops smiling and starts to scream. Even as he rises, his body is on fire. I see him trying to shake the staff out of his hands, but it is stuck tight. A blue glow emanates from the staff, and I see the writing illuminated in the darkness. The man or whatever it is, is now fully alight and burning alive. But it's not a natural fire that is consuming the man, everything around him is untouched.* And as suddenly as I see this scene unfold, I'm back to the present. I look down to Ayesha and see that she has removed her hand from mine. She smiles at me, without saying a word. 'A woman of very few words.'

"Nice trick," I whisper, giving her a wink, knowing exactly what I need to do.

"Six, give me the staff, that's all I want," the big man says again.

"OK, OK!" I say, as if it wasn't a big deal. "The staff is yours," I say moving towards the entrance with it in my hand.

"What are you doing, Godiven?" Arthurs says angrily, his eyes never leaving the gunmen.

As I pass him, I whisper, "trying to save your arse, numbnuts. Be ready," I raise my eyes momentarily. Being from the military, he gets my quip and tenses again, ready for action. 'Just don't go too soon, Arthurs, I've got a lot of questions for you? And I don't want you dead!' I think.

I glimpse towards Susan, who had moved to stand next to Ayesha and Billy. She was holding them close, as if she could protect them by willpower alone. She has eldritch powers, I know, but to stop point blank gun fire, I wasn't so sure.

As I near the crypt's entrance, I see the two gunmen step in front of the man, guns pointing towards me. Perfect, just as I'd hoped. Roberta Sands, back in the hallway, shuffles nervously, her stiletto heels clicking on the stone floor. I still can't see the big man's features, he is standing in the shadows, his face concealed from me. Yet his large frame and voice seem to resonate in my senses. His body language and accent seem familiar. Have I met this man before?

"Here you go," I say nonchalantly, reaching out the staff lengthways, so both gunmen reach for it at the same time. One of the gunmen has his firearm trained on me, while the second one now has it trained on the group behind. Both reach for the staff at the same time, probably trying to be the first one to secure the staff for their superior.

The thing that happens next, even though I know it was going to happen, catches me by surprise. As the two gunmen touch the staff, the staff lights up, the words inscribed along its length, illuminating in the shadows, like a beacon of hope in the darkness. The two figures stand transfixed, as if caught in an alien tractor beam, reptilian eyes showing an unearthly fear. They scream as one, a scream I'd heard in the vision, shown to me by Ayesha. A blue burning flame encases the two and starts to consume them. Before my eyes they shrivel and wither, burning to bone and then dust. I stand only inches away and yet feel no heat. The staff hangs in the air within the blue light as the two figures dissolve, then the light begins to fade. I reach out to the flame and grasp the staff, just as the light flickers and disappears.

"By the Gods!" I hear Billy say.

"He's gone!" Arthurs says, reaching me and not stopping. His gun is out and he's all military now. "Come on," he says to me. "We've got a bad guy to catch." Could he get any cornier, I ask myself, although he is right, we do have a bad guy to catch, one that was happy to kill all of us without a thought.

In all the excitement, the leader and Roberta Sands had slipped away. As I leave the crypt, I see the stiletto's lying on the floor, beside a pair of thick gloves. I glance back to Susan who says, "Go," and I'm off following Arthurs up the spiral staircase, as fast as I can go. Arthurs is faster than me, his strides eating up the stairs three at a time.

"Arthurs, wait," I say as he leaves the stairs and runs into the nave. As soon as I enter the ghosts are on me like a rash. I scream at them, "Not now!", and they return to their goldfish like state floating around the rafters, amongst the pigeons. Poor pigeons, I hope they can't see or sense them.

I race out of the Cathedral entrance into a deafening torrential downpour. A figure flies through the air, and I haven't got time to move out of the way before I'm bowled over onto the wet stone paving. My head hits the ground hard, and I see stars for a few seconds. I look down and see the still form of Arthurs lying on top of me, a gash across his face that was already beginning to heal over. Three deep cuts had ripped his cheek to the bone. I bet that hurts, even though I knew it would heal over quickly. Werewolves had almost as much regenerative power as me.

I look up from my prone position and see a figure, wings spread, lift into the sky and disappear moments later into the downpour, a body huddled in his arms. 'The demon king!' I think to myself in disbelief.

5

THE HARKNESS INSTITUTE

I am standing on a tarmac road, high hedges on either side. The road and the hedges are overgrown, covering most of the tarmac. Large cracks in the road have been forced up by the power of nature like an erupting volcano spewing forth green vegetation, rather than molten lava. The road looks old, unused as if left for nature to reclaim it. I blink, shake my head, my mind swirling with the image, but it's real. I see insects, larger than life bees and wasps buzzing among the flora, their noise denoting a constant hum of activity. Where am I? I look down at my right hand. I'm holding a gun. It has 'Browning ADVT1' stamped on the handle. Behind the trigger a small screen is integrated into the handle. I look more closely. The screen shows a half circle with a series of lines showing distances in metres, counting down to a spot at the centre. Even as I look, a blinking dot appears on the top of the screen, signifying a distance of fifty metres. Another dot appears followed quickly by four more, all heading towards the centre spot on the screen, which can only be me. Somehow, I sense this is not good and I start to move away from the approaching dots on the screen. The more I glance at the screen the more and more the panic rises, the faster I move, the faster the dots are closing. What the hell is going on? Tension wraps itself around me as I race along the road, brushing the vegetation aside as I run, moving with as much haste as I can. The road turns to the left, and as I turn the corner, I can see a wall of brambles blocking my path. Without a second thought, I climb up and over the nearest hedge and find myself in a field of tall grasses. The tall grasses bend in a strong wind, the colour changing

Plate: 9

as the beautiful shades of green move in a metronomic fashion, almost hypnotising. Beyond the open field, clumps of bright yellow gorse cling to the land, before they disappear into the sea. No human, no man-made object, greets my stare; it is like mankind has never existed, and I am an imposter. I'm wearing black faux-leather trousers, boots and some sort of white shirt and top, covered by a khaki coat. I feel out of place here, a man out of time. It is early morning; the sun is just rising on a bright and sunny day. Somehow, I know this is a dream or vision, but I'm sensing every bit of it as if I'm there. Why am I suddenly getting these visions? Is it the staff, or Ayesha, who has instigated this? Listening to these thoughts I know I'm not there, but it feels real.

The tracker begins to pulse, the dots beginning to flash, signifying that whoever is following me is now within twenty metres. I push myself forwards through the long grasses, which are higher than my head. My heightened senses realise that the rustling is noisy, but I know that I must keep moving, I must get away. I can hear my pursuers now, moving through the grasses on the other side of the road. A strange humming coming from all around, that rises above the gentle sounds of nature, scares me to the bone. Somehow, I know it to be the noise of the creatures that are hunting me. No human sounds like that. I push on, through the grasses with one eye on the tracker. The sky grows dark, and I look up to see storm clouds approaching, at a speed I've never seen before, as if they had been filmed and played back on fast forward. The temperature turns icy cold as the sun disappears behind the bank of dark clouds, and I feel rain in the air. The wind starts to get up, swishing the tall grasses even more, pushing them this way and that as if they are being toyed with by some unseen giant hand. The rain hit me then, driven in by the wind, cold and with a hint of salt in the air. I look at the tracker and see the group of five are now on my side of the hedge, getting too close for comfort. The creatures have spread out and formed a semi-circle, with the two leading dots now level with me, and only metres to my left and right, hidden by the swaying grasses. Instinct makes me lift my gun, and fire without stopping. I pull and hold the trigger, and I hear a barrage of tracer bullets rip into the grasses to my left. A screech, and one is down, denoted by a dot disappearing on the tracker. My heart is beating fast now, my lungs arguing for me to stop, but to stop is not an option. In one swift movement, I fire in the direction of the other leading dot just as I see a faint shadow of movement through the grasses. Another one goes down with a screech, leaving three still on my trail. Again, I know this is not the first time this has happened, it's as if I am inside someone else's body re-enacting a scene from their life. But this is different. This vision, I can feel and see, sense and smell everything as if I am actually there.

I keep moving, the ground rising towards the gorse bushes I'd seen earlier. I break out of the grasses and find myself in the open, standing in a clump of ferns with a bank of gorse in front of me. In an instant, I turn and fire, keeping my finger pressed and spraying a deadly delivery of bullets into the grasses. I keep my finger on the trigger for a few seconds, until all three dots disappear. There are some inhuman screams as the bullets find their marks, and as they do, so the dots on the screen blink out, leaving me alone, panting for breath but alive.

I turn and stumble forward through the gorse towards the edge of a cliff, to see a series of stones protruding from the cliff face, winding down towards an small dark opening. Without hesitation, I race down the stone steps, leaping from one to the other across the gaps that would take me to my doom if I slipped. Fifty metres below me, the sea is crashing against the rocks in its eternal battle with the land, the noise loud enough to cover my escape. White foam is thrown up as the waves crash in a monotonous rhythm and I can feel the wetness in the air even from my lofty position.

I look down at the tracker to see a moving mass of white dots appear across the top of the screen, so many that they form a continuous white blob. Inexorably, they start to close in on my position. My heart starts to beat faster at the realisation that there are just too many of them. This is it, no escape! How long have I been doing this? Where was everybody else? And what was it that was hunting me? I reach the bottom of the steps and enter a cavern. I glimpse two forms, instantly recognisable, huddled together, holding a baby in their arms. The baby is shining with an almost angelic glow, showing the faces of Susan and Arthurs.

I am going to die; I hear myself thinking. But I've survived so long, how can it end here?

Even as I think that, I hear the grating of rock and turn to see the stone steps I had just ascended, retract back into the cliff face, leaving no path down to our location. I *look again at the gun and watch as the white dots fill the screen. I know they are directly above me, looking for any sign but finding nothing. And then after what feels like an eternity, they disperse, leaving the screen blank. Only my ragged breathing and the quiet cry of a child within remains. We had survived.*

"John, John!" Susan is saying from the doorway to my bedroom, trying to rouse me.

I sit up shaking my head. 'That was one strange vision,' I think. Shall I tell the others? No, not for now. I will keep this one to myself unless something arises to change my mind. I'd seen the future, I can see that now, and I'd been hunted as if I was the last man on the planet.

"Christ, don't you knock," I say with more anger than I wanted to show.

"You we're making noises in your sleep, John. Anyway, it's time for a debrief and a chat," she says. "I'll see you in Elizabeth's study in a short while. Hope you slept well," she adds.

"Yes, great," I say sarcastically.

"I thought you sleep with one eye open?" she asked with a twinkle in her eye.

"Not every night!" I reply, "But I might have to, if you keep interrupting my sleep," I said rubbing my head and wincing.

"Bad dream?"

I look at Susan and see the picture of her and Arthurs holding the baby. "Something like that," I say. Something in the way I am looking makes her pause, her eyes fix on mine, as if she wants to say more, but she stops herself and turns away.

"Take your time, big guy," she just says and disappears down the corridor.

We are back in Elizabeth's study, sat around a table, the staff resting on top of it like a trophy, which by the sound of it, seems to be as important as the Holy Grail. How long had they been searching for it, I wondered? My shield and sword lay on the same table, gleaming under the electric lights as if they had been recently polished.

"OK," I say, "time for some answers. We nearly got killed down there, last night. If it hadn't been for the girl here..."

"I'm a woman," Ayesha says, interrupting me. "My name is Ayesha, remember."

"Apologies, everyone is a girl when you've lived as long as I have," I say with a lop sided smile. "If it hadn't been for Ayesha here, doing her thing, we'd all be dead by now."

"Really?" Arthurs replies arrogantly, "I don't think so," he adds.

"Really," I say slowly and clearly, looking him in the eye. "What was that trick, by the way?" I ask Ayesha.

"It's no trick, it's a gift, sometimes a curse. I have the ability to show someone a possible future outcome. In this case, I chose wisely."

"Yes, yes, you did," I stutter, taking in her words. "You saved us."

"No, you saved us, I just showed you the way," she replies with a quick smile.

"What did you see?" Susan asks me.

"I saw all of you dead, myself trapped, he wanted to kill us all and take the staff. I saw the gunman pick up the staff and burst into flames, so when Ayesha released me, I knew what I had to do. Who were those people, they weren't human, their eyes looked reptilian?"

"That can't be? I don't believe it," Arthurs replies again, interrupting. Obviously picturing himself dead, didn't agree with his ego. "I don't die easily!"

"I know what you are, Arthurs. And, more importantly, they knew what you are, they came prepared. So, before we leave this room today, or go on any more missions, I want to know exactly who you all are and why I'm here... so get the coffees and pizzas in, it's going to be a long day. And I like my coffee black, strong and with two sugars, please."

"Pizza for breakfast, Yuck!" Ayesha says, her face contorting into a look of disgust.

"All the more for me," I say and smile, then I see the serious look on Susan's face. Susan stood and looked me in the eyes, then turned to look at the others. "It seems we were not prepared for what happened, I'm sorry, I take full responsibility for the protection of this group and I failed, it could have been a fatal mistake," she says solemnly. "I trusted a woman who I thought I knew. I've known her for many years."

"Hey, you're not the first person that has been duped by a broad, and you won't be the last," I reply, trying to make her feel better. "Anyway, how were you to know that those guys were going to show up."

"We should have had it covered," Arthurs says quietly, then more loudly, "I should have had it covered." He was still holding a bag of peas wrapped in a tea towel to his face, where the talons of the demon king had cut deep. The wounds were healing, the scars already fading, but it had left some heavy bruising. 'Man, that must have been difficult to spit out for Arthurs,' I thought.

"Listen, what's done is done, we survived, we are here, so no harm done. Ayesha, you want to tell me about your little gift and how you came about it?"

"I think I was born with it, I'm not sure," she says matter-of-factly. "I didn't know what I had, until I was a teenager. I stopped a man being killed by a group of kids, showing him the outcome if he confronted them. In the end, he walked away after I showed him the worst-case scenario."

"And, is it always the worst-case scenario? Does it always have to involve death, or could it be something more mundane than that, less life threatening, like winning the lottery?" I ask thinking how useful she could be to the team. I realise I was already thinking as if I was part of this team.

"I think it only works when death is a possible outcome. It is as if I am the Grim Reaper's alter ego or something, there to predict people being killed?"

"Nice analogy," I reply. "And your gift did save us. That guy wanted us dead, no witnesses."

"And you Arthurs? I read your file, but it doesn't say anything about what I know you are. And how? I haven't come across a werewolf in over a hundred years or more!"

"Perhaps I can talk on behalf of Arthurs," Susan says looking at Arthurs, who nodded.

"A government programme was set up in the 60s during the Cold War. Every government was looking for the next 'Super-Spy' or 'Super-Soldier'. We had DNA, and bloodstock, from a werewolf and a vampire. So, two separate programmes were set up at remote locations, to alter human DNA with werewolf or vampire cells..."

"You bloody fools," I say, shaking my head at the stupidity of it.

"The werewolf programme took off fast. After only a short while, we created a dozen full-grown werewolves. The only problem was that we couldn't control them. The facility was not secure enough. One night the creatures' decided to make a break for it and they were all gunned down. Only Arthurs survived, we found him curled up in his cell, he hadn't moved. Instead of destroying him, I interceded and promised to look after him here at the institute. Now he is head of security here, and a true asset..."

"And your lover?" I say aloud before my mind had time to stop me.

The whole room went deathly still. Arthurs lowered his bag of peas and turns to look at me wide-eyed. I see Susan's face blush red with embarrassment, and her eyes bore into mine with enmity for a brief moment, before a smile forms across her lips.

"Yes, Arthurs and I are an item. Very observant, John."

"Like I said before, it's all in the body language, that never lies."

"What's that? Your main superpower?" Arthurs asks sarcastically.

"One of many," I reply, with a wink.

"Children, children," Susan says, like a school teacher chastising her pupils.

"And the vampire programme, I suppose that went well too?" I ask with incredulity.

"We lost contact with the place, four weeks in. By the time, we got there, the place was deserted, not a soul alive. All the staff had been killed or left for dead, or that was what we thought. It wasn't until sunset that they started to awaken and kill our recovery team. Only then, did we realise that they had been left, as a trap."

"Well, that sucks." I say, which got a chuckle from the boy, who wasn't a boy. I saw Ayesha giggle and put her hand to her mouth to stifle a laugh. Arthurs just looked at me stony-eyed.

"Arthurs here was the only survivor from the two programmes."

"That's not entirely true, is it. How about all these new age vampires that are out there?" I ask.

"They were rounded up eventually, and dealt with. Every one of them."

I nod my head. "Good skills. Must have taken some doing?"

"They were all tagged. They weren't getting far. We'd doctored the blood, so that human blood would taste awful to them. They had to return eventually, as we had the only blood that could sustain them."

"Very clever, pity about the staff though."

"Collateral damage," Arthurs says coldly.

"So, we have a witch, a werewolf, a lady that can foresee the future... so, what about you?" I say turning to the boy, who had his head in his hands, his elbows resting on the table.

"You know my name's Billy," he says, sitting up straight in his chair to face the group and in particularly me. "I'm an alien..."

"Now that's something you don't hear every day," I say in amazement. "care to elaborate."

"Not really," Billy replies and holds my stare.

"Well, you don't look like an alien to me," I say. "And I've seen a few in my time," I add, watching as Susan and Arthurs both tense at my reply.

"So, it's something to do with our friends from the stars, is it?" I wondered. "But that was back in 1665 in Sweden, a long time ago." I added to see how they would react. I'm not going to mention my Area 51 encounter, or my earlier encounters in the wild west, that one at Area 51 really affected me. I'll keep that for another time. Again, they shuffle in their seats, Susan's hands gripping the folders even tighter. "And you don't look anything like the one's I saw."

"That's because they were probably from a different planet to mine!"

"Billy, he needs to know. He needs to trust us, and he can only do that if he knows who we are," Susan pleads.

Billy paused, looking down at his hands. "Very well," he says. "You know about Roswell in 1947 right, the crash. Well did you ever wonder what they were doing here? No, well, they were coming to get me. I'd been helping the US Government with some stuff and had fallen ill. In fact, I was dying. Just like one of those sci-fi movies, but this one was true. When they crashed, they and everything that could save me was destroyed. The only way I could survive was to transfer my mind into a human body. But I wasn't going to steal another human just to save myself. The agency searched far and wide and found a young orphan boy who had a terminal illness. They brought him to me, and we spoke. I promised him, he would live on through me. I knew I could keep his body alive, his mind in stasis. I made an oath that one day, I would find a host for him. I didn't realise he would stop growing! And here I am," Billy said, a frown upon his youthful face.

"Wow, and I thought my story was strange enough," I say in amazement. "So, this is a mighty strange and eclectic group of individuals, not exactly the X-Men, are we?" I add, looking at Susan with a smile.

"You've watched the X-Men films?" Ayesha asks.

"I might be nearly a thousand years old, but I still like TV, it's one of the best inventions ever," I reply.

"I like John, he's cool," Ayesha says, and then blushes when she realises what she had said. I see Susan smile to herself.

"This is a team, right, that's what we are, yes?"

"Yes, it's a team, John. We've always had a team, ever since Elizabeth's time."

"Wow," I say, "I never knew." I was speechless for a few seconds.

"John, we need you, we need your help, your powers, what you can provide us with."

"And what can you provide, big man, what powers do you have?" Arthurs interrupts again.

Straight to the point and as blunt as ever, I think.

I look around the room. They want me on the team. I don't do teams, but we've already experienced a life-or-death situation and come out unscathed. I am naturally curious, always have been, and I know it's definitely too late to change now. Something big is going down, I can sense it in Susan's words, the way she talks, and her body language. Everything points to someone that is desperate. What do I do, my mind is in turmoil? At last, I know who I am. I know what I can do, I know I can take care of myself but what are they up against, why do they need me? "There's still lots of unanswered questions, and what's with the staff? And who are those guys with the... reptilian eyes?" I say out loud, looking at Susan.

"They are the remnants of a forgotten race, shape changers who have infiltrated the human race for centuries, living amongst us, unnoticed. Have you not come across them? They are not from here, they are from..." Susan pauses to open a folder and look at something, but before she can finish her sentence, Billy finishes it for her.

"Niribu," he says quietly.

"Niribu, I've heard of that before. And these shape changers, could they be the same ones I mentioned in my encounter with the demons from 1350. The ones who came from the stars as slaves. The same ones that tried to overthrow their masters?"

"More than likely, John," Susan replies.

I see Billy tense at this then lean out and look at my sword and shield, his eyes narrowing.

"What else do you have up your sleeve, Billy?" I was going to say but thought better of it. "Is that your real name, or the boy's name?" I add.

"Neither, it's a made-up name. I thought it improper to use the boy's name, it's his body, but my mind. And my real name is unpronounceable, hence Billy."

As he said this, he reaches out and touches my sword. I see a tiny spark come off it, but no one else seems to notice. "This material, this metal is not from Terra," he says.

He picks the sword up by the hilt, struggling with his young arm to hold it aloft. He pulls the sword to him and rests the blade on the edge of the table, tip pointing upwards. He very gently touches some of the symbols on the blade, then places his two middle fingers halfway up on the flat of the blade and drew them down to the hilt. To my utter astonishment, the blade retracts, leaving just the hilt. A second later the two hand guards also retract and disappear.

"As I thought," he says smugly, "A Slithian blade."

"Well, this is another day full of surprises," I say, looking at the hilt of the sword in his tiny hand. "I hope you can get that back out again, otherwise I might make you eat what's left." Billy looked at me confused, with his mouth agape, until I crack a smile. He lets out a sigh of relief. "You can make it into a sword again, right?"

"No, I can't, but you can. Anyone can retract a Slithian blade, but only the one twinned with it can open it."

"OK, care to let me know how?" I ask slightly bemused.

"You are joined. All you have to do is think it and it will be done."

"Really," I say, disbelieving what he said. But I thought about the blade opening, and with a swish, the blade appeared; the sword dropping out of Billy's hand to clatter on the table. A chair screeched on the floor as Arthurs, who was opposite Billy, slides back and stand in one fluid motion.

"Christ, Godiven, watch it!"

"Oops, sorry," I say, and I see Ayesha smile again. Arthurs sits down with a snort of disgust.

"The shield and your armlet are made of the same stuff." Billy continues.

"Slithian?" I ask.

Billy laughs, "No, Slithian is a particular sword make. The metal has a name that is again unpronounceable in human language, it has qualities that make it change its molecular structure, a bit like Nanotechnology."

"So, the shield can retract, as well?"

"Yes, of course. The armlet, no, the sigils on it don't allow for it, only to attach and bind to their twin on first contact. How long have you had these for?"

"Since 1191," I reply quietly.

Arthurs snorts, and adds incredulously, "and you didn't know about any of this?"

"How could I? I was dead at the time, remember, then got woken up with these things around me."

"OK, OK, I was only kidding," he replies, "just trying to lighten up the mood." I shook my head. He couldn't lighten up the mood if he'd swallowed a mouthful of laughing gas!

"You need to show me the sequence please, Billy," it's difficult talking to someone that looks like a kid, but is actually an adult, and an alien at that. It was difficult getting my head around it.

"No problemo!" he replies. He reaches for the shield, re-enacting the sequence and, hey presto, I have a mini shield. I look Arthurs in the eye, thinking about the shield returning to its normal size and it pings back, rocking around on the table like a spinning wheel, before I reach out and stop it with the palm of my hand.

"Don't want to scratch the table now, do we," I say jokingly.

"Cool," Ayesha chips in.

"Show off," Arthurs adds, and he's actually smiling a little, amazing; I didn't know he could do that.

"Your armlet?" Susan asks, "what powers does it have?"

Again, I realise they need to know about me, as much as I need to know about them.

"It senses anything supernatural. It pulsates, warning me of anything in the vicinity, it has come in very handy on countless occasions. The vibrations it gives off are different depending on what is within range. I'm so used to it now that I can feel which supernatural creature is close by, good or bad, before I even see it. Take Arthurs for instance. As soon as he starts to transform, the armlet goes crazy, telling me a supernatural being is present. It's also pretty cool as a weapon. Hit someone with this and they stay hit, trust me. Whatever force is in this metal, magnifies my power by a lot. I can clear a room in a matter of minutes with this bad boy," I say, holding it up to the light.

I glimpse up to see Susan taking notes, just like Elizabeth used too. Has she got a diary too, I wonder? Am I the centre of its attention?

"So, tell me, how long have you been looking for this staff?" I ask, picking it up.

"About as long as you have been looking for your ancestry," Susan replies. "All our teams have searched for it over the centuries, with no success, until you came along. Elizabeth was looking for it!"

"Wow, that's a long time," I exclaim with a whistle. "Why? Why is it so important?"

"Because, it's the only thing that kills them, the only weapon they fear."

"They?" I ask.

"The reptilian creatures, the vampires, other beings. You've seen what it does to them. They are our greatest fear now. We need to harness the power from this staff, find out how it works, make more..." Susan was almost lost in her words. Her passion and fear were there for all to see.

"Not going to happen, I'm afraid." Billy replies, putting his hands together and playing with them, almost kneading them.

"What's with the hands," I ask.

"Oh, sorry," he says, pulling them apart and putting them out of sight under the table. "I still can't get used to those two extra fingers." he says and smiles, then continues more seriously. "That staff comes from a race of beings so powerful, they devour worlds. They are called the Drasil, they are like locusts who swarm upon an entire world, and devour it in days, leaving it barren and lifeless. The staff is made of the bone of the creature, joined together by alien technology, it is one of the most powerful weapons ever created in the universe. That staff is indestructible, nothing on this planet can harm it. The power it harnesses is immense. In the right hands, that is? It has found its way back to you after all these centuries, John. You had it in your previous life before 'you died'. Do you remember how you got it?"

"Not a clue, I can't remember anything before I died, only the last day."

"Have you ever tried hypnosis?" Susan asks.

"Yes, sure, I've tried that, many times."

"But not holding the staff?" Billy says in a questioning way.

"No, no I haven't." I pause, mulling over the idea.

"Can you die? "Ayesha asks.

"Well, not as far as I know. Some pirates once tied a rope to me and threw me overboard, where I spent quite a bit of time with the fishes. Anyway, when they hauled me up, I was wet, but well and truly alive, and very pissed off. I took control of the ship soon after but got marooned on a desert island by the crew, after a heavy night's drinking. They sailed off into the sunset never to be seen again, leaving me behind to die. Anyone else would have starved to death. I didn't. Sure, I was hungry, I like my food as much as the next man, apologies, next person; that's what I'm meant to say now. Well, eventually someone picked me up,

Plate: 10

and recognising me as one of the pirate crew, I was taken back to Charlestown and hung for being a pirate. Christ that hurt, trying to play dead, it made my feet and hands go all numb.

And then there was the case where I fell into a bear trap, in Romania. I was impaled and stuck on a pointed wooden pole for nearly twenty-four hours. When the villagers found me, I was cursing like a good 'un, I can tell you. It took some convincing to get them to come down and free me. They thought I was some sort of demon, which I suppose I was. One of the elders wanted to fill the bear pit up with earth, with me still in it! Fortunately, he got out-voted, because they needed the trap. Anyway, I convinced them that I would sort out their bear problem if they would be kind enough to free me from my predicament."

"And did you?" Billy asks.

"Did I what?"

"Sort out the bear problem?"

"Yes, that was easy. I found the bear; it was only trying to protect its young. It had a broken arrow in its side, and it was in pain."

"Did you kill it?" Arthur's asks?

"No, of course not! I sedated it, kept the young fed. They were cute, they liked me," I say with a smile to Ayesha. "Then I removed the arrow, tended to the wound and made sure it was clean, before covering it up. A few of the villagers had followed me and observed my work. When the bear awoke, it somehow realised what I had done. I don't know how, but it didn't attack. It was amazing, the next time I passed through the village I was treated like a god. They had erected a huge wooden totem to the bear, and left food offerings to keep the family happy. They had even filled in the bear pit! How things can change?"

"How about if you lose your head?" Arthurs says in a completely deadpan way.

"Why, are you offering? I'm sure if you got those claws out, you could give it a go, couldn't you, Arthurs?"

"It was a justifiable question," he replies, his eyes unwavering.

"No, I've never lost my head and if anyone has tried, I've always managed to stop them," I say, staring at Arthurs. Why do some people just rub you up the wrong way right from the start?

"So, what's your superpower, big man?" Arthurs asks with a sneer.

"What, apart from being able to keep it up all night?" I reply with a wink towards the man. I hear Ayesha giggle and see her put her hands to her mouth. I see Billy look at me with astonishment.

"That was uncalled for, John," Susan says sternly.

"Just kidding. Here, why don't you give me the file you have on me, and I'll fill in the gaps. I assume you've all read it, right?" It would be interesting to know how much they knew about me anyhow.

Susan glances at Arthurs who nods, then she hands me a manila folder, without saying a word, her eyes on mine, telling me more than I needed to know. This was 'Top Secret' information and even though it was about me, I still shouldn't be reading this.

I take the folder and look on the cover, a brown printed standard government folder with 'Top Secret' stamped in red across the cover. Below it, is typed my name followed by a code name, 'Knight Eternal', which looked like it had been added recently. Nice name, kind of catchy, I think.

I flip the cover over and start reading.

Subject: John Godiven   **Code name:** Immortal Warrior
Sex: Male   **Height:** Approximately 6 ft 4in
Hair colour: Black with a red streak.
Eye colour: Grey   **Stature:** Muscular
Dependents: Unknown
Family: Unknown *Richard Plantagenet (Lionheart)*
Born: Sometime before 11'91 First appearance: 1571
Status: Alive and well, looks in his mid-thirties
Defining features: Scar on neck
Reasons for Longevity are unknown

Subject must be monitored at all times, and his story kept secret from the public.

And then it went on to list a lot of stuff I'd done over the years that they had somehow found out about. All my missions during both World Wars, and quite a lot of stuff I'd actually forgotten. It looked like somebody had been keeping a close eye on me for quite some time.

"Very impressive," I say, closing the folder and handing it back.

"We know about your time with Elizabeth in the 1570's to the turn of that century. We have a lot of information on you from the turn of the 20th century, but for all those years in between, we have nothing! What happened, John, where did you go?"

"Why do you need to know?"

"It could be important to us."

"Us?"

"To you as well, to all of us."

"Care to explain."

"Something has happened, something big. Worldwide big. We think with you and that staff helping us, it might just tip the balance in our favour."

"You know, Susan, you are talking in riddles, why don't you just come out with it, for goodness' sake." But I was already thinking about this when I spoke to my father in the vision, about what he warned about. Susan was almost repeating his words.

"All the nuclear missile silos have disappeared, all over the world. Unbeknownst to the public, all the nations are on a war setting but not with each other, with something else."

"Disappeared?"

"Sunk into the Earth, destroyed. There's not one nuclear missile remaining, they are all gone."

"Well, that's a good thing, right," I say trying to pick out something positive. "At least, we can't blow ourselves up anymore."

There was no reply, so I reply to her earlier question. "You know about my sword, shield and armlet. The shield can repel any bullet, even grenades, it's pretty impregnable. The armlet you know magnifies my punch. My senses are heightened and are continuing to improve, but apart from that I'm pretty normal. Oh, and bullets don't seem to penetrate for some reason."

"Apart from the fact that you are immortal," Arthurs states.

"Oh, and that, yes," I add with a wink to Ayesha.

I pull out my Magnum 45 and place it on the table. "This is my favourite modern-day weapon," I say. Susan looks at the gun, then back to me and is about to say something when there was a knock on the door, hopefully heralding a well-earned cuppa and some food, but a young smartly dressed man enters and goes straight to Susan, with not a cuppa in sight. She looks towards me while the man speaks quietly in her ear. Susan nods when he finishes.

"Thank you, Tony," she says, and he leaves the room.

"It looks like we will have to cut this short until another time," she says. "It seems we are going to Egypt, something else has come up, that needs investigating immediately. We are getting on a plane first thing in the morning, we are off to see the pyramids!"

"What?" I exclaim, "How about the demon king, those reptilian eyed men?"

"That will have to wait, we have a date with the Sphinx. And I have a feeling, we won't need to find him, he will find us." The thought made a chill run down my spine.

"No one is going anywhere until I know more about this team," I say, slightly louder than I wanted to. "We got lucky last night, tomorrow, we might not be. Have any of you done any military training? Can any of you handle a gun?"

"We have all had military training, John," Susan replies, handing me some files. I take a quick glance and see they are files on all the team, the real ones, this time. I nod back.

"Except me?" Billy butts in, "I don't need it," he said matter-of-factly.

"Why is that?" I ask, "because you are bulletproof?"

"No," he replies slowly, "because I can do this." And he disappears before my very eyes. I look at where he was and see a very faint shimmer in my vision, as if the place I was looking was rocking ever so slightly. And just as quick as he was gone, he's back again.

"And you were going to tell me this when?"

"You hadn't asked till now!" Billy replies and shrugs nonchalantly. "It's all in the file, if you bother to read it this time!"

"Are you sure that boy inside your head hasn't taken over?" I say feeling a little exasperated.

"Positive," he answers with a smile.

"Rrr, so how does this work?" I ask, biting my tongue.

"I have the ability to change my DNA, to blend and become invisible, a bit like a chameleon can change colour to blend in with it's surroundings."

"Does it make you bulletproof as well?"

"No, of course not."

"And you've had no training?"

"I have the body of a boy."

"Then you are staying on the plane until we return, we can then make you fit for action."

"Who put you in charge?" Billy replies angrily, with a face that made him look like a child for once.

"I agree," Arthurs says. "It would be difficult explaining taking a boy into Egypt, anyway."

"I could always stay invisible." he says.

"No!" Susan, myself and Arthurs say together.

"Looks like I'm staying on the plane then." he replies in annoyance.

"Before we go, we've been working on a new gun and tracker at our research facility in North Yorkshire. We'd like you to try it out for us," Susan says looking at me. "Arthurs has already tried it, but he's happier with what he's got at the moment."

My thoughts drift back to my vision. "Is it a Browning?"

"Yes," Susan replies, frowning, "but how..."

"With a motion tracker fitted into the handle, that picks up anything within a fifty metre radius, that is bigger than a dog."

Susan's face drops. "How did you know? This is beyond 'Top Secret'. Only our scientists at the research facility know about this. Not even the military know?"

"I had another vision, maybe a picture of a possible future, I don't know. It probably wasn't going to end well. In the vision, I was holding this gun you just mentioned... which means something about this vision was real," I explain. "Look, I don't know if it is the staff or whatever Ayesha has done to me, but I'm seeing things now. Something has happened and I'm not liking it, not one bit," I add.

"Nothing to do with me!" Ayesha adds, holding both hands up, palms facing forward.

It is late into the night when I put the last file down and sit staring at the walls I know so well. I am in my original room, one in which I had not slept in for centuries. Just thinking that still makes me raise my eyes at the incredulity of it all. But here I am back at the institute, with another Harkness at the helm and a new team waiting and primed to go. It seems like history does repeat itself. I shiver, I just hope the outcome isn't the same. I get ready for bed, knowing that an early call was due for a trip to Egypt, and the start of another adventure. I look at the gun on the table, pick it up and feel it's weight. The motion tracker automatically switches on and the sensors pick up heat signatures all around the house; some moving, some still. Two dots close together might signify Susan and Arthurs; I know that's only a guess but probably a good one. I touch another button and the screen changes to a much closer and detailed view with the dots becoming almost human. I see two bodies entwined, which makes me think my assumption is correct. I see one body as a red light, the other blue and wonder who is who? I wonder how much Arthurs has to control his instincts in order to remain in human form, especially at night time. Starting to feel uncomfortable, I quickly put my finger on the screen and move it to another part of the institute. Now I pick up a smaller figure, moving around. This figure seems a little strange, it's highlighted with a bright yellow glow, making it difficult to see a definite shape. I see the figure stop and then move again, as if entering a room. A second later I see the figure stop again, and then it seems to grow, its colour changing from yellow to a burnt orange. I look at the screen for a few more seconds before placing the gun back on the table, which automatically turns the screen off.

I stare at the gun for a while wondering what I had seen, my thoughts dark, my brain working overtime. Could what I think I saw be true or was my tired mind playing tricks with me. Time to do a bit of detective work!

I look at the magazine, it's only the size of a normal pistol but holds fifty rounds and has a quick-fire trigger option that releases bursts of five to ten rounds per second. Nice toy, I think I'm going to like this beauty. Could it stop the demon king, I doubt it, but it might slow him down for a bit. How has he survived for so long? What is he doing here, is he trying to get the staff? And why can't I remember anything about my life before the incident that made me immortal? It's as if my mind had been wiped clean, reset by that event. Even now after knowing my lineage, I'm a Plantagenet, I'm royalty! That sounds almost as incredible as living forever! And what were those creatures that looked human but had reptilian eyes? Were they somehow related to the story I had lived through all those years ago? My senses tell me so, and my coincidence meter ran out a long time ago. With all these questions buzzing around my head, I was amazed that tiredness crept up on me as it did, like an old friend, wrapping its arms around me and dragging me down into the realms of the sandman. My eyes feel heavy, and I wonder whether I will have a peaceful sleep, or more visions, or nightmares. Only time and the oblivion of sleep will tell.

6

EGYPT

"Wow, that is a lot bigger than I thought it would be?"
"You mean to say, in the thousand years you have lived on this planet, this is the first time, you've seen the pyramids?" Arthurs asks.
"Yep, definitely worth the wait."
"There are even bigger ones than these on Niribu," a voice says from beside me.
"Jesus Christ, Billy!" I whisper to where I think he is, "you are meant to be staying on the plane!" I notice one of the security guards lift his head to look in my direction. The Guard frowns and is probably thinking, 'Crazy Englishman,' or something like that.
We are standing on a shelf of sand, looking towards the Great Pyramid of Giza, Cheops. It is 3.00pm, and the sun is still high in the sky. Not a cloud is visible, and the area shimmered like a mirage in the dry 40-degree heat. Before us, tourists mull around taking photographs and selfies, while camel ride and desert excursion guides try desperately to get everyone's attention, by shouting louder than the man next to them. Kids scamper around attracting attention from any tourist that happen to catch their eye. A light breeze played with the sand, chasing it to and fro along the road.
A posse of bodyguards, Egyptian Special Forces, stand in a line on either side of us, keeping everyone at bay. Dressed in tan suits, with black slicked back hair and sunglasses, they look to me like they should be on some Reality TV show or sci fi 'B' movie. The semiautomatic machine guns, slung over their shoulders

and held in one hand ready for anything, remind me that they were the real deal.

Beyond the pyramids, the desert stretches for as far as we can see, while behind them and across a small road, the city of Cairo sprawls like an invasive weed, stretching further and further into the sands.

"OK, Susan, we are here, so what's this all about?" I ask.

"We had a call from someone from 'The Egyptian Museum of Antiquities' yesterday, and said they had uncovered something that only we should see, it relates to our search. They have been excavating and restoring around the Sphinx, when they uncovered a hidden chamber. Something near the right ear of the Sphinx triggered a small hidden alcove, that has led to a larger chamber being uncovered beneath the statue. That's all I know, so, let's go in there with our professional heads on and see if we can help. They sounded scared and the way the Egyptian authorities fast-tracked us here, this sounds big!"

"Big!" I exclaim. "How big? Earth shatteringly big or cosmic big?" thinking of what I'd been told the day before.

"Let's go and find out shall we," Susan said, looking towards a large taped off area to our left. More security guards and police surround the entrance and as we near, I can see the unmistakable shape of the Sphinx beneath the covered and fenced off area. 'Wasn't it meant to be twice as old as the pyramids,' I thought? Razor wire surrounds the place, and it reminds me of the security surrounding Area 51. From the pictures I had seen of the Sphinx, this was not normally here, and looking at it, it seems to have been hastily erected. 'What was going on here?' I wonder with a wry smile; I was looking forward to this. I was on a mission in the desert with my new team, I was about to go into a hidden chamber beneath the Sphinx that hardly anyone in the world had ever seen, to explore a mystery that was somehow attached to what, the staff or something else. For the first time in a long time, I feel adrenaline flowing through my veins, the sense of adventure stirring feelings inside me that have remained buried for too long. I feel alive again.

A short rounded Egyptian man dressed in khaki trousers and top, with a lanyard around his neck that stated he was Professor Alfredi from 'The Egyptian

Museum of Antiquities', greets us at the entrance gate. He is clean shaven, has a round friendly face and deep-set brown eyes. He seems to be sweating more than all of us put together, his clothes are soaked through, and he wipes droplets of sweat from his eyes with a dusty handkerchief that had once been white. "Hello, hello," he says quickly in perfect English, looking from one to the other of us until his eyes fixed on me. No, not me, the staff I held in my hand. Instinct made me pull it closer, concealing it beneath my clothing when I notice the professor's wide-eyed scared look.

"Professor."

"Oh, oh, a thousand apologies, my friends," he replies in a fluster, "this way, this way, I have something of great importance to show you," he says with a wave of one sweaty hand.

We are led into a large tent and towards a table at the back. No one notices the small imprints of a child's shoe in the sand, and I do my best to stay behind Billy, treading on his imprints with my large size 11 boots. Three or four other people from the museum are sitting down at desks, working at laptops or on artefacts that they had uncovered. Some look up but others are so enrapt with their work that they didn't seem to notice our strange looking entourage. Most of them look like students, hardly out of their teens'. The security team remain outside the tent, guarding the entrance. Electric fans, powered by a generator, blows cool air through the tent, lowering the temperature, so that the tent feels like the proverbial 'breath of fresh air'.

"This way, please," Professor Alfredi motions, as he faces a semi-clear plastic flap that he starts to unzip. It was then that I catch the smell, not strong, but a distinct smell of age and decay that seems to waft out from behind the flap. The Professor stops suddenly and straightens up, then turns to us with a stone-like look on his face.

"We found and opened this entrance a week ago. Someone working on restoring the Sphinx triggered a small hidden alcove. Inside that alcove was a stone tablet that had a map of how to find this chamber, and how to open it. We had a new mobile ground penetrating radar unit which showed a chamber within, and it was decided we must investigate. Further scans showed a large tunnel leading off into the desert, which seemed to go deeper and deeper into the Earth until the radar could no longer pick it up. It stretches for miles, just one tunnel leading from the chamber. The tunnel is incredible, yes, but what we found in the chamber is why we have called the Harkness Institute."

The Professor takes one more glance at me and finishes unzipping the plastic covering. Cables lead underneath the plastic giving artificial light to the chamber for the first time ever. The entrance was surprisingly wide, almost double door width. A long line of stone steps leads downwards to a dimly lit area. Sand scrapes under our feet as we descend, echoing through the chamber, magnifying the sound so that it feels to me like we were in a large endless cavern. The steps stop on a stone floor, and I let out a breath, I didn't realise I had been holding in. I had the urge to shout 'echo' but thought better of it. I straighten up and immediately bang my head on the stone ceiling.

"Ow!" I say, reaching up to rub my head. "Sorry." I raise my hand in apology when everyone jumped a little. Arthurs is bent over, looking at me with a frown, both hands out, palms facing upwards as if to tell me to concentrate.

The roof was very low, and we had to stoop and keep moving. I've hated confined spaces ever since someone locked me in a cave and decided to leave me there to die! So, this place, despite the excitement of the occasion, isn't doing it for me.

The cavern was hexagonal, and a layer of sand covers the stone floor, disturbed now by the team that had entered before us. The roof was made of stone blocks held up by beautifully carved columns. An area in the centre had been lit up and behind that a large opening, which could only be the entrance to the tunnel which was encased in two stone blocks holding up an even larger stone lintel. Susan steps eagerly forward towards the closest column and starts inspecting it, with the light of a torch she produces from her pocket.

"My goodness, these aren't Egyptian hieroglyphs, this is ancient Lemurian, this predates from a time before Egypt became the power it was, before the first pharaoh." There was an excitement in her voice that makes me smile. Elizabeth used to get so excited about such finds. Out of the corner of my eye, I sense Billy move towards the column, his feet making shallow imprints in the sand covering the stone floor.

"This way, please," Alfredi shepherds us on. Susan takes one more glimpse back at the column before catching up with us. Ayesha and Arthurs stand shoulder to shoulder, quiet, reflective and on edge, their eyes darting around the chamber, as if they are being watched. I am impressed by how Ayesha is behaving. She seems to have come into her own, as if the sense of adventure has stirred her into life. Her files had already told me how good she is in the field.

Beyond the rows of columns, I could see a dais with a grey stone sarcophagus at its centre, lit by two spotlights. We seem to be drawn towards this like the proverbial 'moth to a flame'. And as we near, sound seemed to become muffled, silence now seems to become palpable, as if we are in some sort of vacuum. 'What?' I think, 'what is going on here?' I can feel a pulse drumming in my ears but everything else seems to have disappeared, as if I had noise cancelling headphones on. I even reach up, pinch my nose and try to clear the feeling by blowing through my ears, but nothing changes. I turn to see if the others are feeling the same, when I see Susan drop to the floor on her knees placing one hand to her ear in pain. I reach out to help and tap the floor lightly with the staff, and as I do, a distant boom ripples across my conscious mind, dispersing the sound somewhat. I see the others struggling to stand, the pain beginning to take hold. Above the vacuum, Susan, looks at me, eyes wide in pain. She had seen what had happened and motions me to do it again.

"The staff, strike the staff on the floor," she screams above the noise, but I can only just hear her.

I look at her, eyes wide, and follow her instructions, striking the floor with the staff. Another shockwave of sound opens up. Sensing this, I lift the staff and strike the floor again, with more vigour this time. Each time the staff strikes the floor, the vacuum of silence seems to dispel, so that on the last blow, there was a loud crack on the stone floor and the spell seems to be broken.

Alfredi looks about him stunned, "What just happened?" Sweat was pouring from him again. 'Poor guy,' I think, 'you should have been born in Antarctica or something.'

"Not sure, Professor, we are working on the go here!" I say. He's staring at the staff now, as if he was a man possessed.

"If I am not mistaken," the Professor blurts out," that is the Staff of Solomon, said to have been crafted in Hyperborea in the Second Age of Man as a weapon against all the foes of mankind." We knew it wasn't, of course, but we didn't interrupt him, I couldn't exactly tell him it was made from the bones of a world devouring locust and one of the most powerful weapons in the universe, now, could I? He continues, "Handed down through the warrior kings of ancient Lemuria, that fought an eternal battle for their survival against a race of reptilian like beings of ancient times, said to have been defeated by a great warrior king who hunted them down and wiped them from the face of the Earth, or so he thought? The few remaining reptilians were scattered and on-the-run, but far from helpless. You see, they could shape change into anyone or anything, and so they hid among us, plotting and planning, rebuilding, regrouping and surviving in the shadows. You often hear far-fetched stories; you must have come across some yourselves?"

"I hate shape changers, slippery little bas...," I grumbled under my breath to Ayesha who just smiles and says, "grumpy pants!" She is definitely beginning to come out of herself.

"We might have, Professor," Susan replies, "forgive me, but this seems far from the sort of expertise I would expect from you? How come you know so much about these things?"

Alfredi could not have seemed more agitated if he tried. He kept glancing about him in fear that something was going to happen. I think he might blow a gasket if he is any more on edge, a heart attack looks a certainty. I was about to try and calm the guy down, when he reaches the dais, walks up the few steps and looks at what lies inside.

"Because of some stone tablets we have found and deciphered, but more importantly because of this," Alfredi exclaims wide-eyed in fear and revulsion.

"Good God!" Susan exclaims.

"Damn, that's something you don't see every day!" I breath in, while whistling through my teeth.

"You keep saying that, you know!" Ayesha points out.

"Interesting," Arthurs whispers his eyes looking over the sarcophagus into the darkness beyond the lights. What does he sense out there?

"Is that what I think it is?" Ayesha asks tight lipped.

It isn't until we all stand beside the sarcophagus that we realised how big it is. At least twelve feet in length and about three feet wide, it is the largest sarcophagus any of us have ever seen. And what lay within was a thing from out of a distant time, a forgotten era. A creature I'd seen in my visions coming out of an ancient ship. The skeleton is at least nine feet long and adorned with a suit of armour made from solid gold, interspersed with silver. The armour formed a mesh of metallic scales, which covered the whole torso and part of the bottom half to the thigh bones. Naked bone continued to the feet which looked like they had something on them which had turned to dust over the ages, exposing three sharp pointed talons and an appendage that was almost doglike. The arms were adorned with solid gold wrist bands, similar to the one I wore, that reached up to the elbows. The hands were made up of three talons and one thumb. The nails looked sharp, almost filed to a point. But it was the head that everyone was staring at, for this is where the similarity to humans abruptly ended. The skull had been encased in a ceremonial death mask which lay to the side of the head placed there by an unbelieving Alfredi, no doubt.

The skull was oblong in shape, with a large nasal area and a mouth that was full of sharp pointed teeth, almost vampire like. The cheekbones seemed to draw inwards, the ear cavities disappearing more behind the head than a humans', giving the features of a thin aquiline snakelike head that was somewhat out of proportion with the rest of the body. I look at the death mask and shudder. I have seen a lot of scary stuff in my time, but this thing gives me the creeps, it looks so damned real, almost alive. What the death mask was made of, I don't know, whomever made it or painted it was a genius because when placed back on the skull, it would have looked almost as if the thing was still alive. A green skin like texture covered the head, folding and overlapping like a sheet. No hair was visible. The ears were mere slits, and the nose was non-existent, apart from two small holes above the partly opened mouth that showed a gleaming set of razor teeth with two prominent fangs that were set above an exposed forked tongue. The eyes were the things that would give me nightmares in days to come, as they seemed to stare into my very soul. Green slanted eyes with yellow pupils, which looked hypnotic to stare at, confirm the snake like genes of this creature. Nothing human could look like that. Yet, why had Alfredi specifically asked for the Harkness Institute to come?

As if on cue, Ayesha said, "Hey, John, you'd better come and have a look at this?"

Ayesha had moved around the dais to get a different view and was staring down at something resting against the sarcophagus. The lid was broken in two pieces but the inscription and pictures upon it were plain for all to see.

"Oh my," I mutter. The writing was Lemurian, and Susan starts reading it aloud, her voice faltering a little. I look in shock at the pictures that paint a story that none of us want to hear.

"Here lies Toth Sakin, Lord of time and space, sleeping until the time of rebirth. Whoever wakes the priest shall wake an army that will destroy the scourge that is mankind. The horned god shall lead us from the darkness to reclaim our rightful place as rulers of Hyperborea...," Susan stops, and looks up at me but I was looking at the painted column beneath the inscription which shows rows and rows of lizard like men kneeling in prayer before a creature that could only be one person, Toth Sakin. And in his hand was the unmistakable Staff of Solomon.

"We know you have been looking for the staff, Miss Harkness," Alfredi says. "That's why we called you. We didn't know you had found it."

Out of the corner of my eye, I think I can see something move behind Arthurs. A darker shadow among the other shadows, somewhere near the tunnel's entrance. Was that Billy? A trick of the light perhaps or fraught nerves I think, shaking my head. I sure am on edge today, it must be the confined space or lack of sleep, or both.

"The sound thing, what was that?" Alfredi asks. "That never happened when we entered the chamber before." He seems to be a little calmer now, that's good news! I didn't want any more deaths on my hands. And he looks quite heavy to carry out if he falls ill, or something worse happens.

"I'm not sure. It must be something to do with that," Susan says looking at the staff in my hand. "It was like we entered a vacuum and when John used the staff, it broke the seal and everything dispersed, odd, very odd! It was when I saw John drop the staff end on the floor that made me realise what effect it had!" she adds looking at me for an answer. Alfredi raises one eyebrow and turns to me.

I was about to reply when the lights go out, and we all realise that we are no longer alone down here. The sound of shuffling steps come from all about us. Despite the heat, I feel an icy cold chill run down my spine. The smell comes again, the same musty earthy smell of decay and death. I feel, rather than see that there was lots of movement in front of us.

"Susan?" I cry in the darkness, remembering where everything was, and heading behind the nearest column towards where I thought the Professor stood.

"Got it, John." In the darkness, Susan flicks her torch back on and it reflects off the hundreds of snake eyes that are now staring at us in the torch light. I didn't have that in mind when I called to Susan, but that would do for now. Perhaps she didn't want to expose her unearthly or witch-craft powers in front of Alfredi. I know she can summon light with a casting spell. Alfredi screams, running into the sarcophagus and falling over. 'Shit, I hate working with amateurs,' I think, as I pull out my new gun, backtracking towards Alfredi. Arthurs, standing behind the sarcophagus does the same and holds his gun in front of him, both hands on the pistol's handle, his body braced for action. No sign of the inner werewolf in him now. Today, he was undercover and doing a good job to control his powers.

'Where is Billy?' I think with worry and annoyance all mixed into one. My eyes dart around the room until I feel a gentle tug on my trouser leg to signify where he is. I lean down and whisper.

"We are going to have some serious words when we get out of this."

"Wait!" Susan shouts, moving in front of the group, towards the mass of creatures. I move towards her as fast as I can and stand shoulder to shoulder, staff in one hand, my new gun in the other ready to protect her.

My motion tracker is going nuts, it's just a blur of white. The things that stand staring at us in the semi-darkness are so closely packed that it was almost hard to discern any anatomical features, but it was clear that these things are not the same as what was in the sarcophagus. 'Maybe relatives but definitely a few gene pools down from the big dead guy,' I think. The creatures, for that was the only way to describe them, were shorter, squatter with a pale hairless complexion. 'Damn, these guys need to get some sun on them.' They stand stooped over, their arms hang loose, their talons almost touching the floor, as they shuffle forwards. Then they suddenly stop, spreading out around the front of the dais. Snake eyes glint in the darkness, and behind those eyes I could see that the heads are narrow and almost featureless. The teeth were not so pronounced but still show a menacing array of sharp pointed incisors. A distant murmuring hiss rose from their ranks as forked tongues dart in and out in anticipation of what would happen next.

The creatures' number about sixty in all, I reckon, but I felt more arriving and others hiding out of sight; one must have cut the electricity. They carry no weapons, but I feel that their superior numbers, their talons and sharp teeth were adequate enough to make up for that. They stand in front of Susan and I, swaying to and fro with an almost hypnotising rhythm, and I notice that they stood in a perfect semicircle before the dais, seemingly held there by some unseen force and afraid to get any closer. An unintelligible chittering emanates from them now, sending another icy spike of dread running through me, 'these guys are as creepy as the mask.'

One of the creatures pushes forward and although not getting any closer, it steps out a fraction and speaks to me.

"You wield the Staff of Solomon but you are no king." It hisses in Lemurian. It raises its head sniffing at the air, turning its head to the left then the right and sniffing again. "And, you have set free the ancient one with your ignorance, how fitting that the staff that nearly drove us to extinction will bring about our rebirth. We will take our leader and leave you in peace… for what little good that will do to you in the end." With this my hands shake and the staff quivers. I take a step towards him as the creature turns its head and sharply hisses a few orders. Four of the creatures, lumber forward towards the dais just as Arthurs appears

KNIGHT ETERNAL

Plate: 11

from behind the column and into the light of Susan's torch, pistol aimed at the creatures.

"That's not going to happen, guys," he shouts and pulls the trigger. The noise in the chamber is almost deafening, and in shock Susan drops her torch which shatters on the floor. In the instant before it went black, I saw the shot strike the leader in the head killing the creature instantly. Arthurs fires again, two flashes to my right, and we all hear the squeals as the bullets strike home. We hear and feel the horde charge forward, I fire, keeping my finger on the trigger, while reaching over and grabbing Susan, lifting her clean over the sarcophagus and out of the firing line. I holster my gun, tuck the staff under my waistcoat and draw my sword and shield. Then I shake off my coat to reveal my armlet. My eyes are already getting accustomed to the dark. I see the dark form of the unconscious, or dead, Alfredi slumped across the sarcophagus and make a point to protect his body.

Before I can move, Susan steadies herself, turns to face the horde and speaks an incantation that casts an eerie white light around the chamber. I take a step back when I see the metal of my sword, shield and armlet glow as if reacting to the light that Susan cast. The metal gives off a red hue that gleams in the white light like a coloured light bulb.

By now, the moving mass of reptilian flesh was almost upon us when they suddenly stop, staring towards me with some sense of awe in their snakelike eyes. As one, they stoop and kneel before me, their heads bowed in subjugation.

My eyes widen as I turn to look at the group.

"Looks like you have a new fan base, John!" Ayesha says, breaking the silence.

"Very funny."

"It's what's on the sarcophagus lid," Susan says, "look?" I backtrack slowly, one step at a time, and look out the corner of my eye at what's on the lid. Another image shows Toth Sakin fighting off a horde of humans. My eyes go wide when I see what he is wearing and holding, a red glowing shield, sword and armlet all etched upon his fighting form. In his other hand, he wields a long thin spear, it's tip glowing, shown by a series of lines emanating from around its point. More riddles, I think.

Ayesha pulls out a torch and switches it on, the unnatural light blinks out a moment later as a hand appears on the rim of the sarcophagus, followed by another, then a voice speaks out feebly as Alfredi pulls himself up, a nasty cut on his head is bleeding. "It's gone," he whispers in shock.

My gaze never leaves the subdued bowing crowd in front of me. "What's gone, Professor?"

"The mummy and the mask! They're gone!"

Two bodies lay close to Arthurs where he had shot them. The other two, in all the pandemonium, must have slipped past picked up the mummy and mask and disappeared.

"Damn!" I shout. "You slimy bastards are taking the proverbial. Get up!" reaching the first two and pulling them up to their feet. Their skin feels cold, oily and looks almost translucent on closer inspection, and it took some guts to keep touching them. "Get up," I shout again, lifting my arms, palms outstretched. "Get up." They all rise eventually, with no show of aggression towards me, still seemingly in awe of my appearance. They turn to me, and I speak to them in broken Lemurian. "I am not your god I am not your saviour. The only place I will lead you to is your death. Leave us, take your leader, you are welcome to him. Do not threaten us again, otherwise you will face all of our wrath." Arthurs joins me and I see his eyes go red, gun still drawn, a quiet growl coming from his mouth. The closest creatures withdrew, their eyes wide in fear. Susan steps forward controlling the light. I sheath my sword and with my right hand, hold the staff out in front of me. "Now go, before I change my mind and kill you all," I scream.

The creatures turn as one, and without a backward glance scurry off collecting their fallen comrades as they depart. It took a few minutes before the noise of their departure could only just be heard down the tunnel. A few moments later and all was silent.

"Nice speech, John. Didn't understand a word mind you!" Ayesha puts in.

"Thanks, that means a lot," I reply sarcastically.

"You know, John, I understood what you said and I think the ancient kings of Lemuria would have been proud of you. But this is far from over, I think this is just the beginning. I believe that that staff should stay close to you now, John, don't let it out of your sight. I feel unseen arcane forces at work here and if anyone was going to don the mantle of a Lemurian warrior king, then I can't think of anyone else more suitable than you?" says Susan.

"I agree," Arthurs voice says out of the darkness.

"It looks good on you, John, almost Gandalf like," Ayesha said with as much sincerity as she could.

I stood there looking into the darkness of the tunnel. Where does it lead to? I'd love to know. The adventurer in me wants to know. Thoughts rush through my already troubled mind, then a course of action seems to appear.

" You know, I'm fed up with these guys already," I say walking over to the dais and placing the staff upon it. I then reach down to pick up one piece of the sarcophagus's lid in both hands. With a great effort, I pick it up and stride towards the tunnel entrance. "You'd better get everyone out of here," I say to Arthurs, straining under the weight of the rock. Everyone backs away apart from Ayesha, who holds the light steady for me.

I lift the slab as high as I can and fling it at the mantle above the entrance. I hear a strangled cry of anguish from Alfredi before some comforting words from Susan, and an arm around his shoulder led him out of the chamber.

The slab hit the mantle full on with an almighty crash. The lid shattered and the mantle cracked. The two side columns holding up the mantle now lean inwards, but it doesn't collapse. Dust billows everywhere. I return and pick up the other piece of the lid. One more mighty throw and it strikes gold. The mantle cracks and splits, the two side columns fall in on themselves and the tunnel wall collapses, covering the opening with stone and rubble. I sense and hear the tunnel collapsing in on itself on the other side of the entrance. 'Good,' I think. When the dust clears, I admire my handiwork, and turn to Ayesha. Coughing a little I say, "That should stop the hero worship for a while."

Walking out of the chamber with Ayesha, who was carrying my coat, I see the students, who hadn't batted an eyelid when we entered, look at me in amazement. I was still carrying my sword and shield, the staff now tucked under my arm, and was covered in a layer of dust that must have made me look like the ghost of a long-lost warrior king, all I need is a crown. I lift my thumb up, pointing back the way we had just come. "Big cave in, be careful," I tell them with a smile, winking at Ayesha.

On the plane trip home, I sit in silence, the Staff resting across my thighs. Along with the ancient lettering, intricate carvings cover the strange white bone. The metal band holding it together is of the same metal as my sword, shield and armlet, so I know there is some connection. What creature of space did this bone come from, I did not know or could not guess, I only had Billy's word on it, but the structure and consistency of the bone looked different from anything I had ever seen. The whole staff gives off a real air of antiquity, as if it had come from the very dawn of man. The more I stare at it, the more I seem to see things within the shape of the bone. The grain almost seems to move and slide into different shapes. I close my eyes and shake my head, thinking this an illusion brought on by my overworked imagination, but things still seem to ripple within the grain, when I peer again. I make out a part that looks like a beautiful, spired city, with a man in the forefront, a crown on his head and a sword in one hand and what looks like the staff in the other. The carvings were so detailed they almost looked 3-D. I peer closer and can almost make out the features of the man. For an instant, I thought I could see the long hair ripple as if in some imaginary wind. And then as quickly as I am trying to view it, so it disappears. Another figure appears, as I twist the staff in my hand, trying to catch up with the kaleidoscopic movements within the wood. A tall, white, gaunt looking man dressed all in black stood on some African savannah with a black man beside him handing him this very same staff. The man had a sword in a scabbard around his waist, and what looked like a flintlock pistol tucked into his belt. His high brimmed cap covers most of his face as he stares out over the horizon, towards a vast jungle that lay before him. I twist the staff again and the same figure is standing beside an ancient building deep in the jungle, holding the staff aloft to ward off some nameless horror from escaping its tomb! Again, the scene changes and I see a young man, who could be me, staff held aloft. My eyes feel suddenly heavy, I blink to stay awake but the more I strain to keep awake, the more the staff seems to hypnotise me into a deep sleep. I feel my eyes shut and suddenly I am somewhere else. Eons pass in mere seconds, I feel like I am being drawn back through the ages, across the distant pasts of mankind to an ancient time, to a seminal moment in history.

I open my eyes and feel I am now standing, the drumming of the plane is gone to be replaced by another plain, a plain on the Earth. Before me stretches a vast open tundra that leads to fir covered foothills and then beyond that to a range of snow-capped mountains. Upon this plain, a battle has taken place, so large in scale that I feel that no other battle could match it. Upon the battlefield, locked in the eternal embrace of death, were countless humans and reptilians. The coppery smell of death hung heavy in the air. Before me, an army of human warriors, dressed in armour and with billowing red capes, moved through the battlefield putting to death any reptilians that still lived. In the distance, beneath the backdrop of a line of the snow-covered mountains, a cavalry, a thousand strong, wearing the same uniform were chasing down more of the army of reptilians. Vultures squealed above, riding on thermals, biding their time before the feast.
"*We have won, Your Majesty! They are on the run, it is over,*" *an old voice said in Lemurian from behind me. The voice sounded familiar!*
I looked down at myself, my arms were now bare, and my armlet was nowhere to be seen. I felt incredibly tired and weary. In my right hand was a massive double-edged sword, that I now leant on for support. I was bleeding from countless cuts and scratches. Blood still rolled down to mingle onto the earth beneath my feet. Hundreds, no thousands of reptilian creatures were scattered about me, their bodies, twisted and contorted in their final embrace of death. Before me, lay what must have been their leader, his head now shorn from his body by a massive swipe of my sword. In my right hand I held the staff. It gleamed bright and new, the sun high above my head, producing a shining aurora around the weapon.
"*It worked,*" *the voice said from behind me again.*

Plate: 12

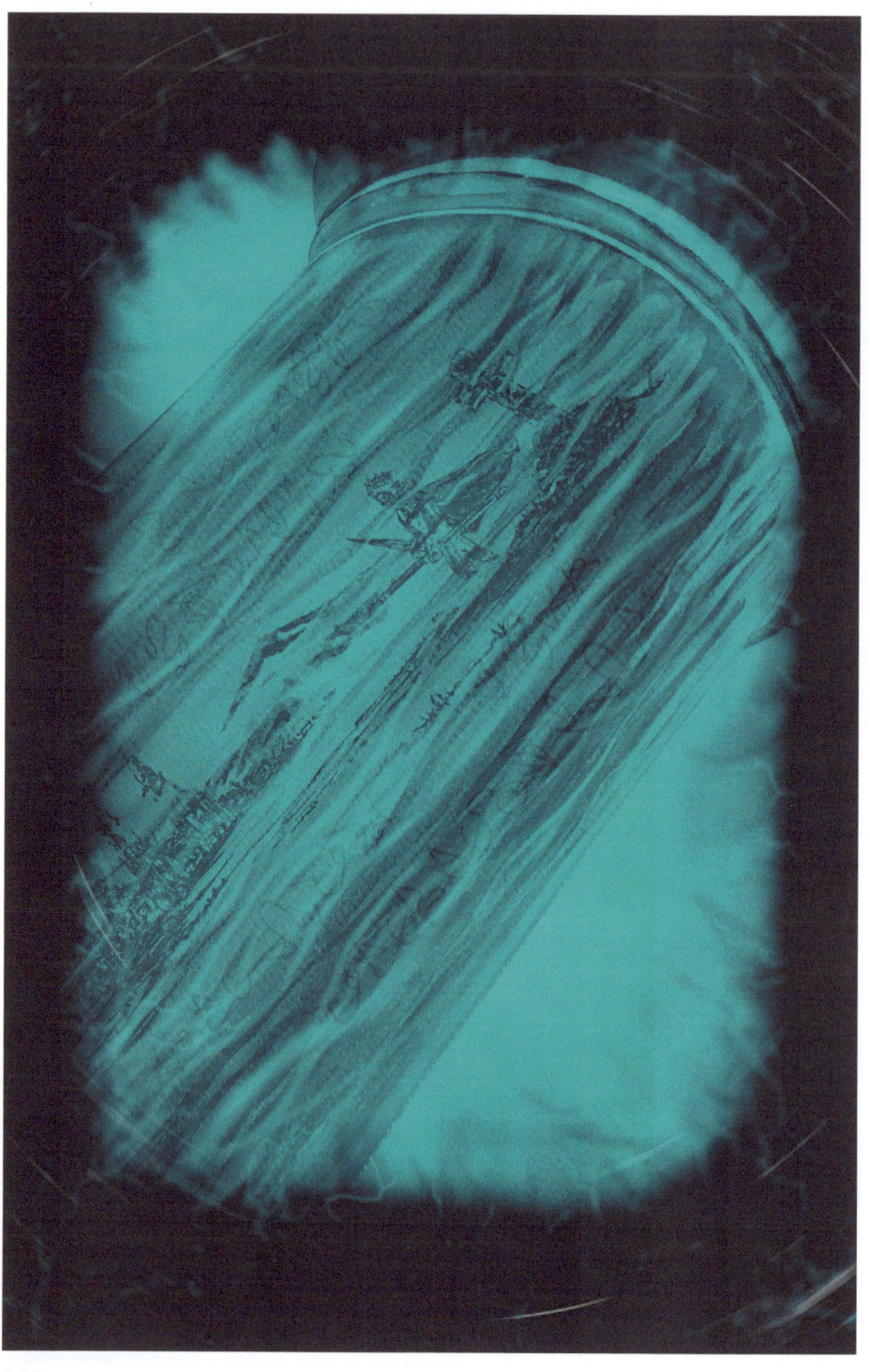

I turned to face the person. The man was dressed in a light robe and sandals. The robe was tightened at the waist with rope. Under his right arm, he held a book that looked ancient. In his left he held a long straight wooden staff that was taller than him.

"My King. Are you all right, Your Majesty?"

Blood was dripping from me somewhere, and straightening up, lifting my hand to my head, I felt the slick slippery touch of blood beneath the Crown that rested upon my head. The cut was deep, and I could feel bone. My arms were gashed in a dozen places, my chest had been pierced by something and I felt the steady flow of my blood mixing with that of my mortal enemy.

I smiled at the figure. "Just a scratch, counsellor, nothing to worry about," I said with a voice that sounded like mine, but somehow wasn't. Behind the counsellor, a massive walled city with gleaming spires, shone in the daylight. On the battlements, I could see figures waving red cloths in the air, and shouts of joy could be heard on the breeze. I thought that I had never seen a city so beautiful. I collapsed then, falling to the earth as my legs gave way. "My friend, make this a proclamation and implement this immediately, we must hunt those fowl creatures down and destroy them. If we do not, one day they will return and wipe out mankind for good. We must..." I reached up and grasped the man with one bloodied hand, pulling him close. "kill every last one of them, they are a scourge that must be wiped out." I let go of the counsellor, leaving a bloodied handprint on his cloak, and fell to the floor. I pulled the staff towards me and as I did, I looked at the staff, seeing the grain shimmer and oscillate before my bloodshot eyes. I heard the counsellor's voice echoing through the ages as I slipped away into the realms of the sandman. "It will be done, my King."

Around my fallen form, I feel power ripple out of the staff and into me.

'Was I dying?' I wondered as my eyes started to close.

"Hey, John, you nodding off there?" a familiar woman's voice, says from my left. The drone of the plane returns as I open my eyes and look around. I am back in the plane, Ayesha sits on my left, Arthurs to my right and Susan across from me, with Billy beside her. My eyes meet Susan's, then go down to the staff and back to Susan. Susan smiles at me. My mind remembers every single detail of what? What could I call it? Another vision; no not a vision, a past life perhaps. Who knows? But I had been there, standing on that battlefield as an ancient warrior King. Had I died on that battlefield or recovered to hunt down the reptilian creatures. Will I ever know, probably not? I hadn't succeeded in wiping them out, but I had turned the tide in the favour of the humans, for centuries and centuries. But for how much longer. I seem to be living in three realms at the moment, my mind seeing visions of the past and future while I live in the present, I've found my identity at last and have found a new purpose. Susan was right, this wasn't over, this wasn't over by a long shot, this was just the beginning, I could feel that now. And I had a part to play in this, in that I was also sure. I look around the plane at my companions and then back to Susan. Is this the new Battleborn, I think, with a wry smile on my face.

7

ASSAULT ON THE INSTITUTE

We travel back to the institute from the airport in silence, our thoughts our own. Jet lag was kicking in and tiredness was showing on our faces, except Billy, who seems to have the energy of a teenager, even though he wasn't.

As we near the gates I see an armed guard, with his machine gun tucked in under his arm, wave us down. He hadn't been there before, so I know immediately something important must have happened. Arthurs wound down the window and the security guard approaches the car, one finger poised by the trigger of his gun.

Susan leans across her seat and speaks to the armed guard who seems a little nervous, his face deathly pale, almost as if he is in a state of shock. He is wearing unmarked black army fatigues that made him look like a Black Op and looks incredibly young to be a security guard. I must be getting old, I think, chuckling to myself.

"What's happened, Michaels?"

"Something breached the perimeter last night, ma'am. No one was injured, and everything's quiet now, but..." he pauses, taking a deep breath, trying to compose himself, "we got one of them, ma'am. It's in the doctor's surgery?"

'Them?' I thought to myself.

"Is it alive?"

"No, ma'am," he said, shaking his head, "It took a lot to take it down though. The others got away. Majors has posted extra guards at all the entry points and is awaiting your orders, ma'am."

'If he says ma'am again, I'm going to get out of the car and shake the kid until he stops saying it,' I think. Susan really was the top dog here for sure, I was impressed. There had been no file on her, so it looks like I'm going to need to do some investigating on my own to find her story.

"Very good, Michaels, keep vigilant and radio in if you see anything unusual. We will get more orders to you shortly."

The gates were already opening as Michaels steps aside, and Arthurs drives us in. We park up, get out and instead of turning towards the entrance, we take a gravel path around the side of the house to the doctor's surgery, a separate building that had once been stables. I hadn't walked this way for over four hundred years, and the last time was carrying the silent form of Elizabeth.

Another guard was stood outside the doctor's surgery, in his Black Op fatigues, and he salutes Arthurs before turning to Susan.

"At ease, soldier," Arthurs says.

Susan nods then walks past the guard and opens the door. The room looks very different now, but the autopsy table that I had placed Elizabeth on still looks the same. I could still picture Elizabeth lying on the table, but now there was a different figure lying there, something not quite human. A man in a white uniform was bending over the thing, his back to us, partially blocking our view.

"Ah, Doctor Johnson," Susan says. This made the man turn and greet us with a warm smile, as if we were all just meeting in the pub for a quiet drink. The doctor looks remarkably young; Christ, do they only employ school kids here! He had a naturally tanned face, which looked like he was born in a country where the sun shines more than the week of summer we get in England. Either that or he fell asleep on a sun bed! His piercing blue eyes and blond wavy hair make him look more like a surfer than a doctor. He is tall and muscle bound, and he carries himself with the bearing of someone supremely confident in his trade. Every action was unhurried and relaxed, despite what lay on the table in front of him.

On the table, lay a figure that was half reptilian, half human in appearance. Parts of the creature, the extremities, looked reptilian in appearance, while other parts still showed what looked like the human clothes that had been the disguise. The transformation was incredibly detailed, its feet and hands which had obviously been human looking, now showed the three taloned fingers and sharp thumb, the same with the feet, with the big toe being replaced by a large, curved claw.

At least seven bullet holes could be seen puncturing its thick scaly hide, parts of which were still covered by a black uniform. Dark blood stains cover most of the torso. Its head had started to turn reptilian, the ears were gone, replaced by small holes, while the nose had started to form into a snout. The snakelike eyes had started to slide to the side of the head, to allow for the snout to protrude. Even in death, they gave me the creeps. There were no eyelids for me to close over, either!

"Good morning, Susan," the doctor replies, his Aussie accent giving away his heritage, and then seeing that we were not looking at him, he continues. "It seems to have tried to transform back into its natural state as it died, hence the half change."

I look at Arthurs and wonder what he was thinking about this. Him being a werewolf and all!

"It's probably natural to revert back to the original form, when you are dying. The system that makes it appear human wouldn't cope with the pain and would switch off."

"You are correct, doctor," Billy agrees.

The doctor peered at Billy for a second and looks as if he was going to say something but thought better of it. He must know Billy is an alien.

"Report, please, doctor!" Arthurs requests, all military like. Johnson was obviously a military doctor or had been, although he looked too young to be a 'had been'.

"It seems that there were three of them, as far as we know. Cameras and sensors picked them up coming into sector five. The lads were there quick but they split-up as they came over the wall, and we lost them for a few minutes."

"Lost them?" Susan says with a hint of anger in her voice. "How?"

"There are some black spots in our camera areas, they seemed to know where

they were." I raise my eyes to Arthurs who was looking at me and thinking the same. 'Someone gave them this information, we have a traitor in our midst.'
"They tried getting into the house through one of the upstairs windows."
"Upstairs windows," Susan asks, astonished.
"They seem to be very good climbers."
"They are," Billy replies nonchalantly. We all turn and look at him.
"An alarm went off and there was a gunfight, and we took this one down, but the other two escaped over the wall and into the woods. A party went after them but found nothing. Everyone is pretty shaken up, especially those that saw this guy."
"Was one of them Michaels?"
"Yes, ma'am."
"Relieve him and get him back to the house, he needs to know, everyone needs to know now," she says, making up her mind over something.
"Susan," Arthurs pleads, "Now, might not be the best time," he adds quietly.
She contemplates a response, then issues an order to Doctor Johnson, "Michaels?"
"Right away, ma'am," he makes to go, then stops and turns back. "There's one other thing…" he says, swallowing hard, for the first time looking uncomfortable.
"You see the burn marks on the skin," he says pointing to some dark marks on the scales that none of us had realised were burn marks. On closer inspection I see how the skin was blackened and shrunk, as if burnt by an extremely high heat.
"Well, when we carried the corpse out of the house to the surgery, we passed through some sunlight. We were in the sunlight for less than a few seconds, and the thing started to burn. We all dropped it in haste and watched as the reptilian parts started to smoulder and burn, while the human parts did not. Realising we might lose our specimen I dragged the creature into the shadows and covered it up before we got it indoors. It's like what you would see if it were a vampire, that is if vampires existed, of course," he adds with a nervous laugh. When we all look at him with no response, he asks, "they exist, don't they?"

Susan ignores his question. "Good work, quick thinking, Doctor Johnson."
"Here," he says, moving back to his tray, "I've two samples. Watch, I'm going outside to show you. In my left hand is a part of the human looking flesh, in my right is the reptilian flesh." He picks up two metal bowls, both containing a strip of flesh. He moves to the door and beckons us to go over to the window to watch. He is in his element now; he'd got his arrogant swagger back and was enjoying being the centre of attention. He steps outside under the overhang, and turns to face the window, with a smile on his face. He holds both trays out at arm's length, and slowly walks backward into the weak sunlight, his eyes never leaving ours. As soon as he got into the direct sunlight the tray in his right hand almost jumps out of his hand as the flesh inside starts to smoulder. Smoke appeared, then a tiny flame and a moment later the whole piece was alight and burning to a crisp. The part in the other tray did not react at all.
"Pretty impressive, Huh," the Doctor shouts. "Even when the things dead, its skin still reacts to sunlight."
He comes back in, the smell of burnt flesh wafteing in behind him making us wrinkle our noses up at the smell.
"It means that while in human form, they can move freely in the daytime, but when they change back, they can only move freely at night," Billy adds to the conversation.
"Thank you, Doctor Johnson, now bring Michaels in, and tell the rest of the men to meet me in the operations room in one hour."
"Yes, ma'am," he says, his face taking on a more serious look, as he salutes and leaves the room.
"Oh, and doctor, that experiment you just did, does that have any relevance? Or were you just showing off."
The doctor looks uncomfortable for a second, then gathers himself. "Very relevant, ma'am, and it was pretty cool right?"
"Michaels?" Susan says again in a slightly louder tone which makes Doctor Johnson speed up his departure.
"Arthurs," I say, getting his attention. "Those three, last night, are you thinking

what I'm thinking?"

"A scouting party?" he says, his eyes narrowing.

"They will be coming back, probably tonight," I say "and in bigger numbers. We need to get all non-military personnel off the estate and prepare as best we can. They are coming for this," I add, holding up the staff. "So, that's what we are going to give them," I say, a plan already forming in my mind. "We fight them on our terms not theirs."

Arthurs raises one side of his mouth in a half smile, his eyes light up with the thought of a fight. He almost enjoys this stuff too much, I think, then remind myself that he is a werewolf.

"We create a kill zone," he replies coldly.

"Precisely."

An hour later and we are in the operations room, which used to be the old dining room area when Elizabeth was in charge. Four specially trained operatives sit in a double line of armchairs facing Susan, Arthurs and another guy, who was Captain Majors. Thank goodness he wasn't a Major! I saw that Michaels was one of the four. All non-military personnel have already left. Four more are guarding the perimeter while two are in front of the surveillance cameras, making ten in total. Not exactly an army but it will have to do. 'Less to lose', I think sombrely. Ayesha asked why we couldn't inform the police or army, or anyone else who could help, but Susan tells her this is a fight we have to take on ourselves. I wonder how many would survive the night. There's a hamlet two miles away, a small village a mile further on, apart from that we are out in the sticks, far from civilisation and, I suppose, an easy target if the force was big enough. They are coming, I can sense it. I know it, as certain as day follows night. Are they watching us now? Probably, but they may not have to with a traitor within our midst. How quickly things can move. Arthurs and I discuss our tactics and instruct the men on what we could be expecting. Within a few hours, a lorry arrives with the supplies we need, and everyone gets to work. I was surprised to find that the institute had a firing range and separate quarters for the security guards. I was also intrigued to find that the men had all done military service, in some form or other, but had been forced to drop out, either for disciplinary reasons or for something undisclosed. It seems that Susan and Arthurs had recruited well. The Royal liaison had been contacted, with no reply forthcoming. We were on our own, fighting our own battle; just how I like it.

We keep up a constant pace, busying ourselves for the probable onslaught. Arthurs keeps the men on their toes and working hard until everything we needed is done. The surveillance cameras covering the grounds were under constant supervision for anything untoward.

The day had been dull, grey and overcast with a mist falling as the temperature dropped in the evening. Good, less visibility, I think. Heavy rain was due through the night. Would this put them off or make them postpone it? I don't think so, it would give them extra cover, or so they would think.

I meet with Susan and Arthurs and discuss my plan and after much wrangling, we eventually came up with something we were all pleased with. I find out that Michaels is the best shot, so I take him to the range and speak to him privately about what I expect from him. He nods, his complexion pale, his face taught. Michaels is from Northampton and is fair of skin, with a smattering of freckles across his young face. A squat boxer's nose sits between his unwavering grey eyes. He wears his crew cut like it was a rite of passage, denoting that he was now a rightful member of this select group of heroes. His nervous tension was infectious. I could feel myself tightening up just by being in his presence, so I teach him some breathing exercises to help calm him down, and myself! His aim was amazing, he never seemed to miss, just like Staunton had been with the bow, I thought with another chill.

I am now standing, looking out from the side of the low Victorian windows towards the wall and entrance gate, barely visible through the drizzle and evening light. The lights are low, and we are staying out of sight. I look around at the group. Arthurs is deep in conversation with Susan, Ayesha is sitting at a grand piano, one finger playing a solitary note. Billy is standing by the doors to the hall, a small backpack strapped to him, with my shield strapped around it. He looks almost top heavy with the backpack and shield strapped to his back, but

Plate: 13

it's necessary if the plan is to work. Doctor Johnson is not in the room, but I know he is by the front doors ready to let Billy and myself out when I make my move. Four of the security guards are spaced out around the house entrances, while Michaels is on the flat turreted part of the roof, a rifle at the ready. Majors is with the rest guarding the old servants' entrance. Apart from the main door, all the others have been boarded and blocked off. If they come in, it will be on our terms.

Double doors from our room lead to a large entrance hall. This has a beautiful wide central staircase, which splits halfway up beneath a large mosaic window, with each staircase leading to the second level. The floor is marble and two lion-headed stone statues adorn the beginning of the grand staircase. Doors lead from the entrance room to other parts of the house. A set of grand looking old oak double doors lead out into the gravelled courtyard, and the front lawn and gardens beyond. The cars have been moved to the large garage beside the house. A stained-glass window at the top of the first flight of stairs lets in a kaleidoscope of colours on a sunny day; but tonight, even the moon, which is hiding behind the clouds, sheds no light through. Ironically, the picture within the glass is one that could adorn any church, it shows an angel, all winged up, kneeling and holding a vase to heaven. I've seen it a thousand times before, but only now do I wonder at the significance of the image.

Minutes pass, but they feel like hours. My mouth is dry, and my hands are clammy. Tension hangs in the air, as I turn to see the sensor lights in the garden come on in a blaze of glory. Ghostlike figures appear out of the gloom, their forms bent over and moving in an inhuman fashion. Ayesha moves to one side of the window to peer out, just as a hail of gunfire rips across the front of the house. Bullets smash through the windows, sending glass flying everywhere and letting in the cold damp breeze. The piano gets shredded, causing it to wail out its last note. The shutters on the windows now show an array of bullet holes but they still stand, for now anyway. We are all crouched low, the thick stone walls giving us good protection. Through the broken window I see dozens and dozens of creatures coming across the lawn towards the house. These creatures are a hundred percent reptile, they have not even tried to become human which makes me wonder if it means they won't be taking any prisoners, and that they are certain that they will win. Yet, despite the fact that they are in their full reptilian state they still hold guns, which actually makes them seem even more scary, more surreal, as if they had been plucked out of some 50s sci-fi B movie. I could almost expect them to stop and peel off their masks, but I know the only mask they ever wear is a human one. The number of creatures appearing takes my breath away, there are so many, more than I guessed. What have I done? Am I leading all these people to their deaths?

Behind them, a dark winged figure swoops down out of the gloom. The shooting stops and everything goes silent as the creatures pause just shy of the gravel parking area.

"Time to welcome our guests," I say rising and heading for the front door, staff in hand.

"Be gentle with them," Arthurs says. I'm warming to the guy. He can't be all bad, he seems good for Susan, I think, as I enter the hall.

"We don't need to inflict any more suffering," a voice shouts, "just give me the staff and we will leave you in peace," the Demon King continues as he approaches the house, his followers parting before him like Moses parting the waves.

He reaches the gravel, crunching to a halt as Doctor Johnson opens the door and lets me out before closing it again, giving the invisible Billy just enough time to join me. The sound of my heavy boots conceals the smaller and lighter steps of Billy. It's raining now, heavy and loud, and I'm drenched in seconds. The Demon King stands there in all his grandeur, his ebony form glistening with the water. His wings are furled and tucked behind his back, the tall fins sticking out above his shoulders. He has aged since I last saw him face to face. Parts of his skin had lost their shine and had become dulled, well, that is what several hundred years does to some people. In places, his once powerful physique now looks less toned and saggy. He still looks an imposing figure, but he was past his best. It seems that age even catches up with demons.

Behind him, I estimate that there are more than a hundred reptilian creatures, all armed and facing me. The odds don't look good.

"Is that all you've got?" I ask, looking at his army, my voice loud and brash, despite my heart beating fast with the adrenaline of fear. It doesn't matter how many times you face death, it never goes away, that tightness of dread that signifies that these could be your last moments alive.

One side of his mouth lifts slightly as he clicks his fingers and more creatures appear out of the gloom, spreading out and forming a circle around the house. "Your sense of humour remains the same, as does your arrogance. You haven't changed have you, in any way, Godiven? I think that's what they call you? You look the same as the day we first met!"

"Pity I can't say the same for you! And, yes, my name is Godiven, it's a good name and it's growing on me," I reply. "I don't have the pleasure of your name, Demon King?"

"Your gibes won't save you this time, Godiven. Your sun is hours away and I don't think you can last that long. My name is Korvak, high priest to the Celestial Enlil."

"Well, that makes it all crystal clear. Why do you want the staff so badly, Korvak? What's the big deal? You seem to have power and wealth, you control these creatures, what else is there?"

"You have no idea, Godiven. The staff is my bargaining tool. The Celestials are awakening, the Earth will be ours once more and that staff," he said pointing towards it, "is going to be my path to gaining the Celestials confidence."

"What, after you tried to overthrow them and failed?" I say with a sneer. By now I am hoping Billy has reached Korvak. I dare not take my eyes from Korvak to check otherwise or he might guess what's going on.

"What," Korvak exclaimed wide-eyed, the red glow shining through the gloom, "what do you know of this? How, can you know of our past?"

"You really think that they are going to forgive you? You and these creatures betrayed your masters, whoever they are? Do you really think giving them this is going to make them forgive, and trust you? I don't think so. You are deluded," I hold the staff aloft and I see his eyes narrow.

"Now," I say into my concealed microphone, expecting the garden area to light up in a different way. "Now," I say again, reaching up and tapping the concealed microphone, as if it wasn't working.

151

Korvak is laughing, a deep bellow of a laugh that makes me want to shove something down his throat to stop him laughing ever again.

"You are waiting for a light show perhaps? I think you will find you need one of your humans to flick the lights. Unfortunately, no one is alive to help you with that request. And you need electricity to help you, yes." He says as the lights go out in the house and all around the grounds. "Your little light trick won't work now, Godiven," a voice says from the darkness.

We had rigged ultraviolet lights along the inside of the main wall, hoping to bath the creatures in them, inflicting the same damage that the sun would do. We had tested it earlier on some of the reptile flesh from the dead creature and it had worked. But then in an instant, everything went pitch black.

"Looks like we are going to do this in the old-fashioned way," I say, drawing my gun and firing in one fluid motion towards where the Demon king had been. I roll to my left, turn and run for the house, hoping Billy is keeping his head down.

As I burst through the front door gunfire erupts behind us from another part of the house. I don't give that another thought, I can't afford to. If Majors doesn't hold out, we will not last for long. The reserve generator that only I, Arthurs and Susan know about, kicks into action, illuminating the front of the house in a dim glow, from the security lights. I race back into the room, to the window and open fire on the oncoming horde. I hear the bang of Michaels' gun from the roof, and I see a creature drop, then get up again. Another shot and the creature is down again and stays down this time. Good lad Michaels, keep it up. I spray the first rush of creatures who go down but are instantly replaced by more. Arthurs fires from the other side of the window, his assault rifle kicking into his shoulder as he holds his finger down spraying the horde as they reach the window and attempt to burst through. He's screaming as he's firing. The gun clicks, it's out of ammo, and Arthurs throws the weapon at the nearest creature, knocking it to the floor. Before it gets up, Arthurs has transformed his hand into his wolf talons and rips the creature's head off. He is still screaming, but now it's turned into a deeper roar as he transforms. The reptilians near him back off, which is the worst thing they could do. He leaps forward, slashing with both hands, creating carnage. Susan and Ayesha are also firing handguns while backtracking towards the hallway as planned. The noise is deafening, the losses great, but still they come on in a relentless wave that could overwhelm us in seconds. I bludgeon one creature away with my armlet, taking four more out as it bowls them over. It would almost have been funny if this wasn't life or death. Arthurs is among them, and I see his blood rage is full on. . His eyes have turned orange, his face, a rictal grin of concentrated bloodlust as he plows into them. They don't stand a chance as I see his taloned hands swiping back and forth, spraying blood everywhere. Even as they fall around him like wheat under a scythe, more of the creatures are pouring through the window and creeping around our flanks.

"Everyone back," I shout.

The creatures are crawling over their own dead to get to us. I notice that in their rage most have thrown down their guns, their primal urge to wrench and tear with their great taloned hands and razor-sharp teeth overcoming the thought of firing a gun. I see a bloodlust in the creatures' eyes, a berserker rage; a rage that has been in all our DNA since the dawn of time, but one that most species have learnt to control. They want to shred us to pieces until we are nothing more than chopped meat.

We backtrack and fire as we go, pushing through the doors to enter the large hallway, leaving scores of dead or dying creatures behind us. We race up the stairs and turn to stand framed by the stained-glass window. The front door bursts open, nearly knocked off its hinges by the Demon King's brutal strength. Loads of the reptilian creatures burst though and stop, massing together at the bottom of the stairs, awaiting the Demon King's orders.

"Where are you going to run to, now?" Korvak asks sarcastically.

"Nowhere," I say smugly, "we are exactly where we want to be. Doctor Johnson, the lights please."

The doctor is hidden at the bottom of the stairs, in the shadows. He presses a button on a hastily erected console, and the whole hallway is bathed in an ultraviolet glow, coming from concealed lamps all around the entrance area. The lights outside had been a ruse. We'd guessed that either someone would be giving them information or watching us from the woods, so we set up a second killing zone that only a few of us knew about. And the result was instantaneous and gruesomely effective. The creatures begin to screech and burn, dying on the spot as the fire spreads from one to the other, consuming all within the room in barely a couple of minutes, leaving a solitary figure standing before us. *My mind reels with the picture, my guts tighten, and I lose my focus as my thoughts race back towards the end of the Second World War. I was with a group of American soldiers that helped liberate one of the death camps. What we came across and witnessed within that camp, was evil on a scale you could hardly imagine, something you couldn't imagine humans doing. Grown men, battle hardened soldiers, had knelt down and wept at the sight. I had entered one of the huts to find a pile of dead naked humans. With only the light from the opened door, I saw what humans can do to fellow humans. I'd seen brutality before in many forms over many centuries, but this was something else entirely, something truly evil. The smell was appalling, the silence even worse. I noticed the scratch marks on the walls next, where frantic hands had clawed for a way out, but finding none. I stepped further into the hut as if drawn to the unbelievable horror, hoping that my eyes were not seeing what I thought they were seeing. The bodies were skeletal: male, female and even young children holding onto each other in their last moments. My knees buckled at the sight, I fell forward and instinctively reached out for balance, and in so doing I touched one of the corpses. The poor man's last few minutes entered my thoughts, his screams a dying echo from a dark time in humanity's history. I remember thinking how could depravity like that can be unleashed on our own species.*

Seeing these creatures burning like this had taken me back to a horrific moment in my life, as if it was yesterday. They writhed and tried to shake off the flames that consumed them. Unearthly screams came from the hundreds of mouths, but it was like they merged, and our senses were assaulted by a single howl. The noise was so loud the window behind suddenly exploded and glass rained down about us.

As I'd expected, Korvak was impervious to the ultraviolet lights. But he was still stunned. He'd just lost most of his troops in one foul swoop.

"I believe you have me at a disadvantage," he says calmly, as if he were playing a game of cards and he had a bad hand.

"Worse than that," I say. "Billy?" The alien materialises next to Korvak, my staff in his hands, pointing at him.

"I was pretty sure the ultraviolet wouldn't affect you, but I'm damn sure that staff will. I remember seeing you wearing thick gloves in the catacombs and thought it odd at the time." I say, throwing my fake staff to the floor.

"He's like a 21st century Sherlock Holmes," Ayesha says to Susan, with a little awe.

"He has been around for a long time," Susan replies.

My eyes go wide, "Ladies, I'm right here," I say with a smile, "trying to save your asses," I add.

A twitch of fear crosses Korvak's face when he sees the staff, his eyes narrow in anger, and he looks around for an exit. Distant gunfire continues.

"That's the sound of your forces being destroyed. So, where are you going to run to now, Korvak?"

Korvak smiles at me, which took me a little by surprise. He turns to look at Billy, who gradually lowers the staff.

"Billy, what are you doing?" Ayesha screams.

Billy takes his eyes from Korvak and turns to the group, and gradually starts to transform before our eyes. His body expands and lifts, his frame and torso growing at the same time as his arms and legs extend. In seconds, he is as tall as Korvak. The appearance of his clothes change, although I notice the backpack and shield, which I'd put on with elasticated straps, remained in place. Calf length golden boots appear on his long muscular legs. His body is partly naked, tanned and toned like a body builder. A thin linen tunic covers his shoulders, and a pair of dark linen shorts cover his valuables, if aliens have them! Golden armlets cover his forearms, stretching from his wrists to his elbows. They make my one look second class in comparison! As his face starts to change, so he reaches his full height, towering above Korvak, who has sunk to his knees in adulation and was murmuring something in fear. The Demon King was bowing in abeyance before this ancient deity from a lost time, as if he were now a mere reptilian slave.

The face and head start to shimmer, and change last, becoming part human part reptilian, a hundred percent alien. The nose disappears as the skull becomes more oblong, pulling the cheek bones in and creating a snout that shows rows of sharp teeth with two holes where the nose should be. The ears almost disappear into the side of the head forming tiny slits. The green slanted eyes with yellow pupils move more to the side of the head and get bigger and seem to blaze with an inner light. The head is hairless, the skin upon the face green and scaly. Billy talks and his forked tongue appears from his large snout. I shudder, I can't believe I spent time with this guy! His voice is different, deeper, menacing and with that slight hiss you'd expect from a guy with a forked tongue! But he's not talking to us, he's facing a cringing Korvak, who is visibly shaking in fear. I can't believe it!

"You think that by returning this, we would forgive you your rebellious actions." his voice is deep and authoritative now, so different from the high-pitched voice of Billy. "Time is meaningless to us. What you did, you did as if it were yesterday and forgiveness is not in our nature," Billy says lifting the staff in both hands and swinging it in an arc that strikes Korvak's upheld arms. The second it strikes, Korvak starts to burn. He screams, "Master, please," one time and then his voice is gone, his body consumed by a blue fire that engulfs him and continues to burn while his body withers, shrivels and turns to ashes.

"Insolent pup!" Billy says with disdain as he pulls the staff out of the fading light. Korvak is gone, turned to dust before our eyes by…?

"Billy?" Ayesha says quietly, finishing my thought.

"I don't think he's Billy anymore, Ayesha." I say staring at a live version of the creature we had seen entombed under the Sphinx. The resemblance was so close, it could have been an identical twin, but this was far worse because this guy is alive and kicking. And I'm pretty sure, he's not called Billy. Lucky I've got a back-up plan!

I notice Arthurs standing in front of Susan, protecting her. Ayesha has a handgun pointed at Billy. 'Don't shoot, Ayesha,' I think, looking her in the eyes, 'Stick to the plan.' She seems to understand with a gentle nod, so I turn back to the new pretender.

"There was no kid, was there, Billy? You just took a young boy's body for your own, with no concern for his welfare?"
"The boy was a nobody, what does it matter to you."
'He was a somebody to someone,' I reply. "In fact, he was a young boy called Chris Latham from Missouri. Parents, Sam and Angie Latham. Chris was reported missing over six decades ago."
My sentence is greeted with a snarl of rage. "So what, what difference does the disappearance of a mere boy make, I am one of the gods, returned to my full majesty, I care little for your human existence, they are fleeting and insignificant. When we are all joined in union, the human race will become our new slaves."
"So, you've been playing us from day one, good on ya, Billy," I say with a smirk.
"My name is not Billy, I am Enlil." he said raising the staff, high above his head. "God of wind, air, earth and storms." The writing on the staff lights up with a blue tint, and tiny lightning bolts race up and down the length as if highly charged.
'He's definitely not Billy anymore,' I hear Ayesha say.
"Oh, just shut the fuck up, will you, you overgrown pompous ass." I shout at him, while my thoughts concentrate on one specific thing. His eyes go wide, his back constricts, and his stomach pushes out away from the pain.
"What have you done?" Enlil screams, his voice quivering slightly with a hint of fear.
"You know that shield I put on your back for protection, yes," The question is rhetorical, so I continued on, "and I padded it out with the rucksack? Yes? You remember, don't you? Well, inside that rucksack is my sword which you ever so kindly showed me how to retract. Thank you for that, by the way. Now the base of the handle is wedged firmly against the shield, while the open slit is facing into your back, and pointing at your heart. You do have a heart, I assume? I mean, even Alien Gods have hearts, right?" I say. "I've just released the point far enough for you to feel it at the moment. It wouldn't take much for me to think more and get it to pierce your heart. And I'm also guessing that sword can even slay a god? Am I right? Arthurs says 'No'. Ayesha and Susan weren't sure. So, I'm

Plate: 14

really keen to find out, because I've just about had it up to here with false Gods and Prophets."

Enlil is pontificating now, his rage barely concealed within his huge frame. He's visibly shaking with anger. The staff crackles again and he begins to raise and point it menacingly towards us.

"How dare you try and trick a God. Don't you realise, we created you. And if we can create you, so we can destroy you," he replies angrily as if talking to a child.

"Hey Billy, we didn't try and trick you, we did, so not bad for a human, eh?"

"Why you..." he says, lifting the staff to point at us.

"This is for Chris," I say solemnly and put a thought in my head.

A sword point suddenly appears out of Enlil's chest, blue blood showing on the blade. The staff drops from his opened hand. Enlil's eyes go wide, and his gaping jaw opens in a silent scream. His legs buckle and he falls forward onto his knees as he starts to choke on his own blood. He tries to speak, but just gurgles once, frothing more blood. For a moment, he stays upright, his eyes fixed on mine, hatred emanating from them, and then like a felled tree, he topples forward onto his chest and lies still.

For a moment, we all stand in silence, realising that we had all survived this night. It was a miracle. I hear Susan calling to Majors on a walkie-talkie and she puts a thumbs up to me that they are all good. Incredible, we hadn't lost a single person!

"You've just killed a God!" Ayesha says to me. "Wow, you're my favourite," she adds sarcastically and laughs nervously.

"He was no god," I say, looking at the still body, "just another power-crazy despot, no different from any of the others I've come across, even if he did come from another world. It seems whatever worlds there are out there, the same rules apply. It makes me sick to think of it, but Enlil was definitely no god."

"Whatever, you're still my favourite." Ayesha replies and winks at me!

8

SAINT JOHN

I awake to the sound of men working, look at my watch to see it was 6am and realised that the work to restore the building had already started which was quick off the mark. When I reached the scene of last night's confrontation, I was amazed to see that all the stained-glass fragments had been cleared, the window boarded up and the doors were now off their hinges being repaired. Susan was standing in the doorway with two workmen looking at some drawings. She looked up at me, smiled and waved. Again, I got that 'so like Elizabeth look', that it shook me for a second before I responded.
"You don't hang around, do you?" I ask.
"Early bird catches the worm," she replies with another smile. Somehow, it seemed like a burden had been lifted from her shoulders, her confidence was back, the threat gone, for now, and she had been the one orchestrating this group to a victory over foes that were not only more numerous but could well be more powerful. Adrenaline was still flowing through her veins; she probably hadn't even slept. I've often noticed in the past that it's after a battle has passed that the survivors tend to look on things differently as time goes by. Good on her, I thought. Arthurs walked past the open door with Majors, and a group of his mercenaries, looking all macho and as if any future existence depended on them.
I wander down, grab some breakfast and a coffee then head up towards Elizabeth's study. The door is open, it always was. I found that a nice touch, it was

as if to say, my door is always open for anyone that wants to come in, we have nothing to hide here. Elizabeth truly was one of a kind and it seems that Susan is following in her footsteps. I amble over to the bookcase and run my fingers along the books, before turning to the desk. The shutters are open, casting two lines of sunlight across the wooden floor.

Elizabeth's diary is on the desk, its leather cover facing upwards, the small insignia of the institute embossed onto the cover. The picture is of a crow holding a stick between its clawed feet, a simple logo, of which sadly I am unaware of its origins. Why a crow? And holding a stick? What significance does this have or is it just a random choice? No, Elizabeth was fastidious about everything. To her, everything was done for a reason. I pick it up and take it into the sunlight, peering more closely, trying to fathom out some sort of meaning. The crow's eyes are blue, which I hadn't noticed, and the stick in its clawed hands was no ordinary stick, it had a faint resemblance to the staff! A thin glint of a different colour between the clawed feet signified that it could be the metal between the two ends of the staff. But how could she have known what it looked like if she hadn't had it in her possession? Or had she seen it before?

I move to the desk and sit down knowing I am going to find something out, even before I open the diary. I flick though the pages to the last entry, reading her words before that horrible fateful day.

I flick back to the previous entry, my heart beating a little faster now.

I close the book with a purpose and look up into the eyes of Ayesha, who is standing in the doorway.

"Hi," she says.

"Fancy a trip to the country?"

"We are in the country," she says, raising one eyebrow.

"A different part of the country," I reply, getting up and heading towards the door.

"On an adventure into the unknown with a fabled intrepid explorer, yes sure. Does it involve death-defying chases, and life-or-death situations?"

"I think we've had more than enough of those for now!" I answer.

"Then what?"

"We are going to find a church in a village called Cannock Green, and find out a bit more about the origins of the staff and my past life, all in one fell swoop."

"Well, if you put it like that, I'm in," she replies with a smile, "sounds like an adventure to me?"

"Do you always have to have the last word?"

"Yep."

"You sure."

"Yep."

"Not this time," I say shaking my head.

"I'm pretty sure, I'll have the last word. See you in a mo," she jokingly adds and skips off up the hallway.

"I'm saying something now," I say out loud as she disappears around a corner. Her head pops back around the corner, "I know, last word!" and she is gone.

I smile to myself at the pleasant interaction. It's good to have company, I never realised how much I'd missed it.

I head to my room and pick up the staff then head downstairs to the operation room, and mention to Susan what my plans are.

"Good idea, the more we know about that staff and your links to it, the better. Any visions last night?" I nod my head, and she continues, "I'm too busy here, Arthurs is also busy reinforcing security and getting things online, so it's just you and Ayesha on this one. You sure you can handle this between you?" she says with a wry smile.

"He'll be fine," Ayesha says, walking into the room, "I'll look after the big guy," she says with a wink to me. She's all dressed for action now. Before I had seen a shy girl, perhaps a little thin and weak, I now see a new Ayesha, a lean mean fighting machine; someone ready for anything life can throw at her. She is wearing tight leather biker's trousers, a white T-Shirt beneath a khaki cotton jacket, and was also carrying a black leather jacket in the crock of one arm. I could see the bulge of a handgun tucked in under her jacket. She was taking no chances.

"You look like you're going biking," I say.

"I am, and so are you. You can ride a motorbike, can't you? I mean, you have been around for ages. Surely, you know how to ride a motorbike?"

"You have a motorbike here?" I say to Susan, as a wide grin forms across my face. Susan nods, "It's Frank's, but I'm sure he won't mind as long as you bring it back in one piece, and without a scratch."
I turn back to Ayesha, "Lady, I was born to ride," I say, and we both laugh out loud.

An hour later we are on the road, my legs wrapped around a Ducati Streetfighter, with Ayesha holding on tight behind me. I can feel her heart beating as I speed up and take the bends without braking, but not once does she ask me to slow down. The day is dry and bright, and the roads are quiet, it is a weekday after all. The feeling of speed and freedom feed my soul like a battery recharging, it feels so good to be so alive again. It took us three and a half hours to reach the start of Cannock forest, and my mood changes a little as I recall the last time I was here. The spot where the incident happened is now a dual carriageway, with a service station tucked into the wood on the northbound side. It seemed surreal to look at it now. I slowed, pulling off the carriageway and coasted down a side road until we found a place to stop, with the woods on both sides of us. I pull off my helmet and shake my hair, feeling my senses coming back to life after the constant drone of the bike.
"You OK?" asks Ayesha.
"Yes, thank you, just exorcising a few demons," I reply.
"Go right ahead, big guy." she answers, removing her helmet. "It's lovely here. So peaceful."
Despite the constant hum of the passing cars on the highway, the place was beautiful. Apart from the road running through the woods, it looks untouched as if it had not changed since the dawn of time. I close my eyes, hearing the birds, the grinding of one tree on another as the wind rustles the tops of the firs. I feel nothing unnatural here, no ghosts, nothing. That was a good sign. The staff sat upon my back in a fishing rod case, and I was tempted to take it out and

KNIGHT ETERNAL

Plate: 15

see if anything happened, but I didn't. 'What's done is done,' Elizabeth used to tell me, 'you can't undo the past, just try and make a better future through the knowledge of what you learn from your experiences.' How true, and that is why we are on this mission, to find knowledge of the past to help us with our future.
"Time to go," I say, putting my helmet back on.
I sense Ayesha put her helmet on and feel her slim arms wrap around my waist, and I start up the engine with a roar.

We reach the village of Cannock Green by noon, parking the bike and dismounting in the village square, outside a busy thatched pub full of people enjoying a lunch time snack in the sun. As soon as we had entered the village and pulled up in the square, I got this strong sense of Deja vu. I looked at the square, the old cottages dotted around, the church partly hidden by an ancient oak that took centre stage and I wondered what events this gnarled old beauty had witnessed over the years. The smell of food and beer drifted on the wind, and my taste buds tingled at the thought.
"Fancy a beer?" I ask Ayesha.
"I don't drink beer."
"Of course not," I reply with a hint of an apology. "Your body is a temple, and all that," I add.
"No, I just don't like beer, a glass of wine will go down nicely though. And don't forget you're driving. You might be eternal and indestructible, but you can still get pulled over by the police."
"Yes, ma'am," I say and salute, "Just one then."
The day was warm, so we sat down outside on a circular park bench, our food ordered and pints in hand. I faced the tree and somehow, my eyes drifted to its intertwined branches and aged trunk as it if were someone I recognised but couldn't remember the person's name. I pull myself away when I sense Ayesha following my stare with a frown. I had something to ask her that had been playing on my mind, so I thought now was as good a time as any.

"So," I say turning my gaze to her. "What's your real back story? I know, I Know, I've read your file from the institute, but it doesn't say much. In fact, out of all of us, it hardly says a thing. There must me more to you? You have a gift, similar to mine but different, so how come?"

Ayesha looks at me, weighing up what to say, her thoughts shaping her pensive expression. "There was an accident," she starts then pauses, her eyes dropping to her wine glass. "I lost my parents when I was eight, the car skidded off a road and hit a frozen lake. There was a blizzard and visibility was poor. Mum was asking Dad to drive slower or turn back, but he wouldn't listen. They were arguing when he lost control to miss a stag that was in the middle of the road. Amazingly, I remember the car skidding across the ice before plummeting under. I recall my mum's frantic screams, Dad freeing himself from the seatbelt and reaching behind to free me. He ignored Mum and looked into my eyes for the briefest of seconds and spoke, even as the car started to fill with the freezing cold water. "Make your life count, make a difference," was all he said, before winding the window down. Water gushed in taking my breath away. I was crying and screaming and reaching for Mum but somehow, he pushed me through the window and out. I took one last breath and kicked for the surface, the tug of my clothes and the cold attacking my senses so that I could hardly tell what was up and what was down. A faint light beckoned me up and I headed for that, my lungs bursting. I reached the surface only to feel a layer of ice blocking my way. I remember bubbles of valuable air leave me as I opened my mouth to scream, the fear of being trapped to drown beneath the ice, too much for my young mind to handle. I felt the brackish waters enter my mouth, filling every part of me in seconds. I remember trying not to swallow, but it was useless. Through wide suffering eyes, I look up through the frosted ice to see a figure standing on the ice. In the delirium of what I thought was my last dying seconds, I see the figure, a man, reach down and strike the ice with his hand. The ice shatters as if it were millimetre's thick rather than inches. I see something shining on his arm as he reaches down and pulls me out with one strong hand. I remember the feeling of being carried and then put down and then I blacked out..." she pauses, lifting her head to look into my eyes. "They said that when they found me,

I had been dead for at least ten minutes before they resuscitated me. They said the cold stopped my heart and that was what saved me. The emergency services couldn't understand how I had climbed free and reached the shore, but when I told them a man had pulled me out, they said that there was no sign of him. They said that it was unlikely there was any man there. They thought that it was my own mind making things up due to lack of oxygen! I know what I saw!" she paused again. "Was that you?"

The question startled me so much, I nearly dropped my pint. A swish of beer fell from the glass to land on the wooden table. "No, no, of course not! I...I.."

"That's good, I didn't think it was, just checking!" she said with a smile.

"So, did they get your folks out?"

"No, the lake was very deep. They sent divers down to retrieve them the next day, but they couldn't even find the car!"

"That's a bit odd, don't you think?"

"I didn't question it; I was eight at the time remember and I'd just lost my folks!"

"Yes, sorry, must have been tough for you?"

"That's when Susan turned up and brought me here."

"What? Why did she turn up out of the blue? How did she know you had special powers? Where you aware you had this gift before then?"

"No, not as far as I know, but I can't honestly remember."

"Maybe she had somehow sensed you or been tipped off about your powers. Otherwise, it's a bit of a coincidence Susan turning up though, isn't it?"

"Yes, I've thought of that over the years but never got around to asking her?"

"Well, now seems to be a good as time as ever to find out. We will speak to her when we get back."

She nods quietly, "Are our powers somehow linked? I mean, you touch a corpse and see its last few moments. I touch someone alive who is possibly going to die, and that scenario is played out in the persons mind, enabling him to change the outcome. Surely, they are linked in some way?"

"Good point, kiddo," I say, shaking my head in agreement and raising my eyebrows. "Something else we need to look into, if we ever get time! Now, I think it's time to do some investigating."

"Like Sherlock Holmes, no, like Starsky and Hutch. No, they are both male, like..."

"Mulder and Sculley, perhaps?" I say.

"Perfect," she says with a thumbs up. "On our own X-File, yay."

"God give me strength," I reply with a smile, which makes her chuckle.

After a snack and one beer, we head towards the church, my gaze lingering on the old, gnarled oak as we walk by. It has a green painted iron fence around it, and on the fence is a plaque with an inscription.

The Cannock Oak
"This tree is the oldest known tree in the country, dating back to the Middle Ages. Cannock is derived from two Anglo Saxon words meaning Powerful Oak."

The old church is tiny, its grey steeple bent, one end of the nave has started to sink into the ground which seems to happen a lot with old churches. In front of the church is a small graveyard, and everything is surrounded by a low dry-stone wall. An old rusty iron gate lies open, a pathway of slabs leading between the gravestones towards the church. The grass is closely cut, the graves neatly kept and tidy with not a weed in sight.

"Built by the monks in 1142," Ayesha says.

"How the hell did you know that?"

"Google," she says holding up her phone, then looking at it again. "Apparently, two monks bought the surrounding land, built an abbey and church for the locals then disappeared, leaving the land for the king to reclaim. Legend says the church was once the centre for a powerful healer who blessed the local spring, producing the finest and clearest water in the land. It is said that the water had special healing properties, and that anyone that drank a cupful was blessed with long life."

"I must have drunk quite a few pints then," I say, making Ayesha chuckle.

"It was also foretold that if the spring ran dry it was a bad omen, and something disastrous would happen. It also says that before the time of the Great Plague, the spring ran red foretelling an end of days."

"OK, OK, enough, let's go talk to the vicar. You don't have his name on there, by any chance?"

She looks at the phone then back to me and shrugs, "No, sorry."

The vestibule is made up of two arched doors and in the left-hand door is an open panel to enter the church.

Pews line both sides of the narrowest church I have ever seen, a jumbo jet's cabin was probably wider. Barely three or four people could sit on either side of the aisle, which led to the front of the church, the altar and the presbytery. A pulpit stood to our right. The walls were all stone with small arched stained-glass windows running along both sides at regular intervals, the sunlight casting a kaleidoscope of colours across the pews. A large font that seemed almost out of proportion to the rest of the church stood at the back. A small organ rested against the left-hand wall. There was a tiny door behind, that must lead to the vicar's sanctum.

"Were people smaller in the old days?" Ayesha whispers to me, reading my thoughts. Why does everyone whisper when they enter a church, I thought?

A lady appeared from the shadows in the back, her dog collar confirming that she was the vicar. "Can I help you?" She was in her mid-forties, short cropped light hair, her face a mass of freckles. She stood about five foot tall and was probably of average weight. Her voice was welcoming and smooth with a hint of authority to match, and her smile was warm and sincere.

"Hi," Ayesha says.

'Uh, hello, my name's John, this is Ayesha, we are here looking for something, and wonder if you wouldn't mind us looking around."

Her manner showed a slight trace of concern before her smile returned.

"I'm Samantha Cuthberts, Vicar of Cannock Chase, if you haven't already guessed."

"Nice to meet you, Samantha."

"What are you looking for, if you don't mind me asking?"

"No, not at all, we came here trying to unravel an ancient mystery and I think this church is the key," I say, thinking on the go, without wanting to lie to a woman of the cloth!

"Um, sounds interesting. Come on then, what are you looking for?" Samantha says and beckons us down toward the front.

"Well," I say, trying to think of something, "we are looking for an old inscription which pertains to a legend about this area, and relates to this."

I take the staff out of the case on my back, nearly taking out a votive candelabra in the process.

"John!" I hear Ayesha admonish me with a tight-lipped whisper, as the candelabra sways to and fro.

I see Samantha take an involuntary step back almost as if she had lost some of her confidence, then I see her compose herself and step forward again. Perhaps she thought I had some sort of weapon.

"We mean you no harm," I say as convincingly as I can. "We are just looking for an inscription, a picture, a message; something unusual, that can help us unravel a mystery. Do you know of anything here that fits the bill?"

I think Samantha was trying to hide her shock, but her face was not quite as relaxed as when we'd arrived. Poor girl, she probably thinks we are about to rob her church or something. Then I look at her again, more closely this time, and sense something isn't quite right here, her body language is all wrong; is she shocked and afraid, or is this just some kind of act? My armlet isn't tingling so there's nothing supernatural nearby. Perhaps the beer was off or something. Maybe after yesterday my mind could still be on edge; seeing things that aren't there. I shake my head, chastising myself for being paranoid.

"I don't know, I'm afraid, I'm relatively new here, sorry." The sorry came out with a slight slur, and I realised she had a lisp. "You are welcome to have a look around," she adds.

"Thank you," I reply, my gaze never leaving hers for one second.

Ayesha moves to the left of the nave, me to the right, to look for an inscription, a picture, anything that could give a clue to my early life. As we move forward, Samantha steps back, away from me, into the shadows and keeps her distance.

"I'll just keep out the way," she says, "call me if you need me," she shuffles back further towards the presbytery, and that's when I see the eyes glinting in the semi-darkness; so, I wasn't being paranoid after all.

I lower my staff as casually as I can, then pounce forward and place one end inches from the vicar's face. Out of the shadows, I see her snakelike eyes look at me with a thousand years of hate.

"If you have killed the real vicar, I'll do the same to you," I snarl, moving the staff closer. I feel it thrum to life at the close proximity of the reptilian shape shifter. Its head stretches back until it strikes the cold stone wall behind, giving me a clear view of the presbytery. I could see the body of the real Samantha, crumpled up on the floor, unmoving, her blank face a mask of fear after coming face-to-face with this creature.

"She's unconscious out cold, that's all, she fainted."

I see Ayesha pull her gun, eyes peeled on the presbytery doorway, searching for any slight movement. She wanders over, senses on high alert and slowly pushes the door open a little wider, gun trained forward. Scanning the room, she sees the silent form, bends down and checks for a pulse, before nodding to me.

"You're too late human, the gods are rising, the Earth will be ours again."

"You know, the last guy that told me that, it didn't turn out too good for him, he was one of your so called gods. Well, he ain't now."

The reptile's face changes to one of utter disbelief. "That cannot be," it hisses, reverting back to its natural voice.

"Ayesha," I say, without taking my eyes off the creature.

"Died pretty easily for a god," Ayesha says over her shoulder.

"Thank you," I reply to her, "You see, these gods of yours aren't true gods like our God, they are just powerful beings who thrive on fear and control. You were their slaves once; do you really want to be their slaves again?"

The creature looks at me, its face one of confusion.

"If I let you go, will you leave this place and never come back?" I ask.

"John, what are you doing?"

"Yes," it hisses, cringing and backing away from the staff.

"Then go," I say lowering the staff to my side.

"John!" Ayesha says to me, questioning my actions.

KNIGHT ETERNAL

Plate: 16

"I can pick you out in a crowd, if you are nearby or follow us, I will hunt you down and show no mercy next time, do you understand?"

"Yes," it hisses again.

"Then begone and never return," I yell, pointing towards the entrance. The creature shambles forward and disappears out of the door. Ayesha follows and watches it go out the gate, and up the road, before returning to stare at me wide-eyed. Before she can speak, I raise my forefinger for the chance to explain.

"That creature now knows one of its gods is dead, signifying that it is not actually a god. Every creature last night was destroyed, so there were no witnesses to their so-called god dying. It's going to go back to some hole in the ground and start telling its kind what it's witnessed and heard. That's going to have a massive effect on them, don't you think?"

Ayesha mulled it over, then holstered her gun. "And you thought all that up on the hop?"

"Yep," I say smugly.

"Then you're cleverer than you look," she replies giving me a lovely smile.

"Gee, thanks for the vote of confidence. How's the real vicar?"

"Out cold, she's in no danger."

"Time to explore then."

We both return to the altar, where something we see stops us dead in our tracks. Beneath the tabernacle we see a plaque with some Latin words carved into the stone. Beneath the words is etched a very faint line of figures depicting a scene from a distant time.

I translate it out aloud, "The well of enlightenment needs the key of Solomon to open its riches."

"I'm impressed," Ayesha quips.

"What, again?"

"Looks can be deceiving," Ayesha says with another of her butter wouldn't melt in my mouth smiles.

"Do you have any filter inside that brain of yours, I do have feelings you know."

She pulls out her iPhone and turns the torch on, panning the small light upon the plaque. In the middle of the picture, a figure sits under a tree. He is surrounded by people, on one side looking infirm, on the opposite side the same figures now transformed and looking healthy. This was depicted quite naively in the carving, but the meaning was obvious. A well was there and you could see a cup in the hand of the central figure, while in the other was a staff with a shining centre piece, carved as if there was a light coming off it. Seeing the picture, my thoughts drifts back to a different time in the past and a map of the world etched into a cavern wall in Africa. It had been there that I had found the famous fountain of youth and learned of its curse. Could this be one of its outlets, I ponder? It would make sense. A more diluted amount might give the effects depicted!

"Earth to John," Ayesha says, breaking my reverie, pointing the torch light at one particular bit. "That's your staff," Ayesha says in wonderment, "and that looks like you, too?" she says pointing to the figure in the centre.

I peer more closely seeing the long red wavy hair, the set of the face, and I feel myself tremble.

"That looks like me, but I can't remember anything about this place, it's somehow been wiped from my memory."

"Perhaps you have Alzheimer's?"

"Filter, and not funny," I say chastising her.

"Sorry, it was just a joke, you are like a zillion years old!"

As she moves, the light of her phone falls upon a small dark hole, dead centre between the writing and the picture. I look at my staff, trying to measure its diameter. Wasn't this staff called the 'Staff of Solomon' in ancient times? My vision mentioned it, as did Enlil. I stand and turn the staff in my hands before putting the tip of one end towards the hole in the stone.

Ayesha moves back, her eyes wide. I gently push the staff into the hole, and it fits perfectly. I keep pushing until it can go no further, it goes about a foot into the stone, but nothing happens. I look at Ayesha.

"Nice trick, now what?" she asks.

"Any ideas?"

"This is like an Indiana Jones movie," she says again with one of those smiles.

"That's not helping."

"Try turning it."
I gradually lean against the staff testing if it would break, the thought of returning with a broken staff was too much to think about. The staff felt solid, so I lean into it a bit more, turning it clockwise. Nothing budged.
"Try the other way," Ayesha says.
This time I don't reply, I just stare at her, step to the other side of the tabernacle and turn my staff anti-clockwise. Immediately something gives and I hear a grinding of stone. I almost lose my footing as the entire wall with the tabernacle, slides open to reveal a spiral staircase that disappears into the darkness.
"Well, that's something you don't see e...."
"Don't say it," I say to her, raising a finger.
I pull the staff out and look at Ayesha.
"Now, I feel like Indiana Jones! Come on, get that torch on, we're going underground."
"Isn't that a song?"
I raise my eyebrows in disbelief and point downwards.
"After you," Ayesha says.
"You've got the torch?"
"There might be spiders down there? I hate spiders!"
"Hold the light in front me then, I'll go first."

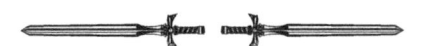

The stairs led downwards for around twenty steps before we enter a tiny room. Ayesha pans around the room with her light to show a line of tiny alcoves with small items placed in each. Her torch moves to the left and stops on an open well full of water. On the rim of the well is a small plain looking chalice as depicted in the picture under the tabernacle. She pans back to the alcoves and we both move closer to look at them.
"No spiders," I say, "it's been sealed for centuries."
"You do realise that if this is on a timed mechanism, we could be locked in here for all eternity."

"Good point, why don't you head back up and make sure it doesn't?" I say to Ayesha.

"Nah, I was just making an observation, we'll be fine."

"These must be gifts given to the healer for his help. He kept them here," I say looking at all the tiny offerings.

"You! You kept them here," Ayesha points out.

"We don't have proof of that yet," but even as I speak, the words feel false. Something had started niggling in my brain, a distant long forgotten memory. We turn to the well and Ayesha points her torch downwards.

"My god, it's so clear," she exclaims.

"Crystal clear," I add looking at the water. It was so clean and clear that you could almost not see it. Only the magnified reflection at the bottom showed any sign that water was in the well. Ayesha picks up the chalice and scoops up a cup full. Ripples spreads across the water.

"I'm not sure if this is a good idea," I tell her, as she puts the cup to her lips and drinks deep, downing it in one go. "Are you sure you don't drink beer?" I ask her sarcastically.

"That is delicious, so refreshing," she says, passing me the chalice.

I put the staff down across the edge of the well and take the cup from her and repeat the process. I hold the chalice in front of me before lifting it to my lips. I can feel the coolness of the water through the thin metal of the chalice. I open my mouth and drink deep, feeling the liquid coursing through my body, rejuvenating my senses. *Images flash through my mind, visions of me speaking a sacred oath and blessing people with the staff. I see crowds massing, waiting to be seen, and peddlers selling their wares. I take another swallow see a face coming through the crowd with a trio of crusaders in full battle armour. I sense myself being lifted to my feet and a face is pushed close to mine.* "Time to do what your meant to do, John, the King has summoned you to Acre, and we have been assigned to get you there, so get your belongings, we're leaving now." one knight says.

I come too with a start. I look at the cup, the well and then Ayesha.

"John, you OK?"

"That was me in that picture, I was there. I had some ideas from extracts I had read in Elizabeth's diary, but to go back in time and witness it, leaves me in no doubt as to what I was and who I am.

"You really are old?" she says and we both laugh, bringing me back to some sort of normality.

"I think it's time to leave." I say, pushing her ahead of me. She goes to reach for the chalice.

"No, leave it here, it's where it should be," I say, looking around the tiny room, one last time.

"OK, big guy, it's your call."

We head up the stairs and I place the staff back in the hole and the tabernacle wall slides back into its normal position. Then I remove the staff and place it back in my fishing rod bag.

Ayesha leaves me to check on the vicar, and I run back to tell her that she is coming round.

"Time for a quick getaway," she says racing towards the church doors with me close behind.

She's ahead of me when she opens the church door and stops suddenly and raises her hands.

"Oh dear!"

I step through into the daylight to join her.

"Police, stop right there, don't move." An armed response team have surrounded the entrance, guns trained on us. I slowly raise my hands and Ayesha's hand brushes mine. I tell her, "nothing happened, and I have had no vision."

She slowly turns to me and smiles again.

"At least no one is going to die this time," she says.

"They have got guns trained on you as well, you know. I'm the one that's not going to die. Are you sure about yourself?" I give her my best ever smile, knowing she can't say a thing to wipe away my grin.

"You are under arrest, anything you say…"

"Yeah, yeah," I say, "just get on with it."

"We had reports of a break-in."

That double crossing reptile had gone to the police, very clever, hadn't thought of that.

At just that moment, the vicar tumbles out holding her head, before looking at us, the armed police and fainting again, falling to the grass like a bag of spuds. 'Amateurs!' I think.

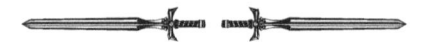

It was evening by the time Susan had got us out of jail and returned us to the institute. Arthurs who had been driving the car, had almost pushed me over the edge with his constant mickey-taking and laughing. But we deserved it, so I let it go, even I could see the funny side. His pride and joy Ducati was being released from the police pound and would be delivered back to the institute. It wasn't until Ayesha told them the whole story of the encounter with the reptilian that the seriousness of the situation became apparent. The car went silent until Susan turned to me.

"You made a brave choice there, the correct one, despite its trip to the police station." Arthurs snorts again in derision, from the driver's seat. "The story will spread like wildfire amongst its kin. And that's a good thing. It's going to create doubt now, something they have never had before. Now tell me what else you uncovered on your sojourn please, I'm keen to know."

9

VILLAGE OF THE DAMNED

We are sitting around a long antique dining table that I had used centuries before, when I had been with Elizabeth and the original Battleborn. It still felt strange, the sense of Deja vu, but I knew it was just my mind playing tricks with me. Ayesha had told our story at the church in great detail, and I had mentioned my flashbacks confirming that it really was me there, back in the twelfth century. The meal had finished, and we were all sat back in our chairs, letting our meals go down, waiting for the coffees to arrive when Arthurs turned and looked me in the eye.

"There's been something, I've been wanting to ask since Canterbury?" I nod for him to proceed. "What are your thoughts on where these ghosts go? If, as you say, you are helping them out of limbo towards heaven or hell, then surely that must mean there must be a divine spirit that rules over this place and us. You said, you had no faith when we first met, but that goes against everything you've told us now."

"Everyone loses faith sometimes. The things I've seen, the things I've done, the evil I've witnessed. But there is something out there, definitely, whether it is the god that we envisage it to be, I'm not sure, but there is power in its word, of that I am a hundred per cent sure of." I look at the frown on Arthurs face and realise that he is struggling to come to terms with what I've told him. I forget how much of a shock the truth can be to some, especially when it's against what they believe, and chastise myself for being so insensitive. The years do tend to desensitise you somewhat! "You lose faith eventually. Then something happens to make you think otherwise, it's a conflict that's happened many, many times. It might be a small thing, something trivial or something big, a person, an event; but it's just enough to make you realise that there is something out there."

"So, you do have faith in God?" Arthurs said.

"I told you, I believe in something, I'm just not sure what exactly, but I've seen things you people wouldn't believe. There is some divine power in the Word of God, I've seen the truth of that. The power of sacred ground. Here's a story that's not in Elizabeth's diary that will get you thinking about your faith in a divine being. If you don't believe in something, then perhaps this tale might change your mind." Everyone, turned to look at me, as if I was the court jester ready to entertain when the banquet was over. It took me back a second to a different time, and to an evil jester who manipulated the whole keep to his ill-gotten gains. That adventure had not ended well for him. I blink, my thoughts returning to the story I need to tell, to remind these people that we need faith in something if we are to be successful.

"Elizabeth had sent me on a solo mission to find Kane Manor located on the rugged north coast of Cornwall overlooking the Celtic Sea, as it was called then. She had asked me to meet the Lord of the Manor, a certain gent who was synonymous with adventure, and invite him to join us at the institute. I never got there in the end, perhaps things would have turned out differently if I had. The day was cold, windy and damp; the type of weather you only get in north Cornwall. I'd stayed the night in a small fishing village, finding accommodation at a local inn near the headland of Steeple Brink. I'd heard that the Cornish coastline was a honeypot of smugglers and because of that it was monitored by the crowns officials, for smuggling was a way of life for many living along the coast. Many of these so called officials were paid to look the other way or faced a knife in the back. The south coast as it was closer to France and with a path up the channel towards many of the large ports of the south, was the busiest of the coast lines, its shallow coves and beaches rife with the art. The rough rugged north Cornish coastline, interspersed with long sandy beaches was less ideal for a smuggler but it was still a thriving business with many a local land owner as thick as thieves with the smuggling fraternity.

I had risen early with the squawks, cries and squeals of the gulls waking me as if calling me forth to an encounter that was going to affect my faith in more ways than one. The locals had looked at me suspiciously as I walked into the inn the night before, their dirty weather-beaten faces peering from above their drinks as if I were from another world, after all I was well dressed and clean. When I had entered the inn and asked for lodgings for the night, the place had gone as silent as a Wild West saloon when a stranger walks in, and when they did talk most of them used a language I didn't understand. I ignored these things; this wasn't the first time it had happened, nor would it be the last. Now, with directions towards the manor and an inquisitive raised eyebrow from the landlord, I left the inn behind me and headed west along the cliff tops towards my destination. The manor was still way off, and I knew I had another day's journey before I got there. Clouds sped by overhead casting long fast-moving shadows across the landscape. Towering cliffs greeted my gaze, the sound of the sea below a constant reminder that it was a force not to be trifled with. Gulls swirled on thermals, squawking away at each other as if fighting for the rule of the skies. From the edge of a cliff, I looked down to see a small beach and beside it a few houses, that I assumed must be a small fishing village. I turned to look inland and saw a few more houses with a church and in the distance a manor house, this must be Shilston Manor if the landlord's directions were correct. An offshore wind was whipping sand off the beach, making the sea a little hazy. Out in the bay I glimpsed a ragged line of rocks jutting out of the sea, and within the rocks I glimpsed the wreck of a ship, it's single mast still protruding out of the sea, pointing towards the heavens at an oblique angle. Waves crashed against the rocks, and as I squinted and peered towards the wreck, I could have sworn I saw some movement out there. I'd heard the stories of wreckers, and I shuddered at the thought of the crew that had met their fate in the depths. The smell of the sea was in the air and the taste of salt was strong. I clambered down the cliff and walked along the beach towards the village, the feeling of sand beneath my feet and the beauty of this rugged unspoilt coastline giving me a spring to my step. The air was still cold though, the wind sending an icy chill through my bones. As I approached the village, I could see a young man sitting on the beach, he was barely two yards from the sea with his head lowered as if he was in prayer; it was almost like King Canute trying to stop the tide. I looked around me thinking that this might be a trap, but there was no cover for any brigand and the village was only a short walk away. Looking towards the village I couldn't see any sign of activity or movement, not even on the quay. I headed towards the man and as he heard me approach, he turned his head and spoke. The lad was barely out of his teens, his long black hair was wet, his clothes soaked. He wore a pair of dark breeches, a white shirt and waistcoat. His feet were bare, his shoes obviously lost to the sea. A piece of seaweed, a thin green line of it, sat on his shoulder. The lad's eyes were as dark and mysterious as the sea, his skin, white and deathly pale. The first signs of stubble were forming onto a face that would never feel the growth of a beard. There was a dark welt on his forehead.

"She's gone," he said with a strong educated voice.

He was holding something in his hands, a thin silver chain with a locket that was open. "This is all I have," he said painfully, "at least, they didn't take everything."

"They?" I ask.

"The wreckers, the villagers." he said, nodding his head towards the distant line of cottages. I looked towards the village, feeling a sense of foreboding. My armlet tingled once and went silent. A sea mist was sweeping in now and the village seemed to shimmer in and out of my vision, like a mirage in the desert. Although the village looked deserted, I could hear the sound of singing drifting on the wind, a faint whisper then silence as the wind swirled around us. Was it Sunday? Was the sound coming from the church?

"What happened here?" I ask him.

"Up at the manor we knew about what they did! Father turned a blind eye on their activities even when the soldiers came, it was to his advantage of course. He said it wasn't our village but another further down the coast. He actually protected them."

I stared at him, wondering how I could help. He sat with his legs crossed in front of him, his hands clasped together around his knees. He was shaking as if

VILLAGE OF THE DAMNED

Plate: 17

he were cold, but he was beyond that now, it was like he was in a trance.

"And then they did this to us! How ironic, eh? Father didn't take it well."

I look around me once more, then sit down beside the lad.

"What's your name, son?" I ask, my gaze drifting out to sea.

"Jon Matthews," he replies turning his head to peer at me with a look as if I had suddenly just appeared. "Are you an Angel or something? The Lord God Almighty come to judge me? Saint Peter, perhaps? Then I am truly doomed."

"I'm not here to judge anyone." I answer, "but I am here to help you find your way, if that's what you want? Can you tell me what happened? From the beginning, please, Jon."

"We set sail on an evening tide, my new bride and I, plus ten other passengers who had booked their place on a voyage to the new world. For me, it was a chance to start afresh, away from the constricting influence of my father. My mother had died in childbirth, and I think it was this that defined our relationship. He seemed to resent me living while his wife, and true love, had died giving birth to me. The older he got, the more bitter and twisted he became, his only solace, the greed of wealth. I never realised he did it for me, until it was too late. He worked his staff to the bone, treated the villagers like slaves and took most of the profit from the smuggling and wrecking for himself, leaving barely enough for the people to survive," he pauses, peering at the locket.

"I met Beth in the village. Everyone said it wouldn't last, a fisherman's daughter and the lord of the Manor's son would surely not survive, but true love found a way. Father was furious, of course. So, I booked our passage to the new world on a ship that had pulled into the harbour for repairs and supplies. Little did I know the ship was irreparably damaged. We left the port with my father's curses drifting across the quayside, his rage so rife that everyone shied away from him leaving him a solitary figure that dwindled to nothing the further we got from the quay. We left on the evening tide, and it wasn't long before a storm rose up out of nowhere. Giant waves crashed across the deck, thunder roared overhead, and we were tossed from one side of our cabin to the other as the boat rocked and tried to right itself against the raging storm. I heard one mast creak and shatter with an awful splintering of wood. I heard the cries of the sailors as the mast crashed across the foredeck, crushing some and casting others into the cold depths. I heard the captain shouting orders to turn for home. I remember water swishing across the room, my beautiful Beth deathly pale with fear. I felt the boat gradually turn and head for the safety of the harbour. Night was upon us as I left my beloved below decks and headed up to help. Rain was falling in torrents and lightening crackled against the dark sky. A lookout shouted, 'Land ahoy', pointing towards the dark bulk of the land in the distance. A light flickered, followed by another, and we steered towards this knowing that the calmer waters of the harbour were not far away. Visibility was poor, all we could see were the two lights at the entrance to the harbour. It was only when the boat shuddered and screamed, with the splintering of wood, that we realised that we had been lied too. Everyone was thrown forward, me included. My head struck something solid, then darkness. When my consciousness returned, all I could see was an empty deck, everyone must have abandoned ship, after we were smashed against the rocks. As my senses returned, I heard the screams of my beloved, then I realized I had been left for dead and Beth must have been forgotten. The water was now all around me on the deck and the ship was broken in two at the centre, a ragged dark tear that gushed water and the odd barrel of supplies. Rats ran about my feet looking for an escape, their tiny squeals of fear heightening my own sense of dread. I could hear the splintering wood above the noise of the storm, as the ship was being ripped to driftwood. I heard Beth's scream again, her frantic cries for help, I must save her. I saw that the main mast had slid down the deck blocking the doorway to the cabins, much of that part of the ship was completely submerged. I raced to the door and screamed to Beth that I was going to get her out. I tried with all my might to shift the mast, but I couldn't budge it an inch, so I tried to find another way to reach Beth. As I was searching, I noticed more lights coming from the harbour, part of me wanted to believe it was a rescue party, in all probability it was the villagers coming out to do what they do best, entice ships onto the rocks with misplaced signal lights, to drown all and reap the rewards from the salvage. How ironic, eh. Eventually I found a large porthole that I knew lead to our cabin, it was just under the water, so I held my breath, smashed the glass and swam through. Through the porthole I emerged into a room half full of water, furniture and our belongings, floating and swirling around as the ship started to tilt. Amazingly, by the door a candle was still burning and beside it I could see the huddled figure of my beloved Beth. I reached her and held her tight, even as the boat creaked awfully and started to slide into the depths. She looked pleadingly at me as if she knew what was about to happen. She placed the locket in my hand, and I tucked it into my pocket. Without a word, I dragged her into the water and pushed her through the porthole. I followed closely behind. I was a strong swimmer and knew Beth could swim as well. I grasped her hand and kicked. I felt the tug of the sea as the ship sank into the depths. A dark shadow swept towards us as we swam towards the surface. Out of the gloom, one of the masts' that had fallen, which was still attached to the ship by its ropes and sails, swept down, entangling us and pulling us further into the depths. Frantically, I pulled free and tried to help Beth, but just as I freed her, something else struck her. I felt Beth's hand snatched from mine and watched as she was pulled into the depths. I screamed and swallowed a mouthful of sea water, diving again to try and get to her but Beth was gone. I kicked upwards, broke the surface and screamed again, spluttering water and crying to God for deliverance. I managed to grab hold of some driftwood in the churning sea, treading water, my mind numbed by the fact the I had lost my one true love. I had no idea how long I stayed there, seconds or minutes, who knows. The sea was throwing me this way and that, but I'd got to the stage I didn't really care whether I lived or died. I looked landward and saw figures with lanterns on the rocks. I saw long poles in their hands, some reaching out and dragging barrels and bundles towards them. My instinct to survive kicked in. Fighting the sea, I swam towards the nearest light. As I neared, I raised my hand and cried for help. I saw a figure, twist the pole in his hand and felt a thud against my head. I went under, swallowing more water, and came up again closer to the rocks. I started to shout for help again, when I bumped into a silent form floating beside me. It was Beth, she had survived! My heart leapt until, I saw the open but lifeless eyes and the thick swollen welt on her head. A thwack in the water beside my shoulder brought me to my senses. The man had missed this time. Before he could remove the wooden pole, I grasped it, hoping to pull him in, but my hand slipped off. I remembered that as a kid I had been shown around the village I had noticed some poles with a hook at one end and a wax covered flat wedge at the other, and I wondered what they were for. Now I knew, the hook was for collecting salvage and the flat end was for clubbing survivors, and the wax was to stop anyone grabbing the pole to pull the wrecker in. I looked up at the dark silhouette of the figure as he raised his pole one last time…"

"Damn!" I say when, he didn't continue, "that is one sad tale."

"It doesn't end there," he replies, "it gets worse!"

"Worse! How much worse can it get?" I ask, my eyes wide. I'd liked Cornwall until now.

"I know what I am," Jon said, "but I seem trapped here for all eternity, as if my sins have sent me to one of the nine circles of hell, to remain here forever."

"You are not in hell," I reply quietly, "you are in a place of limbo and something is holding you here, something that won't let you move on until you see closure."

"Revenge, you mean."

"No, not revenge, a reckoning, an understanding of events so that you can be at peace and move on. I need to head into the village and ask a few questions."

"You won't find any answers in there," Jon says, looking towards the deserted quayside.

"They are all dead, aren't they?"

"Almost. One man is still alive?"

"Your father?"

"No, not my father, a different father."

"The local priest, you mean."

"Yes, Father Joseph."

"Then, he's the man I need to speak to."

"I'm coming with you," Jon says, turning to look back towards the sea. "She was a fisherman's daughter, but she hated the sea. She always said it would be her doom."

'Sounds like a cheerful, girl,' I was about to reply, but thought better of it.

We headed towards the village, a sense of dread drifting across my senses. I

Plate: 20

wish I'd listened more to Elizabeth about how to deal with things like this, but for now I'd just have to take it one step at a time. I'd crossed Europe, helping trapped ghosts find their way to wherever they should be going so I was no novice to this, but this event was certainly a bit different.

I stepped up onto the quay and looked about me. Fishing boats, rocked on their moorings, swaying to and fro on the calmer waters. A line of small cottages encircled the tiny quay, with rows and rows of similar cottages dotted about the hillside. A single cobbled road leading between two cottages led uphill towards the church and then to the manor. Not a soul moved. Even the gulls had deserted this place. The singing came again as if on cue, and I looked at Jon who shivered again.

"Guess that's a calling card." I said and headed for the road. Fishing baskets lay empty and tumbled along the quayside with not a single fish in sight. My boots made a loud noise on the cobbles, and I felt conscious that I was announcing our entrance well in advance. Somehow, I thought that this didn't matter, whatever had happened had already happened, I was here to tidy up the pieces.

We made our way up the steep road until we came to a fork. In the middle of the fork, lay a small stone church, its double doors shut, its single bent spire pointing towards the heavens. My armlet pulsed once, signifying a supernatural presence nearby. I'd already had an idea of what I might find but the armlet confirmed it. I could hear singing coming from the church, many voices joined in a hymn I didn't recognise. The words spoke of the power of the sea, and the life or death hold it has over all who dare venture upon it. I'd heard enough.

"Right," I said, plucking up courage and walking up the steps to twist the iron ring and open the door. The singing stopped instantly with a gentle sigh. The door creaked open, casting dim sunlight into an empty church. Not a single pew was occupied. No one rose to their feet to stare at my intrusion, the church was empty, bar one solitary figure who sat on the altar beneath a large cross.

"Damn," I said again, at the mystery. I stared upward into the rafters and saw a multitude of ghosts swirling around, their blackened faces and burnt clothes a sign of what had happened. "Now stay up there, until I find out what in God's name is going on," I say to them.

"You shouldn't speak God's name in anger," a Scottish voice spoke from the front of the church.
"Father Joseph?" I enquire, ignoring the telling off!
"That is me, and you are?"
"Godiven, John Godiven."
"Welcome to my humble abode, John Godiven."
The door slams shut behind me, and at the same time all the candle on the walls lit up. I smell something then, the rotten smell of death and decay.
"Nice trick," I say, walking up the aisle towards the altar. The air turned cold, and I could see my breath in front of me, I felt myself shiver as the temperature dropped.
Father Joseph rises and turns to face me. The man looked middle aged, wearing a full brown hooded robe, tied at the middle by a double circle of rope. The man was incredibly thin, almost skeletal, his big round face almost out of proportion to the rest of his body. A large dark beard covered most of his chubby face, where a pair of deep set black eyes poked out from above his rosy cheeks and button nose. He held a staff in his hand and was using this to hold himself upright. His dog collar looked dirty beneath his unruly beard. He looked pretty good for a ghost. He spots Jon beside me, and I see him take a step back.
"Jon," he stammers.
"Father," Jon replies from one ghost to another.
"Nice congregation," I say, looking upwards. "Mind telling me how they came to be all burnt up like that?"
Father Joseph smiles, an evil smile that makes his eyes narrow to pinpricks.
"With pleasure," he says licking his lips and clasping his hands. "It was only when the villagers pulled the silent forms out of the sea to salvage anything they can from the bodies, that they realised their mistake. I knew already, of course. Ironically it was Sol Hardy who pulled his own daughter from the sea. He was crying uncontrollably at the loss, it was a nice sound, it certainly helped my mood." I heard a sob from beside me.
"When they pulled master Jon out next, the whole wrecking crew went silent. I was there, watching from the beach. I ordered the men to take the two bodies

to the church, where we would give them a proper burial. We sent for Lord Shilston, and it wasn't long before he and his men arrived. By now, the whole village, man, woman and child had entered the church. When Lord Shilston arrived, he burst through the doors and marched up to the altar where the two silent forms lay. For a few moments, he stood there looking from one to the other. His grief was almost palpable, it was delicious, like a fine flagon of wine, I could hardly console myself."

My own rage was starting to boil over and I took a couple of long deep breaths and gathered myself for what was to come.

"My God," Jon says, "what are you? We've known you all our lives, Joseph, you were even present at my birth."

"Ah, another delectable moment, your birth and the death of your mother all in one glorious day. I fed off that for months. In fact, your fathers sorrow kept me going for some time. Every time I visited him and spoke about things, I fed off that grief, he truly loved your mother, as much as he loved you," he snorts with a shrug of arrogance towards Jon's open-mouthed stare.

"But we welcomed you into our homes, made you a part of the village elders. You were friends to us all, you were our priest." He added in disbelief.

"I know, it was so easy. Joining a scheming landowner, a bunch of washed-up fishermen and their families who had turned to wrecking, I fitted right in here. I'd found my place in the world at last, happily feeding off the grief the sea handed out and the everyday hardships of the villagers, my soul was truly full."

"You are one sick bastard," I shout.

"Well now, laddie, profanity inside a church, that really won't do. Shall I finish my tale of woe, it does so lighten my mood."

I nod, biding my time and planning.

"Lord Shilston turned to the congregation, then marched down the aisle and out the doors, without saying a word. He ordered the doors shut and they clanged together with a crash, as if shutting the gates to hell. He ordered his men to fasten the doors, including the back door. He'd gone quite mad by now and I was feeding so much off the energy of his hatred, I never realised his plan until it was too late. He ordered his men to set light to the wooden roof with fire arrows. By now I was in a state of euphoria as the frantic screams, and fear of the trapped villagers, overloaded my senses. Most died quickly from the fumes, the rest were crushed to death as the roof and retaining walls collapsed, killing every last one of them."

"And you?"

"Yes and me, a sad oversight laddie, but I'm still doing good. You know Lord Shilston poisoned all his men, then hung himself at the manor. Quite sad really," he says without a semblance of compassion. "I bet if you went up there, you might..."

"You are a trickster, aren't you?" and then I correct myself, "or were? It's you that's holding all these souls here, isn't it? And you are doing this on purpose, so you can feed off their sorrow for all eternity, reliving their horror to sustain your twisted soul. That's what beings like you do, isn't it? Well, not on my watch they don't!" I didn't know ghosts could do that, but it seems that you learn something new every day. "I know where beings like you end up and I'm going to be more than happy to help you on your way."

"Gallant words, Godiven, but pointless."

"Really," I say, moving past the priest. I see behind the altar a pile of corpses, all burnt and heaped together as if consoling themselves in their final moments. These were God fearing people who lived off the land and sea, but had been turned by the lure of riches, to wrecking. Where they would end up, heaven or hell, it wasn't for me to decide, but they needed to be set free. The smell is strong here, the scent of death suffocating and nauseous. I reach down amongst the corpses and pull out one with a dog collar still fastened around its neck. The corpse is incredibly light, the face in death still grimacing as if in its final glory.

"One sick, bastard," I say under my breath, heaving the corpse free.

"What are you doing," his voice has an edge to it now, a hint of fear. "You can't do this," he says with even more panic, "They are mine, mine to command."

"You've had more than enough fun to last a lifetime. I'm going to send you to hell and free these souls to journey on to whatever fate God has planned for them. Now get out of my way," I say walking through the priest's ghost. The icy shiver of someone walking on your grave passes through me and then I'm free and marching for the doors. I hear his screams but drown them out and focus on getting out of the church as fast as I can. The ghosts travel down, swirling round me, whispering and chattering, but I ignore them and open the doors wide before stepping out into the daylight. As I step out of the church, I'm startled to see that the sun has broken through the mist, casting the village in an eerie light. As soon as my feet touch the road and I'm off holy ground, the illusion vanishes. I hear ghostly screams that tell me not all the ghosts are happy about where they are going.

"Damn," I say, looking at the ruined church with its roof and steeple gone, the walls caved in. Beyond the church, there is no sight of the mansion, that too must have fallen into ruin. Weeds had forced their way up through the cobbles. Some of the cottages had collapsed and fallen into disrepair. I wandered down the street, seeing the place for what it really was, a ghost village that had been filled with the damned. The corpse under my arm was now just a ragged pile of bones, kept together by some rotten moth-eaten clothes and a dog collar. Even the smell had gone.

"Beth," I heard a voice cry out in joy from beside me, making me start a little. A ghostly apparition is floating up the road towards us. I look at Jon whose face is one of wonderment and joy. But even as I watch, he is starting to fade, to continue on his journey. He looks at his hand, seeing it fading. "No," he says and moves towards his beloved, sensing that his time was short. I see the girl coming up the street, her form also fading, almost as if the sun is wiping them from existence, but I know it's something far greater than that. "Jon," Beth cries out and reaches for him just as their forms start to change. Their hands entwine and lock together as one, and, as one their forms blend into a single form of light that drifts upwards towards the heavens and disappears. I stand there for a moment looking towards the sky. All this suffering because of one man who had manipulated this whole village, and under the guise of a priest no less. Why did God not put a stop to this. The fact that removing Joseph's body from holy ground had released everyone else to meet their fate, confirmed to me that there is something out there, some high-level deity that is pulling our strings.

I strode down to the quayside and walked out to the edge of the jetty facing the

VILLAGE OF THE DAMNED

Plate: 18

sea. The fishing boats that had been in the quay were now half submerged, the wooden frames rotten and broken. Not a single boat floated upright, it was a real graveyard of a port lost in time.

I lifted Joseph's corpse in the air and without a moment's hesitation, flung it out to sea. A wave caught it as it hit the water, tossing it skyward. I wasn't sure if I imagined it, but I swore I saw many pairs of skeletal hands reach up and grab the form, pulling it down into the depths. I thought I heard a gull's cry or was it Joseph's final scream, I wasn't sure. Waves crashed against the harbour wall in an endless tirade while the sun beat down, its rays warming my bones and charging my soul, all in one. I headed out of the village following the path Jon and I had been on but noticing that there was only one set of footprints. I peered out to sea. The rocks still jutted out of the water, causing waves to crash into them, but no wreck was visible anymore.

I'd had my fill of ghosts and needed a beer and some human contact, so I headed back to the inn I'd stayed the night at. When I looked for the village, I stood in astonishment at the sight.

" Damn," I say under my breath. The village was in ruin, its buildings lost to the ravages of nature. I'd slept in a ghost inn! How did I not realise they were ghosts, too? The illusion had been watertight, and I must have been tired for that to slip past me! I wandered down the overgrown road to the inn and looked up at the sign that was hanging half off, swaying to and fro. The door was ajar, hanging by one hinge, the shuttered windows closed. "Damn," I say again. The name on the sign read in old English, 'The Travelling Monk Inn', and I shivered at the sight of a figure etched in the wood beneath the writing. It seems Joseph's twisted power had stretched further than I thought."

I paused, looking towards the group.

"So, you see not all endings have to be hard fought and brutal, sometimes all you need to do is know what to do. In this case, it wasn't all hacking and slaying. So, yes, I do believe there is a God out there, or up there, but I'm not sure what to expect from him next. I know I said otherwise, but I didn't know you then. There is power in the holy word and sacred ground, which proves something. I've been involved in too many incidents over the centuries to affirm that there is a deity with a higher purpose, and one day, I look forward to meeting him, but not yet," I say with a half-smile. "Now, that tale has made me thirsty, I need a beer. You do have beers here, don't you?"

10

ROYALTY

The following weeks passed in a blur of activity and by the end of the summer, the house had been fully restored, and things, for once, were going well. I had settled into my new life, and had got to know the new 'Battleborn' on a personal and operational level, they were a good team and getting better with every mission. I was even getting to like Arthurs. The threat of the Lizard men and their false gods continued to loom over us on every outing, their presence felt by all, as if they were hiding in the shadows, waiting to make their next move at any time. Susan's comments about the nuclear arms being destroyed hung heavy on my mind, as if it was another piece of the puzzle that needed to be fixed before it was too late. It was too similar to what happened to the werewolf clans in the past for it to be a coincidence.

Elizabeth's diary seemed to hold the key to some of this, I was sure. Many hours I spent going over the adventures we went on and the creatures she documented. Her observations on myself were of much interest as well as was her continual search for the staff which had eluded her to the end. The staff, she seemed to think, had immense power. Even then, she was mentioning of a great threat to the land and how the staff could be used to stop this threat.

Susan's background still remained somewhat of a mystery, although I knew she was related to Elizabeth, which had come as a bit of a shock, when informed by the doctor one drunken night, but understandable on reflection. She was so similar in so many ways, it was almost like I was looking at her double. I had

ROYALTY

Plate: 19

some concerns about her powers and having been on some missions together recently, I had questions that needed to be answered.

I had got up early this morning, my mind restless, a sense that something was about to happen in my thoughts. It was late September and there was a thin dew on the lawn, when I crept out the back door, and headed down the path towards the cemetery. White dew covered cobwebs danced on a cool breeze, making it look like the grass was almost alive. I was only thinking about the similarities between Elizabeth and Susan when I heard the patter of footsteps coming down the path. Looks like someone else got up early.

"We've been summoned," Susan says with an authoritative air.

"Summoned?" I reply, my eyebrows raising.

"By our benefactor."

"Ooh, a royal appointment," I say with a hint of excitement in my voice.

"This isn't over, John, not by a long shot, we can all feel it," she says, chastising my light-hearted response.

"I meant no disrespect," I reply quickly. "And while we are alone, I need to ask you something."

"Oh," she replied, taking an involuntary step back.

I'd been standing in the house cemetery, peering down at Elizabeth's gravestone, contemplating past events and friends, I'd been doing that a lot recently, when Susan had approached and asked if she could join me.

"I've seen no records about you, you never passed me any when I saw the ones for everyone else. I saw you in the catacombs and again under the Sphinx and all you did was summon a light spell, a spell anyone could learn to do. You didn't see any ghosts in the church… you don't have any powers, do you? They are dormant in you, aren't they?"

She looks away from me and towards Elizabeth's grave, her lips tight, her head lowered.

"Yes," she says quietly.

"Elizabeth spoke to me about this, she said it happens once in every few generations. It means that your offspring will be very powerful, they get the powers you never had, plus whatever powers they are born with." My mind drifts across

the vision I had and I see her huddled form holding a child in her arms, Arthurs sat beside her. If that is her child from Arthurs, it would be immensely powerful.
"I don't have any offspring," she replies, her voice shaking. She looks fragile now, as if the events of a few months back had knocked the stuffing out of her. I certainly hadn't noticed, but, today, she looked different, her whole demeanour carried an air of resignation. She had a traitor in her team and that must have hurt, must have hit her hard. I've felt that same gut wrenching feeling a couple of times and it knocks your ability to trust anyone for a while. Her confidence looked shot; she needed a boost. Immediately after an event, the adrenaline is still flowing, but with time, comes contemplation, and she had had too much over these last few months. Surviving a near death experience does has an effect on you, I know that all too well. I curse myself for not noticing this sooner, I had been preoccupied and had missed the tell tale signs.
"To run an eclectic team like this you need strength and a clear quick mind to be a leader, to take what's thrown at you and come out the other side intact. We didn't lose a single man, you know. Even I thought we were going to cop it, at one stage!" I say, raising one eyebrow.
"You don't need superpowers; you need to be one step ahead of the game to be a good leader. And you have those special qualities in abundance. I see how everyone looks up to you, I see the confidence and trust, they have in you. You don't need any special powers to get my vote or anyone else's."
Susan looks up at me, her green eyes glistening, a thin smile on her face.
"I suppose we'd better not keep Royalty waiting," she says, with a glint in her eyes, more like the Susan I know.
"Yes, boss," I reply, as she places her hand on my shoulder and we turn and walk away from the graveyard. I still feel the tingle that she was a witch and somehow that feels reassuring, despite her lack of powers.

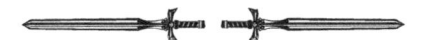

An hour later, we are on our way to London in two cars. When we enter the outskirts, we drive into a warehouse and change into two black Range Rovers with tinted windows, which I would also guess are bulletproof.

I seconded Michaels into the team, and he is driving one of the cars, while Arthurs drives the other. The doctor is with us, obviously to give his medical opinion on things, and Michaels, just in case we get into any scuffles. Two palace guards take over as drivers, conversing with Susan before giving us all the once over. They approach the rest of us and speak quoting a short sentence in a strange language that sounds like ancient Sumerian. They stand for a moment, their body language showing that they are tensed for action, and then they relax and turn back to Susan. The cars look brand new, and I wonder why so many people drive an off-road vehicle in suburbia, when they are meant for mud and dirt tracks. I reckon ninety five percent of four-by-fours never actually drive on anything but tarmac.

As I was thinking this, we were driving down The Mall, before Buckingham Palace and then on to the Tower. A guard waves us straight through the gates, and the driver's take us through a side entrance and into a large garage, big enough to play a full-size footie match. A few minutes later, we are escorted into the Tower's lower levels, and ushered into a waiting room full of antiques with a wooden floor covered by beautifully crafted rugs. A suit of armour stood upright in an alcove, and I almost expected to see a pair of ghostlike eyes staring through the slit in the helmet.

"Ever been in one of those?" Susan asks.

"Yes, absolutely ridiculous, totally impractical, you can't move and you can't see a bloody thing. I ditched mine pretty quickly and fought without it. I never understood what they saw in it. A lot of good soldiers died in those ridiculous cases who probably wouldn't have, if they didn't have them on."

A door opens further up the corridor and two figures appear; one I recognise immediately.

"Ladies, Gentlemen, at ease, please, you can speak freely here," Prince Hubert says in his cut-glass English accent, seeing us all straighten and face him. He is wearing a grey three-piece suit, which fits him perfectly. He looks a little flustered, his face red, a frown forming lines across his forehead as if he is carrying the weight of the world on his shoulders. Three of our crew Arthurs, Michaels and the Doctor all stand to attention and salute. Prince Hubert is their Commander-in-Chief. He salutes back, waves their hands down and turns to me.

"You must be Godiven, very pleased to meet you, Mr Godiven, or should I say Plantagenet, which actually makes you a royal as well. I'm glad you are not here to take the Crown, now that would make it an interesting day," he says calmly, while smiling and holding his hand out. "My goodness, a true immortal, at last?" he says, as we shake hands. "Perhaps all is not lost as we thought, eh, Susan?" His handshake is firm and assured, showing a strength of character that the public don't see.

"No, Sir," she replies curtly.

"This way, please. Chamberlain, stay out here and don't let anyone else in, whatever happens."

"But sir," the tall gangly man who had accompanied the Prince, replies as if he has a piece of fruit stuck in his throat, "this is against royal protocols, sir?"

"Chamberlain, do you not think I know the Palace protocols, I wrote them!"

"These people mean me no harm, I can assure you of that. In fact, I've never felt so safe in my life," he adds as if to validate his order.

We enter a side room, and as soon as we are all in, the Prince swings a bolt across the door; before moving to a large fireplace where he withdraws the poker and sticks it in a tiny hole halfway up the wall. A double twist of his wrist, and with the noise of some levers moving, a secret door opens in the wall to the left of the giant fireplace.

"This way, please," he says, ushering us in.

We walk through the small opening, bowing a little to get through the door and enter a large size room full of computer screens, all with different views of a world seemingly on the brink of Armageddon. I walk to the line of screens and stare at the pictures, my eyes wide. What was I looking at? Could this be the end of the world, I was witnessing on these screens? No wonder he looked flustered! Each screen had a clock running in one corner showing the time, while another line showed its location. They are running live feeds from all over the world, showing what I guessed were missile silos, though they looked more like giant mole hills or sink holes.

"Every nation is on high alert. All the missiles are gone across the whole world, not one remains. They even took one from us that only I and a couple of other people knew about," he says in annoyance. "How could they know?" Prince Hubert adds with a hint of anguish.

I didn't reply, which was probably against royal protocol, but we had probably gone beyond that by now with what I was looking at.

I walked over to another bank of screens that showed more sink holes dotted around the world.

"The factories that make the weapons, all gone." Prince Hubert says walking towards me, his shiny black shoes clicking on the concrete floor. "All the munition factories, everything that produce weapons or bombs… all gone," he whispers in denialism.

"The Palace is being evacuated. We are heading to Scotland by helicopter after this meeting is over. We have a secure place up there that could withstand a nuclear blast if it comes to it."

"Good for you," I reply, perhaps a little disrespectfully.

The Prince turns to look at me, his face unwavering. "Someone needs to keep order after it happens."

"IT happens?"

Another bank of screens entices me forward and on them are all the major cities, around the world, in live feed again.

"We are too late," Prince Hubert says from behind us. "it's just a matter of time before anarchy kicks in, it won't take long. It will become dog-eat-dog in a short while. Civilisation is on the brink. It's lucky North Korea lost their nuclear weapons because they didn't believe us, even when all the NATO countries said that it had happened."

I look at the screens again and I'm drawn to the one of Cairo with the pyramids and the sweeping sands in the background. I remember another distant time, an exotic queen of a lost city in the desert. I shiver at the thought of the murderous sand devils. I recall the warmth of her embrace, and the offer to sit beside her as her King for all time…

"Godiven, are you still with us, man," the Prince says with his irrepressible stammer. I nod in reply and turn to another line of screens showing pictures of the world leaders.

"Seven of the world leaders are reptilian shapeshifters," Prince Hubert says.

I hear Susan gasp. "Many shapeshifters have become aides to most of the other world leaders, they are everywhere. If it had only been one or two, we could have sent the SAS in to take them out, but it's too widespread, we are being overrun from within."

"So how do you know we are not shapeshifters? How do I know you are not one?"

"Because you would have been dead by now. And I cannot vouch for myself, but I don't think I'd be showing you this if I was now, would I, old chap?"

"How? How would we be dead?"

"The words that my drivers uttered. If you were one of them, it would have caused a reaction."

My eyes go wide, I look to Susan, my thoughts confused. "Care to explain, Your Highness?"

"We found something a day ago, a team of archaeologists that had been assigned to find everything we can about the threat we face. We were running out of ideas. Susan knows how desperate we have been, that's why we called you in, back into service."

These words are not lost on me. I smile inside, thinking how recently I'd heard those words in a short vision in Cannock Green, from a Knight from the twelfth century. It seemed that I was always in the service of the Crown, ever since the time of my birth, whether I liked it or not.

Prince Hubert moves to another computer and punches a few keys on a keyboard, bringing up a picture on the screen.

"This was in the vaults of the Natural History Museum, it's been there for years and I think it had been overlooked, we have many unknown artefacts down there, you know."

I move closer, feeling the others close behind me, peering over my shoulders. The picture shows some sort of object sitting on a table. Prince Hubert taps a few buttons on the keyboard and the picture pans in closer.

"A broken spear?" I ask, looking at what looked like an ancient wooden shaft with a metal tip. The shaft had been broken off about two feet from the end. As soon as I see the metal tip, I know it's alien, the same material as my staff and weapons.

"How did they come to find it now?" Ayesha, asks, and then adds, "Your Highness?"

"Good point, young lady. It actually started to thrum. A janitor was cleaning the floor when he heard a noise and notified security. My team have been all over it ever since. It's on its way here now," he looks at his watch, "pretty soon, actually." he adds.

"But that still doesn't explain the words your team said to us?" I enquire.

Prince Hubert stands, raising his chin to look down at me. "It's what's written on the shaft that's given us some hope. It's ancient Sumerian. He pulls a sheet of paper from his breast pocket, then pulls out a pair of half-cut reading glasses, puts them on and reads out what's on the sheet.

"Speak the words that the forked tongues cannot, unlock their detection, strike the spear deep, avenge the King. Leave no enemies standing, show no mercy for they have none in return, Thorfram sacondis farganus."

"What the hell does that mean?" Ayesha asks.

"It's not from this world," I reply, "I don't know what it means, it's not a language I've ever heard. What does it do to the shapeshifters?" I ask Prince Hubert.

"The words have an amazing effect on them, they shy away and lose their human appearance, they revert back to their natural reptilian state."

"Wow," Ayesha says, "that's pretty cool."

"If only we had had this earlier," Susan adds, taking out a pen, a notebook and copying it down.

"We've got it now," I say, and she nods.

Arthurs hasn't said a word since we entered the room, he is still staring at the screen, his eyes fixed on the spear. "We need that spear," he says without taking his eyes from it. "I bet it's another weapon to beat those bastards with, like your staff," he says, twisting his head to look at me.

"I agree, the aliens brought many powerful weapons with them, this could be another one of them."

"It's on its way, gentlemen," Prince Hubert states. "You will have it and may God give you the knowledge to help us in our time of need."

"Thank you, sir," Susan responds.

Behind me, I notice one of the screens go blank, making a faint buzzing noise, the one from Rio de Janeiro. Now, all it shows is a fuzzy, black and white, horizontal line. Even as we watch another feed goes down from Mexico City, then Adelaide blinks out.

"My God, it's started. It's happening all over the world," Prince Hubert says, stunned.

"It could be a dodgy cable," Ayesha says with a lop-sided nervous smile, but no one smiles back. I've realised this is her way of dealing with a situation when she is out of her comfort zone, it's something I often do myself, making light of a dire situation.

We quickly move back through the secret entrance and Prince Hubert resets the door, before walking to and unlocking the door into the corridor. Chamberlain is still there standing at attention, his face a picture of concern.

"Thank goodness, Your Highness," he says with relief, "the team has arrived from the museum, but we've had a problem, we've lost one of the men."

Prince Hubert beckons him into the room, "lost one of the men?"

"He picked up the spear with his bare hands and he dropped to the floor dead."

"What, was he a shapeshifter?"

"No, sir."

My mind is starting to put a few threads together as I hear this conversation. I look at the staff in my hands and realise no one else has ever touched it, except Enlil. I look at my armlet, then to the doctor. And then, I realised how close Ayesha was to it on the bike. A cold sweat runs down my spine at the thought of what could have happened.

"Doc, you still got those armlets from Enlil with you?"

"Right here, Boss," Johnson replies with a grin, lifting a silver-grey case in his left hand.

"Get them out, I think we might need them." I've sort of taken command of the situation and if reading my thoughts, Susan looks at me and nods for me to continue.

"I'll try to make this as simple and quick as I can. None of you have touched the staff yet, thank goodness. Enlil held the staff, right?" Everyone nods, "It didn't kill him, not because he was a god, but because he had those alien armlets on, like me," I say raising my arms to the sky. "Remember, Korvak was wearing gloves in the crypt. "Somehow, they block the power and channel it in a different way. The spear in the museum, the curators or archaeologists would always be wearing gloves. Unfortunately, your man," I say to Prince Hubert, "didn't!"

"We could all have been killed if we touched it?" Ayesha says, her face going pale. "I was leaning against that thing for hours!"

"I know!" I said, wide-eyed, "it's lucky you had some clothes on," I say and smile.

"Not funny," she replies.

At the same time as the doctor pulls out the armlets, there is a knock at the door and Chamberlain ushers in three men who all look white faced and in shock. They stood stiffly to attention in front of Prince Hubert not saying a word. They are all wearing gloves. One is carrying a case.

"I am sorry for your loss, gentlemen," Prince Hubert says, "Please, speak freely here, we are beyond protocols now. Time is of the utmost urgency."

The tallest of the three, a thin man of about fifty years of age, a Doctor Canter, places the case on a table and opens it, revealing the spear. I go towards it, and they shout a warning, but I tell them it's OK. They look at the Prince and he nods approval. Without hesitation, I pick the spear up and am amazed at its weight, it's about the same length as my staff but much heavier. The shaft is made of the same petrified bone as my staff. The tip, the same metal that binds my staff, and makes up my sword and shield. I hold it as if to throw it and feel it's weight balance out along the shaft, to give me a perfect throwing weapon.

"Michaels," I say, fixing my eyes on the young sharp shooter. I see him stand to attention.

"Yes, sir,"

ROYALTY

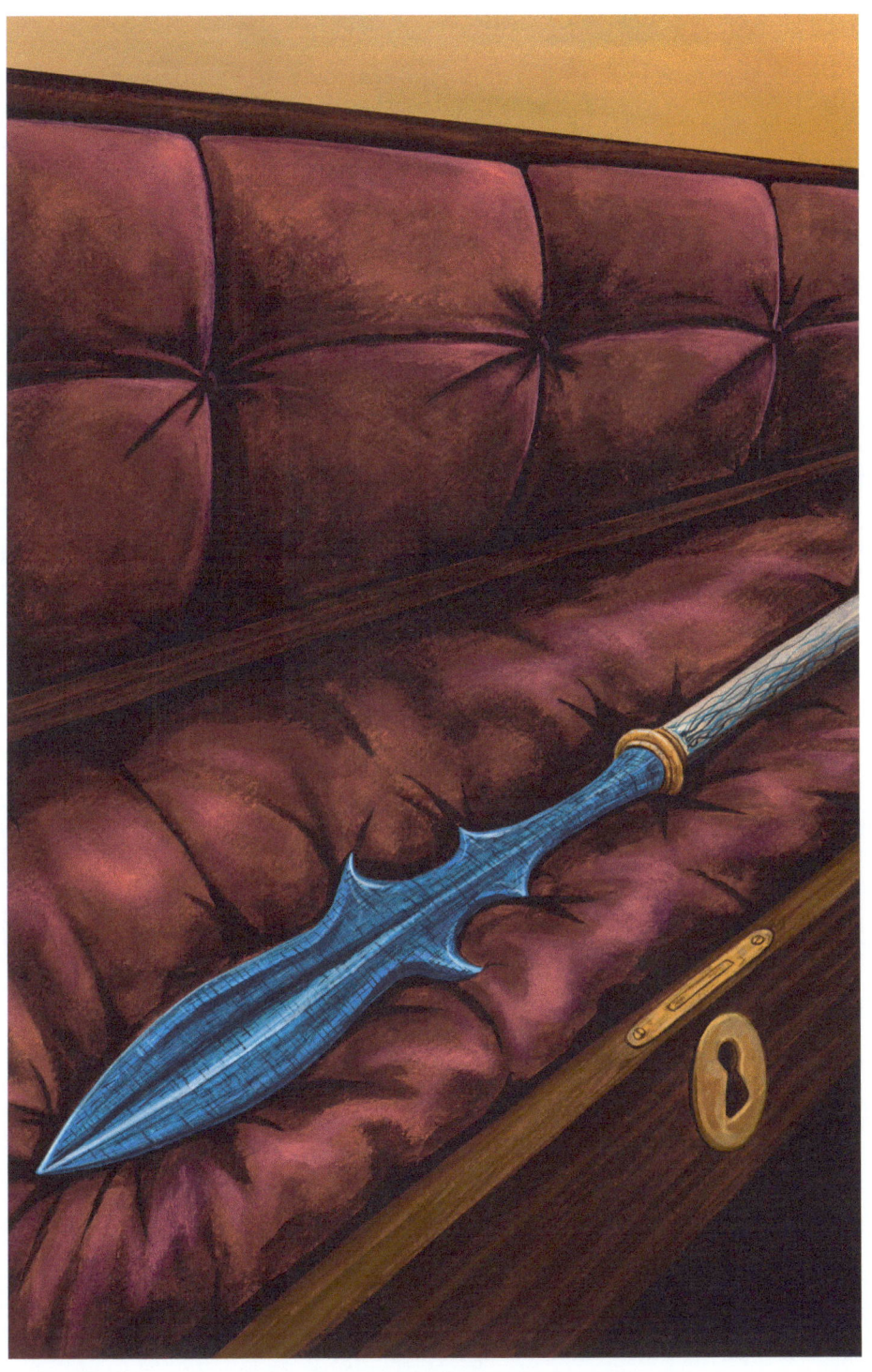

Plate: 20

"Put those armlets on, please."

"Sir?" he stammers looking at Arthurs and then Susan.

"Do as he says, soldier," Arthurs orders.

"Yes, sir."

Doctor Johnson hands him the armlets and he rolls up his sleeve, crumples his hand up and slips it though the armlet, pulling it up until it is tight on his forearm.

"What the hell," I hear him exclaim as the armlet, clicks and grinds into place upon his arm, changing its properties to attach snugly to him. His face goes wide in fear of the unknown.

"Relax," I say, "I've always wanted to know how mine attached. The other please, Michaels?"

He repeats the process, and the same thing happens again. He stands and faces us, both arms held out, palms to the sky, his face an expression of disbelief.

"Now what am I..." he starts to say, but I interrupt.

"Here catch," I say, throwing him the spear.

His reactions are quick as I knew they would be. Before he can think, he's caught the spear and is looking down at it as if he was holding a live rattlesnake in his hands. I see him about to drop it, but I look him in the eye, calming him with my hands.

"You're safe, soldier, that thing can't harm you with those on," I said pointing to the armlets.

I turn to Susan and Prince Hubert and smile, the 'I know it all smile', but I get that look that tells me perhaps I should have talked it though first.

"What?" I exclaim.

"That was a pretty stupid thing to try, John," Susan says tight lipped.

"We haven't got time to mess around, and anyway, I was ninety nine percent sure it would work... and it did," I said, pointing to Michaels, "He's still alive, isn't he?"

Michaels looks at me with a bemused look, and I just shrug. "Now remember, no one touches these things without gloves, understood."

"Or armlets!" Michaels adds, raising his arms up.

I turn to Prince Hubert to speak when Susan's phone goes off.

Her face drops in shock when she hears an anguished cry and the sound of destruction in the background, then the phone line goes dead. She frantically rings the number back, trying another when she can't get a reply, but no response comes from the second number either. Then, as she goes to type in another number, a call comes in and she sinks to the seat nearest her for support, head in hands.

"Something's happened at the institute, we've had a breach."

"Another breach?"

"That's all I've been told," Susan answers, her eyes distant.

11

DEVASTATION

The journey from the Tower passed in a panicked blur, with very little information to go on. Prince Hubert with his aides headed for a helicopter, while we were driven to the warehouse where our cars were parked up, our thoughts on getting back to the institute. The day was just dawning, with dark grey clouds giving us a glimpse, a foreboding, of what we might find. Even as we near the turn off to the institute and go up the drive towards the gates, we realise something big had occurred. Six fire engines sat on the verge in a line of three on either side of the road. The flashing lights of police cars and ambulances shine brightly through a thin mist that hangs around the edge of the forest, causing the scene to look as if it had been whitewashed. Camera crews and news people are shuffling to get a good shot or story. I hear the distant moan of a helicopter whirring over the site.

We are waved down by an armed response police officer, who points us off the road. Arthurs is up and out of the car faster than you could blink, talking to the officer, who he seems to know. The rest of us exit the car and head towards the gates. We shuffle past emergency staff who don't seem to even notice us until we reach the gate. Two other armed response officers guard the gate.

"You can't go through there, ma'am," the closest officer says to Susan who was about to push her way through.

"It's not safe," the other officer adds, with a face as blank as a stone wall. We all reach the gates together, spread out and look at the devastation before us.

"That's a little more than a breach," I say and then regret it.
"There were twenty people in there, John, maybe a few more!"
"Twenty-two, ma'am," Johnson replies coldly, his face, for once, looking sombre and showing signs of shock.
"Oh my," was all I could think to say, "I'm sorry."
The house was virtually gone. Only a stacked line of chimney pots protruded from the earth now, it looked more like an ocean liner on the horizon than the institute we knew. The land, most of the drive and gardens had all sunk into the earth, swallowed up by a giant sink hole. A few fires could be seen smouldering away and I glimpse an electric cable fizzing and crackling from the moisture in the air. Water was gushing from a pipe now sticking out from a muddy cliff that dropped into the pit, that was once the Harkness institute.
Arthurs joins us, his lips drawn tight, his eyes wild looking and distant. His head lifts ever so slightly and I could sense him sniffing the air.
"They haven't found a single body," he says, turning his gaze to the devastation.
"We need to go in," Susan says.
"You can't, it's unsafe, they won't let us." Arthurs answers, tight-lipped.
"But it's our people in there, our property, our belongings," Susan pleads.
"We go in tonight, just myself, Arthurs and Michaels." I say, feeling an anger, I hadn't felt for a long time starting to boil up. Arthurs looks at me and nods, his face grim and determined. I look a Michaels and he also nods, his eyes looking through the gates towards the devastation.
"I had friends in there," Michaels says quietly.
"We all did," Susan answers.
Susan continues, "Was it a coincidence that this happened at the same time as what we saw at the Palace?"
"There are no coincidences, I'd given up believing in coincidences hundreds of years ago." I replied stoically.
"They are blaming it on a sinkhole located under the house, which is bollocks! They say it's the biggest sinkhole ever recorded in this country. It's on the National news," Arthurs adds.
"Can you sense anything?" I ask Susan, wondering if the rest of the group knew

her witch powers were dormant.

"Nothing!"

"I see no ghosts," I say quietly.

"Meaning?" Ayesha asks.

"They are not dead," Susan interrupts.

"If they died so horrifically as this, I would see their ghosts, there's nothing. It is as if they have vanished off the face of the earth."

"Or under it." Arthurs replies, sending a cold shiver up my spine.

"It's like before, isn't it, like in the forests in Germany," I say, thinking of Le Loop's story, looking at Arthurs. Do I sense a touch of fear emanating from the man?

"Yes," he replies coldly, "sounds just like that."

It was just past midnight, when the three of us clambered over the perimeter wall of the institute and headed towards the sunken ruins of the house. Arthurs had spoken to a few of the security guards who were to turn a blind eye if we were spotted by them. I'd made a harness on my back for the staff. My shield and sword were both retracted and tucked out of sight, and my gun was in my hand, motion detector on.

"It's clear," I whisper to Michaels and Arthurs, putting my gun away. Their guns are holstered. We all know we are going to need both hands free to get through the mess that is left of this once great house.

"I need that diary," I had told Susan when we had holed up at the local village pub, waiting for opening time to come around so I could get a beer. "We will go in tonight, retrieve it and see what else we can find. Anything you need?" I ask her.

"All of it," she says with a smile, then adds, "my team back, they were good people."

"I'll see what I can do."

"John, if you find an entrance, don't go in. We heard from your story what happened to the ones that did." Was she protecting me, Arthurs or both of us, I wasn't sure?

"Sure, we will come straight back out," I tell her.

"The diary, nothing else."

"Promise, cross my heart and..."

"Don't say that," her voice starting to stammer, then composed herself, "I think it's bad luck to hope yourself dead, don't you?"

"Well, when you put it that way, I suppose so," I reply.

We had been keeping close tabs on the news, but nothing had appeared as of yet. The world seemed as normal and as chaotic as ever according to the news channels but nothing new, no cataclysmic events seemed to be taking place, despite what we saw at Buckingham Palace. Perhaps, Ayesha had been right after all, perhaps it was a dodgy wire! Maybe someone had just cut the lines. But I did have this sense of dread, as if something big was going to happen, I'd felt it before and had been right most of the time.

I found out from Susan we had a safe house, a second base of operations, none other than Ashworth Castle in Yorkshire where I had gone on my first mission with Elizabeth. We were relocating there immediately after we find the diary. It seemed fitting that we were going there, as if my life with the institute had gone full circle. I looked forward to visiting the cairn of stones to see how it looked now.

We turned our head torches on and walked through the undergrowth towards what was left of the lawn. At times, giant mounds of earth blocked our way and uprooted trees lay across our path. It didn't take long to break through, then we could see what was left of the driveway and lawn that used to be in front of the house. A half-moon was visible in the clear night sky. Our torches picked out great strips of lawn and soil that had been ripped out of the earth, flung and pulled apart by whatever force had destroyed the house. We made our way across all this like explorers traversing a glacier, jumping from one flat area to another, looking for the quickest route towards the sunken ruins. We reached the edge and looked down at the submerged house, it's roof just below the surface, the chimneys' jutting out above our heads. The electric and water had been cut, so no waterfall descended into the depths from the burst pipes, no cables waiting to electrocute us. I could hear the sound of water somewhere, but my light couldn't reach far enough to pick it out. An eerie silence hung over the place, like a mausoleum. I pull out my gun and the motion tracker bursts into action. Nothing moves on the screen, it's blank, no heat signatures. I holster my gun with a sigh, this was going to be a long night, I could sense it. The emergency crews had already been in, of course, finding no survivors or bodies. They had found the house very unstable, so the crews had been ordered out.

I look at the roof and the ledge at the bottom of it, then pan my torch up to a hole in the roof, smashed through by the emergency team. I point to it in silence, and two more beams of light reflect off the tiles, pinpointing the hole. "That's our way in," I say quietly.

It took another ten minutes to reach the opening and find a rope still in situ, from the morning's rescue attempt, dropping into the darkness of one of the upstairs rooms. I recall the doctor telling me how the three scouts had broken into the house through the upper rooms. Something about that had piqued my curiosity and I wondered why they had tried to enter that way. The surveillance room with the two operatives who ran it had been found dead, by Billy's hand, no doubt, but they were on the ground level, so there was no reason for the scouts to come in from the top levels, unless they were after the diary. But that had been left untouched. So, why? Something didn't add up and I was in the right place to find out why.

We dropped down the rope like firemen down the pole when called into action, sliding down slowly until our feet touched the wooden floor of the attic. The house was at an angle, so the floor tilted away from us, like a listing ship. Ar-

DEVASTATION

Plate: 21

thurs went first and secured the bottom of the rope, helping us down until we all stand together, breathing hard and leaning against a beam.

"Time to explore," I say.

"The diary!" Arthurs replies, knowing what we came for. "And then we are out of here."

"There's something else I need to check on, Frank," I say. We are on first name basis now! "Those scouts that came in, did you ever wonder why they came in through the top floor?"

"Less chance of being seen?" Michaels questions. "Dodging the cameras?"

"I get that, but why go to all that hassle to climb the building when they could have found countless other entrances on the ground floor?"

"What are you getting at, John?" Arthurs whispers in annoyance. "This is meant to be a quick in and out operation, nothing else."

"Humour me! Something doesn't add up. You head for Elizabeth's room and get the diary, I'll head up to where they came in, check it out, and see you back here at 01:00 hours, OK. What can possibly go wrong?"

"Everything's gone wrong since you turned up!" Arthurs says raising his eyes to the sky.

"Coincidence." I reply with an exaggerated smile.

"You don't believe in coincidence, remember?"

"You've got me there, it's lucky I'm here to put things right and save all your arses, then." I see Michaels smile at the interaction, he's not confident enough to join in but he will one day, if he survives long enough. I hope he's not wearing a red shirt under that body suit. The red topped security guys in Star Trek never survived an episode.

Arthurs shrugs, looks at his watch, "01:00 hours, no later, stay in contact." he says to me, putting an earphone in, asking me and Michaels to do the same. "Now let's get to it," he adds and pats Michaels on the back, while moving along the wall towards a doorway. I follow, trying to get my bearings, trying to remember where I am and where the scouts entered.

It took me a lot more time to tread through this once proud old house, which was now a graveyard of broken furniture and crumbling walls, than it did yes-

terday. Occasionally the house creaked and groaned, and I would stop, tensing for something to happen, but when silence returned, I would move on. I can hear the odd word of command from Arthurs on the commlink, but apart from the faint crackle of the signal and a few words I hear nothing. No ghosts interrupt my movements. The place is in utter darkness, only the beam of my torch showing me the way forward. I turn a corner and recognize that this is it, this is where they came in. At the far end, I pick out the window, all boarded up. My beam scans the carpet and I see dark splotches that could only be blood. I see a solitary shell lying against a skirting board, twinkling in my light. I pick it up and put it in my pocket, thinking it might make a nice good luck charm. I walk up and down trying to get a feel for the shoot-out. I see that one of the scouts, possibly the one that was killed, must have been coming back towards the window. I see a few spots of blood outside one of the doors and some bigger spots further down the corridor, as if it had been shot and injured at the door and killed further down the corridor as it tried to escape. It was a guess, but it felt as close as I would get to the truth, so I went with it. My hand settled on the round brass doorknob to twist it open, when a thought crosses my mind. Damn, I should have touched the alien corpse and found out it's last few minutes, I could have seen what it was up too? It wouldn't have been nice, but it would have been useful. I curse again when I hear the commlink crackle, and Arthurs voice comes over loud and clear.
"John, we have the diary, I repeat we have the diary and are returning to the exit point," he says all military like.
I am about to reply when I hear Michaels voice in the background, "Hang on a minute, what's that?"
"It's moving, back away, Michaels," Arthurs says loudly in my earpiece, forgetting he's talking to me, making me raise my hand to my ear.
"There's loads of them." Michaels says with panic in his voice.
"It's a trap," Arthurs says, and I hear the sound of gun fire through my earpiece and from somewhere close by. "Covering fire," I hear Arthurs shout and his machine gun chatters away, followed by another one. My head darts around sensing movement nearby but I see nothing, my hand still on the doorknob.

"Get back to the exit point," I shout, pulling up my gun, the motion tracker now a mass of white moving dots, some nearly on top of me. I look at the ceiling and fire instinctively and the ceiling crumbles in, bringing a dead reptilian through, no, not a dead reptilian, something else, a different breed of monster entirely and it is still alive! Before I have time to even compute what I am facing, it springs up and pounces, pinning me to the door with its bulk even as I bring the gun up between us and fire point blank into its chest. Through the moving light from my head torch, the creature is propelled backwards into the corridor wall. I look at its chest, black shining ebony, without a mark and see the bullets dropping to the floor, they hadn't touched it. These were different again from the one lying on the slab in the morgue. In the light I see it now in all its glory. It's huge, at least eight foot tall. No wonder it came through the ceiling! In some ways it looked sort of human, similar to the Demon King but better, the wings were much larger and looked like they were made for a long-haul flight! Everything about it spoke of an evolutionary step up from what I had met previously. Its whole body was wrapped in a thick shiny ebony hide, that I now knew was bullet proof. Even its head and wings were of the same thick black hide. The head was smooth, it's ears and nose, non-existent, just holes where they should be. Big, luminous, unblinking red eyes stare at me. Its lipless mouth opens and hisses, showing rows of sharp incisors, filed to points. In the time and space it took the creature to recover, I had drawn my sword and without a thought thrust it into the same spot. This time the effect was different, the sword slipped in like a knife through butter. A strange look appears on the creature's face, one of disbelief followed by pain. I lean into it more, feeling the blade sink deep. It's eyes stare at mine, its hand reaches for the sword and its mouth opens in a scream; the same scream I'd heard from one of my visions. So, these are the creatures that want to inherit the Earth. "Not on my watch you won't," I say aloud into its screaming face. I see the eyes dull over, feel the body slump and fall towards me. I pull the sword out and take a step back, my weight pushing the door ajar. The body crashes to the floor with a thump and lies still. I open the door and glance into the room as I hear a noise like the unfurling of many wings. I see a bunch of black bodies cocooned within their wings. So, this is how they were undetected, they don't give off a heat signature, until they unfurl their wings! Great! I count at least ten at a guess. The first one unfurls and launches itself at me in a blur, it's wings somehow propelling it forward at an incredible speed. The creature crashes into me before I can even raise my sword. My feet trip on the dead creature on the floor and before I know it, I'm pinned back against the opposite corridor wall. I drop the sword and grab one of its taloned hands as it swipes down to take my head off. Its face is inches from me, and its bloodshot eyes stare into mine with savage hatred. The other taloned claw reaches up for my face, when I sense movement to my left. Something enters the creatures head from the side, killing it instantly. Red glowing eyes dim, roll upwards and its body convulses then drops to the floor.

I see Arthurs reach the door and spray his gun at the advancing creatures, knocking them back into each other. He pulls a grenade from his side, pulls the pin out with his teeth and throws it into the room and closes the door all in one fluid motion. "Fire in the hold." he shouts.

Michaels pulls the spear free, kicking the dead creature aside and pulls me up, even as I grab my sword. He drags me away from the door and looks at me with a wry smile.

"Going to save our arses, eh?" he says with glint in his eye.

I don't have time to reply as the grenade goes off. The door explodes open, flying into Arthurs and knocking him into the far wall with an almighty crash. A second later, the creatures appear at the opening, fighting to break through.

"Jesus Christ," Arthurs shouts over the din, "It didn't touch them," he says, wide eyed, rising to his feet, a big gash across his forehead, dripping blood.

Again, I don't reply, I step forward and slash at the first one. It's got nowhere to go to get out of the way and slumps to the floor, it's head half hanging off.

"We need to go," Arthurs shouts, as I see Michaels step past me and spear the next one that was trying to climb over its fallen brother. That one too goes down with an awful screech and lies still, blocking the way out for the others, or so we think? A dart of blackness flies out above the bodies and knocks Michaels and I to the ground, the creature on top of us. I hear its wings unfurl and it starts to rise and swing one arm towards Michaels, when I hear a roar behind me.

Plate: 22

Arthurs has had enough of playing soldier. He's in full werewolf mode now and he looks magnificent. He's grown to his full size in a matter of moments, his clothes ripped to shreds. His gun and equipment clatter to the floor. His head is touching the ceiling and he dwarfs over us like the god of all werewolves. His face is now the face of a wolf, a snout full of sharp teeth and with huge orange eyes that stare with bloodlust at the fight to come. Arthurs is standing on two powerful hind legs made for walking upright, the muscles beneath the fur, twitching and ready for action. His body is covered from head to toe in a thick silver-grey hair, that actually makes him look even larger. For a heartbeat, he stands framed in the corridor, his eyes scanning the scene, his snout sniffing the air, then he pounces on the creature and swipes it's head off with one massive, clawed hand, before it even knows what's happening.

Blood gushes over us as I try to rise and see Arthurs head for the doorway, the creature's body still twitching as it topples between us, never to fly again. He is so fast it's frightening, he's easily as fast as these creatures, if not even faster and far more agile in the enclosed space. I hope he doesn't lose control completely; he might kill us in his bloodlust frenzy. We look at each other in astonishment, our eyes wide, our faces covered in blood and gore. I reach out and grab Michaels by the arm and we pull each other up between the dead bodies. I look at the back of Arthurs, framed in the doorway and wonder, could one werewolf be a match for these fiends.

He stands at the door and roars at the creatures, and I see them shrink back, they weren't expecting this. Arthurs pulls the corpses out of the doorway with ease, flinging the last one back into the mass cowering inside giving himself time and space to enter, to continue the killing spree. He roars another challenge and dives in. I sense movement down the corridor and see four more of the creatures coming up towards us, blocking our exit.

"We are trapped," Michaels shouts in panic.

"Then we fight our way out," I say to him, "follow my lead and I assure you we will live to fight another day." I draw my staff and stride forward, meeting the first one full on with the staff pointed at its chest. It tries to grip it, before it realises its fatal mistake. Perhaps the creature didn't see what it was, or didn't know what it did, but it dies as soon as it touches the staff, its body consumed by a blue glow as the flesh turns from black hide to skeleton and then to dust, in only a few seconds. I walk through the glow and the dying figure, and stand facing the remaining three, I am feeling calm and in complete control. I know exactly what I am going to do. They stop, as if hitting a brick wall. I raise the staff again, roar at them and charge. This roaring is catching, after all I can't let Arthurs have all the fun! They backtrack and scuttle down the corridor, disappearing into the darkness in the blink of an eye.

"Cowards!" I yell at them.

Behind me, I hear the noise of utter carnage within the confines of the room. The screams of the creatures intermingling with the roars of Arthurs, make a merry song of death and pain. Sounds like Arthurs is having fun!

"Good skills," Michaels says to me, as we turn and enter the room, weapons drawn.

Inside the room is a mass of dead and dying creatures, and body parts. Arthurs seems to have found a weak point on these creatures; their heads don't stay attached to their bodies that well! Obviously, someone messed up when they were created. Blood is everywhere, dripping from the ceiling and covering the room as if someone had exploded a balloon full of blood. Our two headlight beams pick out Arthurs, who is dealing with the last two creatures. They are trying to blindside him by keeping apart from each other and spreading his vision, but now we are here they don't have a hope in hell. Arthurs has cuts all over his body, and I see great tufts of hair on the floor where he has been struck, a cut on his head is bleeding badly, but he doesn't seem to notice any of this. He's limping slightly as if he is injured, but this is still one helluva sight to behold, he is one perfect killing machine. One creature moves while the other pounces. Michaels pulls his arm back and throws the spear, it strikes one creature plum in its chest throwing it backwards into some overturned furniture. As it rises, it unfurls it's wings and prepares to dart forward. Before it has time to get up to speed, I step into its approach and dispatch it with my sword. It's wings were making ready to spring the creature forwards, but it has no chance, the sword digs deep, and it topples back into the pile of other dead bodies, Michaels spear still protruding from its chest. I hear an almighty roar, a spray of blood splatters across the room and a head bobs across the floor in front of me. I look towards Arthurs who is covered in blood, some of it his own, but most of it from these repulsive creatures. His wide orange eyes fix on me and then shift to Michaels, I see no sense of recognition in those wild berserker orbs. I notice his body tense, bracing to attack.

I put one hand out, fingers spread. Tension and the smell of death hangs in the air. 'Don't make any sudden moves Michaels, otherwise it might be your last.' I think, raising my eyes to Michaels.

"Easy, Frank, it's us," I say calmly, standing still. I hear the heavy panting of the werewolf starting to slow, I hear the creaking of bones and the wrenching of muscle. "We are on your side, buddy."

"Could have helped," a growling voice says.

I see Arthurs trying to control his voice as his body groans with the effort of changing back, but his vocal cords are not quite back to normal.

My eyes gaze in awe as his body transforms, the human skin still showing the signs of the brutal fight. He collapses to his knees, completely naked. He has deep cuts and tears in his flesh when he changed back, but already they are starting to heal. It's remarkable, before our eyes the wounds are starting to knit together, the hair regrowing.

"Having fun!" I ask.

He looks at me again, his orange eyes dimming and changing to their normal colour.

"Something like that," he says gruffly. "A new species, do you think?"

"I think the same, but just a slight evolutionary step up, as if they had been supercharged."

"They still die the same."

"That's because we caught them off guard, they didn't expect us to take the offensive." I see Arthurs struggling to rise. "You OK?"

"The bump on the head hurts the worse."

"That's because it dented your ego, not your body," I say with a wry smile.

Arthurs curses under his breath but returns the smile. I see Michaels put his

foot on the torso of one creature and pull the spear out with a squelch.
Around us are littered the dead creatures, mostly body parts, scattered about the room as if they had been toy soldiers whose owner had decided to pull them apart, especially their heads. In the middle of the room, something glistens in my headlight.

"What the hell is that?" Michaels asks. He's keeping an eye on the corridor, scanning his headlight up and down checking for any movement, but his torch had picked out something bright on the floor between the bodies.

I quickly pull out my pistol and check the motion tracker for any movement, seeing none and put it back in the holster. What's worrying is that if these creatures are dormant the motion tracker can't pick them up. I turn my attention back to the glistening object that is lying in the middle of the floor. I move closer and am joined by Arthurs. It is some sort of square plinth each side about a foot long, and about an inch high. It seems to be made of some gold-coloured metal. I bend down to take a closer look and I notice an inscription, words similar to those on my sword, running along all four side's.

"It's alien technology," I exclaim.

The top looks like a flattened pyramid with four triangular sides. In the very middle is a solid gold square. The metal seems to be humming and I can feel that same effect from when we were under the Sphinx. It is giving off some sort of energy signature, but what for? Is this what they were coming to collect or was it a trap set for anyone that happened to come along? But what does it do? The more I look at it, the more it seems to look like the pyramid was now extending upwards to form a genuine 3-D pyramid.

"Now that's something you don't see every day?" I reach down to pick it up and find that it is quite heavy, heavier than it looks.

"We need to tag it and bag it, and get the hell out of here," Arthurs says, all business like.

"And you need to get some clothes," I add, not taking my eyes off the thing.

"My rooms just up the way, I'll go get some," he says picking up his weapon.

"If you shoot anything with that, you are going to burn yourself," I tell him. "Take Michaels."

He peers at me again then looks at Michaels, before lowering his head. "Come on Michaels, let's go get some clothes," he says, then turns to me. "Don't leave this room or wander off anywhere," he says, "there could be more of those things out there."

"I can handle myself," I reply, slightly aggrieved. "But I'll stay here, I promise!"

As they leave, I pick up the object in both hands and stare at it. It feels solid but I sense that inside this box is some sort of device that had many moving parts. I shake it, holding it to my ear but feel nothing loose inside. I look at the top, and it really does look like a pyramid when viewed from above. So, we have an alien puzzle box to decipher. Where's Billy when you need him? Oh, of course, he's dead, because he was a double-crossing alien demi-god scum bag, killed by his own technology, how fitting.

Michaels and a newly dressed Arthurs return, and we head off in silence. I keep my gun out, the motion tracker on. We reach the room we had entered by without any more encounters with the creatures then haul ourselves up the rope, one by one, until we stand on top of the roof, feeling the cold night breeze ruffle our hair. It felt good to be outside, being inside and under attack had felt very claustrophobic, one of my fears that has never gone away, and I suspect never will. Nothing moves in the silence around us, only the distant sound of an owl, breaks the night's solitude.

We climb back onto the land, cross the ruined lawn and clamber back over the wall.

Ten minutes later, we are in the car with Susan and Ayesha heading towards a small private airfield and an awaiting helicopter.

"Change of clothes," Susan says to Arthurs, raising one eyebrow. He was still hobbling a bit and looked exhausted, but he was going to survive.

"I had a bit of an accident," he replies with a hint of humour, as he slumps down into the back seat, next to the two girls. What is wrong, Arthurs is getting a sense of humour, have I missed something! The doctor had gone on ahead.

Shame, we need him now. Michaels took the wheel, and I rode shotgun.

"Are you going to be up for flying the copter?" I hear Susan ask Arthurs. Before he can reply, I speak up. "I'll do it, I haven't flown a helicopter for ages, should be fun."

"Fun!" Ayesha replies from the back. "Do you have any qualifications?"

"I've flown hundreds of times," I say, it was a small white lie, it was probably about a couple of dozen times but that's just splitting hairs.

"But probably not recently," she replies.

"What's it with you, anyway? Don't like flying?"

"I don't like heights, especially as I have no wings!"

"Well, nor do I."

"When was the last time you have flown a copter, John?" Susan asks in all seriousness.

"It was in Vietnam. We flew in to help evacuate civilians from the worst hit areas. We weren't part of the war; we ran parallel to that. The Americans' used it as a propaganda piece eventually, so I quit. That war was an evil war, all wars are of course, but that one was the worst. Death could creep up on those soldiers from just about everywhere and anywhere. The jungle hides the enemy like a chameleon changes its colour. One minute you are alive and the next... I saw some crazy shit out there I can tell you. Stuff that would make you think twice about what is real and what is not. And some of the things I found in that jungle... Well, let's just leave it at that, shall we."

"That still doesn't explain how qualified you are to fly this copter." Ayesha pleads, "it was bad enough hanging on to you on the back of that bike," she adds, and I smile.

"I'll tell you what, you do your thing, touch my hand, see that we are not going to die because I'm at the wheel and then we can get on our merry way, deal?" I say reaching my arm back towards her.

Ayesha snorts and acknowledges me without a word, while casually reaching up and gripping my hand. And that's when things start to go strange.

Suddenly I'm in the cockpit of this copter, but no one else is with me. I am fighting for control of the bird with both hands on the joystick. I'm screaming something above the vacuum of silence, then I sense the engine cut out and feel that awful weightlessness as the copter plunges downwards. Somewhere I hear the tolling of a bell and know it's ringing for me. Is this my end at last. And, just as I'm writing my own eulogy, somehow the engine kicks back into life and I wrestle for control again. I cry out in delight, defying the odds as I feel the copter starting to rise, then I hear a huge whoomph and my ears pop. I sense a massive force expanding outwards from the helicopter as if we had imploded and exploded at the same time. I look up to see a bright light above me. I feel that dropping weightlessness again, and then there is nothing but the silence of the dead.

I come back to the present with a start, pulling my arm away from Ayesha and looking her in the eyes.

"John," she says worriedly.

"John, what happened?" Susan asks, leaning forward.

"Arthurs," I say, "if you are up to it, I think you'd better fly us home this time."

He looks at me and nods, "OK, big guy, I've got it."

We get to the copter, strap ourselves in and Arthurs takes off as smoothly and effortlessly as a pro.

My mind is in turmoil. The others are looking at me waiting for me to reply. Ayesha, already fearful of flying and spiders, looks at me pale faced as if it were her fault that I had seen something. Like she said, it is a gift and a curse all rolled into one.

"I don't know what I saw, but I'm glad I did," I said to reassure Ayesha. Somehow, I felt I didn't want to disclose my vision, it seemed almost too personal. And it seemed like it wasn't portraying the immediate present for once. Anyway, now I'd seen it and changed the future, it wasn't worth worrying about. But what had I seen, was it my impending demise? I heard the bells tolling and the white light, they were pretty much a giveaway!

"I can't explain exactly what I saw, but I just know I shouldn't be flying this machine now," I said, giving them my best smile. They didn't fall for it, I could see that on their faces, but they weren't going to push me; they knew if it was important, I would have told them more.

"What, you had a prophesy or something?" Arthurs shouts above the noise, and chuckles. How close he was, I thought. "Something like that." I reply.

"Get some rest, John," Susan says to me and places a hand on my arm, "it's been a long day."

"Tell me about it!" Ayesha says.

She doesn't know the half of it. I lean back and shut my eyes, feeling the reassuring sound of the engine vibrating through the seat. The copter rocks back and forth in the wind, the darkness of the night visible out of the small side windows. I'm taken back to another time, the rocking of a carriage, the closeness of a group, the darkness outside the windows. I see my friends, the Battleborn, rubbing their hands against the cold, cursing in their indomitable way. I want to scream to them to get ready, to prepare, to be on guard, but I know I can't change the past. I see Elizabeth turn to me and is about to say something when I hear the screams of terrified horses. I jerk awake, my head tilted to one side, my neck stiff from leaning awkwardly. 'Damn, that felt too real.

I look around me and see Susan handling the object we got from the institute, peering at it from all angles. It's so heavy, she's having to hold it in both hands. Her eyes flick to mine.

"Any ideas?" she asks.

"Not one, yet, but I'm working on it."

"You think, they were coming back to retrieve it or to place it there, when you arrived and interrupted them?"

"It doesn't make sense, the creatures didn't register on the motion tracker until they moved, so as we didn't pick anything up, I would say they were not putting it there but retrieving it. It wasn't an ambush, we just happened to get there at the wrong time."

"We are just coming in to land now," Arthurs shouts back to us. "It's windy out there, so make sure everything's secure, including yourselves." Through the cockpit window I see dawn is breaking, a thin smudge of light on the horizon that is the start of a new day. A strange thought pops into my mind, and I wonder how many times since the Earth was created had a new day dawned. The copter banks across the sea and starts to descend. I glimpse the dark outlines of a castle and the rugged hills of the moors below us. The copter starts to rock about a bit waking Michaels and Ayesha.

"Susan, the room that we found the object in. What was in there? Could the security team have overlooked searching or finding that thing?" I ask, nodding towards it.

"It was a spare room, stacked with furniture. I suppose so."

"Coming in to land," Arthurs shouts back.

"So, I'm guessing they were coming to retrieve it, not leave it there."

Our eyes meet across the small seating area just as the copter's landing gear touches solid ground.

The object thrums and vibrates in Susan's hands making her drop it to the floor. A vacuum effect as if something is sucking all the noise in the world away, crashes across my senses. Even the sound of the copter is silenced. I see the group as one, put their hands to their ears. The writing on the side of the object lights up, and the centre of the thing starts to expand upwards forming a 3-D pyramid. As it reaches its full size, the sound returns and a bell chimes. I hear a few of the group let out a sigh of relief as everything returns to normal.

"Thank God for that," Ayesha says.

"Everyone out now," I shout, "quickly."

The gold button on top of the device silently drops back in on itself and the ground shakes with an almighty roar, throwing us all over the place. A bell tolls from everywhere and nowhere, and the vision suddenly becomes strikingly crystal clear to me. Michaels who was half-in and half-out of the copter disappears, falling out. Ayesha bumps her head and I see blood and a nasty welt forming. Susan who was still strapped in, unclasps herself and reaches Ayesha. The copter tilts and sways some more as the ground beneath it forms and reforms. I see the castle itself shake, I see rocks falling and the distant screams of people I couldn't even see. Arthurs appears at the hatch helping everyone out and reaching my hand. He pulls me out, his face asking questions.

"What the hell's happening?"

"That thing," I say pointing at the object, "It's a kind of bomb, it's what destroyed the institute." His eyes go wide and a second later, he looks at Susan, then at me. "Get out and shut the door," he says returning to the pilots seat.

"Not tonight, you don't," I tell him, "I've got this one."

"We can't afford to lose you," he says, his voice rising.

By now, the small group that has left the craft had stopped and was staring back at us. Susan had already realised what was happening and had put Ayesha in Michaels care and was starting to head back.

"Look Arthurs, Frank," I say, "you might not realise this, but you are just as important to this operation as me, maybe even more so!"

"What do you mean by that?" he says, puzzled.

"Listen, protect that lady with your life, OK. She's got a big part to play in this as well."

Again, he looks at me with no understanding. "I'm taking this bird up, not you," he says ignoring me, while reaching for the handle of the door.

"Arthurs," I shout getting his attention. He turns to me, and I hit him with all I've got with the arm that I have my armlet on, "we are wasting time." I just finish my sentence as he sails through the air to land at the feet of Susan. Without a backwards glance, I jump into the copter, strap myself in and start up the engine. Arthurs rises and heads towards me as I hear another level of the pyramid drop, causing another bell to chime. The earth also drops this time and rolls almost like a giant wave of soil, stone and turf. I see the company, the new Battleborn, roll to the floor helpless. I see people escaping from the castle only to be thrown to the earth as another tremor unfolds across the countryside. I see the tip of one of the rotors touch the ground and keep rotating until it is just a blur. I pull the joystick back and suddenly I'm airborne and alone with my thoughts. I look behind me at the object, glowing brightly in the back of the copter; now, with only half the pyramid visible. How it works, I have no damned idea, I just know I have to get it as far away as possible from these people, people who I have grown to care for and call friends, the new 'Battleborn'. I veer the helicopter away from the castle and head towards the open moor. I keep rising as high as I can so whatever destructive force is inside that alien time bomb is diffused by the space between. I head towards the rising sun like Icarus on his final quest, both hands on the joystick, my body braced. The vacuum of silence attacks my senses first, followed by a distant sonic boom as I feel and see out the cockpit, the air around the copter waver and roll. The copter groans and starts to buckle with a screaming of tearing metal. The engine stalls and I plummet earthwards. Is this it, is this how it ends, the vision seemed to say so. I'm helpless but I'm still holding the joystick, when the engine somehow kicks in and I pull up fighting for control, the copter swirling round and round. If I can get onto the middle of the moor and bail out, I might just survive. But I know this is just a dream, I know how this is going to end. The helicopter starts to right itself and I pull back on the joystick to rise again and head further away from the castle, and out towards the open moorland. I see a bright light as a new day dawns, as the sun peaks over the moor, my eyes shutting momentarily, a corona of light, emblazoned upon my eyelids. I sense the silent scream of the vacuum and hear the bell toll again, and then suddenly everything goes dark.

12

THE CALLING

September 1599

We are sitting around the long dining table at the institute, a roaring fire in the hearth casting shadows across the high walls of the room. Two candelabras sit proudly upon the table, the candles are half burnt and making flickering shadows on the ceiling. Across from me sits Frederick the German, his huge frame blocking out the light thrown from the fire as well as capturing most of the heat, to boot, on this late chilly September night.
"Move over you big lummox, you are stealing all the heat," says Brother Matthew, chiding him in a light-hearted fashion. Frederick mumbles an oath in German beneath his thick beard and shuffles his stool across a bit to give us some heat. Elizabeth sits at the head of the table watching quietly, her eyes and thoughts mirroring her look, she seems happy. A decade in and we are all still here. True, they have all got a little older, perhaps even a little slower to react, but the Battleborn are a finely honed team, especially with Elizabeth as our leader. She was in her seventies now, but still walked and moved as spritely as she did the first day I met her. Maybe, she has a few extra wrinkles, and her hands seem to give her pain sometimes, but apart from that her mind and body is as active and sharp as a woman half her age.
"Why don't you tell us one of your stories, John, they are always a good listen?" Brother Matthew asks, giving me a nudge.

THE CALLING

"You've never told us of how it all started after you woke up," Staunton adds. "What's your first recollection of waking from your long sleep? Can you remember?" Elizabeth enquires from across the dining table.

"Very well," I say, "it seems that a story is in order, if that is what you desire." I see them nod, so I take a deep breath and let it out slowly, I reach out and take a sip of my beer before continuing. "I'll tell you about that and an encounter I once had with a Queen of a lost city in the desert, and how close I came to becoming her eternal king". The thought of her touch still makes me shiver, and the revulsion I felt when I saw her true form still makes me cringe.

"I remember being in this cavern lit by torches. An altar stands before me; upon it a shield, sword and metal armlet that I know all too well now. I remember seeing a swirling mist and within the mist a creature out of your worst nightmares.

A hideous monster, twenty feet tall was clawing its way from a large well surrounded by swirling mist. The creature looked like a huge male version of Medusa, wreathing, frond-like tentacles for hair above a reptillian looking maw. It's huge muscular form, covered in brown hair, contorted in agony as it tried to escape. Large snake-like eyes fixed on me and I almost froze on the spot as it looked at me with an intense hostility and hatred, staring deep into my very soul. It opened it's long jaw that ran the length of it's face to where small holes denotes where the ears should be, and I saw rows and rows of sharp teeth dripping with drool. More small protruding horns were visible on it's chin and I get the feeling that this demon, or whatever it is, was not fully grown.

The thing roars, trying to escape the mist trapping it, keeping it at bay. I see for the first time that someone is standing on the altar chanting, arms raised. Something moved towards me from my left, a blur of movement and the sound of a blade passing through the air. I ducked, as a gleaming scimitar swishes just above my head. I remember throwing something then towards the figure, as I see out of the corner of my eye the arc of the scimitar destined to leave it's mark. I feel a faint sharp sting followed by the warm flow of blood on me. My knees go week and I fall back onto the dias and lie there, sensing my life seeping away. And then I am awake, my eyes open, lying on my back against the cold stone of

Plate: 23

the altar. I remember opening my eyes and hearing the shrieks of people nearby. I look up to see a roof in ruin barely a few feet above my head. The people that found me thought me a demon, which was quite appropriate. I kept saying "God in Heaven," but with the dust in my mouth and a dry throat, it came out sounding more like, "Godiven." Someone had been talking to me asking my name, but I couldn't recall that. I remember trying to rise, choking on the dust and the dryness in my throat. I felt my heart beating fast as if to make up for lost time. I remember looking down at my armlet for the first time, wondering how it had got there. A glistening sword, I couldn't recall ever seeing before, rested in one hand, while in my other hand a metal shield was strapped in place. I remember lifting up the shield to look at the markings on its front. My neck was stinging and my body ached with every move.

"W... water," I ask and one of the spectators' throws me a goatskin pouch. He stood wide eyed and in fear for his life, not saying a word, despite the fact his mouth was permanently hung open in surprise.

"Thank you," I try to say through my parched lips, but it comes out more like a croaky whisper. I feel the cool liquid as it enters my mouth and throat, the feeling as it passes through my system, one of almost ecstasy as if I had travelled many days in the desert without water and suddenly been handed the amber nectar of life.

He quickly paced back to stand with the others who were all looking at me as if I had two heads. Seven people stood there, immobilised by fear. They all looked thin and emaciated, most were local, apart from one man who looked European. It was him who I addressed.

"Where's Richard?" and then not forgetting my place I add, "where's the King?"

"King?"

"King Richard?" I ask, pulling myself to my feet, brushing dust, sand and rubble off my clothes with the back of my hand. I sheath the sword in a scabbard that hung around my waist, so as not to intimidate him. I watch as the figures all take a step away from me. I see one look over his shoulder and I follow his gaze to a shaft of light above some rubble. The place looks like there had been a gigantic cave-in. Large stone blocks and columns lay scattered across the floor.

The roof hung at a strange angle, tilted downwards into the darkness behind me. Some sort of altar protruded out of the rubble and darkness, where I had lain. I spotted a square block of stone upon the floor, which seemed to have recently been moved by the signs of footsteps and movement about the altar. A human skeleton sat on the floor beside the base and a scimitar lay beside it, glinting in the dim light cast by the torches within the ruined chamber. Parts of clothing hung off the skeleton, shredded and torn to tatters over age. What has happened here? What am I doing here? How did I get here? Remember, John, I say to myself. My mind seems muddled and confused with shifting thoughts of battles, a siege and a mission. I was on a mission for the King to stop the ritual to summon a demon. I wasn't carrying a sword or shield, just my staff... where is my staff now? I look around, it is nowhere in sight, probably hidden beneath some rubble or destroyed. Then I remember the Mamluk with the scimitar and him turning to dust, it must be here somewhere. Did I dream I was holding a staff, I could not remember, but surely, I would not have gone into battle with a mere staff. But I remember the mission, or parts of it. Where was the rest of the group? Why weren't they here? Why can't I remember what happened?

"King Richard? King Richard died years ago."

"Died!" My mind went numb, I only saw him a few days ago. I look at the man again, his clothes look different, his face is pale, and he is looking at me as if I am a ghost. His accent is Italian, his words echoing around the room like a reminder of what he is telling me. "How many years ago?" I ask him as my mind attempts to piece together what is happening. My eyes wander to the skeleton and the evil looking blade of the scimitar, a dark stain covering its sharp edge. My body tenses as I recall a scene of intense fighting, and I reach up and run my hands across a long scar that stretches from one ear, down my neck and across my throat. I feel a thin ridge of flesh that has healed over the wound, it wouldn't be till later that I see how ugly the scar looks; and how lucky I am to still be alive. And also, how fatal it looked! The scar tingles and stings as if it had recently happened but my touch tells me otherwise, it must have happened some time ago.

"Signor, I do not know exactly, but King Richard died many, many years ago, after the end of the last crusade," the man spoke nervously.

"What year is this?"

"Signor?"

"Year, what year is this?" I say louder.

The man cringes back towards his fellows. I raise my hand in apology. "The year?" I repeat, more quietly.

"The year of our lord 1290, Signor." he replies sheepishly.

My knees go weak, and I collapse to the floor, the shield clanging on the stone, but keeping me from falling. How can this be? One hundred years had passed, I should be nothing more than a pile of bones. I feel a beating pulse throbbing in my neck, a roaring sound in my mind, what's happening? My friends will all be dead. The King dead. No one I know will be alive! So, how come I am alive? I raise my confused and questioning eyes towards the Italian.

"How did you find me?" I see the man's eyes move to the altar behind me. "Tell me everything, please? I need to know?"

"Signor, we found your body on the altar, a huge piece of stone on your chest. We thought you were dead but could not understand why you looked so alive. I mean, it looked like it had just happened, your body looked perfectly preserved. We lifted the stone from your chest, it took four of us," he said looking at the block of stone on the floor beside the altar. "As soon as we did, that thing," he said pointing to the metallic armlet, "lit up, then you let out a huge sigh and started breathing again. The sword and shield that were lying against the altar shot into your hands as your eyes opened. It is magic Signor, or... the work of the devil!"

With the help of the shield, I pushed myself up to my full height. Again, the spectators' shuffled back. "I am no work of the devil," I say to them with a smile, "but the devil might know why I'm still alive. And I intend to find out. Now show me the way out, I'm thirsty and I'm in need of a good draught of beer. And you," I say to the Italian, "No more talk of the devil, he has nothing to do with this. Now take me to whoever is in command around here."

A few hours later, I'm standing on the ruined battlements of the city of Acre, watching a constant stream of bedraggled humanity leave the city, looking for safer places. The hustle and bustle of the evacuation is clear to see. Children lost in the crowds are crying for their mothers, mothers are crying back, their voices tinged with panic. Sellers stand at the sides of the road, trying to get every last bit of profit from the fleeing masses. But despite all that, there is an orderly fashion about the occasion as if this had been done before. Everyone seems to know where to go. Camel herders shepherd their camels along the route, treating their animals better than any human that got too close. Dust hung in the air, forming a dirty haze that hung above the crowds like a cloud. The sun is high in the sky and not a real cloud can be seen. It's so hot I feel my clothes and armour sticking to me like a second skin. The air feels like you are standing too close to a raging fire and seems heavy and dry with dust and sand. Word has gone out that the city, the same one we had laid siege to a hundred years earlier, was about to fall to the Mamluks.

Peter de Severy, commander of the Knights Templar stood facing me. He was six foot tall and wore clothes and armour that were not that dissimilar to mine. His wizened old face is one that has seen many battles. His eyes gleamed with a fiery intensity that spoke of a steely determination.

"Your story," he says in a deep voice, looking out over the hubbub of the city, "is one I find difficult to comprehend, friend John, if you were not standing here before me," he pauses. "Were it not for the workers who found you who tell the same story, I would believe you a spy?"

I start and take a step back, my hand going toward my sword. The two Templar guards standing close by spring into action and come toward me, but Peter raises his hands, "Relax, if I thought you a spy, you would be dead by now, your head will be adorning the walls on a spike," he adds in, his eyes moving to one of the city walls. I follow his gaze and see dark specks dotted on the wall, with the unmistakable stains of blood running beneath each head. I shake my head.

"You do not agree with our actions. You, who were a part of the King's inner circle on one of the crusades."

"I seem to have lost the appetite for fighting when I see that after a hundred years nothing much has changed. It seems the innocent are the only ones to suffer." I said looking towards the departing masses.

Peter's bearded face turned into a frown. "You speak wise words, my friend. So how come you were here?"

"I can't remember much. In fact, I can not remember anything of my previous life before I was awoken, I can only recall details of the quest I was on. That final day before whatever happened is quite clear. The King, King Richard, needed my skills on a mission. He ordered a small group of us to head into the city ahead of the main force to stop an ancient ritual from happening. The King was not someone to trifle with, or question. He ordered this mission personally, so who am I to disobey an order from the King."

"Yes, good, good," Peter replies a little absentmindedly, not thinking over my reply. "Friend John, I might have need of your services if you are up for it, it might save us all from the forthcoming siege. Even as we speak, the Mamluks are pushing ever closer to the city. Our forces can't hold them back. I am ordering as many as possible to flee down the coast to regroup, while we rebuild the city and ready it for the oncoming siege. The less townsfolk we have cooped up, the less mouths we have to feed. We were looking for stones to rebuild the outer walls, which is how we found you. We will hold if reinforcements come. I have sent word for help, it will come."

"Need of my services? You want me to remain here and fight with you?"

"Ha, no John, I have enough fighting men to know that one more will make no difference. No, I need you to find something for me, a place in fact? No one knows you are here. If we have spies within our midst, they will not know of you. You can move more freely than any of us. You know this land?" he asks.

"I do," I answer.

"It has not changed much in a hundred years, I assure you, maybe even in a thousand years."

"Then what it is you want of me that is so important?"

"We need a relic, something that will raise terror into our enemy and create a religious fervour amongst our fighting force, something that they will fight to the death to protect. I want you to find this relic and bring it back to me. And in recompense, I will grant you safe passage back to England. Do we have a deal, friend John?" he states lifting his chained mitten covered hand towards mine. From the deadpan look in his eyes, I knew this was a deal I could not refuse.

I nod, "Where do you want me to go?"

"We found this map on the body that was beside the altar they found you on. It tells of a lost city where there maybe secrets that might help us with the fight ahead. You head south through the desert towards this oasis, then it's a day's ride from there to the city. This map shows the way through the sands to the lost city of Ubar, a city lost until now. The Templars have been searching for this city for a long time, most never return. Legends abound about its beauty and fabled riches...," he pauses, and I can see from his body language that he is holding something back, but perhaps now is not the time to press.

He held out an ancient brown parchment in both hands, "take this and return with something that can be of value to us and I will make good my promise. My men will get you supplies and a camel," he nodded towards the two knights, and one of them turned quickly and paced off. "May God watch over you, my friend," his voice was smooth and the words sincere, but I had the feeling that this deal was rather one sided.

A few hours later I'm leading a straggly camel out of the city, through the throng of humanity and towards the dirt road that led towards Jerusalem. The smells of the food stalls, sweating bodies and city waste was an intoxicating mix that stung my senses. Everything seemed so sharp and fresh, everything I peered at looked crystal clear as if I could see better than I had ever done in my life. And the smell of the camel definitely made me think my sense of smell had increased. Was it that I had been asleep for a hundred years or was I truly feeling a difference?

I wore a plain linen overall to conceal my crusader uniform and a turban to cover my reddish locks. If I hadn't, any local would remember me all too well and it wouldn't be long before word got out and I'd have a horde of the mamluks after me. After a few hours, I reached a small crossroads and took the left fork towards the desert. Very few travellers were on this dirt track, by now, the long line of refugees heading along the coast rather than inland towards the desert. Palm trees adorned the sides of the track in large clumps that clung to the desolate ground, creating tiny pockets of green among the barren scrublands. A few travellers were resting under the palms, the shade scant protection from the rolling, dry heat. In the distance I spot the shifting sands of the desert and realise that by nightfall I might be near its edge. I keep a fastidious check that no one is following me. I shy away from any conversation and keep my eyes from making contact with anyone. By my bulk and size alone, I stood out already. By evening, every bone in my body was aching, so that when I passed a lone cart and topped a rise, I stood in awe at the sight before me. I peered behind at the cart and man that was disappearing into the gloom, then turned again towards the open desert that lay before me like an ocean of sand, stretching to the horizon and beyond. The sun was setting quickly, as it does in the desert and the temperature was dropping rapidly. It is easy to get caught out as the sun drops behind the horizon so quickly, and the stifling heat suddenly turns to an unexpected coldness. A red haze shimmered across the intoxicating sands. I saw sand clouds rolling off the tops of dunes, the sand glimmering in the dying sunlight. As the shadows lengthened so it looked like the dunes were moving, like waves on a stormy day. I took out the map and look at it before the visibility is completely gone, then look again towards the huge expanse of the desert. This seems like a foolhardy adventure, if ever there was one; trying to find a lost city by using a map that could have been drawn by anyone. But Peter de Severy is my commanding officer now, so by rights I have to follow his orders however strange they seem. I did not like the man, there was a hint of madness in his eyes, a look of one who had lost touch with reality and what really matters. I will have to deal with him on my return, if I do return. My past seems as murky as his intentions. I can't remember my childhood, my parents and friends or what made me who I am. I remember being called John on that fateful day of the mission. And now, the people that found me think I am John Godiven, because that is what they thought came out of my parched lips. For now, I will

go with that, until I find out who I truly am. In England someone will know.
I find some concealment off the track, light a fire, eat and drink sparingly and wait for the stars to come out. The map was actually a type of code, using the stars. I will travel in the cool of the night and hope to reach the first point on the map by daylight. I have no idea why the Mamluk at the altar had this map, but I sense that this lost city and what happened to me have some sort of link.

By morning, I'm well into my trek when a sandstorm hits from the south. I see it coming towards me like a rolling and ever-changing wall of sand. It's like some primordial force of nature, a wave of destruction that nothing will stand in the way of. It's odd because I can see it, but I can't hear anything, and the sun is still shining down and cooking me to the bone. There is a stillness to the air, the calm before the storm, and then the elements go mad. I automatically look for some cover, knowing full well there is nothing around me apart from the dunes. The wind arrives first, bringing with it the advance guard of sand that strikes me like I'm being whipped. The camel grunts in alarm so I dismount and lead us to the leeward side of a dune. I try to get the camel to sit but the angle is obviously not to its liking.
I dig myself into the slope, while holding tightly to the scared animal's reins. I sit down, my back tucked in, my head covered and await the arrival of the storm. By now, the wind is howling, and visibility has dropped to a few feet at the most. I can't hear a thing over the noise, even the baying terror of the camel is blocked out. It's the screeching and whistling of the wind that is so deafening, it seems to attack my hearing so much that my other senses seem to be affected as well. The full force of the storm hits, and I can feel it sweeping over the top of the dune before crashing down on top of me. I tense myself, lean into the slope and shut my eyes. I have covered my face and am breathing through the cloth, my breaths coming thick and fast, the feeling of suffocation almost too much for my already battered senses. I don't know how long I stay tucked into my makeshift hole on the dune, but the storm abated as quickly as it started. I

try to move and realise I am half buried by a mound of sand. I try to wrench myself out and after some effort manage to get myself free, only to realise I had let go of the camel's reins at some point and it was now nowhere to be seen. This was like a death knell, losing your camel in the desert often meant a long lingering death. From the exaltation of surviving the sandstorm to the feeling of losing your camel in only a few moments is almost too much for me to accept. I could head back, I'd been using the stars as a map until the sun rose, then the sun's position as my guide. But looking at the map I knew I must be closer to my destination than where I had started from. And, another thing I don't quit easily, I'm stubborn. I climb to the top of the dune and see an endless wave of sand stretching to the horizon. Somewhere out there is the lost city, and I'll be damned if a mere sandstorm was going to stop me finishing my quest! The sun was high now it must be near noon, with the heat creating shimmering waves to make it look like the horizon was constantly moving. Drinking a little water to wet my dry mouth and sore throat, I headed off into the desert.

Hours later, I collapsed against the base of a dune that looks like the highest mountain in the world. My head spinning, already I've seen things that would disappear with a mere blink of the eye; mirages that put doubts in your mind, as if your eyes were lying to you. At one point, I swore I saw the shining spires of a majestic looking city glistening in the heat, until I wipe my tired and dry eyes to get a better view; and then only the sweeping sands of eternity met my stare. I shake my head to clear my mind and look again, but nothing is there. I think perhaps I'll rest till nightfall and then start again, but with the pain in my head and no cover from the sun, I feel like I have to move on, I must keep moving. I somehow pick up the stamina to climb to the very top of the dune and collapse in a heap; my body wracked with aches. I must keep moving, don't stop, I tell myself. Another part of me says, just a minute's rest. I raise the bottle to my lips and drink one last drop of water; the goat skin is empty. The sand is incredibly hot on my bare hands, almost burning my skin, but I'm beyond caring now. Just a moments rest, part of me thinks again, as my head drops onto the water skin, looking for the sanctuary of sleep.

I'm not sure how long I slept but my eyes open with a start, as if some inner demon was telling me to wake up, the hardened crust around the edges of my eyes stuck together as I try to blink and see. Something glistens in the distance, rising above the sands on a shimmering river of illusion. Another trick of the senses, another mirage sent to tease my already failing mind. I rise up on leaden legs, every sinew in my body screaming at me to stop, to lie down and rest. But to rest now means only one thing, certain doom; cooked alive in the desert, a meal for the lizards, my bones burnt white by the harsh sands and relentless heat. My arms strain against the shifting sands as I try to rise. I shout at myself to get up and reach the crest of the dune, because, surely, from there, I would see my salvation. I was so disorientated that I then realised I had already got to the top of the dune and was now on the other side about to head back up in the same direction like a lost sheep. How many days now I had been out here, I do not know? The camel is gone, wandered off in the sandstorm, hopefully to safety, leaving me here, lost and about to die in this god forsaken endless sea of nothingness. The sandstorm had come out of nowhere, as if conjured up by some jinn of the desert to thwart my attempt to reach the lost city. All this rushes through my mind as I crawl back to the top of the dune for a better view of the mirage. But is it a mirage? It's still there, a picture of beauty, shimmering in the distance. The outline of the palm trees are clearly visible, their green tops sparkling in complete contrast to the yellow blandness of the sands. I glimpse the reflection of water beneath the trees. Water, drinking water. I started forward, too hastily for my tired legs. I stumble and fall, then I roll back down the dune. I get up with a start, desperate to see the oasis, thinking that it might go if I don't keep my eyes on it. But it's still there, thank the Lord. Adrenalin gets me to my feet as if it were a strongman lifting me up, forcing me to keep going, my guardian angel. I stumble forward through the sands on legs that feel like they are not my own. At one point the vision seems to disappear, and I cry out to God for his help. I then realise I have dropped into a trough between two dunes, and I was rising again, even as I called out for salvation. I reach the top and stare down in amazement at what lay before me. I sink to my knees and thank the Lord for not giving up on me.

A large pool of water stretched before my eager gaze, surrounded by shrubs, cacti and palm trees. The sun reflected off the water like a mirror as no ripple touched its clear smooth surface. At the furthest point from me, a ruined building, built of stone, sat next to the water, confirming that I was not the first human to come this way. Nothing moved within the oasis, it was as if it was a mirage held there to taunt wary travellers to their doom only to disappear when they approach. But I know this is real, I can sense it, I can smell the scent of water on the hot breeze. My eyes check for any movement in the shadows of the palms, but I see and sense nothing. I pace forward and as I enter the line of palms my armlet starts to throb and pulse. I look down at it in amazement and fear. What was happening? The armlet seems to be alive; it begins to beat and thrum like it has its own heart. Instinctively, I try to wrestle it off, but it is stuck to my arm, held fast by some force that had put it there.

I reach the edge of the pool, my shuffling feet kicking sand into the water, causing tiny ripples to stretch out until they disappear and settle to nothing. It is the most beautiful sight I have ever seen. A few steps more and I sink to my knees and drop my head into the pool, feeling its cool waters washing over me. I cup my hands and drink deep, feeling the lifeblood of the water reviving my senses. I drink so much my body aches, but I still drink more; it is like an addiction. I cry out in joy and splash my hands for I had felt I was surely a dead man. The water was clear, the pool so deep I couldn't see into its shadowy depths. All I could see was my smiling face within the ripples I was making. I notice an open area between the palms that led to the water's edge, which I assume must be where travellers fill their water skins and lead their camels to drink. The small stone building sat just to the left of this, tucked into the water's edge, with a row of palms behind it.

Before I had time to explore, the water exploded into a frenzy of activity as if something huge has erupted out of its dark depths. Before I even have time to reach for my sword, a thick wet band wraps itself around me, pinning one arm to my body, pinching my legs together and forcing the breath from my lungs. I feel like I am being crushed to death. I look on in horror as two tiny eyes appear above the surface, about ten feet apart. A thin grey looking protrusion, between the two eyes, is just visible above the churning waters. The thing starts to rise out of the pool, its huge scaly bulk clearly visible. It looks like a giant frog. I was transfixed, held tight, as it rises out of the water. Its head becomes visible first, it's protruding eyes, now clear of the water, look so human. I see a massive gaping mouth with no sign of teeth and realise that its huge tongue was the thing that held me tight. It pulled itself out on four webbed feet, but it was its extra appendages just below its rotund face that astounded me. It has two human looking arms, which make me look on in horror. It reaches the shore and starts to retract its great tongue, pulling me towards its gaping jaws. I suddenly come to my senses and with my free hand try to unwrap the slavering tongue off me. I can't get a grip on its coarse fleshy surface, my fingers digging into its slimy skin like a thick sponge giving no purchase. My feet are pulled from under me, and I land into the shallow water at the edge, with a splash. The dark open mouth rises above my prone body, the smell of death and decay reaching my already battered senses. I glimpse the white of bones within its mouth, human bones and animal bones. I saw glinting specs of what must be some sort of metal and realise that this mouth was a graveyard to the dead, and a fast route to the afterlife. I pull my free arm out of the water and strike the thing in its face in a last-ditch attempt to stop the inevitable. As my armlet strikes the beast, it creates an amazing reaction. I hear the thing squeal and scream in agony, its tongue uncoiling and setting me free in a single moment. I rise to my feet in the shallows and look at my armlet in astonishment. What was this thing? I pull my sword out with my other hand, shaking the pins and needles out of my body and take a deep breath of fresh air.

The beast didn't move, it sat there, its mouth tightly shut; its tiny protruding eyes on the side of its great head, looking at me almost pleadingly.

"I don't know what manner of beast you are, but I'm sure you've killed and eaten many a passing traveller, but no longer, today you will roast in hell."

I lift my sword, my anger granting me the courage to attack this monstrosity without a thought for my own safety. I step forward, sinking to my knees in the pool when I hear a voice that I realise is in my head.

"At last, someone has come who has the tools to end my miserable existence. Please, stranger, I beg of you, do not hold your hand. Kill me now and let me rest."

"What?" I say aloud.

"Strike me down, end my eternal suffering."

"What are you?" I ask pausing, my arm held aloft, sword in hand.

The creature's eyes stare at me and I sense no more hostility coming from the beast, rather a longing for restful oblivion. I lower my sword.

"I am you and something more, created as a mockery of life by those that can, nothing more, nothing less. Left here to live for all eternity in seclusion, surviving on the odd traveller or camel that strayed too close. Now at last, you have come to end my torment."

"I wasn't sent here to end your torment, I came seeking the lost city of Ubar. Do you know of this place?"

"If you seek the eternal city, then go no further, turn back; only death, madness and misery await all who enter."

"Great, that sounds like fun!"

"Do not mock me, until you have been there and seen the monstrosities they have made. Then you will understand. But take my word for it, do not venture inside, do not go to that cursed place. It will be the death of you."

"How long have you been here?" my curiosity peaked. Talking to a giant frog, who spoke back to me in my mind was certainly something I hadn't expected to happen today, or any other day. Perhaps I have been lying out there in the sand somewhere, my mind casting images before my last fateful journey.

"Since the beginning of Earth, before the dawn of man and what you call civilisation. How do I know this? Because every victim I consume, I consume their thoughts and memories. I've seen your race rise from the mire to conquer the planet, never knowing you were just an experiment."

"I don't understand half of what you are saying creature, but I will not take your life now, it is not what I do."

"But you must," the voice said with a tinge of fear and pleading, "you alone have the tools to end my suffering."

"I will not." I said, taking a step backwards.

"If I tell you where the eternal city is will you help me?"

"No, creature I will not," I said loudly, turning my back and stepping out of the water. A swishing sound comes from behind me, and the tongue wraps itself around my legs again, pulling me off my feet and thumping me into the sand. I choke as I get a mouthful of sand. Cursing I twist my body to strike the tongue with my sword, when I am yanked into its mouth and the mouth shuts closed behind me, casting me into darkness. My feet touch the ridged slippery base of its mouth, I find purchase and swing my sword to where I guess the tongue is. The smell in the mouth reeks of death and I gag, to stop myself from being sick. I feel the blade cut deep, slicing through the tongue with ease. Then, much to my relief, I feel the tongue loosen and drop to the base of the mouth. I feel a gush of blood strike me, drenching me in its thick sickly ochre. I nearly lose my footing, but I find my balance with one hand touching the ridged roof of the creature's mouth. The creature screams and I now realise that the first screams were in my head.

"Again," it says in almost unholy ecstasy. I bend forward towards the back of the mouth, slip on some bones, hearing the clink of metal moving beneath my feet in the darkness. I strike upwards and towards where I think the brain is and I hear a faint sigh of relief and a distant "Thank you," sail across my senses, and then the creature drops into the water and opens its mouth with its last dying breath. The light from outside shines in like a torch in the dungeon and I glimpse a small golden urn, barely a couple of inches long, standing in a thin covering of water and blood, beneath my feet. I pick it up and clamber out of the beast's mouth onto the sand. I'm covered from head to toe in green slime and blood. I turn to look back at the creature, but all I see is one tiny glimpse of a closed eye as it sinks back beneath the surface, dropping deeper and deeper into the depths as if being drawn towards the gates of hell. And then all is silent, the pool returns to its normal solitude, the ripples disperse, and I let out a deep sigh of relief that I am, once again, still alive.

"Thanks for that," a voice says from behind me, which makes me nearly jump out of my skin in fright. I dropped the urn and my sword on the sand in front of me. Standing on top of the urn is a thin grey monkey with a white fur covered round face. It balances on the urn on one leg using it like a stalk, the other leg bent at the knee, the foot resting on the supporting leg. The monkey stood about a foot and a half tall, it's head almost out of proportion to its body. A thin hair covered tail was also touching the urn giving it extra leverage. The monkey smiled showing a broad grin that covered most of its lower face. Large round brown eyes stared at me with a hint of happiness crossed with fear.

"Was that you talking to me in my head?" I ask him. Could this day get any crazier?

"No, that was the long suffering Manamet. He is finally at rest, thanks to you."

"I just killed him." I said in disgust.

"There is that, but you do not realise how long he has sought the embrace of death. Even those who have lived for an eternity, tire of life. The finality of death can be as alluring as life itself."

"How can I understand you? And you me?"

"Because language is universal if you know how to use it."

"Well, that explains everything! So, what are you?"

"I am a Jinn, a genie and I am now beholden to your every command until you free me from my bond upon your final wish."

"Wish! Don't tell me, you grant wishes that come true?" I say in disbelief. In the back of my mind, I did realise he has just appeared out of a small urn that had been trapped in a giant frog creature for centuries, so I think there could be some truth in his words, so I decide to give him some slack!

"Only three and then I'm free," the Jinn said with a lilting poetic high-pitched voice.

"Prove it?"

"Then make a wish, but choose wisely, you only have three, do not waste them."

"How? What do I have to say or do?"

"Just say my name which is Tu, 'I wish'... and that is it. Your wish will come true." Tu said holding his tiny arms out, fleshy human-like palms facing the sky, a big grin on his little face.

"Really!" I reply wearily, feeling exhausted and in need of rest. The march to the oasis has taken its toll, the adrenaline rush of the fight has dropped, leaving my body in agony. My body feels like my bones are made of stone, my limbs stiff as a board with the strain of the trek. All I need is a good night's sleep, a wash and a clean shave...

"Ok, Tu, I wish that I would never have to shave again, as long as I live, it's a waste of time and I hate the thought of a knife around my neck for some reason."

Tu looks at me incredulously. "That is all you wish for?"

"Yes, yes," I reply impatiently.

"As you wish. Then your wish is granted."

I tense my body, waiting for something to happen. There is no sudden flash of light or any change whatsoever. Everything is just as it was. I look at Tu who is still balancing on the urn, one paw up, leaning on the leg that is holding him upright.

"What do you expect to happen?" he says to me, "The heavens to open, a great clap of thunder and a blinding light to strike you," he pauses. "It doesn't work like that," he adds with a wry smile, "it's a bit more subtle than that. And by the way, in all the centuries that I have granted wishes, that is probably the worst wish I have ever granted," he says with another winning smile.

"How do I know it worked?" I say, ignoring his retort.

"Well as it was a wish, that will take time; because it was a stupid wish, then you will have to be patient to find out now, won't you?"

I stare at the monkey not knowing what to say. I know it was a pretty stupid wish, one that I know I could have used more wisely.

"I don't know if you are going to be the most annoying companion or the most helpful, but I am guessing on the former at the moment," I say with a deep sigh. "Now, night is coming, I need to wash this slime off me and get some sleep. In the morning I'm going to decide if I turn back or try to find my way to the Eternal city."

"The Eternal city!" Tu says, bringing his hands together, "You are nearly there, it is just over the dunes... but you don't want to go there," he puts in quietly, "it is an evil place."

"So I have been told!" I exclaimed, "Now is there any chance, you can shut up and keep out of my way, while I clean up." Even before I've finished the sen-

tence, the tiny creature has twirled in a blur of motion, and I watched in amazement as the body seemed to dissolve into a funnel of smoke then shoots into the opening upon the urn and disappears. The tiny lid clanged shut with a musical note and then all is silent. I stare at the urn for a few moments longer and smirk.
"Well, that worked, perhaps I can get some rest now." I said to myself.
"I heard that," a tiny voice echoed from within the urn.
"God give me the strength to carry on!" I say, looking to the heavens.
"I heard that too."
I ignore Tu, knowing that it will probably not be the only time this will happen, and look back to the water which is like a mill pond again. Was the frog the only creature in those dark depths? It felt that way, now it felt safe, the creature or whatever it was, was dead. Aching all over, I climb into the water, the feeling so comforting the water so refreshing. I strip my clothes off, cleaning them as I do and throwing them onto the nearest bush to dry. The sun is beginning to drop rapidly now, so by the time I'm out and dressed again the sun is so low, it's peeking through the palm leaves, casting shadows across the sand. I make my way to the stone building and peer inside. It's a single-storey building, but there's nothing inside to give me a clue to what it was used for. One end is open to the elements, which means the inside is covered in a mountain of sand that rises to the roof at the back of the building. The place looks ancient, the stone has been sandblasted over the years. On one wall I see a line of large metal hooks, with rust covered chains hanging from them, their ends disappearing into the sand. I wonder what I might find if I dig into the sand. A coldness creeps over me when I think of what I may find, it's a very uneasy feeling that makes me think I don't want to sleep in here.
I find some shelter beneath the palms, light a fire and eat a little of what food I have left. The night is cold but I'm feeling alive again, almost as if I've had a second chance, or in my case, a third chance after what seemed to have happened in Acre.
"Tu?" I ask looking at the urn, "you can come out now. Is that what I have to say?"
"Just 'Tu' will do." Tu says appearing in a swirl of wind on top of the urn.

"Do you always stand on top of that thing?"

"No," says Tu, hopping off and sitting beside me, "the sand would have been too hot on my paws earlier in the day."

"I have some questions?"

"Oh good, I love questions." Tu replies clapping his hands together like he's part of a travelling side show.

"I need to get to the Eternal city, can you lead me there?"

"Of course, but I'd rather not. If you die and you haven't taken your third wish, I could be trapped in there forever."

"Do you actually exist in that urn?" I ask with a frown.

"That is a very good question, almost makes up for your poor first wish but that will take some doing," he replies with one of his cheeky grins.

"So, where do you go when you are not beholden to someone?" I press.

"All I can explain it like is that I am aware I'm inside, I feel no physical body and I'm not aware of time as you are. Today could be yesterday as easily as it could be a thousand years from now," he stops, lifting his face to the sky, his eyes wide and searching, "My, you humans have changed over the years! Humanity is on the cusp of a great new revolution, one where the world will be so different, you will think you are on another world entirely," he looks back at me now, his gleaming brown eyes reflecting the flames from the fire. "But that will happen sometime in the future, it is the present that preoccupies us now."

"What would happen to you if I die before my final wish?"

"I would be stuck forever in limbo without any chance of rescue. Even though I don't realise the passage of time, I know I am trapped inside, confined within the limbo of nonexistence. There are hundreds of us trapped out there inside some lamp or urn, waiting till the end of time to be set free. We are everywhere, here we are called Jinn, in some places Djinn and others as a Genie."

"That's a horrible way to live."

"You could say that."

"How do you know this happens?"

"As soon as you released me, I see all that has gone before. I can sense where my trapped brethren are," Tu pauses looking sombrely towards the stars, "they are

THE CALLING

many. To you humans, it will look like any old lamp or urn, to us it is a prison. You would never know there is a trapped soul within. Coming out like this is the only thing we have to look forward to, and even that has its consequences if you die. That's why we make the most of it!" Tu said with another big smile, his mood brightening quickly.

"Then we must make sure that never happens? I don't particularly want to die either. And do you always appear as a monkey?"

"No, we appear in whatever form is suitable to the person who has released us." I look at Tu in surprise, "I don't understand, so why a monkey for me?"

"That's one answer, even I don't know, it is a mystery to me. Perhaps in this form I will be helpful for you in your quest ahead."

"Perhaps, so how much do you know of the City of Ubar? Have you been there?"

"I haven't been there, but I know that it is the 'first' city, so ancient that to most it is just a myth, a legend, much sought after for its riches. But the allure of wealth always has its consequences."

"What do you mean by that?"

"Only that all who have sought the city have never returned. Would you mind making your next two wishes before you head to the city, I really don't want to spend all eternity stuck in there please?"

"No, I will not, I need your guidance to get there first, then I might need those wishes to help me."

"That is a good point, but no good if you die in the meantime." Tu replies.

"Enough," I say out loud, making the monkey shrink back towards the urn. "Tomorrow, we are going to find Ubar, whether you like it or not. Now, I need to get some rest, so you do whatever you do, but I'm going to sleep."

"In that case, I will watch over you, I am in no need of sleep," Tu says, his eyes gleaming in the firelight.

"Thank you, I feel safer already."

"That is unkind!"

"Apologies, it's called sarcasm. And thank you, I appreciate your offer," putting my head down and turning to look at the stars.

253

Morning came with a gentle tug on my sleeve. My eyes open to see Tu, standing there with a handful of dates in one outstretched paw. He smiles when he sees my eyes open.

"You snore," he remarks.

"Thank you for that observation."

"It's loud enough to wake the dead. Even those ghosts from the building heard you. I had to chase them off a couple of times."

"What? Ghosts. What ghosts?"

"I believe you should be able to see them as well," he whispers, a frown forming on his face.

"How am I supposed to see something that doesn't even… exist?" I ask as my gaze shifts to the stone building. This time I see movement there, people are moving about in a manner that almost made them look as if they were blind. About a dozen or so people, no, not people, ghosts! I know they are ghosts because I can see through them! They are shuffling around beside the edge of the water as if they are lost sheep. Some of the bodies look misshapen and deformed, some are without limbs and there was one that looked like two bodies have been joined together. One even seems to have two heads. My mouth drops open, my eyes opening wide.

"I can see ghosts," I stammer out, "in daylight too!"

"Well of course you can, didn't you know that?" Tu replies looking at me, "No, of course, you didn't. It's no big deal they are mostly harmless, just lost souls looking for someone to lead them to the afterlife. They are stuck, waiting for someone to release them to complete their journey."

I close my mouth with a grinding of teeth and rise.

"It would be best to leave them, they won't bother us, they are not a pretty sight to behold."

"They are already dead, and are bound not to look very nice!"

"Precisely."

I look once more at the ghosts and think about Tu's words. "Very well, this mystery will have to wait for another time. We will talk further on this, Tu."

"As you wish, my friend." Tu says handing me the dates.

A short while later we are on our way. Tu sits on my shoulder, his tail, wrapped around my neck for balance. I had checked the map by the stars last night and had a good idea which direction to take when we set off. All the goatskins I carried were full of water and we had a fresh supply of dates, so we were well stocked for our journey. I still carried some dried beef and some biscuits, but they were nearly gone. The sun was up, and it is a blisteringly hot morning. Everything shimmers in the early morning heat making the sand look as if it was moving, right up until the point you stepped foot on it. Tu's urn was tucked in under my shirt in a concealed pocket that was normally used for a hidden knife.

"If you fall off, don't strangle me!" I say to Tu.

Tu laughs, "You know for someone that made the worst wish in the world that is very observant. Perhaps there is some intelligence in there somewhere," Tu says, tapping my head with his paw.

"Oi!" I say, a little hurt.

"Just testing to see if it's hollow."

Morning turned to afternoon, and still no sight of Ubar. Only the rolling dunes greeted our eager stares. Sweat continually trickled into my eyes, stinging me with its salty contents, making me blink and cry out in annoyance.

"You know, you never asked my name?" I said to Tu as we reached the top of yet another dune. The top of this dune was flat and seems to go on for miles so, thankfully, I could walk for a while without the stress of going downhill and then climbing again. The going was still incredibly tough as every step sunk into the sand, my legs ached with the strain, but I felt we must be close now, so we ploughed on.

"I already know your name and where you come from, you are John..."

"What is that?" I say interrupting him, my gaze picking out some movement ahead. "Is that a sandstorm or whirlwind?"

"I don't know, it looks like a small whirlwind but there are lots of them, see."

More were appearing as we looked. They appeared like upside-down pyramids of swirling sand. There must have been at least twenty in all, but it was hard to count because they keep crossing over each other's paths as they picked up speed. From our distance, I could make out a dark form within each moving whirlwind.

"Oh no that's not good, sand devils," Tu says quietly, his tone making me feel that we have just awakened a demon. As we watch, they seem to close formation and head towards us almost as if they had heard us.

"What in hells name are sand devils?"

"They are the protectors of the Eternal city."

"And you decided to tell me this now! And you question my intelligence?" Already they were approaching fast, at a speed as quick as the sandstorm, flying across the sands like twirling marionettes, covering the distance between us in a heartbeat. I could hear them now, skittering across the sand, the noise coming from within the whirlwind like a mini sandstorm, each one magnifying the sound to a crescendo of noise. As they drew close, they spread out to surround us, some passing us, cutting off our retreat. They close to within twenty feet of us and stop, forming a semi circle. Within the swirling sands I see a more solid dark form at its centre, human like in appearance, but somehow different. The arms proportionally too long almost as if they had huge gloves on the end of each hand. I see movement and hear a cracking noise that sends a bolt of fear into my frayed senses. I take a step backwards withdrawing my sword.

"Tu, any ideas?" I shout above the din. Sand is being whipped up about the forms sandblasting us and making it hard to see and speak.

"You could always make a wish?"

"Nice try, but I've wasted one I'm not going to use another one until I'm completely sure."

"They don't look very friendly to me." Tu replies.

"They haven't attacked yet. You said they are the protectors of the city? Then we must be close?"

"Yes, the sand devils have protected the city from the day it was built. Created by the celestials as protection from all who might seek to take the city. I did not think they would still be alive. I apologise for my oversight."

"It's fine as long as we survive this encounter!"

I involuntarily take another step back, and one of the sand devils moves towards me. The form within the swirling sands seems to slide forward out of the centre of the cyclone, staying within the whirlwind but close enough to the edge for me to see it in all its ugly glory. I'm sure the body was humanlike once, but it isn't now. Its skin was red from head to toe. Two white sightless eyes greeted my stare.

The body was covered in a red skin, but as the thing moved, it seemed to concertina like the armoured shell of an armadillo. Just visible behind the form, I glimpsed a huge stinger attached to its back, like the tail of a real scorpion. This twitched and span around as if it had a life of it's own. It was one of the most horrifying sights I have ever seen. Its movements were clear for me to read, no doubting their hostility. There will be no retreat, we were being shepherded forwards. Good, if they lead me to the city, then great, we have a royal escort. But when we want to leave, then that could be a different story entirely. One, I would have to deal with when the time comes. The line of sand devils behind moves forward, pushing us in the direction they want us to go in, the ones on the side move forward in perfect synchronisation, like professional dancers. It was an eerie sight that was giving me a strange feeling. Now I know how lambs feel being led to the slaughter.

"All right, all right, we are coming," I say to the nearest ones but no reply is forthcoming. I sheath my sword, feeling it will be of no use against these demons anyway. As long as we follow them, they are not going to attack. "Tu, it might be best to disappear for a while, I may need you later."

"But..." he starts to say.

"Begone," I tell him quietly, watching as Tu dissolves into the urn hidden in my shirt, which was actually quite a strange feeling.

We climbed to the top of another line of dunes, and suddenly there before us was a great city of shining spires and marbled roofs, all encased within a huge circular outer wall made from white stone, which glinted in the noon day sun as if it were a ring of sparkling diamonds. Above the city wall, I glimpsed circular

Plate: 24

turrets that gleamed in the sunlight, their walls encrusted with sparkling gemstones. An ancient stone inlaid road led through the sands towards a strange looking gate set into the massive white wall. To my horror, bones littered the outside of the city walls in their thousands, some skeletons with ragged bits of clothes attached, others bare and exposed, others of camels and humans closely grouped together. I grimaced at the sight and think that it looks like an entire caravan had been killed on this spot. Yet more skeletons became visible as we approached the city, masses of them. Most half covered by the shifting sands, but others exposed to the elements; a stark warning that thousands had died here over the centuries. Scattered between the skeletons, scorpions skittered about, singing a dance of death with their fiery tails twitching if we got too close. Lizards, like tiny armadillos, shrink away from the scorpions streaking over the sun-bleached bones of the dead like they were stuck to them. Metal swords and armour glinted from within the elephants graveyard of bones: scimitars, giant two-handed broadswords, shields, breastplates and helmets that had fallen to the sands in the final moments before their owners took their last horrifying breaths. I see an old Roman standard, it's golden eagle half covered by the sands, surrounded by a plethora of Roman shields, swords and armour. My God, Tu was right, no one seems to leave this fabled city, well not alive anyway. But all this paled into insignificance when I saw the mass of ghosts floating above the battlefield, swirling around like fish in a pond. There are so many, it is like a cloud blocking out the sun. It's like a swarm of hornets, buzzing around in tight circles, and when they see us approaching, they all turn and shoot towards us, only to stop short when the sand devils close ranks around us. A moment later and they are floating above the battlefield again, barely a few metres from the sands, our group forgotten. I glimpse other ghosts wandering between the skeletons, one coming close enough to call out, "save us," it screams. The ghost wore full Roman armour and still wore a helmet, his face was swollen and blistered, his eyes red and bloodshot. I could see no mortal wound on his body, though his arms looked swollen and red, almost like there was too much blood in his veins. "Save us," he calls pleadingly. "In the name of Mars and Mithras, end our suffering." A sand devil sails towards the ghost who is clawing its way over the bones as if it is still alive. "I'm not afraid of you, you can't kill me twice, you monster."

The sand devil stopped, twirling on the spot in front of the ghost, then shot forward in a blur covering and consuming the Roman. I hear a fateful scream and then the ghost appears again walking through the sand devil, his face a grimace of determination. "You see monsters, you can't kill anything twice," the ghost says as it approaches me. I stumble backwards, shrinking away from the apparition, tripping on some bones and falling to the sand. My hand reaches out for balance and comes to rest on a half-covered sand blasted skull.

Suddenly I am somewhere else. I hear screaming from all about me, the panicked cries of the doomed. I look around, the ranks have broken, my square has dissolved into a mass of screaming and frightened men. Hardened warriors, seasoned fighters of many campaigns swing their swords in the untrained manner of those who had lost all control. Shields fall to the ground forgotten. I see the standard waver and topple before this unseen enemy coming from within the sands. "Hold your line," I shout the order, but it's too late, it's every man for himself. I dodge a sword swing from one of my own men, push the jabbering wreck aside and stand firm to meet my foe. A tumult of swirling sands and flashing pincers shoot out from the sands at me. I parry one pincer but feel the other strike my lead arm. Instantly, I feel the poison start to take effect. I see more of the swirling devils coming towards me, through eyes that are already starting to see a way to Elysium. I swing my sword in a wide arc, hoping to die as a Roman legionnaire should. As my senses start to dull, I feel the puncture wounds of more devils as they land on top of me and thrust their poisonous barbs in...

And then I'm back to the present. What in God's name happened there, it's like I was reliving the last moments of that Roman legionnaire, right up to his bitter end. I lean over and throw up what little breakfast I had had into the sands. I see a lizard scurry towards it and a scorpion dart in to intercept it, the theatre of life and death shadowing the past, present and probable future.

"What in God's name was that?" I shout out loud.

"I'll explain later," replies a tiny voice from inside my shirt, which makes me jump again. I feel the proximity of the sand devils behind me closing in, forcing me ever onwards.

I'm moved on, pushed on by these devils that lurk within the swirling sand, the killers that I have seen in the vision. I notice that where I had been sick, one sand devil swerves to the side at the last minute, to get out of its path. I shake my head, thinking this strange but think nothing more of it for now. The city is nearly upon me, the towers hidden behind the huge diamond like white marble wall, polished to a smooth sheen. Apart from the main gate no opening, no archers port, nothing showed on its gleaming outer surface. It almost looked like it had been made out of one massive stone, cut, hewn and polished to a shiny finish. What a simple way to stop invading forces, I thought. The only way in and out seems to be the huge metal looking gates that were gradually beginning to open on creaking hinges, as if they had not been used for a very, very long time. As the sun had now passed its zenith, so shadows from the great wall stretched out into the desert towards us. I notice the lead sand devil stop short of the shadows and drop into the sand, disappearing in an instant. More follow, all dropping into the sand as I approach the entrance. I step into the overhanging darkness of the gates, a deep sense of foreboding crossing my already fractured mind. At least I was out of the boiling sun for once. Some sand devils are still behind me, and they draw to a stop, swirling on the spot, waiting for me to enter the city.

The gates are huge, at least fifty feet high and made from some sort of wood inlaid with a metal that looked similar in colour to my sword, shield and armlet. Each gate must be about six feet thick. I could see the intricate detail and the fine engineering skills that had gone into the building of these gates, and was astounded at its ingenuity and strength, far beyond anything I had ever seen before. I had seen the huge siege engines wreak havoc to the city of Acre and thought that this was a set of gates that would take some toppling, the siege engines had met their match. The metal seemed to be plaited across the doors in a crisscross fashion, encasing it in a solid mass of hardened steel that looked impenetrable.

No party greets my stare, no sound comes from inside, it is as silent as a tomb. There is an unearthly eeriness about the silence as if the city itself is holding its breath waiting to come alive when the next traveller passes by or is escorted there! Have the occupants fled, are they in hiding or are they all dead? I see steps leading upwards into semi darkness, huge wide steps almost too high for me to step up easily, as if it s built for taller beings than me.

Instinct makes me draw my sword and pull my shield off my back. The metal is remarkably cool despite being in the sweltering heat all day, as if it could absorb the full heat of the sun and still retain a cool temperature. I look back at the remaining sand devils, who slip into the sands like dolphins slipping beneath the waves, their job done; another lamb led to the slaughterhouse! I hear the cranking as the gates start to close behind me. I tackle the first two steps as the gates boom shut, sending a cloud of dust billowing past: no escape that way. I hear more clanking of what sounds like cogs, and a final clang and then it dawns on me, I'm locked in the largest dungeon in the world, with no idea of a way out.

13

THE LAST WISH

I wait for my eyes to become accustomed to the gloom and realise that despite the fact I'm under cover in a building of some sort, there is light coming from somewhere. I clamber up the steps and stop, panting for breath after the climb. I am in a huge chamber with a white marble floor that has a series of black veins running through. Massive lines of basalt columns stretch into the heights, their tops barely visible against the darkness of the roof. Alcoves with strange apparatuses line the walls. In places, the floor is covered in a thin layer of sand and when I peer closely, I see small circular indentations that although are not footprints, they are a definitely a sign that I'm not the only thing alive in this giant acropolis. The temperature in here is totally different from outside, it's notably cooler. I feel a faint breeze coming from somewhere which is cool and refreshing. Each step I take on the gritty floor echoes through the chamber, making me think that if anyone was unsure as to whether I had entered, they wouldn't be now. I see a line of ornaments sitting upon the floor, spaced out and stretching the whole length of the room, a covering of cloth upon each. I walk to the closest one and reach out, touching this cloth which is as thin and light as silk and as dark as the night. I pull the sheet off the ornament to reveal a huge circular mirror that spins slightly on some sort of podium. I walk further into the chamber keeping my eyes and ears alert for any kind of life; but I see nothing and all I hear is the echoing of my own footsteps. I reach the end to see a line of chairs running along both sides of the columns with a large, raised Dias with three further chairs upon it, set against the back wall, denoting that this could possibly be a throne room. Everything looks too big, as if built for a race of beings larger than humans. The chairs, the dais and steps are all in proportion with the steps outside, everything far too large for the average human, it felt as if I had shrunk! All the seats are smooth, have no markings, and could fit two of me; the three on the dais are even bigger again.

No person sits upon the throne, nothing but empty seats meet my gaze. The place has a smell about it, a pungent but sweet smell of which I am not familiar with and not something I have come across before. A door behind the throne room lies open so I creep towards it keeping my eyes open for any movement, my sword held out, my heartbeat and breathing coming faster with the tension. What forgotten race lived in these marbled halls? Where had they all gone? Were they friendly?

With trepidation, I enter the next room and peer upon a much-changed scene. I see a thin cloud of smoke hanging in the air. The smell is stronger in here, much stronger, I breath in feeling it fill my lungs, the feeling intoxicating and rewarding all in one. Before me is a small antechamber that is in semi darkness. I look around the room and see fine lines of silk hanging from the ceilings and walls. More of the material is draped over divans made from a material and form that looks almost like it had been created by animals rather than humans. I see yellow flowers dotted about the room in pots, their stems moving on a cool breeze. It seems that the floor is mysteriously moving but looking closer I notice the gentle hypnotic movement is actually a fine yellow mist swirling around, concealing the floor beneath a couple of feet of haze. I hear a scraping noise which startles me but somehow doesn't alarm me. I sense some movement within the room. Am I hearing things, is the smoke some sort of drug? I can hear skittering noises coming from all around, but with my blurred vision I can't make anything out clearly. A figure rises lithely from behind the divan, it's form partly obscured by the silk hangings. A dim light emanates from the back of the room casting the silhouette of a human body. My mind swirls with visions, my brain hurting as I strain to see the figure facing me. My eyes sting with the strength of the strong aroma, which is heavier as I walk towards the back of

THE LAST WISH

the antechamber, my legs feeling heavy. I blink, rubbing my eyes, making them sting more. All of a sudden, I feel dizzy and tired, what is happening to me? Again, I see the outline of a figure, the torso, slim and definitely womanly. As I draw even closer, I look into the eyes of one of the most beautiful women I have ever seen. The light glints off her tanned and smooth skin, a tiny slip of silk covering her shapely breasts. I look deeper into her eyes and am lost in a heartbeat. Long black sweeping hair, high cheekbones, a full wide mouth with thick red lips, are all lost on me as I stare at her like a lost puppy. The eyes seem to swirl and change colour, solidify to one colour then change again, swirling around so that I feel my head was spinning in time with the changes. In an instant I have been mesmerised by her beauty.

"Welcome, Traveller," the woman says in a quiet and seductive voice. "You have travelled far and must be in need of rest. Come, lay your tired body here and I will attend to your needs."

I shake my head and close my eyes, feeling her words enticing me forward. Some sixth sense is telling me that something is not right, but my other senses tell me otherwise.

"You must tell me of your journey, the outside world and what is happening. But I am getting ahead of myself. Come," the 'Come' sounded almost a command than a gracious show of care. "Rest your head on my lap and I will relieve you of all your worries." The 'relieve' resonated on my already entrapped mind but I was already lost. I reach the divan and sit down, then stretch out as I feel her cold hands place my head in her lap. I look up again into those eyes and see a galaxy of stars spinning across the cosmos.

"My name is Sheeba, I am the Queen of Ubar and I welcome you," the voice, sensual and seductive. My eye lids droop shut, the weight of them so heavy, nothing in me could stop them closing. In seconds my tired mind succumbed to the rigours of the adventure and the welcoming sleep of exhaustion grips me. I dream of Sheeba laying with me, her lithe form swaying in the ecstasy of lovemaking. I felt tiny pinpricks of delight running across my body, as if a thousand needles were pricking me all at once. I'd once seen an Indian medicine man who had tried to heal someone with a set of pins that he placed on certain parts of

Plate: 25

the man's body. I didn't understand at the time, but this dream feels like this was happening to me. I see her cry out and throw herself around me, her cold arms gripping me in a vice like grip. I see her eyes go wide and her mouth open showing more teeth than I would expect to see. Her face changes when she sees my startled expression, her mouth clamps shut and again I feel the ecstasy of her touch. I drift off into another world where my senses are pushed to new limits of delight, far beyond anything I knew before.

When I woke, I felt like I was still in my dream. Sheeba lay beside me, her naked body covered in the silk material. The mist floats all about us and I reach out, seeing my hand moving through the yellow mist forming swirls and whirlpools. She smiles and looks at me, like a cat playing with a mouse.

"Your mind is strong, your willpower and belief even more so. Tell me of your travels and the outside world, it has been so long since we have had a visitor."

Sitting up, I notice that I am naked, my clothes and equipment resting on the floor beside the divan. I see my body is marked from head to toe with tiny scratches and pinpricks of blood, as if I had run naked through a bramble bush. My mind is still fuzzy, my eyes clouded as if covered in some film that stops me from seeing properly. The intoxicating aroma is all about her, and over me. My eyes lock on hers and again I am a pawn to her every word. As if from a distant dream, I tell Sheeba all about how I came to be here and more stories of the outside world. Then she asks me to dress and follow her.

I watch as she walks in an ungainly fashion towards another door at the back of the room. Part of my mind thinks there is something strange here, but most of me longs to be intoxicated by her beauty. I strain to look away from her eyes to look at her legs, but all I can see is the yellow mist swirling around her.

We enter another room of swirling mists and silk like hangings, a larger room where the strength of the perfume is less strong. Standing in this room are a group of people, a hundred or so strong. They mill about the sides of the room forming a gauntlet for us to walk through. In my dreamlike state I can make out that they are figures, but I can't make out their faces they are just blurs. One thing I can notice is how they move in the same ungainly fashion as the Queen.

"Your story is an interesting one, John of England. Rather than searching and returning with an artefact, you have returned some to their home."

I didn't understand her words completely, but the meaning was patently clear. "Why would you want to continue your life as it is, all the hardships you have been through, all the pain and suffering, when you could stay here with me as your Queen, live a life of harmony and pleasure as my eternal King."

By now, we had entered another room, where the mists had cleared somewhat, and the silk hangings were sparse. The yellow lotus flowers were everywhere, their pungent smell making me sway and almost fall. I reach out towards one of the hangings and it comes away in my hand. I feel a sticky mass of string like webbing stick to my palm, like touching a spider's web, which brings with it a feeling of revulsion at its touch and a moment of clarity that somehow brings me back to my senses. I go to wipe my hands on my clothes when I feel the bulge of the urn beneath my shirt. 'Tu', I think without saying it, I had almost forgotten about him. A quiet voice says, "Resist and see," as if from a league away, but again, clear thought gives my mind an idiom of clarity.

I look again at Sheeba, she is half concealed behind a dais where another set of divans sit all wrapped in the same silk like material, the same material that I had just felt on my hand in the centre of the room.

"What is happening," I blurt out. Something about how she looks, the way she is standing doesn't seem right, and shivers run up my back.

"I say again, relinquish your quest, stay with me and live a life of luxury as my King. You will not regret it, I assure you," the last sentence was said in that same seductive tone, the one that made me her slave before.

"I... I... cannot relinquish an order, my oath is to my own King and country, not to here, and not to you."

"Then, I have no further use for you," Sheeba says callously. I see her pull a lever beside the dais and before I can react, the floor disappears beneath my feet. Instinctively, my arms go wide as I drop into the darkness clutching for anything but only grasping thin air. As I fall, seeing the light from above disappearing, I have time to think that this long a fall will kill me unless I land in deep water. A recollection of people falling from the walls of a besieged city as the walls collapsed around them crosses my frightened mind. I remember the sickening thud and the way the bodies turned to mere shadows of the person they were before. I remember watching with unholy fascination as the blood spread from beneath the unmoving bodies as they lay still amongst the invaders who were threatening to take their homes. Was this to be my fate? The fear of death grips me like an iron hand around my throat, choking me, causing not a word to escape my lips. My heart leaps in my chest as if it wants to escape the ominous outcome. I land with a sickening jolt, my body landing on what feels like solid rock, the air escaping from my lungs as my rib cage collapses and then all is silent; the stillness of death wrapping its eager arms around my broken body.

I wake up a good time later in complete darkness. My eyes flick open, and I take a long gasping breath as if I had just been born. Recollection crosses my jumbled mind. I remember the beautiful Queen, our wonderful union, her eventual betrayal, and then realise I should be dead. The fall should have killed me, so how am I still alive. In the darkness, I lift myself to a sitting position and check for damage. Remarkably, I feel fine. I can't see anything, but I can't feel or sense breaks! How can this be? Had I dreamt this? It felt mighty real at the time. My hands feel across my body, my left hand coming across a bulge which momentarily makes me panic thinking it a protruding bone, but then I recognise the shape of it. Relief kicks in like a shot of adrenaline.

"Tu?"

"Yes, John," the monkey says from the darkness.

"I can't see," I say with a hint of panic.

"You can see, it's just very dark down here and your eyes are clouded over," he replies with a hint of sarcasm.

"You know what I mean," I said with a hint of annoyance.

"It's lucky then, that I have perfect eyesight in the dark," Tu says smugly, "otherwise you would be lost down here forever."

"So, that's why you appeared to me as a monkey, so you could help me out of here." I ask him, posing the question to the voice in the darkness.

"It seems that way," Tu replies quietly.

"Tu, how did I not die from the fall? And why do I feel like I have woken from a deep slumber, as if my mind has somehow been in a dream?"

"I think you will find it is more of a nightmare, when you see things for what they truly are?"

"What do you mean by that?"

"I will explain later. Promise me one thing, if we are going to get out of here don't shut me up in that thing again; when you do, I can't stop your actions. I'm not allowed to intervene until you ask me to."

"OK, OK, so how am I still alive, you know don't you?"

"I do, but we need to move immediately, something is coming along the tunnel to our right and it's not come to say 'hello.'"

I turn my head and listen. I hear a faint shuffling, out in the darkness, an ominous sound of something large moving towards us, something I could not see. It sounds far off but, it is definitely getting closer, a dragging sound followed by some heavy laboured breathing. I reach for my sword, but all I grasp is thin air. The fear of the unknown, the blackness and the shuffling sounds were an unnerving experience. Facing a foe, being able to see it and fight it, was a bad enough experience, but at least you knew what you were up against; but here in this dark dungeon or whatever it was, my assailant was invisible and could strike at any time, and I had no weapon to protect myself.

"A sword wouldn't do any good, anyway," Tu tells me. "We need to move."

I rise to my feet, shaking my head as if ridding myself of the last vestiges of a dark dream. My head felt clear now, my senses somehow tuned to the present; as if over the last few hours, they had been dulled by some unseen force. Of course, the yellow lotus flowers that gave off that pungent sweet smell.

"Had I been drugged?"

"Yes, yes! Time to move remember," Tu implores gripping my leg, which makes me yelp in fright; not knowing it was him at first. My cry reaches our unknown pursuer, and it stops. All is silent for a moment. I hold my breath and then I hear the creature shuffling again, the movements getting faster.

"Lead on, Tu," I say with a hint of fear in my voice.

"Keep moving towards my voice," he instructs, "unless I tell you to stop. The floor is quite even ahead, I can see a staircase leading to a door, we need to reach that. I'll tell you when we reach the stairs. Now move," he orders.

I stumble forward in the darkness, a sighted man as blind as a bat. Tu's voice echoes off the walls, telling me we are in some large underground cavern. The floor is incredibly smooth and feels almost metallic to the touch. There is a smell of dampness in the air, and I can hear running water coming from somewhere ahead.

Every few seconds Tu, says, "This way," repeating it time and time again. As I grow in confidence, so I start to move faster. I sense the creature behind me, the sound of its movements dwindling, as if it can't keep up. I almost wonder what evil monstrosity might be lurking in these Stygian depths. Perhaps it is better that I can't see. We keep moving for some time, in what seems like a straight line, before Tu shouts for me to stop.

"We are at the foot of stairs," Tu tells me.

"Tu, I think I have been blinded, I still can't see a thing, surely, by now, I should be able to see something?"

"That is because you have been seeing through the eyes of the yellow lotus. The poison it generates clouds your mind and vision, it forms a film across your eyes that makes you see things differently. There is a pool ahead, you need to wash the poison from your eyes and get it out of your head before you face Sheeba again. It is safe here for now, I will watch out for you, but be quick."

He leads me forwards and then stops me with a sharp tug on my clothes. I can sense and hear the faint sounds of water in front of me, a plopping that's echoes around the cavern.

"It is deep and clear, it will heal you of your ailments," Tu tells me in a reassuring fashion. "Walk in, immerse yourself, there is nothing to fear. After that, you will be able to see more clearly."

Without hesitation, I step forward, feeling my feet splashing in the shallows. For the second time in as many days, I immerse myself in the waters, feeling the calm warmth of the liquid washing away the grime and poison that had clouded my mind and blinded my eyes. I rub my eyes, blinking beneath the water, my eyes stinging but I immediately start to see some sort of light shining through the darkness.

I rise out of the water like some ancient Titan, feeling better than I had felt for quite a while. I can see now, well slightly. I glimpse a small silent unmoving form sitting at the edge of the water's edge.

"Tu, I can't thank you enough," I say in earnest, "you've saved my life."

"Just protecting my investment," Tu replies. "That stuff that gets in your eyes would eventually blind you, but, fear not, you have not been affected long enough, your sight will return, although you might not wish that later."

Behind him, I can see a winding staircase that seems to go up in segments towards a door set in the wall. The cavern is huge. With my sight partly restored, I can now sense the sheer size of what we were in. Without Tu's help, I could have wandered around down here until I was killed by some unseen monstrosity or died of starvation.

"Thank you, anyway," I say again sincerely.

"You're feeling better," he says cheekily.

I shake myself down and am about to reply, when I hear the shambling sound again. This time I can see something moving out of the darkness towards us. It's large bulk rises many feet into the air, the thing's form wider than a baby elephant. The monstrosity moves like a giant snail, sliding across the floor, making a squelching sound. I can hear it wheezing from somewhere upon its body, it's true form lost in the darkness. Tu jumps onto my shoulder and whispers for me to make towards the stairs.

"Please, help me." I hear in my mind, and I think, not again. I reach the stairs, my wet clothes, feeling heavy and cumbersome, then turn to face the thing. It stops a few paces away and raises itself up. With my eyes getting more accustomed to the light, I see a mass of moving tentacles, no, not tentacles, human looking arms and legs protruding from some sort of jelly like body. No face was visible and for that I am thankful, because I did not want to look upon what sort of tortured face was hidden within that writhing mass of gelatinous flesh and writhing appendages.

"I'm not going to kill you, if that is what you want?" I say.

"I merely seek revenge on the ones that have done this to me. Let me come with you. Set me free so I might seek my revenge or die trying."

"Why is it everyone is so keen to die around here. This truly is a place of the damned, a true city of the lost, if ever I had seen one," I answer with a modicum of curiosity.

"Please, if you can open that door into the next section, I will go about my own business and not bother you. Just leave the door open, that is all I ask."

I had a lot of questions to ask this creature, many that I needed to know, but one thought came to mind.

"What is your name?" I simply asked. I was fed up not knowing.

"I was once Talloon of the Sailif, until they did this to me." The thing was still holding itself aloft, showing me it's mutilated form. I could still hear it's wheezing breath and see it's moving mass of appendages. I sensed a deep longing to help this thing despite what it looked like.

"Very well," I say, "if we can get through that door, we will leave it open for you, but if you get in my way..."

"Thank you." Talloon replied, interrupting me.

Without another thought, I turn my back on the monster and head up the stairs. The stairs grate beneath my feet as if made from metal and I see that there are tiny gaps between each step. Each section we climb, it levels off onto a small platform then ascends again to the next. The staircase is built into the rock on one side while, the other, a handrail stops one from falling to the depths of the cavern. When I near the top, I glance back and see Talloon pulling himself up using his hands and legs as leverage. Talloon was moving at a pace now, propelling himself up at a speed that even I would have been proud off. He's actually closed the gap on us. Despite his lack of threat towards us, I turned to Tu.

"I hope we can open that door."

"It will be once I've been at work on it," he says, pulling something from out of his hair.

We reach the door and what looked like a tiny doorway from the base of the cavern, now shows itself to be a double set of doors that are slid shut, made from a metal with a crossover join in the middle. No handle greets our stare and I see

Tu looking at it with interest from on top of my shoulder. He hops off, landing nimbly on his feet before approaching the closed door. By now, Talloon is two stair levels down and gaining fast, showing no sign of slowing.

The monkey jumps to a ledge to the left of the doorway, chips away with his little pick at the wall and I watch amazed to see a segment drop off revealing a shining piece of metal with a round red circular dot in the middle. He turns to me and smiles with a wide grin, then proceeds to push on the red circle. A faint whirring of machinery crosses our senses before the doors swing open on there own accord.

"I am not keen on magic, Tu," I say tight lipped, drawing my sword. Over my shoulder I see Talloon reaching the same level as us. I grab Tu and without hesitation, walk into the opened doorway. Immediately, the doors begin to close behind us. I turn and reach out with both hands to stop the doors just as pairs of arms reach in and catch the door frame, stopping it in motion. Talloon's body jams it's way into the opening forcing itself through by sheer power of its bulk. My god, what an abomination, this creature was. I could smell its stench from living unclean in the darkness, a human smell of the unclean, one that is different from any other animal on the planet. I turn back to see where we are going when I see ahead of us a corridor between two rooms. On either side are walls made of clear stone, which feel as hard as stone but are transparent to see through. What trickery has this place to create see through walls that are as solid as any stone-built ones. But it's what's on the other side of the corridor that catches my breath.

To our left, as we walk along the corridor, is a massive room full of red flowers. The room is lit by some light source in the high roof that casts an eerie warm glow over the sea of red. Pipes run along the edge of the ceiling with tiny, perforated holes running along them. The plants stand nearly as tall as me and have thick black vein like stems. The flowers seemed to sway as if blown by some unseen wind. I notice that as we move, so the closest ones bend and move towards us but are stopped by the clear walls. It is as if they are alive and aware of our presence, almost as if they could up their roots and march towards our position.

The swaying movement is almost hypnotic, it is like watching a rolling sea on a stormy day. Above their heads, hanging from the ceiling, are metal cages held there by great iron chains. The bottoms' of every cage are open, hanging down, all except one at the end, which still holds a silent form within. At first, I think it is a skeleton, but a faint movement tells me it's alive.

I walk further down the corridor and draw level with the cage and look up into the haunted eyes of suffering. A human form rests against the metal cage. Even from this distance, I can see he would stand at least eight foot tall. He is all skin and bones now, his once white clothes ragged and dirty. His wrinkled face has the look of one who has lost his wits a long, long time ago. Froth drips from his half-opened mouth. One eye is open looking at me curiously, the other blank and staring into space. I notice that below his cage, the red flowers are more numerous. He starts to speak and as he does so the flowers start to move.

Despite the wall, I hear his voice as if he were standing next to me. It echoes around the hallway as if it were coming from all around us.

"More test subjects, good, good, send them in. Come, come, don't be afraid, nothing to worry about here," it was saying towards us.

"That poor man," I say, "we must help him, get him down from there," I say aloud.

"Do not pity that thing," Talloon's voice echoes in my head, "he is the one who created us, myself, Sheeba, the sand devils and many more... I was one of his assistants once, a helper, if you like. I questioned his judgement and for that went from creator's assistant to patient in one quick move." Talloon paused. "That was so long ago." Out of the corner of my eye, I see his huge form shift across the corridor to stare in on the wretch in the cage. "It seems that the prisoners have taken over the asylum," he says, "Sheeba was always the most devious, the one to watch, she was always looking for a way to escape. It seems she got her wish. It looks like the tables have been turned, the inmates are running the place now."

'Wish', I think, I still have two wishes left. My heart beats fast as I decide what I can do, but I must hold back until I am sure. I didn't understand a lot of the stuff that Talloon was saying but I got the idea. I forget the man and turn to look into the opposite room. The room is in semi darkness lit by some sort of light source that runs along the tops of the walls. I walk up to what I think is one of the side walls, misjudging it and very nearly banging my nose on the clear solid material, my arm just touching it in time. Is this more magic? I take a step back as I look within, The room is a mass of cobwebs and white eggs with tiny forms moving inside. The eggs are clustered around an area where it looks like some sort of throne has been made from thick black webs. I'd had enough of this place; it gave me an uncomfortable feeling as if we shouldn't be here witnessing these creations.

"Tu, any idea how we can get out of here?"

"We need to get past Sheeba and out of the city. And we need to get past the sand devils again," he says with a heavy heart. "You are going to die here and then leave me here until the end of time, trapped forever."

"Tu, if you say that one more time, I might just wish that upon you." I reply angrily, regretting my comment as soon as I said it.

"I can help you," Talloon says in my head.

I turn to face Talloon, trying to keep my eyes on the monstrous creature, even though my mind tells me to avert my gaze. Sorrow grips my heart at what this thing had been through.

"There are a series of hidden corridors from which we used to observe the patients without them knowing. They are all sealed from the power of the yellow lotus. To escape from here you can take these tunnels to the throne room. I can show you how to open the gates...and then it's up to you from there..."

"How will we get past the sand devils without being seen?"

"Tu, I have a plan for that, we just need to get out first. Let's go," I say moving forward along the corridor.

"I ask of you one more favour," Talloon asks.

My body stops abruptly, and I feel Tu's tail tighten a little to keep his balance.

"But first you must see Sheeba for what she truly is," he says.

Talloon leads the way, his giant bulk only just fitting through the openings as we head deeper into the labyrinth of the city. At one stage, we enter a room full of discarded armour and there sitting atop a pile is my sword and shield. I eagerly pick them up and despite the fact that they are new to me, I'm pleased to see them. I feel better with them on my person, as if they are more than just a sword and shield. We move on, reaching a long hallway that lies in darkness. Talloon approaches a segment of wall and pushes a stone that reveals a hidden entrance. "We must be quiet now," he whispers. "We are near the queen's lair," The way he said, 'lair,' sent an icy chill down my spine. "Although we can see her clearly, she will not be able to see us. Do not be alarmed, she can not see us, remember." We enter the opening and I walk behind Talloon as he shuffles forward across a solid metallic floor that has a soft lining running along its middle. On one side of us are doorways to large rooms, all unoccupied but containing a litany of grim disclosures. The thick see-through walls disclose so much that I almost wish that they were not clear. In one room, I see a table with a skeleton attached to it, held in place with strange straps. In another, I see cages with skeletons of strange creatures within. Another, I see one skeleton that has two heads attached to its torso, both skulls peering at us, the mouths open in a silent scream of eternal pain. Everything looks like it has been centuries since whatever was happening here stopped. And in every room as we move closer and closer to what Talloon called Sheeba's lair, I see more and more strands of webbing and a fine mist hanging about the rooms, a tint of yellow within its fine clouds.

A sense of dread begins to grip me like a tight suit of armour. We reach another room, and my hand goes to my mouth to stifle a scream, my knees going weak at the same time. Sheeba is barely two paces away from me on the other side of the wall, her back to me, resting in a thick web of netting. I see her eight spider legs kneading the web as she looks out from her throne at her subjects, more spider like creatures! These are full on spiders, huge, each one the size of a man. I turn and slide my back down the wall to sit in a heap at the bottom. Bile forms in my throat and I feel as if I am going to be sick. My God, Sheeba was another monstrosity, a hybrid between a human and a spider. I feel the pricks and remember the marks on my body, and I feel revulsion at the thought that makes me want to scream. The yellow lotus that I had inhaled in her rooms had blinded my senses and portrayed her as an exotic beautiful queen looking for a consort to spend eternity together. My hands were shaking, my mind reeling at the thought of her exquisite touch that had taken me to a different level of ecstasy that I never knew existed.

"Let me tell you about Sheeba," Talloon says from what felt like a long way away. My heart was beating fast, a roaring filled my already over tired brain.

She had made love to me, or it felt like she had. I felt sick to the bone. I wanted to jump back in the waters below and cleanse myself a thousand times over to wash her from existence, but I knew no waters could wash those thoughts away for a long time, if ever.

"Sheeba reigns as the queen here for a hundred years until the reckoning. Near the end of her century, she lays a hundred eggs which when hatched, eat her alive. From this batch only one is a queen, a new Sheeba who has all the knowledge and understanding of her predecessor due to the fact her thoughts and experiences have been consumed and passed on to the next in line. The other ninety-nine remain loyal servants to the queen until they too are consumed by their brothers and sisters when they hatch. And so, the cycle continues every hundred years. The time of the great reckoning is coming for Sheeba, it will happen soon," Talloon informs us. "I ask another favour of you. The flowers you saw, they can walk. If they get out into the world, they will destroy it in a matter of months. If Sheeba continues, sometime soon, she too will escape this city. We can not allow this to happen."

"We?" I ask.

"I can see past your warrior's physique, John, I know you can not leave this place as it is, it is too dangerous to let it remain here. You were the first to break her spell, you have an inner strength within you. I sense greatness in that mind of yours, a warrior's code to do the right thing. Once discovered, this city might bring about the end of the world. This can not happen, and I don't think you want to let this happen either."

I can see past the monster now at the man within, the heart and mind of the man who has suffered so much but still tries to do the right thing. I no longer see him as a monstrosity anymore, it is as if his words had evaporated the way

I look at him, showing me the true soul within. I see he is trying to put right all the wrongs he had helped to cause. I sense a willing quest for redemption within the mind of this person that had once been an instigator of these grim tests on humans.

"Very well." I say. "What do you wish me to do?"

"That's suicide," I say to Talloon, having heard his plan.

"It is what I wish to happen, this place must never be found until all the inhabitants are destroyed. Even then, danger lies with the knowledge within."

I take a deep sigh, thinking how much I wish to get away from this damnable city of the lost and to get back to a world I know better.

"Very well." I reply agreeing to his plans, telling him a little of my plans also. We retread our steps to near where we came in and enter a new room, a small room with lots of strange equipment that was alien to me. I watch as Talloon moves to two pipes that have red circular levers on them. Two hands from two of his many appendages, grip and twist the levers until they can go no further.

"It is time for us to say our farewells," he says in my mind. "I bid you good luck and Godspeed, John. A good and long life awaits you outside."

I look at him, not knowing what to say, my mind again in turmoil and trying to concentrate on what must be done if we are going to succeed and get out alive. In the end, I just say, "Thank you," before he turns and shambles off down the corridor without a backward glance.

We rush back the way we have come, and I stop momentarily beside the chamber where Sheeba is lying. It's an eerie thing to look out at her through this clear wall, knowing that she can not see us, even though we can see her. As if reading my mind, she suddenly stirs, turning and twisting in her web to look in my direction. Tu's tail tightens around my neck, and I can feel him shaking. For a moment I think our eyes meet, but then she swivels again, and the contact is lost. I let out a deep breath and move on quietly, my heart beating so fast that I think that Sheeba would hear it through the walls, if I stayed longer. We reach a door and find the lever that opens into the original throne room.

"My, it's huge," Tu whispers.

"Hurry, Tu, we must do as Talloon instructed."

Quickly and as quietly as we can, we uncover all the concealed mirrors, revealing at least twenty in all. I let out a sigh of relief when we have completed our task. We backtrack to the steps that lead to the gates and head to an alcove tucked in on the first column. A single red button lies tucked in the side of the alcove.

"Ready, Tu?" I say, withdrawing my sword.

"Not really," he says and gulps, his brown eyes wide with fear.

"That's good enough for me," I say, pushing the red button in. Immediately, a screaming sound echoes around the chamber, then an aperture in the roof starts to slide back, revealing the rewarding sight of blue sky. A large beam of light stretches across the room, even as I hear the sound of doors opening further back in the chamber.

I see Sheeba scuttle through and stop dead before the light, seeing me at the same time, her eyes now pinpricks of hatred.

"So you somehow survived and you wish to escape back to your world to complete your quest. How noble of you?" she said in a loud voice that reverberated around the huge room. "Unfortunately," she says, walking towards us through the sunlight, "I can not allow that to happen." Behind us, I heard the clanking of the mechanism that opens the gates. By now the sunlight was stretching all along the giant hallway as the aperture continued to open. Finally, a beam of sunlight hit the first mirror and an amazing effect happens. A beam of light crisscrossed around the room lighting up all the alcoves so that none of the chamber was in darkness. The light shone on all the rest of her brood who were pouring out of the rooms and falling in behind her.

"You silly fool, we are not afraid of the light."

"It's not for you, it's for them, they don't like the dark." I say, nodding my head towards a heaving mass of red flowers that erupted out of the same tunnel we had come from. They moved with a smooth motion, almost sliding across the floor, the tiny roots at their base, like a centipede's legs, propelling them forwards at a pace that was frightening.

I see Sheeba grind to a halt, her legs scraping on the marble floor. She backtracks screaming at us.

"What have you done? You have doomed us all." she screams as I move towards the shadows of the steps. I turn and watch horrified as Sheeba scuttles through the throng of her brood to escape, even as the first plant reaches the front line of the spiders. Pincers thrash and legs pierce through the plants but nothing stops the onslaught as the flowers open to reveal rows of razor like petals that clasp any part of the spider it can get a hold of and rip it to shreds. An awful high-pitched squealing erupts around the chamber as a wave of flowers crash into the spiders and start to eat their way through them. I see Sheeba reach the Dias and race for the open doorway only for a large form to block her way. Talloon appears in all his majesty and literally drops on the screaming form of Sheeba before she can scuttle out of the way. I see the two roll and fight, both struggling for an advantage. I'd seen enough.

"Time to go, Tu," I say, my throat dry.

"Definitely," he says back. I move to the alcove and press the button again then race down the steps, taking them two at a time until we reach the gate and the wonderful sight of the open desert. The gate is already starting to close when we slip though and are free at last. I peer back to check that nothing has followed then let out a deep sigh of relief, we'd done it, now all we had to do was get past our last obstacle!

I slide to a halt within the shadows of the wall even as the sands began to stir and bring forth the protectors of the city. Over a dozen sand devils block our path in a semi circle of swirling sands and clacking mandibles. They stayed just out of reach, basking in the light of the sun, the dark forms visible within the swirling sands of the mini cyclone.

"Out of the frying pan and into the fire," Tu says, gulping, his eyes wide.

"I have never heard that saying," I reply calmly with a smile as if I wasn't alarmed at the closeness to my impending death.

"I hope you know what you are doing," Tu said, from my shoulder. Without

Tu's knowing, I had already informed Talloon of my plans if we escaped and he had quietly nodded his approval.

"Relax," I reply, "I've got a wish to ask of you?"

"I hope it's better than the last one, otherwise…"

"Tu, I wish that it would rain heavily until the city is drowned beneath the moving sands of the desert for all time."

Tu looks at me, realisation dawning in his big bright eyes. "As you wish," he says and nods in approval.

A moment later, this time, lightning crackles above a cloudless sky, thunder roars from nowhere and everywhere. I see the things within the cyclones that were once human, shift within the sands, their forms twisting to find out what was going on. And then I feel a single drop of water hit my hand. I look at it in amazement, watching as the water droplet rolls off my hand and disappear into the sand a moment later. I look up as more rain starts to fall, heavy droplets that splatter onto the sand all about us. I smile and momentarily close my eyes.

The sand devils scream as one, the swirling cyclones of sand disintegrating as the full force of the downpour hits them. In moments, the cyclones have disappeared completely, leaving the pitiful creatures within exposed on the wet sand, blind skeletal humanoids their evil tails fully exposed, their red flesh glistening in the rain. I don't hesitate as I draw my sword and advance on the closest one.

"Tu, take a nap for five minutes, I've got work to do," even as I swing my sword at the nearest form. The creature couldn't see me but could somehow sense it's impending doom. It reached up one pincered hand to block the swing of my sword, but it was to no avail. The sword sliced through the creature, and it fell to the wet sands in two pieces, shedding no blood as if it had been hollow and lifeless from the start, a caricature of life, rather than a living creature. What mysterious powers had kept these things alive for so long, I would never know and did not care either. They could die at the end of my sword, at last, and that was good enough for me.

The others turned towards the sound as a silent scream escaped its dry lips. I just laughed and charged in, my sword singing a merry song of death and destruc-

tion until no creature stood upright, the bodies of the sand devils, lying upon the skeletal remains of so many of their victims in a final harmony of death. Out of the corner of my eye, I glimpsed movement and realised I was looking at a wave of black nothingness flying towards me, a sea of screaming ghosts, released at last from their eternal limbo to travel on to whatever heaven or hell they were destined to go too. The wave swept through the rain, as if it didn't exist, covering a large part of the foreground and it reminded me of the advancing sandstorm from what felt like an eternity ago but was only a few days past. I stood my ground, the hand with my armlet on held out in front of me. Why I did this, I do not know, it was almost as if it had told me to do this. The sea of ghostly figures, thousands of people from different times and eras swept towards me and even as I watched so they started to shimmer and lose their form before turning into tiny pinpricks of light that flashed out of existence like the flickering light of a dying candle. I hear cries of joy, mixed with screams of fear and anguish and then all is silent, apart from the constant downpour as the rain attacks the sands as if on a mission to drown it beneath a sea of water.
"Tu?"
"I'm here," he answers appearing on my shoulder, his tail curling around my neck as comfortably as a scarf on a cold day.
A rumbling stirs my battered senses. I peer behind me to see the whole city shift in the sand. Tower blocks within the great walls sway to and fro. I watch as stonework starts to fall off, revealing shining silver covered columns beneath. The walls themselves seemed to shudder and rock. I watched in awe as cracks appeared along the outer wall. I see giant pieces of the white masonry break off and thunk into the wet sand, only metres from where I am standing.
"I think it is time to move," Tu says quietly.
I clamber forward even as the sand starts to sink beneath my feet. I skip once then jump and land on more solid ground and keep moving until I reach a ridge of sand before turning and looking back through the torrential rain at what my wish was achieving. More masonry fell from the walls, and I realised that the whole thing had been covered in some sort of white smooth alabaster. Again,

another rumbling from within the earth and veinlike tendrils stretched across the walls, increasing in size until a huge column of the wall crashes to the sands, revealing a shining metallic wall beneath. As the city rocks and sways within the churning sand, so whatever had been covering its outer surfaces, starts to break apart and fall off, showing the city for what it was, a metallic circular ship of some sort. Even as I contemplated this so the sands beneath my feet began to move again. I backtrack some more, reaching the top of another dune and watch in open mouthed awe as a huge crater starts to form. At its centre, the circular city is sinking deeper and deeper into the sands. First the metallic walls succumb to the relentless rain and collapsing sands. Within moments, the once gleaming spires begin to drop beneath a lake of quicksand until the last top of the tallest spire sinks below the surface of the rolling dunes, the city disappearing completely from view as if it had never existed. And as quickly as the rain came so it stopped, leaving an eerie silence but a welcome freshness to the air.

"Now, that's what you call a good wish," Tu said with another one of his teethy grins. "You've still got one wish to go," he adds, "I expect a good one now, John, you really surpassed yourself on that last one."

I was listening but not taking it in, I was still watching in awe as the sands began to settle and reform into a solid mass of dunes. Pools of rainwater sank into the depths in moments, leaving the sand, once more undisturbed, hypnotic and timeless.

"I've been thinking about that final wish too, Tu," I said, sheathing my sword.

"And?"

"Tu, I wish that every genie is released from their servitude to grant wishes including all the ones that are trapped within their prisons. I wish to grant them all freedom."

Tu looks at me and I see his body is shaking, his wide eyes, watering. I see him gulp and swallow then speak, "As you wish," then he added a moment later, "my friend."

Even as he says this, I see his form shimmer and change before my eyes then suddenly reform into the same form again. I feel his tail unwind disappear then refasten itself around my neck. I see him looking down at himself, his tiny hands patting his body as if he hadn't known what he was.

"It looks like I am to be a monkey for the rest of my life," he says with a snort, followed by a short laugh. He looks at me then, his eyes staring into mine as if trying to read my mind.

"John, that was the best and kindest wish anyone has ever uttered…and it will truly be the last wish ever granted for all eternity. Thank you, from all of us. I can sense the joy across the whole world with what you have granted, you have truly changed the world today. I am honoured and proud to call you my friend." I nod, suddenly realising what I had done. There would be no more wishes granted ever again. I had used up the last wish! "Thank you, Tu, it is my pleasure. Now, which way is the oasis, we've still got a desert to cross!"

I paused then, looking around the table at Elizabeth and the battleborn, who were completely enrapt in my story.

"So," Staunton says, "how did you get back."

"When we reached the oasis, there, lapping water from the pool, was my camel. I travelled back with Tu as company, taking two days to reach the edge of the desert. Tu and I parted ways then. He hopped onto a cart full of children on the endless wave of humanity that was still leaving Acre. He told me that he didn't like sea voyages and as he knew I would be travelling in one soon, it was best that he got out of Acre before it fell. It seems he could see the future somewhat as well, but I didn't press him on it. In Acre, I met up with a startled looking Peter De Severy and handed him the golden urn, telling him that Ubar was deserted and had already been ransacked of all its valuables. To my delight, he was happy with his artefact and seeing my haunted eyes, he didn't press me for more information. True to his word, he got me a place on one of the last ships that left Acre before the siege began. I remember looking back at the place from the hull of the ship and wondered why so many lives, past and present will be lost on a pile of rubble when there is so much of this earth untouched. And that's how I started my journey back home."

"You know, John, I think you are the best storyteller, I have ever heard," the large German says, "you should write a book, you know?"

"I think it's time to retire, gentlemen," Elizabeth intercedes, "tomorrow is going to be a long day, we are heading off early to Cannock, there is something there I am looking into and I need you all along. We leave at sunup," she says, her eyes locking on mine, a wry smile and show of warmth spreading across her aged face as if she knew something I did not.

I look around the group, the Battleborn, and feel privileged to be here. If this wasn't a family, nothing was. With Elizabeth as the Matriarch and us fellows as her sons. I look at Matthew who is downing his last drop of ale before banging the mug down onto the table and belching out loud.

"Matthew!" A woman's voice utters.

"Sorry, ma'am," he says with a infectious grin. I smile and Elizabeth gives me the stare, so I drop the smile instantly until I see her brown eyes twinkle and smile back. Playing with me like a cat with a mouse, I think.

Staunton follows suit, placing his wine cup on the table, nodding a 'goodnight' to us all, before picking up his trusty bow and heading off. He carries that damn thing everywhere with him, even to the John!

I wait for the rest to leave and sit there for a while longer in contemplation, the only sound, the crackling of the dying fire and the flickering flames of the candles. I was so lucky to have found such a person as Elizabeth, or had she found me, I'd forgotten the detail. With her and the Battleborn, my life now seemed complete. The little fact of not knowing my true identity seemed to pale into insignificance compared to what I had here. It didn't matter who I was, but who I am now. I had a purpose, a family and a roof over my head, what more could a man ask for. I knew it would end sometime as they aged and passed away and I stayed eternally youthful, but that was far in the future. For now, we must live for today, nothing more. And tomorrow, another of Elizabeth's adventures to look forward too.

As I look into the fire, it spits and goes out suddenly, the dying flames disappearing before my startled eyes. I turn my head to peer closely and feel a weight

THE LAST WISH

upon my body stopping me. The fireplace starts to go dark, fading into nothingness, the light it gave off, vanishing completely. My eyes go wide as the room itself starts to fall into shadow as if the whole world was folding into darkness with myself as the focal point. I can feel my heart beating fast as I try to rise and escape this creeping blackness that is swallowing the room. It's reached the table, rolling over everything like a black silent wave of destruction. I can't move, I'm stuck in place as if pinned to my chair. The wave races along the table, moving faster as it closes in on me and I call out once before the darkness engulfs my body and oblivion beckons.

Moments later, my eyes blink open as I feel movement around me. I see a tiny pinprick of light that seems to be coming from above me. Suddenly, I hear the grating of rock and a blinding shaft of light engulfs me. Someone is holding a massive piece or rock which he throws to the side, then turns and leans down towards me, his face instantly recognisable.

"God in heaven!" I say, choking as dust clogs my dry throat, making it probably come out like 'Godiven'!

"Bron!" I croak out in amazement. Even as I speak, I see Susan's face appear at the edge of the opening, her face a mask of relief and happiness.

"John!" she exclaims in delight.

I try to rise but realise I am pinned down by a dozen or so large boulders.

"Stay where you are, my friend, I will have you out in a short while. Do not struggle." Bron says calmly.

I see another familiar face at the opening, a beaming smile on her face. "Yay, John, you're still alive." then she turned away and I heard her continue to say, "See, I told you he'd be alive, Frank," she exclaimed to Arthurs whose face appeared moments later at the opening, a wry smile on his face.

"Never should have doubted you, big man," he says, looking at Ayesha.

"How did you find me?" I ask, looking at Bron. "And how come you are here?"

"You sang our song, we said we would come," the giant said.

"I don't recall calling you, singing any song!" I said, as the giant continues to gently lift boulders from around my form. I see him pause and contemplate an

287

Plate: 26

answer, a wry smile on his ancient face. Then he returns to his task of lifting the huge boulders, one at a time. I was pinned beneath them and couldn't move but I seem to be unharmed other than that. My memory started to return, the helicopter, the device, the explosion.

"The calling can come in many forms," he says as if that explained everything.

"What happened?" I ask.

"You saved everyone with your courageous act," the giant replied, in his matter-of-fact tone, while lifting the last stone out of the way. A huge hand then reaches down to mine, and I reach up and grasp it like it was the hand of God reaching down to take me to heaven. I feel myself being lifted out and picked up.

The light hits me first, followed by a cold wind that sweeps across the moorland. My eyes start to grow accustomed then go wide as I see what was before me.

"God in heaven!" I repeat.

I'm standing on shaky legs in the epicentre of a huge crater, the rim only just visible above the rows and rows of giants that are standing around looking at me. I see areas around the crater where excavation work and digging had taken place which makes me frown at the thought of it. Gorse and heather line the rim as if framing the scene for someone looking from space. Susan, Ayesha, Arthurs, Michaels and the doctor are all standing together walking towards me. Ayesha throws herself into my arms and I call out an 'ouch' when something in my back clicks back into place.

"Welcome back, John," she says planting a kiss on my cheek before removing herself from my person.

"It's good to see you, John," Susan says, putting her arms around me. I feel the usual comforting tingle that denotes she's a witch, and then Arthurs appears by her side, one hand resting on her shoulders. I grimace at the thought of our last encounter then look at his face in amazement. I knew he had fast healing properties, but there was no sign of a black eye or any bruising, at least! That cold chill creeps down my spine and it's nothing to do with the wind or the fact that I've been trapped under tons of rock either.

"How long have you been looking for me?" I ask the group.

Everyone looks at each other as if none were happy to talk.

"How long?" I ask slightly louder.

"It's been five days since you disappeared," Susan answered. She was the group's leader after all.

I let out a sigh of relief. "Thank goodness for that, I thought you were going to say two years or something like that, for a second there!"

"Five days was a long time, we thought we'd lost you. Only Ayesha seemed to think you were alive. It wasn't until yesterday, when the giants turned up and started digging that we found you."

I look behind me at the silent rows of giants.

"Thank you," I say and nod towards them, "It is good to see you again. It has been a long time."

"You are welcome, friend John."

The doctor wraps a thermal blanket over my shoulders, "Good to have you back, mate," he says in his Australian drawl. Michaels raises the spear and nods a welcome in silence. In his other hand he is holding my staff.

I nod again, my mind trying to come to terms with the fact that only minutes before I was back in 1599 recounting a story in the desert to Elizabeth and the Battleborn and now here I am, back in the present, still alive, my healing powers somehow protecting me from the detonation that had formed this huge crater.

"Did everyone come through?" I ask.

"Yes, John, thanks to your quick thinking. Now let's get you back and get some hot food in you, you could do with a wash as well, you stink," Susan says with a smile and wrinkle of her nose.

"Just get me a beer and I'll be all right, the hot food and shower can wait!"

THE END

The Knight Eternal will return in...
Book 2
Untold Tales Of The Knight Eternal
Coming soon...

HARKNESS INSTITUTE

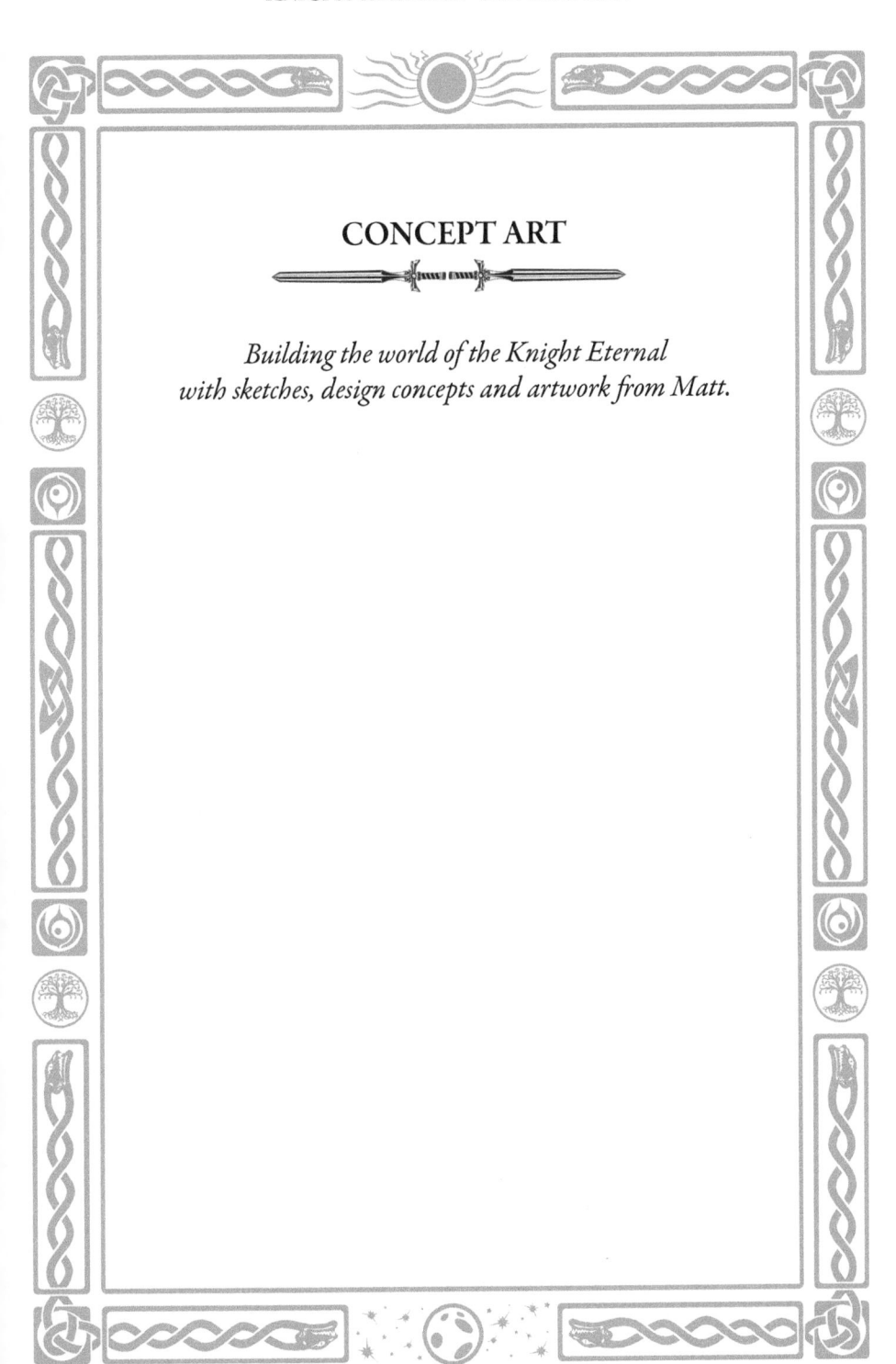

CONCEPT ART

Building the world of the Knight Eternal with sketches, design concepts and artwork from Matt.

CHARACTER DEVELOPMENT:

Original concept art for John, Knight Eternal:
"*This sketch inspired the cover art for the book after we decided we should introduce the reader to John in this first novel as the crusader he was before becoming immortal. The final artwork depicted a scene with the head of the vanquished foe as a reptillian shapeshifter, and not the human we see here.*"

THE GHOSTS:

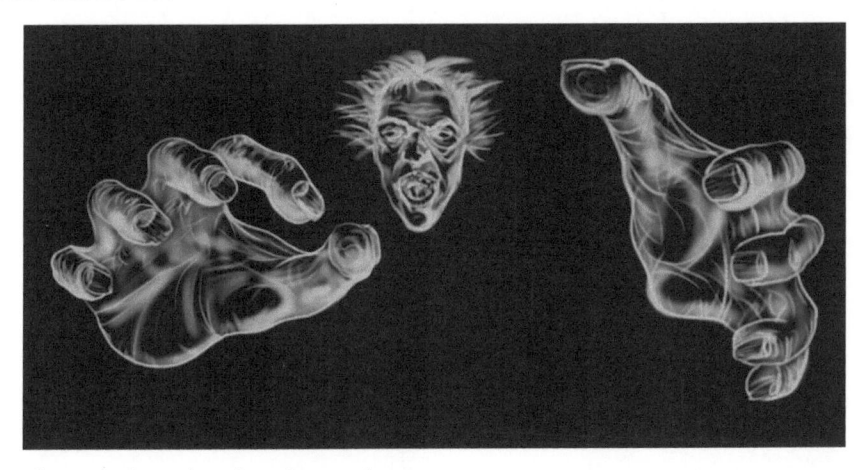

Combining digital and traditional art:
"In order to create convincing transparencies for the ghosts that appear in the book I used Adobe Photoshop to paint the ghosts digitaly before overlaying them on the hand painted background."

KNIGHT ETERNAL - BATTLEBORN

ARTEFACTS & WEAPONS:

"The world of the Knight Eternal revolves around artefacts and weapons from other worlds, all made of alien materials imbued with immense power. Designing these weapons first helped when painting them into scenes, giving them more authenticity."

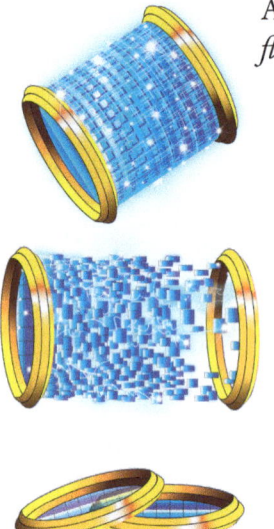

ARMLET: *Made of Slithian pieces that move and flow together to fit the bearer.*

SHIELD: *Made of Slithian, allowing shield to shrink.*

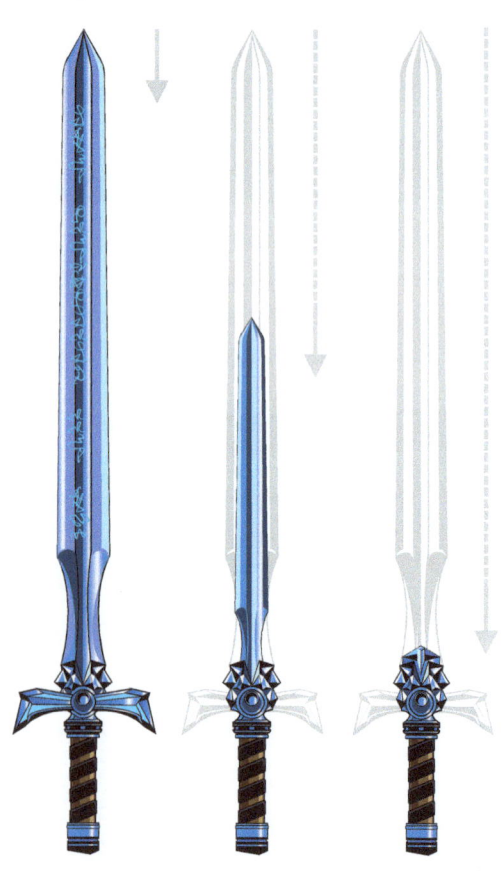

SWORD: *Blade is made of Slithian that shrinks into the hilt. Celestial star script appears on the blade when activated.*

STAFF: *Made from the bone of a 'Drasil', a galactic planet eater; deadly to touch, made safe by wearing an armlet.*

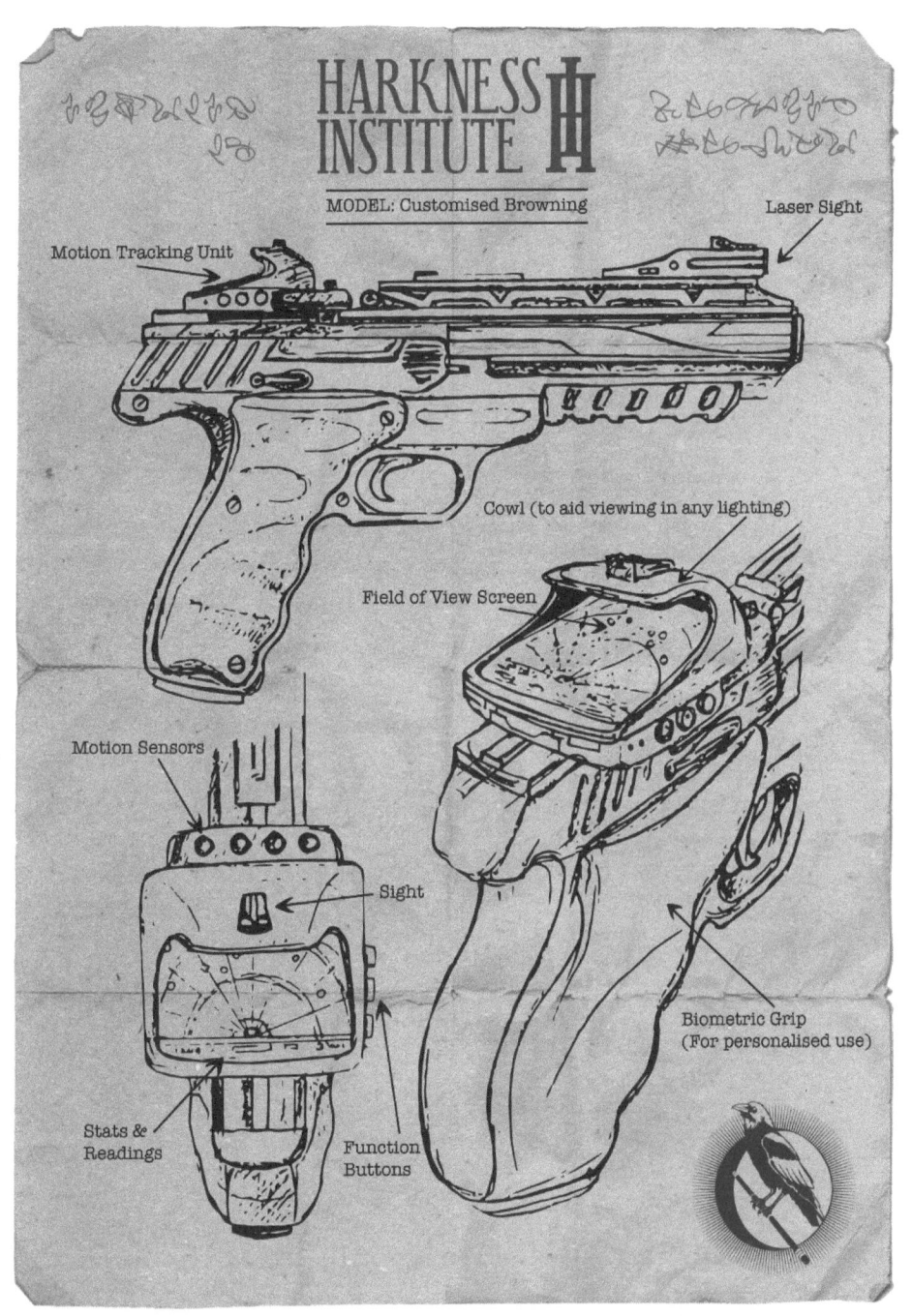

Motion tracker weapon design: This manuscript was found folded into the back of a secret diary belonging to Susan Harkness.

KNIGHT ETERNAL - BATTLEBORN

DEMONS & MONSTERS:
#1 - *Demon King (Vampire)*, #2 - *Sand Devil*, #3 - *Arthurs*, #4 - *Hell Demon*

THE BATTLEBORN

KNIGHT ETERNAL - BATTLEBORN

INDEX OF ILLUSTRATIONS

CHAPTER 1
P.10 ~ Plate 1: The Knight Eternal is discovered, trapped in Acre
P.25 ~ Plate 2: Walking through blood soaked snow to investigate the giant's cairne

CHAPTER 2
P.34 ~ Plate 3: John burries his wife
P.46 ~ Plate 4: The Demon King confronts John

CHAPTER 3
P.58 ~ Plate 5: John and Susan arrive at the Harkness Institute
P.69 ~ Plate 6: Elizabeth Harkness confronts Le Loup

CHAPTER 4
P.86 ~ Plate 7: John is hassled by ghosts in the church
P.94 ~ Plate 8: VISION - King Richard in a future apocalypse

CHAPTER 5
P.101 ~ Plate 9: VISION - Hunting reptilian creatures with motion tracker gun
P.114 ~ Plate 10: A swarm of DRASIL; space dwelling planet eaters

CHAPTER 6
P.132 ~ Plate 11: The Battleborn confront the reptiles in an Egyptian tomb
P.138 ~ Plate 12: VISION - John's staff shows mysterious scenes within

CHAPTER 7
P.148 ~ Plate 13: Reptilian creatures storm the Harkness Institute
P.158 ~ Plate 14: Enlil (The Celestial) meets his end

CHAPTER 8
P.164 ~ Plate 15: John & Ayesha stop in Cannock forest enroute
P.172 ~ Plate 16: Ayesha pulls a gun on the shapeshifter

CHAPTER 9
P.183 ~ Plate 17: Ship battered by the storm
P.193 ~ Plate 18: John throws the evil priest into the ocean

CHAPTER 10
P.197 ~ Plate 19: John & Susan standing at Elizabeth's grave
P.207 ~ Plate 20: The alien spear

CHAPTER 11
P.215 ~ Plate 21: Decending into the wreck of the Harkness Institute
P.220 ~ Plate 22: Arthurs changes into his true form!

CHAPTER 12
P.234 ~ Plate 23: Hell Demon conjoured in Acre just before John is crushed
P.258 ~ Plate 24: John and Tu head towards the sand devils

CHAPTER 13
P.266 ~ Plate 25: Sheeba - in all her glory - a deceptive and beautiful evil
P.288 ~ Plate 26: Bron the giant finds John buried in the rubble in Yorkshire

CONCEPT ART ~ P.293 - 299

Look out for these titles coming soon:

Knight Eternal
~ Book 2 ~
Untold Tales of the Knight Eternal
Eight chilling Tales of the Knight Eternal's travels across the centuries.

And...

Knight Eternal
~ Book 3 ~
The Desolate Earth
The concluding volume of John's adventures in this trilogy.

Sign up to the River Styx Project monthly newsletter and find more exciting titles from Ian and Matt, available at
www.riverstyxproject.com

If you have enjoyed this book, please feel free to add a positive review online, they are invaluable to our commitment to producing more quality books.
Thank you, Ian & Matt.